Outstanding praise for Chris Cavender and PEPPERONI PIZZA CAN BE MURDER!

"The small-town setting, the small-business focus and the relationship between sisters Maddy and Eleanor are all reminiscent of Joanne Fluke's Hannah Swensen mysteries."

—*Booklist*

"Cavender is an ace at writing cozies. His characters are believable, especially the relationship between Eleanor and her sister, and his plots are rock solid. Sure to appeal to fans of food cozies."

—*Library Journal*

"Scrumptious . . . this entertaining series will continue to gain fans with its clever plotting and small-town appeal."

—*RT Book Reviews*

Books by Chris Cavender

A SLICE OF MURDER

PEPPERONI PIZZA CAN BE MURDER

A PIZZA TO DIE FOR

Published by Kensington Publishing Corporation

PEPPERONI PIZZA CAN BE MURDER

CHRIS CAVENDER

KENSINGTON BOOKS
www.kensingtonbooks.com

KENSINGTON BOOKS are published by

Kensington Publishing Corp.
119 West 40th Street
New York, NY 10018

All Kensington titles, imprints, and distributed lines are available at special quantity discounts for bulk purchases for sales promotion, premiums, fund-raising, educational, or institutional use.

Special book excerpts or customized printings can also be created to fit specific needs. For details, write or phone the office of the Kensington Special Sales Manager: Attn. Special Sales Department. Kensington Publishing Corp., 119 West 40th Street, New York, NY, 10018. Phone: 1-800-221-2647.

Kensington and the K logo Reg. U.S. Pat. & TM Off.

ISBN-13: 978-0-7582-2951-9
ISBN-10: 0-7582-2951-8

First hardcover printing: August 2010
First mass market printing: April 2011
10 9 8 7 6 5 4 3 2 1

Printed in the United States of America

To PHM and EHM, my very own M&M's!

My idea of feng shui is to have them arrange the pepperoni in a circle on my pizza.
—Unknown

Chapter 1

My name is Eleanor Swift, and for once, nobody was trying to pin a murder on me, even though it happened in my pizzeria, A Slice of Delight. A dead body in the kitchen—with a large thin-crust pepperoni pizza and a bloody rolling pin on either side of it—could have easily put me in the crosshairs of the police investigation.

But I wasn't completely off the hook, even though I had a perfect alibi.

My delivery man was being accused of the homicide, so I could hardly stay out of it, could I?

At least that's what I kept trying to tell Kevin Hurley, the chief of police for Timber Ridge, North Carolina. And he might have believed me—or even listened to my argument—if I hadn't dumped him back in high school nearly twenty years ago. It was a long time for someone to hold a grudge, but he clutched it like a starving man grabbed for the last donut in the box.

Two days before the murder, my sister, Maddy, came into the pizzeria fifteen minutes late from her allotted hour afternoon break. It was a little after three, and things were generally slow then, but I wasn't about to start any precedents with my one full-time employee, even if she was my only family left. Maddy had been divorced several times, but that never stopped her from looking for her next future ex-husband. When my husband, Joe, had died, she'd come to work for me after her last divorce. I should say latest divorce, because with Maddy, it was hard to say what might happen down the road.

"You're late," I said as I handed her my order pad.

"Sorry," she answered, smiling brightly at me as her body language clearly denied the sincerity of her apology. My sister and I were studies in contrast, and not just because of her record number of weddings and my widowhood after being married to the same man for more than ten years. Maddy was tall and thin, and her hair had been blond so long, I doubted her roots even remembered what color they should be. I was shorter and quite a bit curvier, while my hair was the original chestnut brown it had always been.

"Why don't I believe you?" I asked as I started back to the kitchen. Sometimes I worked the front, but the back was where I was most comfortable, the place that I belonged.

"I just ran into David Quinton," she said with a wicked smile.

That merited a bump on my adrenaline scale, though I wasn't about to admit it to anyone else, not even Maddy. David had been pursuing me for some time, and I'd finally decided to let him catch me. Well, sort of. We had a standing dinner date once a week for the past several months, alternating restaurants and who picked up the tab. It was nearly May, and I couldn't believe the weekly meal had so quickly become a habit for me, something I looked forward to when times were slow at the pizzeria.

"I saw that smile," Maddy added. "Don't bother denying it." When I shook my head, she added in a more serious tone, "Eleanor, you're not being disloyal to Joe if you admit that you like spending time with David."

"Please. I get that same line from him every week, don't you start on me." I bit my lip, and then against my better judgment, I asked, "What did he have to say?"

"He wanted to know how I was doing," Maddy said with that smug expression of hers.

"That's it?" Maybe my part-time beau was getting tired of our chaste dinners and had decided to go after my sister, instead.

She grinned. "No, he asked about you, too. Why don't you call him?"

I shook my head. "We're having dinner in three days. I can wait that long to get together, if he can."

Maddy shook her head. "You're more stubborn than I am, and there aren't many people I can say that about."

"I'll take that as a compliment."

"You can take it however you'd like, but we both know that's not what I meant." We were back by the soda fountain, and for the first time, Maddy looked around the dining room. It was nearly deserted, but I knew what—or, more appropriately, who—was missing.

She frowned. "Where's Greg? He didn't take off on you, did he?"

Greg Hatcher was my main deliveryman, and since we'd just recently started taking telephone orders again after a really unpleasant time, I needed him at the pizzeria more than ever. Maddy knew how much pressure his absences placed on me, and while my sister might take more than her fair number of shots at me, she was always the first one to defend me if she thought I needed it.

"Don't worry so much. I let him go."

"You fired him? Eleanor, we need someone to deliver the pizza, and he needs the paycheck so he can stay in college. How could you do that?"

"Take it easy. I didn't get rid of him. He had an errand to run."

Maddy wasn't mollified. "That's not like Greg to leave you here by yourself. What was so important that it couldn't wait until I got back?" She shook her head, and then added, "He didn't duck out on you to see Katy Johnson, did he?"

Katy went to college nearby with Greg, and they'd been dating off and on since he'd first come to work for me two years ago.

"No. As a matter of fact, they broke up."

"Again? If they're so unhappy with each other, why do they keep getting back together?"

I looked at her and fought the laughter I was feeling. "You're giving relationship advice? Seriously?"

"Hey, several of my ex-husbands would gladly write me references," she said. "Just because we split up doesn't mean we aren't all still friends. Well, mostly," she added uncertainly, no doubt ticking names off her internal matrimonial roster and putting them in columns likely labeled FOR and AGAINST.

"Fine, you're the relationship guru," I said, "but Greg didn't run off on me. I gave him my blessing to take off. He had a meeting with Bob Lemon."

Bob was a local attorney who, despite appearing to be quite sane in most respects, was lobbying to be Maddy's next ex-husband. To his chagrin, he was failing at it miserably, too.

"What's Bob got to do with him? Greg's not being sued, is he?"

"No," I said as I donned my kitchen apron. We'd slowly migrated to the back where my pizza oven and supplies were kept, but Maddy kept the door that separated the two spaces open with the edge of her left shoe. "It's about his inheritance."

"It's finally happening? I thought Wade was still holding everything up. Don't tell me he finally broke down and signed the blasted agreement."

"Not yet, but Bob and Greg have high hopes." Greg's older brother, Wade, was keeping their grandparents' estate open long past any semblance of sanity. Greg had told us his brother's request was simple, and nonnegotiable. He wanted three-quarters of everything, despite how the will read, what their own parents said, or what the letter from their grandparents themselves outlined. Greg's grandparents had died the year before when a gas leak and subsequent explosion in their home had taken them both. They'd ignored their grown children in their joint wills, instead leaving an estate approaching two hundred thousand dollars to their two grandchildren, to be divided equally between them.

Apparently, it was the last part that Wade had trouble with.

"I honestly didn't think he'd ever budge," Maddy said. "I've heard of people who never back down."

"It happens." When our parents had died, there had been just enough money to pay their bills, a perfect arrangement in my mind. They'd enjoyed themselves up to the very end, and while I'd hated to see them go, they'd left this world as close to breaking even as I would have thought possible. In a way, they left us the greatest gift of all, precious memories instead of stocks and bonds. I wouldn't have traded a million dollars for the memories I had of them, and I knew my sister wouldn't, either.

"Trust me, I'm not naïve enough to think it doesn't," she said, "but more than that, it's not uncommon for the eldest son to expect more than his siblings. Some folks believe it's the right way to handle things. They're like royalty. Once there's a successor to the throne, the rest of the boys are just spares. It's got to be tough on Greg dealing with that, on top of losing his grandparents."

"He's handling it better than either one of us would," I said.

To her credit, my sister didn't protest the assertion.

She stood there a second, and then asked, "I wonder what made Wade change his mind?"

I smiled. "Greg thinks he knows. His brother's been counting on getting his hands on some of that money, and from the sound of it, he's taken out some loans that weren't issued by any bank, if you know what I mean. Evidently the collecting agents are getting antsy and applying a whole new kind of pressure to Wade."

"How stupid is he?" Maddy asked. "That's just begging for trouble."

"Hey, it's probably the only thing that's motivating him to come to the bargaining table. Apparently, Wade doesn't make that much working as a bookkeeper for Roger Henderson. Bob's brokering the deal, so we should know something when Greg comes back." I gave my sister a stern look as I added, "Don't interrogate him about it, though. It's his life, and if he wants to tell us, he will. Otherwise, it's none of our business."

Maddy just laughed. "You don't think there's a chance on earth I'm going to agree to that, do you?"

"No, but I can hope, can't I?"

"Whatever gets you through the afternoon," Maddy said.

Greg walked into the pizzeria kitchen two minutes later, a thunderstorm dancing in his eyes.

"Do I even need to ask how it went?" I asked as I handed him his apron.

"What do you think? It's the same old Wade. No matter how much my parents protest the fact that their darling little Wade has finally changed, they just don't realize that the only way he's changed is that he's gotten better at lying to them." As Greg threw his apron on over his head, he added, "He's not fooling me, though."

"Does he honestly want more than half?" Maddy asked.

I would have chided her about the intrusion, but I kept my mouth shut. I wanted to know the answer to that one myself.

"Oh, yes," Greg said. "Only he's not going to get it. I could use the money, but I'm not as desperate as he is. I stormed out of the meeting. You should have heard the garbage I had to listen to from him. I told him I'd rather see the money go to the lawyers than give in to him. He might not have believed me before, but I've got a hunch he finally got the message. You know what? I meant every word of it. If he's going to be this stubborn about it, I'll finish school, pay off my loans when I can, and just let him hang in the wind. We've got three more years before the courts intervene."

"He could sue you, couldn't he?"

"Bob says that Wade would have to agree to a contingency fee if he did that, so at least my brother knows that he'll make even less if he takes me to court. He might be a greedy jerk, but he's generally not that stupid." Greg looked at us both for a moment, then said, "I don't get it."

"Get what?" I asked.

"How do you two get along so well? You're two sisters who work together. If I'm in the same room with my brother for more than three minutes, a fight breaks out."

"We fight," Maddy said.

"Trust me, we do," I added.

"But you genuinely care for each other," Greg said, shaking his head sadly. "I wish I had that, more than I could ever tell you." After a moment of silence, he said softly, "I had a sister. Did I ever tell you that?"

I'd known Greg and his family practically all of his life, but I hadn't known that. "What happened to her?"

"She died three days after she was born," Greg said. "She would have been the oldest, and Wade would have been put in his place. My parents were so happy when my brother survived, they gave him a double dose of love, and I got stuck with the scraps."

Greg wasn't being the least bit melodramatic. Though Wade had been in and out of trouble all of his life, Greg had been the faithful, true, obedient son, for all the good it did him in his parents' eyes. Wade was the favorite, Greg was the spare. No wonder Wade felt so entitled, considering the way he'd been raised. It didn't make it right, but it did make sense, in his skewed family dynamic.

I couldn't take the weight of Greg's sadness. "You know, Maddy and I think of you as family," I said.

My sister didn't say a word. She just reached out and patted his shoulder.

Greg nodded briefly, then wiped at his eyes with the back of his arm. "These allergies are killing me. I'd better get to work."

Greg hurried out into the dining room, but Maddy stayed behind. "That boy got a rotten deal in life, didn't he?"

I nodded. "He hasn't let it spoil him, though. He's tough."

"He's not that tough," Maddy said.

"Then he's coping. Greg's a survivor. He'll deal with his brother, and if he needs us, all we can do is be here for him."

"We can, and we will," Maddy said. She peeked out the door, and then added, "We've got some customers, so I'd better get out there and give him a hand."

"Maddy, don't say anything else to him about what happened at Bob's office this afternoon, okay?"

"I wouldn't dream of it," she said. She started to leave, hesitated, then turned around and wrapped me in her arms. "I love you, Sis."

"I love you, too," I said, startled by her declaration. Maddy wasn't the kind of woman ordinarily to show affection, unless it was toward her latest marriage target.

After she was gone, I got out the broom and started to make another circuit of the kitchen floor before I began cooking. The place could never be too clean for me, and the health inspector had given us a string of nearly perfect scores since we'd opened the pizzeria.

Maddy came rushing into the back as I was finishing up, and she startled me so much that I dropped my broom.

I hoped and prayed nothing had gone wrong. "What is it? Did something happen?"

She leaned down to pick up my broom, then handed it to me as she said, "Relax, Eleanor. A big group just came in, and I wanted to give you a heads-up so you could get started on crusts."

"How many people are we talking about?" I asked.

Maddy smiled. "I was going to call you after you got things started, but I can't wait that long. Look out the door."

I wasn't sure what to expect, and I thought I was ready for just about anything, but I was still surprised to find twenty-five Elvis Presley impersonators milling about the restaurant when I peeked out through the door. The Elvis imitators were white, black, Asian, Hispanic, men, women, and one kid who couldn't even be in his teens yet. "What on earth is going on?"

"They're headed to Graceland in Memphis," Maddy said.

"And they're driving through Timber Ridge?" I asked as I openly stared at them.

"They started in D.C. and they're headed down to I-40 West," she explained. "It's a pilgrimage. Can you believe it?"

"On days like today, I can believe just about anything."

Greg joined us, and I could see him smiling despite his earlier bad mood. "This is so cool." He looked at his order pad, and then asked me, "Can you make fried peanut-butter-and-banana sandwiches?"

"I could, but I'm not going to," I said. "They can order off the menu like everyone else."

"That's what I told them. They said they'd settle for five large specials if you wouldn't do these."

"That I can do," I said as I headed back to the kitchen. As I knuckled my freshly made dough into pans, I started an assembly line putting the pizzas together. I'd have to chop and slice more toppings before the dinner crowd showed up, but I didn't mind. Maybe tonight we'd make up for some of the slow days we had at the Slice every now and then. There was nothing like a stuffed cash register to make me smile. Money wasn't the source of happiness for me, nor was it the root of all evil. It was simply a way to keep A Slice of Delight up and running. Honestly, without the pizzeria, I didn't know what I'd do with myself.

As the pizzas went onto the conveyor heading into the oven, I kept loading the line until each one was waiting its turn. As they cooked, I started restocking our toppings bins for our evening shift.

When Maddy rejoined me, she spotted the first pizza coming out of the oven and grabbed a pair of tongs. "Mind if I give you a hand? The natives are getting restless."

"Be my guest," I said. "Did you leave Greg out there all alone?"

"Are you kidding me? He's having the time of his life. Who knew he was such an Elvis fan?"

"It appears there's a great deal we don't know about him," I said.

Maddy transferred the first pizza to a serving platter and cut it into eight slices. "Keep them coming," she called out to me as she disappeared back into the dining room.

I stopped chopping peppers and took her place at the far end of the conveyor. By the time I delivered the pizzas, I had three new orders for dessert pizzas from the traveling impersonators, so I started on those so they'd be ready in time. It was a different kind of pizza altogether, featuring cookie dough crust with melted chocolate on top and drizzled with icing to finish it off. I also made an apple cinnamon dessert pizza some days, but I was fresh out of ingredients for that one.

As I delivered the desserts, my efforts were met with an appreciative audience. A few of my regulars had wandered in, and I was afraid they'd be put off by the dining

Elvis group. Instead, they seemed to act as though I was providing them with entertainment along with their meal. My husband and I had talked about putting a jukebox in as soon as we could afford one, but the dream had died with Joe. As it was, I couldn't see how the investment would pay for itself, and I had to keep a close eye on the bottom line, or I wouldn't be able to afford luxuries like electricity and water.

I moved to the cash register, and nearly without exception, as they paid for their meals, every member of the Elvis entourage said, "Thank you, thank you very much."

By the time they were gone, I needed a break, and from the expression on the charter bus driver's face, so did he.

Neither one of us was going to get one, though.

I helped Maddy and Greg clean up; then I returned to the kitchen to finish prepping more toppings.

We had a brisk business for the rest of the day, and I kept busy making orders as they came in. We could handle the crowds most of the time with just two or three of us, but there were times when I could have used an extra set of hands. Josh Hurley, the chief of police's son, had supplied that help at one time, but the chief wasn't all that eager to have his only son return to work for me.

I decided that particular foolishness had gone on long enough.

I called the police station, and wasn't surprised when Helen Murphy answered. She was the receptionist and dispatcher for our local law enforcement, and I didn't think I'd ever called there when she didn't answer the telephone herself.

"Helen, it's Eleanor Swift," I said.

"Hello, Eleanor. What can I do for you?"

"I was wondering if I could talk to the chief."

She hesitated, then asked softly, "Do you mean he's not there yet?"

"No, why would he come here?"

Helen was about to tell me when the kitchen door opened, and the chief himself stepped in. "Never mind, he just walked through the door."

"Were you looking for me?" he asked. Kevin Hurley was tall and lanky, and I could see a smattering of gray creeping into his temples, which didn't make me feel any younger, since I was a year older.

"That can wait. What brings you to my pizzeria?"

He frowned at me as he admitted, "It's Josh. He's been hounding me for months to talk to you, and I hate to say it, but my son has finally worn me down. He wants to know if he can come back to work."

"That's always been your decision, not mine," I said. Kevin had forbidden his son to work for me during a recent bad time, and I was beginning to believe that the ban had become permanent.

"Well, he's driving me nuts, and I don't care what his mother says, I think you should hire him back. He's only got a month left until he leaves for his summer college classes, but it would be great if he could spend some of that time working here for you."

"I don't want to cause trouble at home for you," I said. Kevin's wife, Marybeth, wasn't a big fan of mine, and if I was being honest about it, the feeling was pretty much mutual.

"Don't worry about that, I can handle it." He stared at his hands as he asked, "So, what do you say? Can he come back to work?"

"Are you sure you're okay with it?" I asked softly.

"I'm tired of his attitude," Kevin said. "I'd consider it a personal favor."

"Then it's done. Tell him he can start this evening."

"How about tomorrow?" Kevin asked. "He's got a big test tomorrow he needs to study for."

"Why don't you have him call me and we'll work a schedule out."

"He'll call you within the hour." Kevin moved toward the door; then he paused for a second. "What was it that you wanted to talk to me about?"

I wasn't about to admit that it was the same topic of his son's employment. The way things had worked out, the chief of police was going to feel obligated to me, and it might be leverage I would need sooner or later. "I was just wondering if you'd heard anything about the rezoned parking in back. Are they really going to get rid of it to widen the alley?"

"It's not up to me," he said, "but I honestly doubt it. The town council has it on the agenda once a year, but it never passes. If you're worried about it, you could always talk to the mayor."

"I have been, but he's not exactly my biggest fan. I thought you might know something. Thanks, anyway. Now if you'll excuse me, I've got work to do."

"Thanks again, Ellie," he said, and before I could voice my displeasure at the ancient pet name, he was gone. Only a handful of people had ever called me "Ellie," and just two men ever got away with it. I loved the way my name sounded when my husband, Joe, had said it, but Kevin's intonation just brought back the hurt he had caused me in school. Maybe he wasn't the only one holding a grudge about what had happened all those years ago. I'd caught him with the woman he eventually married. The only problem had been that he'd been dating me at the time, too.

"Get over it, Eleanor," I scolded myself aloud. "That was a lifetime ago."

Maddy came into the kitchen and looked around. "Who were you just talking to?"

"I was giving myself a little pep talk," I admitted.

Her eyes widened for a second, and then she said, "All right, that's good to know. When you're finished cheering yourself on, I've got another order for you. Come on, Eleanor, you can do it. Make that pizza. Make that pizza. Rah, rah, rah."

"I love it when you're funny," I said as I took the order from her. "I don't mean now. I mean when you're actually amusing."

I started working the crust into the pan when I realized she was still lingering by the kitchen door.

"Was there something else?"

"Aren't you going to tell me what he said?" Maddy asked.

"Who are we talking about?" I responded, playing as dumb as I dared, and fighting to keep a straight face as I did it.

"Don't give me that. What did the police chief want? And don't tell me he was ordering a pizza. I saw the look on his face when he came into the Slice."

I thought about stringing her along, but I had work to do, and so did she. "He wanted to know if Josh could come back to work."

"It's about time," she said.

"Better late than never."

"Is he coming tonight?" Maddy asked as she looked around at the disarray my kitchen had become.

"No such luck. Maybe tomorrow, though. Do you think you can handle things until then?"

"Are you kidding? Greg and I are acting like a well-oiled machine out there."

"Then I suggest you get back to it," I said as I added the layer of cheese that went down on top of the sauce, and just before the pepperoni.

"Slave driver," my sister said as she darted through the door before I could respond.

All I could do was laugh. It would be good getting my best staff back together, though it was about to change again soon. Josh would be going away before long, and I'd have to hire his replacement. I liked the way a student kept the Slice tied in with the local school, and besides, an eager teenager properly motivated was a blessing to my business. I'd hired a few duds over the years, but they'd quickly quit once they saw how hard the work was. When I found someone I could count on, a hard worker who didn't complain and generally showed up on time, I always figured out a way to bump their pay to keep them happy.

Now I'd have to start interviewing again, a job I dearly dreaded.

But not today.

At the moment, I had a full dining room, two hard workers serving out front, and a plentiful supply of dough and toppings.

It was all I could ask for.

A little later, there was a knock at the pizzeria's back door, but I ignored it. We used it to take in supplies during regular business hours, and sometimes we even got to our cars that way, but mostly having a door there was more of a nuisance than anything else.

The knocking became a pounding, and I got a little aggravated.

"Come around to the front," I yelled through the door.

"Eleanor, it's Paul."

I recognized my favorite baker's voice instantly. I glanced at the clock and saw that it was almost nine o'clock. For a baker, that was like three A.M. for anyone else.

"Paul, aren't you out a little past your bedtime?"

"Tell me about it," he said as I let him in. He was a tall and handsome young man in his late twenties, with a black goatee and big brown eyes. "I'd normally be asleep by now, but I was on a date."

"I don't need to know any more. From the look on your face, it didn't turn out too well, did it?"

He nodded. "Since I'm up anyway, could you make me a small cheese pizza? I can't deal with people out front right now."

As I got out some dough and started kneading it into the pan, I said, "Pull up a stool. Tell you what, I won't even charge you for this, if you keep me company and tell me what was so bad with this woman."

He did as I asked, and as I added sauce and cheese, Paul said, "She's a night owl. In fact, she said she doesn't start coming alive until ten at night. Not exactly a perfect match, is she? Why do I let my mom fix me up with these girls? I'm never going to learn."

"Come on, there's no harm in being a hopeless romantic," I said.

"Well, I've got the first part down pat, I'm hopeless, all right. I need to find a girl who works the same hours I do, but how am I going to do that?"

"It can be a cold world out there, but you can't give up."

He looked sadder than I'd ever seen him. Then he mumbled something so softly, I couldn't quite make it out.

"What did you say?"

"Nothing," Paul said, just a little louder.

"I know better than that. Now tell me, or I'll eat your pizza myself."

"I was out of line, Eleanor. I'll pay for the pizza, if I can get it to go. I'm not fit to be around anyone tonight."

I stood in front of him. "That wasn't our deal. I want to know what you said."

He looked at me steadily, silently pleading for me to drop it, but I couldn't do it. I'd just figured out what he'd said.

"I'm not going to tell you."

"Then I'll tell you. You said that I've given up on romance."

He hung his head even lower. "So you heard me after all."

"It took a minute to figure it out." I took his hands in mine. "Paul, look at me."

He was reluctant to at first, but finally he lifted his head.

When he did, I said, "I found my one true love with Joe. That's what's different about my situation."

He held my stare. "Eleanor, do you really believe we just get one love in our lives?"

"If we're lucky," I said, releasing his hands. I glanced at the conveyor and saw that his pizza was ready. After I sliced it and boxed it up, I handed it to him.

"I still think I should pay for this," he said as he took it.

"Tell you what. Next time I want to indulge in one of your éclairs, you can look the other way when it comes time to pay."

That brought out a smile. "That's what I love, the barter system. Still, one éclair isn't worth as much as one of your pizzas."

"That's a matter of opinion," I said. "But if you insist, I'm sure Maddy wouldn't say no to one, too."

"It's a deal." He took the box, and then as I let him back out through the rear door, he said, "I'm sorry if I ruined your evening. I shouldn't have bothered you on a night when I feel so sad."

"Nonsense. Friends are for rainy days, and sunny ones, too. Anytime you need to talk, you know where I am."

"Thanks."

I let him out, and then locked the door behind him. Paul was a good man with a strong and caring heart, and I hoped that one day he'd find his own true love.

I'd meant what I'd said about mine. For me, it had been Joe, and would always be Joe.

I had a great life, and for the most part, I enjoyed every minute of it.

It was good being me.

At least it was until later that night when someone stuck a gun in my face.

Chapter 2

"**D**on't do anything stupid and I won't hurt you," the masked man said as he poked the handgun toward me.

"Why don't you rob a bank like everyone else does?" I asked, still clutching the deposit bag with the night's receipts. Maddy and Greg had worked so hard during the rush that I'd sent them both home early. Ordinarily, my sister never would have taken me up on my offer, but she'd had a headache and had leapt at the chance to escape.

The funny thing was that I hadn't even been nervous walking at night to my car through the breezeway between two buildings to the alley behind the pizzeria, where I parked my Subaru.

Apparently, I'd been wrong not to expect something.

"Don't make me shoot you, lady," the robber said, his voice muffled by the mask he was wearing. I tried to figure out how I could describe him to the police after this was over, but he was so average in height and build that it was almost painful. It didn't help matters that he was covered from head to toe in black, including the ski mask that had to have obscured his vision. I couldn't even see the color of his eyes through the mask, though I kept trying to ignore the gun shoved in my face. It was tougher to do than it sounded.

"Last warning," he said, and I saw a gloved finger start to move toward the trigger.

"Take it," I said as I tried to give the deposit bag to him in a rush.

The problem was that my hand was shaking so much that I dropped it before he could grab it. He swore as the bag hit the ground and sprang open. I'd been meaning to replace it since the zipper had busted two months ago, but I hadn't gotten around to it.

He knelt down in front of me to scoop up the cash and receipts, and for a second, I thought about hitting him over the head with my purse. It wasn't as bad a choice of weapons as it might have appeared, since it was loaded down with lots of nice, heavy things, but before I could act on my impulse, he looked up at me, gestured with the gun, and then just shook his head.

No words needed to be spoken. He was warning me, and I was going to go along with his silent demand. After all, it was only money, and I could always make more, though tonight's take wouldn't be that easy to replace.

Still, it wasn't worth dying over.

He stood again, then quickly ran down the alley toward a cluster of other buildings before I could even get my breath back.

I called the police dispatcher on my cell phone as I leaned against my car, still shaking from the potentially deadly encounter.

"I need to speak with Kevin Hurley," I said.

"He's clocked out for the day," Helen Murphy explained. "I thought you said he already came by your restaurant tonight."

"Then send someone else," I screamed, not meaning to raise my voice, but having no real control over it. "I've just been robbed."

Helen's voice softened immediately. "Are you all right, Eleanor?"

I took a second to get my breath, and then said, "No, but I will be."

"He didn't hurt you, did he?"

"Not physically, but my nerves are jumping all over the place," I said as I slumped even lower against the driver's-side door. "Just send someone over to the alley behind the Slice as soon as you can, Helen, would you?"

"It won't be a minute," she said. "Stay on the line until someone shows up." I could hear her making a call on the police radio, and she was as good as her word. It couldn't have been sixty seconds before I saw a squad car rushing toward me.

I felt a little bit of relief when I realized it wasn't the police chief. I didn't want to deal with Kevin Hurley, especially not yet, but my joy was short-lived when I saw another squad car closely following the first one.

It appeared that our chief of police wasn't about to leave this for one of his employees.

It somehow made a very bad situation even worse.

"You just can't stay out of trouble, can you?" Kevin asked me after he determined that I was okay.

"Come on, Chief, it's not like it was her fault," the policeman who'd first answered the call said.

Kevin iced him with a deadly glare, then said, "Garvin,

you're new, so I'm going to give you one chance to question my judgment. And guess what? You just used yours up. Now get back on patrol."

The new officer turned slightly green as he made his way back to his cruiser.

"You didn't have to be so hard on him," I said after Officer Garvin was gone, "especially when he was right."

"Don't you start on me," he said.

"What are you going to do, punish me, too?"

"Eleanor, you don't understand. He's got the chance to become a good cop someday, but he needs to learn his place in the pecking order of things, or he'll never make it."

I was mad now, my fear displaced by my anger. "How about me, Chief? Do I need to learn my place as well?"

The police chief took a step back, apparently surprised that I still had a bite to go along with my bark. I didn't know why he'd ever think otherwise. I'd never given him any indication in the entire time he'd known me that he could boss me around.

"I'm sorry," he said after a long sigh. "I'm just worried that this could have been much worse."

"I'm not stupid," I answered, managing to speak a little softer than I had before. "I wasn't about to argue with him. He wanted my money, and he had a gun pointed at me, so I gave my deposit to him. End of story."

Kevin nodded, then said, "I have a thought, if you're in any mood to hear one from me."

"Go on. I'm listening," I said.

"You really should get a safe for the pizza place and take your deposits to the bank the next day on your afternoon break. Eleanor, you shouldn't be carrying money around with you at night when you're all by yourself."

I could tell he was bracing himself for a blast, but I

didn't have any more fight in me. "You know what? You're right. It's a little like locking the barn door after the horse is loose, but I'll buy a safe tomorrow."

"And you need a better alarm system," he added.

"Don't push your luck. I can barely afford to stay in business as it is." I waved a hand at his paperwork. "Are we finished here? I just want to go home."

"Just sign this and you'll be finished for now," he said as he handed me the report he'd been working on since he'd first arrived.

I did as he asked, and he handed me a copy of it. "There's not much chance you'll get that money back, you know that, don't you?"

I nodded. "I know. Right now I just want to forget this ever happened."

"In Timber Ridge? You're kidding, right? You're going to have to tell this story two dozen times before the week is over, and you know it."

"Just let me have my fantasy a little while longer, okay? Good night, Chief."

"What happened to calling me Kevin?" he asked.

"When you come in for pizza, or ask me something about your son, I'll call you Kevin, but not when you're here on business."

He waited until I got into my Subaru and drove away. I half-expected him to follow me home, but he must have had other, more pressing business to attend to besides acting as a police escort to a shaky ex-girlfriend.

I debated calling my sister, knowing she'd left the Slice with a raging headache, but I realized that if I didn't, she'd never forgive me. I pulled out my cell phone and punched in her number as I drove.

"Hey, it's me," I said.

"Miss me already?" Maddy asked.

"I just got robbed."

She laughed, then hesitated. "Don't do that, it hurts when I laugh." There was a brief pause, and then she added, "Wait a second. You're not serious, are you?"

"I wish I were kidding, but I'm not. He got all of today's cash, including the money the Elvis entourage spent, and all of our receipts."

"Forget the money. Are you okay?"

"Yes, I'm fine. He stuck a gun in my face, and that was about all I could see. Not that much skin was showing otherwise. The robber was wearing a heavy coat, jeans, work boots, and a ski mask."

"Did you at least recognize his voice?"

"Do you think someone I know robbed me?" The volume of my voice tripled as I said it. Being robbed by a stranger was one thing, but having someone I knew hold a gun on me was a thousand times worse.

"Hey, settle down. I didn't mean anything by it. It was just a question."

"Sorry, my nerves are a little frayed."

Maddy said, "Come over to my place. I've still got your pajamas here, and there's a new toothbrush still in its wrapper waiting for you."

"I should go home," I said.

"Why?" she asked. "You shouldn't be alone tonight."

"You've got a headache."

"It's getting better by the minute. No more excuses. Come on."

"You know what? You're right, I don't need to be alone tonight," I said as I turned my car around and started for her apartment. "I'll be there in five minutes."

"I'll put the popcorn on," she said. "We'll make it a party."

"Thanks, but I just want to go to bed and try to forget what happened."

Maddy shifted gears instantly. "We can do that, too."

I shoved my telephone back into my purse, and then as I drove to my sister's place, I thought about what had happened. Something she'd said had really shaken me up. I hadn't told Kevin, but I was just beginning to realize that there had been something familiar about that voice.

I'd heard it before, even though the robber had tried to disguise it.

The question was, where?

The more I concentrated on isolating it, the fuzzier it got. I decided that the only way I was going to identify it was to forget all about it and let my subconscious have a crack at it.

But I couldn't help feeling nauseous when I realized that someone I knew had threatened me with a gun and had taken all my cash.

Maddy was waiting by the front door of her apartment, and as I got out of the car, she flashed her lights for me.

I walked up the stairs, fighting the irrational urge to run. Until that moment, I hadn't fully realized just how terrified I was. Stress was like that for me sometimes, hitting me with a delayed reaction long after I was out of danger. It took everything I had not to keep looking behind me, afraid I might see that masked gunman again.

My sister didn't say a word; she just wrapped me in an embrace the second I reached her. "I'm so glad you're all right. We've got to come up with a better way to handle our money."

"I know," I said as I disengaged myself from her grasp.

"Kevin suggested we buy a safe, and said that we should make afternoon deposits instead of night drops. For once, I have to agree with him."

"Hey, even a broken clock is right twice a day," she said with a smile. "Why should the chief of police be wrong every time he says something? Come on in, I've got some hot chocolate simmering on the stovetop."

"I said I wasn't in the mood for a party, and that includes those famous chocolate bombardment bashes you're so famous for."

"This is just a little toddy to help you sleep," she said. "Hot cocoa always did have that effect on you."

"Sure, okay, that sounds good."

I took the mug she offered and sipped it gratefully. It was warm, but not too hot to savor, and just holding the toasty mug in my hand made me feel better.

"Was it horrible?" Maddy asked softly.

"It was pretty scary," I admitted.

She nodded, as if that was enough. "Then there's no reason to talk about it. Let's change the subject, shall we?"

"I'm all out of topics of conversation," I said.

"That's all right," she said with a laugh. "We both know that I can more than monopolize any conversation."

I laughed along with her, and realized that coming to her place had been the perfect decision. Maddy had her faults—I knew them more than anyone else, even her ex-husbands—but she loved me, and she could nearly always make me smile, a rare enough event on days like today.

After the hot chocolate was gone, I stifled a yawn, then excused myself and made my way to her guest bedroom. I was worried that I wouldn't be able to sleep after what had happened, but to my surprise, I was out before my head hit the pillow.

* * *

There was a note on the door of the Slice when we opened the next morning. My hands shook a little as I opened it, but I was relieved to see that it was from David Quinton: *Eleanor. You weren't home last night. Call me as soon as you get this. David.*

Maddy asked, "Who is that from?"

"Nobody," I said as I started to crumple it up and put it in my pocket.

"Come on, don't hold out on me," she said, and snatched it out of my hand.

She read the note aloud as I unlocked the door. "I think it's sweet."

"You would," I said as I started to lock up behind us.

She followed me to the kitchen, where I immediately started making our dough for the day. As I got out the ingredients, she asked, "What are you doing?"

"I don't know. I figure there's a good chance that somebody's going to want pizza today, so I figured I'd better make some dough. I'm kind of crazy that way sometimes."

She shook her head. "You know what I mean. Before you do anything else, you need to call David."

I ignored her suggestion and continued working on the dough. "You can call him if you want to, but I've got work to do."

"Eleanor, it's clear that he's worried about you." She grabbed the telephone and shoved it toward me. "It will just take two seconds."

"You don't honestly think that, do you? Even if it were true, it's two seconds I don't want to spend talking to him. Maddy, I'm not ready to have a conversation with anybody about what happened."

"You talked to me last night."

"Just barely, and you're my family." I attempted to ignore the phone, but the more I tried, the more adamant my sister became that I call him.

I finished adding yeast to the water, mixing the flour and other ingredients together, and turning on the mixer before I finally took it from her. "Fine. I'm calling him right now, so back off, all right?"

"That's all I'm asking," she said.

As I dialed David's number, Maddy asked, "Do you want me to give you some privacy?"

"Why on earth would I want you to do that?" I asked.

David picked up on the first ring, and before I could even say hello, he asked, "Eleanor? Are you all right?"

"I'm fine, David, but I can't really talk. I'm up to my elbows in dough right now." That wasn't strictly the truth, but I had work to do.

"You never came home last night," he said, an undertone of accusation in his voice. "I waited until one A.M."

"You shouldn't have done that," I said.

"I didn't mind. As soon as I heard about what happened, I needed to see you. I had to make sure you were okay."

"I stayed with Maddy last night," I said, cradling the telephone between my shoulder and my neck so I could check on the dough, steadily stirring away in the floor stand mixer.

"Of course you did, that makes sense. I should have looked for you there."

"No, you shouldn't have," I said. My patience was just about worn out with him, and I couldn't keep from letting it show in my voice.

"Are you seriously going to act like you're the one who's hurt? I'm really surprised you didn't call me after what happened to you, and more than a little disappointed. Eleanor, I have a right to know how you are."

"And tell me, why is that, David?" I saw Maddy warning me off, but I was on a roll and wasn't about to stop. She'd wanted me to make this telephone call, so she was going to have to live with the consequences of it. I didn't even try to ease the anger in my voice as I said, "We're not dating, as I've told you a hundred times before. We have a meal together once a week, but if you think that gives you some kind of proprietary interest in my well-being, then you're mistaken."

"Sorry," he said, the hurt clear in his voice. "I was just concerned about you."

"You needn't be. I'm fine, which I believe we already established. Is that all you wanted to talk to me about? I can't really talk. I'm busy right now. I have to get the Slice ready to open."

He paused a moment, then said softly, "The reason I was looking for you last night was that I wanted to tell you that I won't be able to make dinner this week. Something came up at the last minute."

He hung up before I had a chance to say anything else to him.

"How do you like that? He just canceled on me," I said as I hung the telephone back into its cradle.

"Are you honestly surprised?" Maddy asked. "What's gotten into you? You just treated him like caring about you was something criminal."

"He doesn't have the right to worry about me," I said, getting back to my dough. "We're just friends." It was time to turn off the mixer and take the mixture out so I could knead the dough on the counter.

"You didn't have to stomp on him so hard," she said. "I wouldn't be surprised if you drove him off for good."

"I can't do anything about that now, can I?" I said, trying to keep my voice confident as I spoke. I'd been frustrated with David—there was no doubt about that—but I hadn't meant to be so mean to him. It generally wasn't in my nature, but I was still upset about being robbed the night before, and his implication that I should have come running to him didn't sit well with me. I was a little too old to have to check in with someone whenever something went wrong in my life, even him.

Maddy bit her lip; then she said softly, "Eleanor, I wonder if you should call him back and apologize."

I'd had enough of this particular conversation, from just about every angle. "If you want to chat with him, just hit redial. Me, I'm done talking to him at the moment."

"I think I'll work out front a little," Maddy said, even though she still had vegetables to prep for the day.

"You know what? That's just a swell idea," I said, making sure she caught the sarcasm in my voice. As close as we were, there were sometimes when I needed space away from my sister.

After Maddy left the kitchen, I started working the dough. It felt good kneading the soft mass, folding and refolding it again and again. I got out a lot of frustrations that way most mornings, but today it was a little less than satisfying. I felt rotten, and I knew exactly why. Maddy was right. I'd been far too short-tempered with David, and while I didn't need to check in with him every hour on the hour, I did owe him more respectful treatment than I'd just given him. I hated when she was right, especially when it meant that I was wrong. It was pretty clear that David wasn't the only one who merited one of my apologies.

I put the well-kneaded dough in a bowl coated with oil, lightly brushed the top, then covered the whole thing and put it under the proofing lamp to give the yeast a chance to kick in. I had an hour before I had to touch it again, which gave me plenty of time to make that telephone call.

David didn't answer, though I suspected he was listening as I left my message. "Listen, I'm sorry I was so abrupt with you. It was nice of you to worry about me, but I meant what I said. I'm fine. Call me later if you feel like it."

Leaving a message wasn't nearly as satisfying as making the apology to him directly. It somehow felt like I was taking the coward's way out.

That left one more apology I needed to make.

I was getting ready to head out front to take care of it when Maddy started to come into the kitchen.

She stopped short and peeked in through the door. "Is it safe to come in?"

I grabbed the cleaver we used to chop the meat for our steak pizza special. "Sure, I'm just fooling around with this big knife."

"I thought I heard you on the phone," she said as she edged in. "Did you call someone?"

"You have the ears of a bat," I said. "If you must know, I called David."

"You didn't chew him out again, did you?"

"No," I said, putting the cleaver down. "I called him to apologize."

"That's wonderful," she said with a smile.

"He wasn't home. At least he didn't pick up." Maddy frowned, and before she could say anything, I added, "I left him a message, so don't say anything else about it. I was wrong, and I admit it. I apologized to him, and this is about the only apology you're going to get from me about this. Can we just move on?"

To my surprise, she agreed. "The front's all set up now,

so I'm ready to get the toppings going." As she started pulling peppers out of the refrigerator, she asked, "Is Greg coming by today?"

"I'm not sure. He's got class this afternoon," I said.

"So it's just the two of us."

"No, Josh Hurley is coming in sometime. I'm just not sure when." I'd chatted with him briefly on the telephone after his father had come by the Slice, and he'd promised to come by as soon as he could.

"That's great. We can handle things until school's out," Maddy said. "I'm surprised Marybeth and Kevin are letting him come back to work."

"From the sound of it, he's driving them both crazy pacing around the house. Kevin made it sound like I was doing him a favor when I agreed to let Josh come back."

"It will be good seeing him again," Maddy said. "I've missed his odd sense of humor, haven't you?"

"Let's just say I won't mind *not* being spread so thin." Josh and my sister had the same skewed sense of humor, one that I didn't always get. They seemed to find the oddest things hilarious, leaving me in the dark about why some of the moments that sparked spontaneous laughter worked for them and not for me.

Bob Lemon stuck his head into the kitchen an hour after we opened. "You doing okay?" he asked as I was making a specialty pizza–club sandwich.

"I'm fine. How are you?"

I'd already had four telephone calls and two visits, all with the express purpose of checking up on me. It was one of the good things about living in a small town, and one of the bad ones, too. Most folks knew what was going on before the newspaper printed it, and all in all, they were supportive of me, which was a nice feeling indeed, but sometimes it felt like we were all living just a little too close.

"Oh, I'm just dandy, but then again, I didn't get robbed last night," he said.

"Don't feel left out. Maybe he'll get around to you tonight."

Bob laughed. "Lawyers are notorious for not carrying much cash on them. I doubt I'd be worth the bother."

"You and I both know that, but does he?" I asked. I liked that Bob had allowed me to keep the conversation playful. There had been enough hand-wringing to suit me for a long time.

"If he still comes after me, then I'll have to overwhelm him with my skills," Bob said.

I looked him over. "Don't tell me you'd challenge him with your fists."

Bob laughed at that. "Trust me, the last thing in the world you ever want to do is get into a fistfight with a lawyer."

"I didn't realize attorneys were that tough."

"It's not the fight that hurts, it's the years you end up in court afterward being sued. No, my main talent is talking. I'd have him handing me his wallet before the whole thing was over."

"I don't doubt that for an instant," I said. I slid the sandwich I'd been preparing onto the conveyor, and then I asked, "Is there something I can get you?"

"No, I already ate at my desk. I just came by to check on you."

I made a big checkmark in the air. "You can cross that off your list, then."

Maddy came back with an order, and then she said to Bob, "Don't you have better things to do than harass my chef? We're working here."

"Sorry," Bob said, though it was clear he wasn't remorseful at all. He glanced at our clock, then added, "I have to run, anyway. I'm due in court in seven minutes."

Since it was a brisk walk from the pizzeria, I knew he wouldn't have any trouble making it in time. That was another good thing about living in Timber Ridge. Most places were just a stroll away.

After he was gone, Maddy said, "Nancy Taylor and Emily Haynes both wanted me to tell you that they're glad you're okay."

Nancy was our postmistress, while Emily was Dr. Patrick's dental hygienist.

"You know," Maddy said, "maybe it would be easier if you worked the front today and I made the food. It would save everyone a lot of trouble sending you messages through me."

"I probably should do exactly that," I said as I wiped my hands on my apron. I knew my friends were there to support me, and it wasn't fair of me to hide in my own kitchen, no matter how uncomfortable the attention they gave made me feel.

"Funny, I was kind of hoping you'd say no," Maddy said. My sister made it clear that she was most at ease working the front, though she was perfectly capable of preparing everything we offered on our menu. I'd made sure of it right after she'd come to work with me, and while I'd been grieving over losing Joe, Maddy had held the Slice together with all she had. It was something I would be forever grateful to her for doing.

"I really don't have much choice," I said. "We're both going to have to grin and bear it for now, aren't we?"

"I suppose," she said as she put on her apron.

I grabbed an order pad and said, "Thanks, Maddy. I

know I don't tell you enough, but I don't know what I'd do without you."

"I'm not sure either, but I'm absolutely positive that it would include great amounts of suffering on your part."

I laughed at her as I checked my appearance in a small mirror before I started waiting on tables.

Maddy smiled. "Don't worry, you're pretty enough."

"I just wanted to make sure I didn't have any flour on my forehead."

My sister laughed at that. "It only happened once. I know I should have said something, but it was hilarious watching you waiting on tables with a white streak on your forehead. You looked like some kind of deranged unicorn."

"Funny for you, humiliating for me," I said.

I walked out front, thinking that I was prepared for the barrage of well-wishers.

I was wrong.

They nearly mugged me before I could refill the first soda.

And for just a second, I found myself wishing that I didn't live in such a small town after all.

"Is school out already?" I asked Josh Hurley as he walked into the Slice a few minutes later. Tall like his father, he'd inherited his brooding good looks as well.

"I ducked out early," he said. He must have seen my face clouding up, so he added quickly, "We were having an assembly, so I didn't miss anything."

"I'm not sure your father would agree with that."

Josh flashed me a quick grin. "Then maybe we shouldn't tell him." He looked around at the tables I'd been meaning to clean, and quickly grabbed a rag. "It looks like I got here just in time. Where's Maddy, by the way?"

"She's working in the kitchen this afternoon," I said.

Since there were still a few late lunch diners at the restaurant, Josh came close and whispered, "Are you sure that's such a good idea? Nothing against your sister or anything, but she doesn't have your touch in the kitchen."

"We only have another ten minutes," I said.

"Why's that? You're not closing early today, are you?"

I didn't get it at first, but then I realized that he hadn't worked since we'd instituted our two o'clock breaks. "We close every day now from two to three."

He looked so disappointed, I added, "Sometimes Greg stays here and cleans or organizes the inventory. I suppose I could leave you here today by yourself."

"That would be great," he said. "I really need the hours."

"Saving up to buy a new car?" I asked, just joking with him.

"As a matter of fact, I am."

"What happened to your MINI Cooper?" Josh had loved the car his folks had bought for him on his sixteenth birthday, and I couldn't imagine him driving anything else.

"Mom took it back," Josh said with his trademark scowl.

"Why would she do that? Not that it's any of my business," I added quickly.

"I don't care who knows it. When I ran away, she decided that I wasn't mature enough for the responsibility, so she parked it in the garage and hid the keys." With a scoff, he added, "Not that I'd ever drive it again now—not after what happened. I'm saving up to buy my own car, and if all I can afford is a beat-up old Ford pickup, then I'll take it."

It was an awkward situation that I had somehow compounded with my joke. "I'm sorry. I didn't mean to pry," I said.

"You didn't." He looked over at our two remaining customers and asked, "So, how do we get them to leave?"

"It's usually not a problem," I said. The few times it had happened before, Maddy and I had simply waited them out.

Josh said, "Don't worry, I'll handle it."

Before I could stop him, he walked over to the table, said a few words, then the couple who'd been eating threw a twenty on the table and hurried out.

"What did you say to them?" I asked.

"I told them the health inspector was coming by, and we had a ton of code violations we had to take care of before he got here."

"Josh, you can't do that."

I looked at him and saw that he was laughing. "Relax. I just let them know we were closing, and invited them back some other time."

"What else did you say to them, Josh?"

He shrugged. "Maybe I implied that the city was towing cars in the parking lot, but if they thought I meant their car, it's not my fault, is it?"

"In the future, we'll have to figure out a better way to handle it," I said.

"Hey, it worked, didn't it?" He grabbed the twenty, then handed it to me. "Looks like a nice tip."

"Don't kid yourself. It will barely cover their tab," I said.

"Sorry about that. I won't do it again." Then he hit me

with that puppy-dog look that had worked so well for his father. It was just too bad for him that I was immune to it by now.

I swatted him with my dish towel, and then said, "No more stunts like that, or you'll be back on the unemployment line. Do you understand?"

"Yes, ma'am," he said contritely. I hated being called "ma'am," but I couldn't very well correct him, so I let it slide.

He looked around the pizzeria, and then asked, "What kind of jobs do you have for me when you're gone?"

"You can take out the garbage, and then hose down the inside trash cans. After that, there are a few cases that need to be unloaded, and the storeroom could use a good mopping."

"Wow, that all sounds too much like work."

"Then don't do it, Josh."

"I was just kidding," he said in protest.

"Too bad I'm not in the mood for it today. I've changed my mind. Don't bother signing in."

"You're firing me on my first day back?" His expression had turned from light and playful to full-on despair in an instant.

"No, you can come back at three when we reopen." The relief was evident in his face, until I added, "But you've got to take this job seriously. I'm not in the mood for your antics."

"I'm sorry, Eleanor. I guess I'm just a little giddy being back at work."

The boy was starting to drive me as crazy as his father did. "Forget I said that. I don't need any robots working for me, so don't start, understand?"

"I do." He looked suitably contrite as he added, "Dad

told me what happened last night. I should have realized you'd still be shook up by it."

"Anybody would," I said, just a little mollified by his new attitude. "It's not pleasant being robbed at gunpoint."

"I'm sure it's not." He looked around the dining room, then added, "Are you sure I can't get to work on those trash cans now?"

"I'm sure," I said. "Go on, take off."

Josh shrugged, and as he headed for the door, he called out, "I'll see you at three, then."

Maddy came out a second later and saw Josh retreating. "Did he decide not to work, after all? I thought Josh wanted to come back to work here."

"He does, but I told him to take off until three. That's when he's supposed to be out of school anyway, so it shouldn't be any kind of hardship for him. I thought about giving Josh some of Greg's work, but he's paying his way through college, not saving up to buy a pickup truck."

"What happened to his MINI Cooper?" she asked.

"Marybeth took it away from him so he couldn't run away again."

"Why am I not surprised," Mandy said. "If I were Josh, I'd never drive that car again."

"Funny, that's exactly what he told me."

Maddy smiled. "Great minds think alike, what can I say? I took care of the kitchen, so we're free for an hour. More like fifty-seven minutes," she added as she glanced at the clock. "What did Josh say to our customers, anyway?"

"You saw that?"

"I was peeking from the kitchen."

"He implied that they were towing cars in the lot, and that our customers were in imminent danger of losing their transportation."

"At least they're gone," Maddy said. "So, what are you going to do on your break?"

"I really should go shopping for a new safe," I said.

"Yeah, well, I should cut down on my chocolate cake intake, but I don't see that happening, either."

"What's going on? What did you have in mind?" I asked my sister. She was a genius at getting me in trouble, or into awkward situations at the very least.

"I think we should arm you," she said.

"I'm not carrying a gun around in my purse. I've got pepper spray."

"For all the good it did you. Do you want to get robbed again?" Maddy asked.

"You know the answer to that, so why ask it? Do you honestly think that if I have a gun, it will make things any better?"

"Dad always thought so," Maddy said, something I knew to be true. Our father had been a firm believer in having weapons to defend his family and his home, and growing up, we'd been taught a healthy respect for them.

"That was his choice, and going around town unarmed is mine," I said, knowing that the decision was right for me. "But if you want to go Smith and Wesson shopping, by all means, don't let me stop you."

Maddy pursed her lips. "So let me get this straight. It's not the self-defense you have a problem with, it's doing it with handguns, is that right?"

"I guess so," I said after thinking about it for a few seconds. "What other option does that leave me?"

"I've got something that might help, if you're really interested. I know it's worked wonders for me."

Sometimes my sister could be really cryptic. "What are you talking about, Maddy?"

"I think we should check out a site I like on the Internet."

"You know my old computer died," I said. "Josh talked me into getting a new one, but it won't be here for a few weeks."

"That's no problem. I've got my Dell XPS in my bag."

As she got it out and set it up on one of the tables, I asked, "Don't you need a phone line for that, or something?"

"Eleanor, how do you manage? It's the twenty-first century. We'll do what everyone else does and steal someone else's signal."

"I don't feel good about that," I said.

"It's not actually stealing. Someone around here has Wi-Fi, so we're just borrowing a little access."

"I'm not sure I agree with your ethics."

"Don't worry, this will just take a sec," she said as she connected to the Internet. "Look at this," Maddy said as she stared at the screen ten seconds later. I didn't want to peek, since I still wasn't sure it was proper, but my curiosity finally got the better of me.

I don't know what site she pulled up, but if it was any indication of what was out there, it was hard to believe everyone wasn't going around armed with at least something. There was an array of stun guns, Tasers, pepper sprays, knives, collapsible batons, crossbows, slingshots, and a few things that I couldn't even dream what their functions might be.

"Shut it off," I said.

"It's a part of living in the modern world, Eleanor. The sooner you face that fact, the safer you'll be."

"I don't want to overreact because of what happened last night," I said. "I got robbed, and it shook me pretty badly, but I'm not going to go around armed to the teeth."

"It's your duty to protect yourself," Maddy said.

"What if I'd had a stun gun like you carry around all of the time?" I asked. "He had a real one, and I'm not about to start carrying around a revolver in my purse to match weaponry with him."

"Don't be silly," Maddy said.

"At least you're willing to see that much."

"You'd have to carry an automatic," Maddy replied.

I pushed the lid down on her computer. "I'm done talking about this."

She lifted the top back up. "You're making a mistake."

"It won't be the first time, and I'm sure it won't be the last," I said.

"Okay, but have you ever really looked at my stun gun? It's really kind of neat."

"I don't know how it could be."

Maddy reached into her oversized bag and pulled out the thin black rectangular box, about four inches tall. There were two small probes coming out of the top of it.

"I've seen it before," I said.

"But we've never really talked about it. Eleanor, this might not look like much, but it's pretty powerful for its size, and it runs on a nine-volt battery," she said proudly.

"And you actually think that's enough to stop someone from attacking you?"

"It puts out eighty thousand volts, Eleanor. It will do the job. Here, why don't you take this one? I'll get myself another one."

"Thanks, but I'm not interested," I said, afraid to touch it. "I'll stick with my pepper spray."

As I started for the door, she asked, "Where are you going?"

"I need a little fresh air. I'll see you in half an hour."

I walked out of the Slice before she could stop me.

It was a beautiful afternoon, but my sister had nearly spoiled it for me. While it was certainly true that I'd hated how helpless I'd felt the night before, did she really think having one of those gadgets of hers in my purse would have changed anything? The only way it would have done any good at all was if my attacker hadn't been armed. If that were true, I'd either fight him or run as fast as I could. The old "fight or flight" worked just fine for me. At least my job allowed me to wear blue jeans and tennis shoes, both conducive to bolting, should the need and the opportunity ever arise again.

I found myself wandering around the brick promenade in front of the shopping complex of buildings. I didn't do that nearly enough, staying safe locked up in my kitchen and only commuting back and forth to the alley, where I stowed my car. There really was a lot to offer to the citizens of Timber Ridge in our little shopping complex.

I walked past Paul's Pastries, thought about going in to see how he was doing after last night, and then I realized that food wasn't the comfort I needed at the moment. It would be too tempting to bury my feelings in a chocolate éclair. I glanced at his door and saw that Paul had changed his hours. He was shutting down half an hour earlier than he had in the past, and I realized that if I was ever going to get another treat, I'd have to do it during the first part of my break, and not the latter. The display cases—normally overflowing with donuts, pies, and cakes—now stood bare.

For some reason, the shop looked haunted to me, like the shell of something that used to be alive.

Last night had evidently hit me harder than I'd realized.

Right beside Paul's place was a storefront that gave me shivers, even on my best of days. It had housed a clothing store, but the owner had long since departed for the warm climate of Florida. No one had rented the store since, and a cluster of naked mannequins stood in the center of the shop, as if they were gathered for a meeting on how best to overthrow the world. It was bad enough in the daytime, but the security lights inside at night gave them all a weird, otherworldly appearance that never failed to make me pick up my pace whenever I walked past the window.

Slick's Sports was on the end of the row, closest to the side street that ran perpendicular to our shops. Slick was a balding middle-aged man with a full beard. He'd kept in shape throughout the years, and I often saw him running past the Slice, at all times of day and night.

He was adding clothing to a sales rack in front of the shop as I walked past.

"Eleanor, have you finally come to get some running shoes?"

"Not yet," I said. "But I see you keep at it all of the time."

"That's how I stay so fit," he said as he slapped his flat belly under his shirt. "I run six days a week, and I couldn't imagine what my life would be without it."

"At least you take one day off," I said, trying to be funny.

"That's when I ride my bike," he said. "It's good to work different muscles every now and then." He lowered his voice, and then added, "Sorry to hear about your trouble last night. I've been thinking about it, and if you'd like me to walk you to your car at night when you close, I'd be happy to do it. All you have to do is call."

"I appreciate the offer," I said, "but I'm not sure what your wife would think."

Slick and his wife had three grown sons, and had been married, in Slick's teasing words, "all their lives."

"It was her idea in the first place. She was a big fan of your husband." He hastily added, "So was I. You know that."

"I do," I said. "Thanks for the offer, but I'll be fine. I'm getting a safe to keep my deposits in until I can bank the next day, so it won't be a problem."

"That's the smartest thing I've heard all day. Come on in."

I glanced at my watch and saw that I had just ten minutes left of my break. "I'd love to, but I'm kind of pressed for time right now."

"Are you sure? I've got a safe you might like," he said.

"Since when did you start carrying safes?"

"We live in the North Carolina Mountains. Some of my customers have guns, so I started carrying them as a service."

"I don't need to store any firearms," I said.

"I know that, but I've got the perfect unit for you. I'll give you a merchant's price break, so you can't pass it up." We had an informal agreement among shop owners to give each other discounts as a way of fostering team spirit and a sense of community on the square. Paul and I sometimes got the worst end of the deal, since we offered perishable items, but most folks were good not to take advantage of us. And if they did, they'd suddenly find their food arriving at their tables a little later every time, with some toppings appearing and disappearing like magic. It didn't take long for anyone who abused the system to get the point.

"I'm not going to take advantage of you," I said. "It wouldn't be fair to you, since you rarely get pizza at my shop."

"Doesn't matter," Slick said. "My boys do, and you've

always taken good care of them. Why don't you let me repay the favor?"

I was a big fan of his sons, and I had indeed cut them some slack over the years. Why not take advantage of a friend's offered generosity? "Okay, you sold me."

"Don't you want to see it first?" Slick asked, clearly baffled by my sudden turnaround. "I haven't even quoted you a price."

"You're right. I don't have long, though, so we need to make it quick."

Slick grinned, and I asked, "What's so funny?"

"I've heard of high-pressure sales before, but never from the customer."

I followed him inside, and he showed me a stout-looking metal box. "It's nice," I said, "but what's to keep someone from just picking it up and carrying it off?"

"We bolt it to the floor," he said, as though I'd missed something obvious. "I can have one for you by tomorrow, and I'll install it myself before you open for business." He grabbed a piece of paper and wrote a price down on it. "This is ten percent over my cost, to cover my handling fees. Should I order one for you?"

Glancing at the figure, I thought it was a substantial amount just to keep my money safe, if I actually had any left after buying it. Still, it was better than having a gun shoved under my nose. "I'll take it. Thanks, Slick, and thank Nancy for me, too."

"You bet," he said.

I left the store feeling immeasurably better, and by the time I got back to the pizzeria, I was beginning to think that I'd managed to put the robbery behind me.

Until I saw who was waiting for me out in front of the Slice.

Chapter 3

"Don't tell me," I said to the chief of police as I started to unlock the door of the pizzeria. "You found the guy who robbed me already."

Kevin Hurley shook his head. "What? No, we don't have a clue who did it."

I looked at him, startled by the frank admission. "You're actually telling me the truth? What happened to the usual line that you're looking at several suspects?"

He shrugged. "I could tell you that, but would you believe it? Eleanor, I'm afraid it was just a random holdup, and we probably aren't ever going to catch the guy. Have you bought a safe yet?"

"I just ordered one from Slick," I admitted.

"Good," he said.

With the door open, I hesitated before going inside. "Was there something I could help you with?"

He looked almost embarrassed to say what was on his mind, until he finally blurted out, "I came by looking for Josh."

"It was an assembly, Kevin. Does it really matter that

he ditched it to come in early to work? He's missed being here."

That got his attention. "Are you telling me that my son left school early?"

It was clearly news to him. Now I'd gotten one of my employees in trouble without meaning to. "You can't exactly take the high road on this one. I seem to remember that we skipped a few assemblies ourselves in our time, remember?"

He clearly didn't like having the past thrown back at him, but if he was going to bust his son about what he'd done himself in the past, it was my duty to step up and remind him. At least that's the way I saw it.

"That was different," Kevin said.

"Why is that, because it was you, and not him?"

The police chief decided to ignore the question, no matter how valid it might be. "If he's not here, then where is he?"

"I'm not sure. When I closed at two, I sent him away." I glanced at my watch and saw that I had one minute before we were due to open again. "If you hang around for a few minutes, I'm sure he'll be here."

Maddy hurried toward us, and when she got to the door, she asked, "Am I late? I couldn't be. After yesterday, I made sure I had plenty of time to get back."

"No, you've still got a good thirty seconds on the clock," I said.

"Sweet," Maddy said as she looked at Kevin. "Good afternoon, Chief." She looked at me and asked, "Eleanor, is anything wrong?"

"No, everything's fine," I said.

My sister nodded. "Then I'll get started on the dinner prep."

She walked past me, and as she went inside, Maddy

raised an eyebrow in my direction. I shook my head slightly, and she nodded. A great many words were spoken without either one of us saying a thing.

"Sorry, but I need to get to work myself," I said.

"If you don't mind, I'll wait out here for Josh."

"Come on inside. I'll buy you a Coke."

He shook his head. "Thanks, but I don't mind waiting for him outside."

I touched his shoulder, and he turned toward me as I said, "No offense, but I doubt you'll do much for my business loitering around in front of the pizzeria in your uniform. It makes it look too much like a crime scene. Come on in. You can speak with your son the second he gets here. I promise."

To my surprise, Kevin nodded his agreement. "Fine, I'll take a soda, but I'm going to pay for it. You know how I feel about cops taking freebies from the people they're being paid to protect."

"Suit yourself," I said as we went inside.

"You're not going to fight me on it?" he asked as he took a seat by the window.

"I never argue with a customer who wants to pay me," I said. "I'll even charge you double if it will make you feel any better."

"No, thanks. I appreciate the offer, though."

I grabbed his drink, and then returned with it to his table. "If you'd like something to eat, we happen to cater to that kind of customer, too."

I was being flip, but he didn't respond in kind. "The drink's fine." Something was clearly on his mind, but he obviously didn't feel like sharing, and I didn't have any desire to drag it out of him.

He was still staring at the front door when I walked back into the kitchen with Maddy.

She looked up from cutting onions. "What was that all about? Did he find the guy who robbed you last night?"

"No, he pretty much admitted that wasn't going to happen. He's looking for Josh, and without realizing it, I happened to tell him that his son skipped school today."

Maddy laughed. "He shouldn't get too high-and-mighty about it. I remember Kevin missing a day or two himself."

"I reminded him myself, but he seems to have forgotten all about that," I said.

"Parenthood probably does that to you," she said. After a moment's pause, she asked, "Do you ever regret not having kids with Joe?"

It was a serious question from out of the blue, and for a second, I froze.

Maddy must have seen something in my face. "I'm so sorry," she said as she put down the knife in her hand. She started toward me, no doubt to wrap me in one of the embraces she reserved just for me.

I took a step back, and she immediately understood.

After a moment, Maddy said, "Sometimes that gear in my head between thinking something and saying it breaks down."

"You know, it's not like we never talked about it," I said, suddenly feeling like talking about it, much to my own surprise. "But we were remodeling the house right after we got married, and then we were opening the Slice. It was just never a good time, and then he died so suddenly."

"I'm so sorry," Maddy said.

I hadn't even realized I'd been crying until I felt tears tracking down my cheeks. I wiped them with my hand, then asked, "How about you?"

"That's a funny thing," she said. "I loved every last one of my ex-husbands, but never enough to have children with any of them. I'm sure that has to say something about me, doesn't it?"

"Or your ex-husbands," I suggested.

"Good, I like that. Let's blame it on them."

Maddy picked up the knife again and started chopping. I composed myself, and started cleaning up the prep area around her. I knew it drove her crazy, but I couldn't help myself.

When the kitchen door opened, I expected to see Josh, but I was surprised when Greg Hatcher came in. He wasn't working the early shift, but he was scheduled to come in later that night.

"What are you doing here?" I asked, and then I noticed his bloody nose.

"What happened to you?" I added as I wet a washcloth and handed it to him.

"That's what the chief wanted to know," Greg said as he took the damp cloth from me and held it to his nose. "There's a little good news. I don't think it's broken." He took the washcloth away, looked at the blood on it, and then reapplied it to the tender spot.

"Eleanor asked you a question," Maddy said.

"I don't guess either one of you would believe I ran into a door, would you?"

My sister and I shook our heads in perfect unison.

Greg laughed wryly. "Yeah, I don't think Chief Hurley believed me, either. Fortunately, Josh showed up the second after I walked in, and he had something more immediate to deal with than my nose."

"We don't," I said. "I'm just going to ask you one more time. Who hit you?"

"This is nothing," he said. "I'm fine."

"Who punched you in the nose?" I repeated.

"Hey, you said you were going to stop asking." When

he saw that neither one of us was amused by his reply, he admitted, "Wade did it, okay?"

"Your own brother hit you?" I asked.

"Are you kidding me? He's been beating me up since we were kids. This is nothing new."

There was an odd expression on his face, and if I didn't know any better, I could have sworn he was smiling.

"What's so funny?" I asked.

"This is the first time I ever hit him back," Greg said.

"Violence never solves anything," Maddy said.

"You couldn't be more wrong," Greg said. "You should have seen the look on his face when I stood up to him. I just discovered that it's the best feeling in the world bullying a bully. He looked stunned when I popped him right back, straight on the nose, on the same spot he'd just clobbered me. I don't care if it hurts to laugh, you should have seen him scurrying away. I doubt he'll be taking any more swings at me."

"So you're all right," I said as I filled a plastic freezer bag with ice and handed it to him.

"Never better, if you want to know the truth." He traded the bag for the washcloth—which I directed him to drop into the hamper for soiled garments—and gingerly applied the ice to the bridge of his nose.

"What's this going to do to your settlement negotiations?" Maddy asked.

"Who cares? I don't need the money any worse than he does, and I'll be dipped in asphalt if I'm going to be the first one to cave in. I've done it in the past, but that doesn't mean I ever have to do it again."

"What started the fight?" I asked.

"Guess. My dear brother demanded yet again that I give him three-quarters of the estate and quit stalling, or he said he'd whip my tail. When I said no, he hit me. That's when I hit him back. It was a two-punch fight, but at least this time I had one of the swings. That feels better," he said as he shifted the ice on the bridge of his nose.

I studied him carefully and then said, "Don't be surprised if you get a pair of black eyes out of it."

"Totally worth it," he said. "Do you mind if I use your office? I'd like to sit down so I can get a better grip on this ice bag."

"Sure, just try not to bleed on anything. I'd hate to get a health code violation for it."

"Got it," he said, his words a little softened by the effect of the blow to his nose. "I'll be fine to work this evening. I just want to rest a little."

"The rest is a good idea," I said, "but you need to take tonight off. We've got it covered, now that Josh is back at work."

"I'm not so sure he'll be staying," Greg said.

"What do you mean?"

"His dad wasn't all that pleased with him when I saw him," Greg said. "I'll be fine. Just give me a little time to rest up."

I peeked through the door and saw that Kevin was gone, while his son was busy cleaning all of the tables, though they'd been spotless when we'd left them an hour ago.

"Where's your dad?" I asked as I walked out to join Josh.

"He had to go," Josh said. "Sorry I was late," he added. "I lost track of time."

"No problem. Is everything okay?"

He shrugged. "As good as they're ever going to be. I don't want to talk about it, if that's okay with you."

"Trust me, it's fine," I said.

I started back toward the kitchen when Josh asked me, "Is Greg all right?"

"You know what? I don't think I've ever seen him this happy."

Josh stared hard at me. "He got socked in the nose—you know that, don't you?"

"I don't think that's why he's so happy," I said. "But if you want to know what's going on with him, you're going to have to ask him yourself."

Josh dropped his rag on the table he'd been cleaning and headed back to the kitchen. I hadn't meant for him to ask immediately, but everything was set out front, so we were ready to reopen for our dinner customers.

I grabbed the rag and then flipped the sign to OPEN just as Greg walked out of the kitchen area.

"If you don't need me, I think I'll take off," he said. The ice pack was gone, and his nose had stopped bleeding.

"That's not a bad idea. You might want to take some Excedrin when you get back to your place."

"I'm way ahead of you," he said. "Maddy already fixed me up with some."

"Would you like one of us to drive you home?"

He shook his head, and I saw him wince from the motion. Clearly, the elation he'd felt at fighting back had been replaced by the reality of a hard punch in the snout. "I'm good," he said. "See you tomorrow."

"If you're up to it," I said.

"Are you kidding? I wouldn't miss a shift for the world."

After he was gone, Josh came back out front. "Maddy said I should relieve you out here so you can go back to the kitchen."

"You've got the dining room," I said as I walked back to join my sister.

"What's up?" I asked as I put my apron on.

"That's what I wanted to ask you. Can you believe Greg? I didn't know he had it in him."

"You know I don't approve of fighting," I said.

"Pushing a bully back is important. It took a lot of guts for him to finally stand up for himself."

"Just what we need around here, more drama," I said.

I started working up a few crusts so we'd be ready when we needed them, knuckling the dough into their pans. I admired the fancy tossing I saw some pizza makers do on television, but it wasn't a skill I ever planned to learn. Even if I could throw crusts with the best of them, there was no one in the kitchen to see me do it. I'd tried it a time or two, but all I'd ever managed was pizza dough on the floor and an imprint on the ceiling, where an errant crust had struck when I'd tossed it too hard.

Ten minutes later, we had our first customer, and the evening hours flew past in a steady blur of pizzas and sandwiches. Maddy and Josh kept busy out front, and I was hopping all night in the kitchen.

It was the kind of evening I lived for these days, but the joy didn't last for the rest of the night. We had a visitor who upset our happy moods the second she walked through the door.

Katy Johnson—Greg's on-again, off-again girlfriend—burst into the kitchen like she was running away from a fire. Tall and curvy, Katy had flaming-red hair and an attitude that matched, most of the time.

"Where is he?" she snapped at me as she looked wildly around the place.

I knew who she was looking for, but that didn't mean I had to answer the question. "Sorry, Katy, but customers aren't allowed back here."

"I'm not buying anything. I have to find Greg."

"He's off tonight," I said. "I'm going to have to ask you to leave."

She stared hard at me, and then to my complete and utter surprise, Katy started crying. It was the strongest display of vulnerability I'd ever seen in her.

"Eleanor, I've got to find him. I did something stupid, and I can't fix it," she said through her tears.

"I don't know much that can't be repaired in this world," I said, my voice softening. The girl was obviously in some serious pain.

"This is too much. Greg caught me with Wade," she simpered.

"Are you talking about his *brother*? Are you kidding me?"

"We were just kissing," Katy said as she dabbed at her tears. "It was all pretty innocent. Honestly."

"I'm sure Greg didn't think so," I said. "Katy, what were you thinking?"

"Greg was getting tired of me," she said, nearly wailing the words. "I had to show him he couldn't just throw me away like an old pair of shoes."

I lost a lot of my sympathy for her then. I hated relationship games, and always had. "How did Greg find out?" Not that he needed much of a clue. Small-town living was notorious for gossip, and Timber Ridge was no exception.

"Wade set me up!" she screamed.

Josh came into the kitchen and looked straight at me. "Eleanor, is everything all right?"

"It's fine," I said, more out of habit than actuality. Katy was anything but fine, but she'd brought it all on herself.

Josh nodded, glanced sideways at Katy, then took the wisest course of action he could; he left.

"Katy, how did Wade set you up?"

"I was at his place, you know, to talk," Katy said. "He excused himself, made a phone call, and then he came back in with drinks. The next thing I knew, we were on the couch making out. I would have stopped it—I suddenly lost my taste for revenge—when Greg crashed in. He was furious, and Wade admitted that he wanted his little brother to see that he could have me whenever he wanted. Greg's face just died. He wouldn't listen to me, no matter how much I begged him to give me another chance. Now I can't find him, and I have to make it right between us."

"Good luck with that," I said.

"That's it? You're just going to stand there? Don't you care?"

I stared at her for a few seconds, and then said, "I care about Greg, and you hurt him. Don't expect any sympathy from me."

"Wade did this," she said petulantly. "Why can't you see that?"

"You were the one on the couch with him, Katy."

"I wish he were dead," she said, her voice barely above a whisper.

"Be careful what you wish for," I said.

"You're useless to me—you know that, don't you?"

Before I could reply, she slammed the kitchen door open and stalked off. I grabbed my cell phone and called Greg the second she was gone. It sounded as though he needed a friend right now.

He didn't pick up, which was no real surprise. When the voice mail came on, I said, "Greg, Katy was just here. I know what happened. If you need to talk to somebody, I'm here for you. Call me. I don't care what time of night you get this. It's going to be all right," I added, then ran out of things to say. It was in his hands now. If he needed me, Greg knew where to reach me.

Maddy came in as I hung up. "What was that about?"

"I'm surprised you didn't come back for the fireworks," I said as I started cleaning up my station.

"I would have, but I had a table of customers that wouldn't let me go. What did you say to her, Eleanor? She shot out of here looking like you'd smacked her in the face with a pizza pan. You didn't, did you?"

"No, though it was probably what she deserved. She and Greg had a fight." Wow, that was the understatement of the year.

"There's more to it than that, though, isn't there?"

My sister had some kind of radar when it came to conflict. I nodded. "She went to Wade's house to make Greg jealous, and Wade called him. When Greg got there, Wade and Katy were kissing on the couch, and Greg left before Katy could say anything."

Maddy shook her head. "Boy, I can't even imagine how she could have killed the chance of them ever getting back together better than that. Greg hates his brother."

"Katy knows it, too, so it's not like she's innocent in all of this."

Maddy said, "That's true, but Wade has reached a new low, even for him. I can't imagine what Greg must be feeling. We should call him."

"I already did, but he didn't answer. I left him a message to call me if he needed me, but there's not much else I can do."

"Young love. Who needs it?" Maddy asked.

"Hearts seem to break easier then, don't they?"

Maddy nodded, and then started to leave. She stopped at the door, looked back at me, and said, "I nearly forgot. I need two large specials with extra anchovies, capers, hot peppers, and pineapple."

"You're kidding, right?" I've been known to throw almost anything on a pizza, but even *I* had my limits.

"That's what took me so long. I tried to talk them out of it, but they insisted."

"To each his own," I answered as I made the pizzas. As they went through the oven on the conveyor, I couldn't help worrying about Greg. Seeing Katy with anyone else would be bad, but finding her with his brother had to kill him. I just hoped he didn't do anything stupid because of it.

We finally got our last customer out of the pizzeria, and I still hadn't heard from Greg. Knowing him, I figured he was out driving around, trying to figure out how his love life had managed to fall apart so quickly. I wouldn't trade places with him for anything in the world.

Maddy came back and was pleasantly surprised that the kitchen was clean. "You started without me," she said.

"We had a lull, so I thought I'd take care of the dishes while I had the chance."

"Good. I'm beat," she said.

"Go on home," I said. I'd already sent Josh home, since he had a test the next day that he'd admitted he'd failed to study for.

"No, I'm good," Maddy said. "I'll hang around a little longer."

I started to say something, when I finally got it. "You're not going to leave here until I do, are you?"

"What's wrong with that? I work here, too."

"There's more to it than that," I said. "Don't even try to lie to me. You're going to hover over me until I go home." I was kind of psychic when it came to my sister. She could fool a great many people if she put her mind to it, but Maddy had never been able to lie to me.

"It's my fault you got robbed last night," Maddy said, her voice breaking with the confession.

"Were you the one holding a gun on me? The thief wasn't as tall as you, and don't try to tell me you slouched down. Besides, I would have recognized your voice, no matter how hard you tried to disguise it."

"Don't be ridiculous."

"Then if you weren't holding the gun, how was it your fault?"

Maddy was fighting the tears, and I gave her time to compose herself. After a minute, she said, "If I'd been with you, he wouldn't have risked taking on two of us."

I hugged my sister, and then I said, "Maddy, I know in my heart that it wouldn't have stopped him. He had a gun, and neither one of us did. The only thing it would have accomplished is that both of us would have been terrified."

"Even so, you shouldn't have had to face it alone," Maddy said sternly. "I left you."

"I'm the one who told you to go home, remember? Listen, we can debate this all night, but nothing's going to change the facts. There wasn't anything either one of us could have done to stop him."

"I'm still staying," she said as she leaned against the wall and crossed her arms over her chest.

"Fine. But I'm not ready to go yet. I have to balance

the register receipts, make out the deposit, and sweep up the front."

"At least that part's done," she said. "Josh and I cleaned up the dining room after the last customer left."

"Good enough. I suppose if I can't talk you out of staying, you can watch me work. I always did like having an audience."

"Liar," she said, finally releasing some of the tension that had been between us.

I laughed. "Okay, I hate attention, but I'll make an exception for you."

As I ran the report on the cash register, I counted the money we had. It balanced on the first try—miracle of all miracles—and I filled out the deposit slip and slid it into the bag, along with the money we were banking.

"Now what do I do with it?" I asked, more to myself than to my sister.

"One thing we're not doing," she said as she took the pouch from me, "we're not walking out the front door with it."

"Agreed," I said. "So, where does that leave us until the safe arrives?"

My sister looked around the kitchen for a minute, nodded, and then slid the pouch on the conveyor into the heart of the pizza oven. Unless a crook knew where to look, it was doubtful he'd be able to spot the bag there.

"What if somebody breaks in because they're craving a pizza?" I asked jokingly.

"Then they get a bonus for their trouble, but do you honestly think that's going to happen?"

"No, but then again, I never thought anyone in Timber Ridge would rob me."

"We can put it someplace else, if you'd feel more comfortable," Maddy said.

"That's as good a spot as any," I said. "Come on, let's get out of here."

"I agree."

As we walked outside, Maddy said loudly, "There's no money on us tonight. Just two poor gals going home after a hard day's work."

I looked around to see who she was talking to, but there was no one in sight. "What's that about?"

Maddy smiled. "If the robber came back to steal again, I wanted to give him fair warning that we weren't carrying any cash on us."

Just then, someone stepped out of the shadows, and I felt my heart drop to my knees.

Maddy's hand dove into her purse, but I stopped her before she could pull out her stun gun.

"It's okay," I told her. Turning to the uniformed officer I'd met the night before, I said, "Good evening, Officer Garvin. Thanks for coming by to check on us."

He nodded. "I'm supposed to make sure you get to your car safely."

"We're fine," Maddy said.

"I can see that, but it's the chief's orders, and I'm not about to ignore them."

As the three of us walked toward the back parking lot together, I said to him, "I'm sorry if you got in trouble last night. It's not fair, the chief putting you on the graveyard shift just for standing up for me." As I said the last part, a shiver ran down my back. "Graveyard" probably wasn't the best choice of words.

"It's absolutely not a problem," he said. "To be honest with you, I kind of like working this time of night. Everything's quiet, you know?" He paused, then added, "Well, at least it usually is."

We were finally at our cars, and after I thanked him for

the escort, the officer nodded his head toward us and walked away.

"He's nice," Maddy said. She'd been oddly quiet during our walk.

"He seems to be."

Maddy added thoughtfully, "I wonder if he's single?"

"He's not exactly your type, is he?"

Maddy said, "He's not too young for me, if that's what you're thinking."

"No, but I can't imagine that he's rich enough."

"That's not fair," Maddy said. "My first husband didn't have much money."

"And less by the time you were finished with him," I said.

"You've got a point." She yawned, and then said, "I'm going home. It was a long day, wasn't it?"

"They get that way sometimes. I'll see you tomorrow."

We got into our cars and drove away in different directions. I'd half-expected her to follow me home, and I was gratified to see her drive toward her apartment, instead. I was a grown woman, perfectly able to take care of myself.

But I had to admit that I'd felt better walking to my car with a police escort. I had to give Kevin Hurley credit for that. He took his job seriously, no matter how he was feeling about me at the moment.

I'd been in my house that morning just long enough to shower and change clothes after staying all night with Maddy, so it was good to be home for the night. Whenever I was away from it, I missed it, and not just because of the comfort I felt being around my own things.

No, there was more to it than that. I could sense Joe's presence there more than anywhere else in the world, including the pizzeria. He'd poured his heart and soul into our house renovation, and I could swear there was still a part of him there in it. I was glad I had that. There was no gravestone marking my husband's passing, no monument or memorial. Per his wishes, I'd had him cremated, and his ashes were spread in the Appalachian Mountains, tenderly poured into a stream, where they'd be among some of the places he loved best. It was a fitting end, and one I'd arranged to share with him someday.

But for now, I had him all around me.

I took a quick shower, then headed off for bed. Usually, I needed to read at least a little every night before going to sleep, but Maddy had been right. For some reason, the day had been particularly trying, and I felt as though my energy had been drained from me by more than just work.

At two minutes after three, I was jolted awake by the telephone. The only thing I could think of was that Greg had finally decided to take me up on my offer to talk.

How I wish that was what the phone call had been about.

Chapter 4

"Greg?" I asked as I rubbed my eyes with my free hand after grabbing my telephone. "Is that you?"

"Now why would you say that?" Chief Hurley asked.

"Sorry, Kevin, I thought it was Greg Hatcher. I told him to give me a call, no matter how late he got in. What's going on?" I stared blearily at the clock, trying to make out the numbers. As the fog started to clear, I could see that it was two minutes past three in the morning. That helped wake me more than a cup of coffee. "What's going on? Did something happen to Maddy?" She was the only real family I had left, so it was pretty natural that my thoughts would go straight to her.

"No, as far as I know, your sister's fine. I'm not sure I can say the same about your deliveryman, though."

"Oh, no. Something happened to Greg, didn't it?"

"Besides the fact that I can't find him, I wouldn't care to speculate on that. Do you have any idea where he might be?"

None of this was making any sense. "Hang on a second. Why are you looking for Greg? What happened?"

"You're going to find out soon enough, so I might as

well tell you now. Somebody took a rolling pin to the back of his brother's head, and the way they've been fighting lately, it just makes sense that I want to talk to him."

I couldn't believe what I was hearing. "Do you honestly think Greg had something to do with the attack on his brother?"

"It's more than assault, Eleanor. It's murder. He died on the scene."

"And you think Greg is the murderer."

"I didn't say that I thought he did it, just that I needed to interview him." He paused a second, then added, "I'm not ready to say he's not a killer, either. That's why we need to have a conversation as quickly as possible. The only problem is, I can't find him."

"So you thought I might know where he was," I said, finally clearing out some of the cobwebs left over from being suddenly awakened.

"That's not the only reason for this call," he said. "I need you to come down to your restaurant."

"What's wrong? Are you hungry?"

"No, and even if I were, it wouldn't do me any good. You can't exactly make me something to eat. It's a crime scene right now."

"Please don't tell me you're at the Slice," I said as I rubbed my eyes again.

"I wish I didn't have to. Wade was murdered in your kitchen. I need you to get down here as soon as you can."

"You don't need me to identify the body, do you? Honestly, I didn't really know Wade all that well." The gears in my mind were spinning at an alarming rate, and mostly I was thinking about Greg, and the different ways his brother had pushed him in the last twenty-four hours. Could it have been hard enough to make him commit murder?

The police chief said, "Don't worry, I know Wade by sight, so there's no doubt about that. What I need to know is if the murder weapon belongs to you."

"A murderer isn't likely to carry a rolling pin around with him waiting for an opportunity to use it, is he?"

"Are you coming down on your own, or do I need to send a car after you?" It was easy to hear the weariness in his voice.

"I'll be there in ten minutes," I said.

I hung up the phone and called Maddy. I'd expected to wake her up, but I was surprised to hear music playing in the background when she answered.

"You're not even asleep yet?" I asked.

"I tried, but it wasn't working out, so I decided to make myself a pitcher of margaritas, instead. Come on over, we'll make it a party."

"Not tonight," I said. "Somebody killed Greg Hatcher's brother, and the police can't find Greg."

"Hang on a second," she said. I heard the telephone clatter to the floor, and the music died abruptly. "That's better. Why did the chief call you?"

"He wants me to identify the murder weapon. Someone used a rolling pin on Wade."

"And he thinks you know who owns all the rolling pins in town?"

"Did I forget to tell you? It happened in the pizzeria's kitchen, and Kevin thinks the pin belongs to me."

Without a moment's hesitation, Maddy said, "Swing by and get me on your way. I'm going with you."

"I'd hate to interrupt your party," I said, though I'd been hoping that would be my sister's reaction to the news.

"I can't drive myself, I've had a bit too much to drink, but if you don't pick me up, I'm going to risk it anyway."

"I'll be there in six minutes," I said, hanging up as I reached for a pair of blue jeans and a T-shirt.

I made it in five, and Maddy was out front waiting for me.

"What took you so long?" she asked as she got into the Subaru.

"I had to get dressed first, unlike some people," I said.

As I drove to the pizzeria, Maddy said, "It's just awful about what happened, isn't it? I can't believe Greg's brother is dead."

"From what I've been hearing about the guy lately, I'm a little surprised that it took someone this long to get rid of him." I immediately regretted my flip choice of words. I didn't even know the young man, and here I was slamming his memory. "Strike that," I said. "My only excuse is that I'm still half-asleep and completely exhausted. I hated the way Wade jerked Greg around, but that's no excuse for being so callous about his death."

"It's okay if you talk that way to me, goodness knows I've said plenty of worse things about our fellow citizens, but I wouldn't say anything like that to the police chief."

"I'm not that crazy," I said. "I just wish I knew where Greg was."

"It doesn't look good for him, does it?"

I glanced over at Maddy, who was watching the road as intently as I had just been. Somehow she had managed to sober up from her party night. Finding out about a murder had probably done the trick, and if that hadn't been enough, having Greg as the number one suspect was probably enough to manage it. "Maddy, you don't actually think Greg had anything to do with this, do you?"

"Come on, Eleanor, we both like him, but we have to face facts. First there's the dispute over his grandparents' estate, and then Katy gets caught with Wade on the couch, and that all just happened this evening. Who knows what any of us would do when we're pushed that hard?"

"I don't believe it," I said. "Greg wouldn't kill anybody."

Maddy stroked my arm. "In my heart I don't believe it either, but we have to tell Kevin what we know."

I slowed the car so I could look at her. "Why should we tell him anything? He prides himself on his great detecting skills. Let him figure it out for himself."

"If we're the ones who tell him, we can try to give it a little positive spin. If he finds out on his own, it could be much worse."

"I don't see how," I said as I resumed driving.

"Really? Tell me you can't see Katy Johnson blubbering all over Kevin about how this whole thing is her fault. She'll make this all about her, that Greg killed Wade out of his love for her. Is that a notion we want the police entertaining for one second?"

"No, I guess you're right. It just feels like I'm being disloyal to Greg," I said.

"When in fact, it's just the opposite."

I parked in front of the shop, despite my ingrained routine of parking in back, and saw that three police cruisers had ignored the parking lot completely and were on the brick promenade itself. There was plenty of room there, since the space had originally been a road before the city fathers had covered it with pavers and converted it into a parklike atmosphere.

"This isn't going to be pretty," I said as Maddy and I approached the rest of the way on foot.

"At least we've got each other," she said.

Officer Garvin was out front, evidently waiting for us. "The chief wants to see you inside," he said.

"Thanks," I said as Maddy and I walked into the pizzeria.

Kevin was standing by the door, examining the wooden frame. "Did you lock up tonight?"

"I'm sure I did," I said. "Why?"

"There's no sign of forced entry," he said flatly.

Maddy said, "You were distracted tonight, Eleanor, remember? I'm not at all sure you locked the door when we left."

I looked at her quizzically as Kevin said, "Nice try, but it's too late to cover for your boy. Greg has a key to the place, doesn't he?"

"Not that I know of," I said.

"Are you trying to tell me that a store employee doesn't have a key to your pizzeria? Think hard before you answer. This is an official police inquiry."

"Not specifically," I said. "There's a key on a hook by the kitchen door, in case someone besides Maddy or me has to open."

"What about locking the door when you left here tonight? Do you remember doing it?"

I tried to think back to that evening. "You're not going to like my answer, but I honestly don't know. Maddy might be right. I remember getting my key out, but then we were interrupted, and I can't be sure I locked it." I saw thunderclouds roll across his brow, so I added, "It's the truth, Kevin. I'm not covering for anyone."

"Who interrupted you?" Kevin asked.

"Officer Garvin," I admitted.

"Stay right here." Kevin walked outside, and I glanced back toward my kitchen. Someone had propped the door open, and I could see the body still lying there, a rolling pin—*my rolling pin*—on the floor beside it, along with a thin-crust pizza. I could tell that pin from thirty paces, since it had a stain on it from an earlier disastrous attempt to roll out a dessert crust with blueberries embedded in it.

Kevin came back in. "He doesn't remember seeing you lock the door, but that doesn't mean you didn't do it."

"Even if we had," Maddy said, "someone could have snagged that key, made a copy, and put it back without either one of us noticing it."

"Anything's possible," he said, then softened his next words. "I hate to ask you this, but I need you to identify—"

I cut him off. "The rolling pin's mine. I can see the blueberry stains on it from here."

He nodded, at least satisfied with that part of our conversation. "We'll need it for evidence, but you'll get it back eventually."

"Forget it. I'm going to go out and buy another one. Have you had any luck finding Greg?"

The chief shook his head. "I've checked his apartment, his folks' house, and his girlfriend's place, but he's officially a missing person of interest right now."

"You didn't actually talk to Katy, did you?" I blurted out.

"No, she wasn't there. Why? Should I?"

"There's something you should know," I said. "It doesn't mean anything, but if you hear it first from her, it's going to sound a lot worse than it is."

"I'm listening," he said.

I took a deep breath, then said, "Katy was at Wade's this evening, and Greg caught them together."

"Were they in bed?"

"Of course not," I said, though I wouldn't have put it past Katy. "They were on the couch, kissing. Greg broke up with her earlier, and she was trying to get back at him."

"How'd he know she'd be there?" Kevin asked, his gaze piercing mine.

I reluctantly admitted, "Wade called him. Greg was upset, but not enough to hurt his brother."

Kevin rubbed his chin. "I don't know. That added to the fight over the grandparents' will are both pretty good reasons."

"But he didn't do it," I said.

"If he didn't, why can't we find him, then?" Kevin asked softly.

Maddy butted in. "He probably doesn't even know you're looking for him. It's not against the law to go off by yourself without telling anyone where you're headed, is it?"

Kevin took a few deep breaths; then he said, "Come on, ladies, even you two have to admit that it looks bad for the kid. I like him too, but that doesn't mean I'm going to wear blinders on this case. If he did it, I need to catch him, and the sooner I do that, the better off he'll be."

"I'm not sure of the logic of that," I said, "but think about it. If I knew where he was, would I have mistaken your telephone call for his?"

"Why did you think he was calling you at three in the morning?" Kevin asked. "There's not something going on there I should know about, is there?"

"Kevin Hurley, you should wash your mind out with soap. He's young enough to be my nephew. When Katy came by and told us what she'd done, I thought Greg might need someone to talk to, so I called and left him a message that he could phone me, any time of day or night."

He seemed to take that in, and then finally said, "If you

hear from him, find out where he is. Better yet, urge him to turn himself in."

"I'll think about it," I said.

"Eleanor, that wasn't a request—it was an order."

It was all I could do not to salute him, but I managed to keep still. "Understood." I looked back toward the kitchen, not able to make myself stare at the body again. "When can I have my restaurant back? I know it sounds cold, but I can't afford to just shut down."

"I should be able to let you have it tomorrow," he said. "I'd suggest that you take a day off and enjoy it."

"I can't see that happening. Are you certain I can't have it back any sooner?"

"It might even be later if you keep talking to me while I should be working. I'll call you when I've got a better idea of where we stand on the investigation."

I was about to lash out at him when Maddy grabbed my arm hard enough to hurt. "Thanks, Chief."

She was practically shoving me back to my car.

"Why exactly did we just give up so easily?" I asked.

"Have you ever won an argument like that with him in your life?"

"No, but that doesn't mean I shouldn't at least try," I said.

"Agreed, but let's save our battles for another day. Right now, we both need some sleep. In the morning, we'll be able to think about this with clearer heads."

"I'm too wired up to rest," I said.

"Then come in when we get to my place. I've got half a pitcher of margaritas left, and I can't think of a better late-night drink than that. It surely beats the daylights out of warm milk for a bedtime toddy. Come on, what do you say?"

"Why not?"

"That's the spirit."

I didn't think I'd ever get to sleep once we got back to her apartment, but by four A.M., I was curled up in Maddy's spare pajamas, and drifting slowly off to sleep in her guest bedroom.

At least I didn't have to get up early, since I clearly wasn't going to be making any pizzas that day.

I had a hard time sleeping in past nine, no matter how late Maddy and I had stayed up. On the other hand, she'd probably sleep until four this afternoon, since she didn't have to go into work.

I got dressed quietly, left her a note, and headed back to my place. I was glad I'd been the designated driver the night before. A hot shower helped perk me up, though I still felt a little groggy from not enough sleep. It was funny, but in college I'd been able to stay up all night without any discernable ill effects the next day. Now, if I didn't get at least seven hours of rest a night, I'd feel it for days afterward. The coffee I always set the timer for the night before was waiting patiently for me in the kitchen, and by the time I finished my first cup, I was as good as I was going to get.

As I sat at the counter trying to figure out what to do next, there was a tapping on my kitchen window.

It was Greg Hatcher, and from the look of him, he'd gotten even less sleep than I had.

I opened the window and looked down at him. "Greg, what are you doing here? Chief Hurley is looking all over town for you."

"That's why I cut through your backyard to get here. I need to talk to you, Eleanor."

I looked around outside to see if any of my neighbors

were watching us. Mrs. Huffline, on one side would be fine, but Mr. Harpold, on the other, was born to gossip. Since he'd retired from teaching school, he'd become a one-man Neighborhood Watch program.

Fortunately, no one was looking at the moment.

"Come on, you might as well come in," I said.

He started to climb in through the window when I stopped him.

"Through the back door," I said.

"Somebody might see me," he said. "Move over."

I did as he asked, and Greg surprised me by leaping up and catching the windowsill, then hoisting himself into my kitchen.

"Is that coffee?" he asked as he spotted my mug on the countertop. I noticed that he'd stepped in the dark soil under the window and was tracking up my kitchen floor, but I couldn't very well ask him to clean up after himself.

"It is," I said. "Would you like some?"

"More than anything else I can think of at the moment."

I poured him a cup, which he thankfully downed in quick gulps.

While he started on his refill, I said, "Greg, I don't know how to break it to you, but you're in more trouble than you can even imagine."

"I know," he said as he took another swallow. "I'm trying not to think about it."

"I'm guessing you heard what happened to your brother, then," I said.

"It's all over the radio," he admitted. "Thanks for that."

"The coffee?"

"No, for believing in me. You didn't ask the question that's been hanging in the air since I got here, but I'm going to answer it, anyway. Eleanor, I didn't kill my brother. I wasn't all that fond of him, and he's been driving me crazy the past few days, but I wouldn't hurt him."

"I never thought you would," I said. Maddy's musings didn't need to be voiced during this particular conversation.

"You're going to be in the lone minority, then," he said.

I could see that Greg was a wreck, nearly falling over from his tough night, but I couldn't let him stay there with me.

"I believe you," I said. "Have you thought about turning yourself in? It's too dangerous with everyone out looking for you."

"They can just keep looking," he said. "There's no way I'm going in willingly. If Hurley wants me, he's going to have to find me."

"It might not be that bad, Greg. Kevin might just want to question you so he can eliminate you as a suspect."

"Yeah, and I'm going to win the lottery, too. On second thought, I quit believing in fairy tales a long time ago. I'm going to find out who killed Wade on my own. He was a skunk of a brother, but I owe him that much. At least that much."

"I spoke with Katy last night," I said, trying to be as delicate as I could. "I'm sure the police know what happened with her by now as well."

Greg frowned. "She did something stupid, but she just wasn't thinking. Wade took advantage of that. I wonder if Sandi had any idea what he was doing."

"Sandi?" I asked.

"Sandi Meadows. Wade's been dating her for six months, and, let me tell you, she's one girl I wouldn't dream of getting mad at me. She has the disposition of a hungry grizzly bear, and I don't care how pretty she is, she isn't worth it."

"Oh, I know her. Do you think she might have killed him?"

"That depends," Greg asked. "Do you know how Wade died? They didn't say on the radio, and I couldn't exactly call up the chief of police and ask him."

I searched his eyes, and it was clear to me that he was telling the truth. "Someone hit him over the head with my maple rolling pin," I said.

Greg's face fell. "I hope he didn't suffer. He was a rat, but even he deserved better than that."

"It looked like all it took was one blow," I said. "He didn't even get to taste the pizza on the floor beside him."

"You saw him?"

I nodded. "Kevin asked me to come down to the pizzeria to identify the murder weapon this morning. You don't have a key to the Slice, do you?"

"You know I don't," Greg said. "Why? Did someone say I did?"

"No, but Kevin asked me, and that's what I told him, so we're good there."

He drained his coffee, but he wouldn't take another refill.

I stared at him a few seconds, then asked, "Greg, who would want to see your brother dead?"

"Do you mean besides me?" he asked.

"Let's just assume for the moment that you didn't do it."

"It's the truth, so we don't have to assume anything," Greg snapped at me.

"Hey, I'm on your side, remember?"

"Sorry," he said, his expression immediately softening. "I know you're one of the good guys."

"So, who makes the 'bad guy' list?"

Greg thought about it, then after thirty seconds, he

said, "I'd have to say Sandi's right up there, and if I'm being honest about it, you have to include Katy, too."

I couldn't believe what I was hearing. "You actually think your ex-girlfriend could have done it?"

He shrugged. "I don't want to, believe me, but I keep coming back to the way she acted last night. The second she figured out that Wade had set her up, she had blood in her eyes."

"Who else makes the list?"

"The only other person I can think of is Art Young."

"Why is that name familiar?" I asked.

"He's the one who loaned Wade money. From what I hear, he's all kinds of trouble. What was my brother thinking? Why did he go to a thug like that to get cash?" Greg hung his head low. "Don't answer that. I already know why. He wanted money from our grandparents' estate, and I wouldn't give it to him."

I took his face in my hands for a few seconds so that he couldn't avoid looking at me. "Greg Hatcher, you're not going to blame yourself for what happened, do you hear me? You didn't kill your brother, not by trying to obey your grandparents' wishes, or anything else."

"I just wish I believed that," he said, hanging his head down.

"I can't do anything about that," I said, my mind racing, trying to figure out how I could help him. A sudden question occurred to me.

"Greg, where were you last night? Is there any chance you have an alibi?"

He shook his head quickly. "No, nobody would believe me, and I don't have any way of proving it."

"Why? Where were you?"

"I was asleep in Josh Hurley's basement. He let me in

after his folks went to bed, and I crashed there. I do that sometimes, since he's a friend of mine."

"Why didn't you just go back to your apartment?" As I asked him the question, I realized that if he had, he would most likely be sitting in a jail cell right now.

Greg hesitated, then looked down at his hands as he explained, "I didn't want to be alone. Josh is one of my best friends, and I didn't know who else to ask. I know, it's pretty crappy as alibis go."

"Josh didn't bunk down there with you, did he?"

Greg shook his head. "No, as soon as I got settled in on the couch, he headed up to his room." Greg smiled, but there was no mirth in it. "Funny to think that the police chief was looking for me all over Timber Ridge, and I was sound asleep in his basement. Luckily, I got out of there before he found me. I was getting dressed to go back to my place when I heard it on the radio." He bit his lip, and it looked as though he was fighting back tears. After a few seconds, Greg said, "I can't believe he's gone."

"I'm so sorry," I said as I patted his cheek. "Is there anything else you can think of that might help find his killer?"

Greg looked at me with a wide open expression. "Are you going to try to find the murderer yourself? It's too dangerous, Eleanor, I can't let you do it."

I wasn't sure how he thought he could stop me, but it was a noble thought. "Don't worry, I won't be alone. I'm sure Maddy will want to help out, too."

"Why doesn't that make me feel any better? I'm going to find out what happened to him myself."

"That's going to be tough, with the police looking everywhere for you. You lift your head up in plain sight—the next thing you know, you're going to be in jail. Leave it to Maddy and me. We've done this before, remember?"

I was about to say something else when I heard a car pull up in my driveway. "Hang on a second."

I glanced out the window and saw Kevin Hurley getting out of his squad car. Before he could make it to the first step, I rushed back into the kitchen.

"It's the police," I said. "Greg, do you know what's going to happen to me if Kevin Hurley finds you here?"

"I know. You'll be in the cell next to mine. I shouldn't have come. I just didn't know where else to turn." He looked as though he was going to cry. "I don't have anything. I'm flat broke, and the cops are looking everywhere for me."

Rapidly I said, "Greg, I have a rainy-day fund I keep in my Garfield cookie jar." I figured there was about two hundred dollars there. I knew it wasn't much, but it was the best I could do on the spur of the moment. I looked out the window into the sunny day as I added, "And from where I'm standing, it's pouring outside right now for you."

"I won't take money from you," Greg said.

"And I probably can't give you any without being accused of aiding and abetting a felon. That doesn't mean you can't borrow it yourself and pay me back later." The front doorbell rang, and I added, "I have to go answer the door. I'll be right back." I shoved the cookie jar, with Garfield's prominent ginger belly, toward him.

Before I left, I paused under the archway between the kitchen and the dining room. "Greg, if you're still here when I get back, I won't be able to help you," I said softly. "So unless you're ready to turn yourself in after all, I'd take off if I were you."

"I don't really have much choice, do I?" he said, and I wished I could see even the slightest ray of hope in his eyes.

"If you want to stay in touch, my answering machine might make a good place to leave me a message." I leaned forward and patted his cheek. "Be safe, Greg."

The doorbell rang again, and I went out to talk to the chief of police.

I just hoped Greg was gone by the time I got back.

"Good morning," I said as I finally opened the door and stepped out onto the front porch. I'd made Kevin Hurley ring it three times, and he was about to head for my backyard when I walked outside.

"That took you long enough," he grumbled.

"I had a late night, remember?"

"At least you've been to bed," the police chief said.

He had a right to be grumpy, but that didn't mean I had to mollify him. "What can I do for you, Chief?"

"I wouldn't say no to a cup of coffee," he said.

"Well, I wouldn't wave good-bye to a piece of toast," I replied, still standing between him and my front door.

He looked at me, clearly perplexed, a state I often created in him. "What is that supposed to mean?"

"I thought we were saying what we wouldn't do to inanimate objects. I wouldn't wink at a sprinkler, either."

He shook his head, dropping that particular line of conversation. I wasn't just being silly. I was trying to buy Greg time to get as far away from my house as he could. Just because I had to tell the police chief he'd been there, I didn't have to make it any easier for him. Or did I have to tell him after all? It was possible that I could leave Greg out of it entirely. Kevin might think I was lying about harboring Greg for even a moment, but it was nothing he'd ever be able to prove.

"We need to talk," he said.

"I want to talk to you, too. Can I have my pizzeria back?" I asked, carefully blocking his way inside.

Kevin looked around us, and we both saw Mr. Harpold watching us from his front lawn. He'd been standing at his mailbox the entire time the squad car had been there. When he saw us looking back at him, he didn't even pretend not to be watching. "Eleanor, do you really want to do this out here?"

"I suppose not," I said. I'd stalled as long as I could. Greg had to be gone by now. If he wasn't, it was on his own head. "Come on in. I'll start a fresh batch of coffee."

He nodded thankfully, and we walked inside. I looked back at Mr. Harpold, who waved at me like he was a kid watching a parade.

I managed to stay in front of Kevin, but I still couldn't slow him from getting into my kitchen.

"What happened here?" he said as soon as he saw the open window and the footprints on the floor.

"What are you talking about?" I pretended to see the kitchen in a state of disarray for the first time. "What's going on?"

"That's what I want to know." He approached the footprints, but he was careful not to step in them. As he knelt down beside one, I noticed that there were two mugs of coffee on the counter. If he saw them, Kevin would know that I'd talked with someone—most likely Greg—which would kill the story I was going to try to sell him that this was all news to me. I moved quickly behind him and put one mug in the sink before he could spot it.

"What are you doing?" he asked me. Apparently I wasn't as stealthy as I'd hoped.

I had two choices. I could lie, or I could tell the truth.

I decided to lie. "It looks like somebody got into my cookie jar," I said.

"Don't touch that," he said as I picked up the lid against his orders. "Nice job, Eleanor. You probably just ruined the fingerprints on it."

That had been my intention all along. "Sorry. It's just a habit of mine to straighten things up."

"What's in there?" he asked as he looked at the jar.

I lifted the lid and looked inside. It was nice to be able to tell the truth at least once during our conversation. "Nothing but dust," I said.

He shook his head, and then turned to the window and looked out. "There are footprints in your flower bed," he said. I watched him scan the yard, and then he added, "Whoever was here is long gone."

"I can't believe someone broke into my home," I said, trying not to ham it up too much. "So much for our Neighborhood Watch. Where's Mr. Harpold when I need him?"

"Watching us out front, probably. This didn't happen too long ago." He studied the window, and then said, "This wasn't even locked. There's no sign of forced entry."

"I felt like a morning breeze," I lied. "I was just finishing my coffee when I had to answer the doorbell. Someone must have taken my absence as an open invitation."

"It was Greg, wasn't it?" Kevin asked, staring hard at me. "He was here."

"How should I know? I was out front talking to you, remember?"

"Eleanor, you're not helping the kid by keeping him from me, you know that, don't you?"

I worked up a little insincere indignation. "Search my house if you don't believe me. Greg's not here."

"Probably not now, but he was. Go ahead, deny it."

"I'm not going to stand here in my own kitchen and

listen to you accuse me of things you have absolutely no proof of. You need to leave."

He didn't even look surprised by my outburst. "What happened to my coffee?"

"I hear they have a mean brew down at Emily's Coffee Shop," I said.

"Be careful, Eleanor. This isn't a game, and the quicker you learn that, the better off you'll be."

"Have a nice day, Chief," I said.

He finally took the hint, then tarried at the door. "You want to file a police report on your break-in?"

"I don't see the need," I said. "Nothing's missing. I'll be more careful about unlocked windows in the future."

"You do that," he said.

I watched him leave, and after I was sure he was gone, I called out, "Greg? Greg? Are you still here?"

Thankfully, there was no answer. I wiped off the windowsill, swept up the dirt on the floor, and rinsed the coffee mugs. In three minutes, it was impossible to tell that Greg had ever been there.

But Kevin knew.

And I didn't even care.

It was clear our police chief was focusing his attention on my deliveryman, and if he was wasting his time doing that, he wasn't out searching for the real killer.

That meant that Maddy and I were going to have to do it ourselves, or Greg wouldn't stand a chance. He couldn't stay underground long on the money he'd borrowed from me, and there weren't that many places that he could hide in Timber Ridge.

Chapter 5

"Wake up," I told Maddy when she finally answered her telephone. "We have things to do today."

"Eleanor, why are you calling me on the phone? Aren't you still here at the apartment?"

This wasn't going to be as easy as I'd hoped. "I'm standing in my kitchen. I came home to take a shower and change clothes. While I was here, you'll never believe who popped in."

"It's not that tough to guess," she said. "I'm willing to bet that our chief of police came calling on you."

"He did, but that was later," I said.

"Who came sooner, then?"

"Greg Hatcher," I replied.

That got her attention. "Greg was there? What did he say? Did Kevin catch him with you? What's going on?"

"I'll tell you," I said, "as soon as I pick you up. Can you be ready and standing out in front of your place in ten minutes?"

"Come on, tell me now," she said. "It's not fair making me wait."

"No, I know you. If I tell you everything that happened with Greg and Kevin, you'll just crawl back into bed, and you can't do that, not today."

"Why shouldn't I?"

"Fine, go ahead," I said. "I'll just follow the leads Greg gave me about his brother's murder by myself. Sorry I bothered you. I'll give you a call tonight if I get the chance."

I hesitated an instant, then hung up.

Three seconds later, Maddy called back: "Okay, that is not very nice—you know that, don't you?"

"What can I say? I learned some of my best tricks from my little sister."

"I resent that remark," she said.

"I don't blame you, I'd resent it, too. The question is, are you willing to deny it?"

"You win. I'll be out front. Give me fifteen minutes, though."

I looked at my watch. "Starting right now. The timer's on."

She hung up without even saying good-bye. It might have been cruel of me to hold back the information I'd just gotten from Greg, but it was the only way I could be sure that Maddy would join me in my investigation. And there was no way I was going to snoop around today by myself. A killer was out there somewhere in Timber Ridge, and I didn't want to face whoever it was alone.

As good as her word, Maddy was out front when I got to her apartment complex. As she got into my car, she asked, "Where have you been? I've been waiting like three minutes."

"Sorry for the inconvenience," I said, though it was

pretty clear to both of us that I wasn't sorry at all. "I had to get gas before I picked you up."

"It sounds like we're going on a road trip," she said. "Where did you have in mind? If you need suggestions, I've got a dozen good ideas."

"We're not out on a lark, remember?"

"Absolutely, but I wasn't sure you did. What did Greg tell you?"

"For starters, he gave me a number of suspects he came up with overnight. At the top of his list is Wade's girlfriend, Sandi Meadows. Evidently, she's the jealous type, and she has a temper, too. Then there's Katy Johnson."

"Greg thinks his girlfriend might have killed his brother? That's kind of Shakespearian, isn't it?"

I shrugged. "He said Katy was capable of it, and I tend to believe him."

"So far, we've got two women as our suspects. Were there any men who hated Wade enough to kill him?"

I started driving. "Greg said a man named Art Young could have done it. Wade owed him money."

Maddy whistled. "You're kidding me, right? Was Wade really that stupid?"

"So you've heard of him?"

Maddy nodded. "Bob told me about him a few months ago. He was going to represent the man in a civil suit, but the case was suddenly dropped at the last second, and Art tried to get out of paying him the full amount he owed. This from a guy with illegal loans out all over our part of North Carolina, and who knows what else he's into. Bob said that Art has never been formally arrested, but he's come awfully close a few times."

"He sounds like a real prince," I said. "I can't wait to talk to him."

"Hang on a second, Eleanor. Are you serious? We're going to question him about Wade's murder?"

I glanced at my sister. "We can't really be that choosy about our suspects, can we?" I thought about it a second, then added, "Maybe we'll see if Bob will tag along with us when we talk to him. Do you think he'd do it?"

"For me? I think so," Maddy said. Bob had a never-ending crush on Maddy, and she wasn't beyond taking advantage of it when it suited her.

She looked out the front windshield, and then she asked, "Hey, I don't mean to be nosy, but where are we going?"

"I thought we might have a chat with Wade's neighbors to see if they noticed anything odd over the last few nights."

"He was killed at the Slice," Maddy reminded me, as if I needed that particular fact refreshed in my mind.

"Trust me, I didn't forget," I said. "But if Wade's neighbors are anything like mine, someone might have seen something."

"What are we going to do, just start ringing doorbells?"

I grinned. "As a matter of fact, that's exactly what we're going to do."

We pulled up in front of Wade's place, and I reached in back for something I'd brought from the house.

"A clipboard?" Maddy asked when she saw me bring it forward. "You're kidding, right?"

"This is just to get a foot in the door," I said.

"So, what are we doing, getting petitions to banish the letter *Q* from the English language, or are we trying to free Willy's little brother?"

"Nothing as dramatic as that," I said. "We're going to circulate a petition to create a Neighborhood Watch group in the area. That should give us a perfect segue into asking about Wade, and talking about what might have led to his murder. Are you in?"

"Have I ever said no to you?" she asked.

"More times than I can count," I said.

"Don't be so nitpicky," Maddy said. "It's unbecoming." We got out of the car when we neared his place, and as we started for Wade's closest neighbor, my sister added, "Actually, this is pretty good. I'm impressed with your imagination, Eleanor."

"I was trying to think about what might work to get us the answers we need, and I kept coming back to this."

Before we could get to the first front door, Maddy said, "Let me see the clipboard before we ring the bell."

I had a blank sheet of paper under the clip, and a pen hung down from a string attached to the back. Maddy scrawled a few things on the paper, and then handed it back to me. "There, that's perfect."

I saw that she'd headed the paper *Petition for Neighborhood Watch* and she'd even added a few signatures as well. Below hers, Maddy had scrawled three names: one looked like Abraham Lincoln, one appeared to be Jesse James, and the third could be interpreted as Kevin Hurley.

I started to scratch out the police chief's name when Maddy asked, "What are you doing?"

"I doubt Kevin would appreciate us forging his signature."

She studied it a second, and then with a few slashes from her pen, it was hard to see what name was written there. "I think it's a mistake, but I've made it more unrecognizable now."

"Thanks," I said. My finger was poised over the doorbell when I asked, "Do you want to do the talking, or should I?"

"It's your idea," she said. "You should get the fun of executing it."

"Okay, but feel free to step in anytime you'd like."

"You can count on it."

An older woman came to the door of the Cape Cod–style home, a pair of gardening gloves in her hands. Her hair was frosted white with time, and was cut short and stylish. She wore an old pair of blue jeans, but I could swear I saw a crease pressed into them. The last time I'd ironed my jeans was—now that I thought about it—never.

"What can I do for you ladies?" she asked in a rich and cultured voice.

"We're here about crime," I said. The woman looked perplexed until I added, "And how to stop it. Don't you think neighbors should look out for each other in this uncertain day and age?"

The woman frowned. "I could hardly refute that." She studied us both, and then added, "I haven't seen you around this street before. Where exactly is it that you live?"

"We've both been in Timber Ridge all our lives," Maddy said as she looked at the woman a little closer. "Why, you're Mrs. Searing, aren't you?"

She frowned, and then a smile blossomed on her face. "Madeline, is that you? You've changed so much I hardly recognized you. You're all grown-up."

Maddy moved closer, effectively shutting me out. "Except for your haircut, you haven't changed at all."

"You're a liar, but I love you for it," Mrs. Searing said cheerily. She pointed to me, and said, "This is your sister, Eleanor, isn't it?"

"I am," I admitted. How did Maddy know this woman, and I didn't? My sister cleared up the mystery in a second. "Mrs. Searing taught fifth grade at the elementary school after you left for middle school."

"I needed two more years in the district before I could retire," she explained to me, "and I always wanted to teach at that grade-school level, so I transferred in. Before that, I was at Edgewood, teaching high-school senior English."

"That must have been quite a transition for you," I said.

"Not as much as you might think," she replied. "Teaching is teaching, and children are children."

I thought about adding, *And clouds are clouds, doorknobs are doorknobs, and parfaits are parfaits,* but I didn't.

"We're here about what happened to the man next door," Maddy said, abandoning the Neighborhood Watch front I'd been prepared to utilize.

"It's terrible," Mrs. Searing said. "I must admit, I wasn't all that fond of Wade, but to be bludgeoned to death must have been horrific. It happened at the local pizzeria, didn't it?"

I nodded. "Mine, to be exact. I own A Slice of Delight."

"Sorry, but I never learned to like pizza. I suppose that makes me un-American these days."

"We have other things on the menu, too," I said.

Maddy frowned at me. "Hey, Sis, take it easy. We're not out drumming up business for the pizzeria," she said to me, then turned to Mrs. Searing. "Do you have a moment? We'd like to ask you a few questions."

"Certainly. I'm ready for a break, at any rate. I've been working in my greenhouse out back, and my stamina isn't what it once was."

"I doubt that," Maddy said. "Are you still walking every day?"

"How sweet of you to remember," Mrs. Searing said as she led us inside. The house was neat, clean, and clearly feminine. "Would either of you care for some coffee or perhaps some iced tea?"

"Tea would be great," I said.

Maddy nodded her agreement, and soon enough we were sitting at the kitchen table like old friends, chatting away.

After taking a drink of herbal tea, Mrs. Searing asked, "Now, why are you two attempting to do the police's business?"

She'd said it so sweetly, it took me a second to realize that there was a barb planted there.

"We hate to see an injustice done," I said. "And if we don't act, an innocent man might go to jail."

Mrs. Searing seemed to ponder that for a few moments, then said, "You've certainly got my attention. Go on."

"My deliveryman at the Slice is Wade's brother, Greg. Scratch that, he's more than that. Greg Hatcher is our friend, and we don't want to see him suffer because of a short-sighted investigation."

"I can respect that sentiment," she said, then took another sip of tea. "What can I do, though?"

Maddy asked, "Did you ever see anything odd going on over at Wade's place? Especially in the past few days?"

Mrs. Searing frowned slightly. "I'm not sure I should be telling tales out of school, as it were."

"We're not looking for idle gossip," Maddy said, "though if you have any of that after we're finished, I'd love to hear it."

The older woman smiled at my sister, and I realized yet again how smooth Maddy was at getting people to root for her in whatever she did.

"I'm sure you would." She took another sip, then said, "There was quite a fuss over there last night, I'm afraid."

"We heard some of it," I said.

"I don't approve of yelling, not in my classroom, and certainly not in my neighborhood. The family on the other side of me loves to converse in loud shouting conversations all day long. I wonder at times if they're all deaf, the way they shout at each other."

"Back to Wade's," I said with a nudge.

"Yes, I often get off-track these days. Yesterday evening, there was shouting on that side of my house as well, but there weren't any pleasantries being exchanged. Wade's brother was there, but he left rather abruptly, with a young woman dogging his heels. She had the most unflattering things to say to Wade as she left, and she wasn't afraid who heard her."

"What did she look like?" I asked.

"Let's see, she was tall and a little on the curvy side, with a shock of the most amazing red hair I've ever seen."

"That's Katy," I said.

"She looked nothing like the next girl who came by and yelled at Wade. I must say, he had a rather hard night before he died, with two separate women cursing at him within ten minutes of each other."

"Did you get a good look at the second girl?" Maddy asked.

"I wasn't snooping, but my goodness, they were raising enough commotion to get everyone's attention on the block. I'd never seen the first young lady until yesterday, but the second is a fixture over there. She has blond hair, though I'm certain it isn't the shade she was born with." It was all I could do not to look at Maddy, since she fit that description herself, but I let it slide.

"What else?"

"She was rather petite, and she looked delicate some-how, at least until she slapped him, and then opened her mouth. I've heard sailors use better language." Sandi Meadows came by the pizzeria now and then, and though I'd never heard her curse, the rest of the description fit her to a tee.

"How many sailors do you know, Mrs. Searing?" Maddy asked with a grin.

"You'd be surprised," she said smugly.

"Good for you."

"If I may," I interrupted, "did you happen to hear what they were yelling about?"

"It was difficult to miss," the older woman said. "I won't use her language, since I don't speak like that, but the essence of her diatribe was focused on Wade's short-comings in his faithfulness to her."

"Anything threatening, specifically?" I asked.

"She said she'd see him dead before he went out with that tramp, which I assumed at the time was a reference to the redhead. I must say, there was entirely too much ex-citement around here for my taste."

"It should quiet down some now," I said, not meaning to be harsh.

She nodded. "Fair enough. I stand corrected. I know it's not acceptable to speak ill of the dead."

Maddy shot me a harsh look, then turned back to the former teacher. "Is there anything else you'd like to add?"

Mrs. Searing took a final sip of her tea, then shook her head as she said, "Sorry, no. I'd love to chat, but those flowers aren't going to transplant themselves."

· Maddy hugged her as we all stood. "It was great see-ing you again."

"As it was seeing you," she said. Mrs. Searing put her

hand out, and I shook it, not at all surprised by the strength of her grip.

"Come again anytime."

After we were gone, I put the pen back in the clipboard. "I told you that would work."

We both started laughing as we walked to the Subaru.

Maddy asked, "Is there any reason to talk to anyone else?"

"I'd say we should talk to the rest of his neighbors. Who knows? Maybe we'll get lucky again."

It was not to be, though. The older man on the other side of Wade's house hadn't seen anything, heard anything, and didn't want to get involved. No one else around was home, so the rest of our canvass turned out to be a wash.

"So," Maddy said, "where do we go from here?"

"The main person I want to speak to now is Sandi Meadows. There's a problem, though. I don't know how to find her."

"Let me make a quick call. I might be able to help."

Maddy pulled out her cell phone, dialed a number by heart, and then turned away from me as she held a whispered conversation. As she talked, I looked around at the houses surrounding us. From all outward appearances, it was a quiet little block, one any family would be delighted to live in. But it had secrets of its own, and not just the shouting neighbors next door. One of their own had been murdered last night, though not at home, and it appeared that the rest of the world would go on as if nothing had happened. Everyone here seemed to be insulated in their own world. The more I thought about it, the more I decided that it wasn't so much a neighborhood as it was a series of separate lives, barely touching each other. Soon enough, a FOR SALE sign would no doubt take its place in the yard, and someone else would move in. There was a continuity to it that gave me little hope, a feeling tinged with an underlying sadness that, for better or for worse, Wade Hatcher would be forgotten soon enough. I wondered if after I died if whoever bought my Craftsman-style bungalow would wonder about who had lived there before, or who might have painstakingly restored it to all its glory. My late husband, Joe, had once said that as long as the house we'd rehabbed together stood, a part of us both would remain alive in the world.

But when there was no one left who remembered us, it would be as if we'd never been born at all.

"Why so sad?" Maddy asked as she looked over at me after she'd finished her telephone conversation.

I ignored her question, not because I didn't want to answer it, but because I had no idea how to, without sounding so gloomy and introspective. "Did you have any luck tracking Sandi down?"

Maddy nodded. "She works part-time at Plusters Fine Clothing, but she just took her lunch break, and odds are that she's at Brian's Grill. Funny thing, though. My source said she left the store with a guy. It didn't take her long to replace Wade, did it?"

"Who's this source of yours?" I asked as we headed for my car.

"If I told you that, I'd be breaking my word," she said. "Just take it as the truth. Come on, we'd better hurry if we want to catch her."

I did as I was told, and drove quickly to the short-order grill that was on the outskirts of town. I wanted to size Miss Meadows up for myself, and I was dying to see who had replaced Wade so quickly in Sandi's life.

* * *

It was easy enough to spot her. I saw Sandi Meadows the second Maddy and I walked into Brian's Grill. The café was a dive on the edge of town that had a much more eclectic customer base than I did, one of the reasons I envied its owner, Mark Deacon. The place had a plain concrete floor painted battleship gray, booths from the fifties covered with dull red vinyl, and a paint job on the walls that had last been spruced up sometime two decades ago. Mark had inherited the place from his dad, the original Brian, who'd been quite a local character in Timber Ridge. Mark had gotten a full scholarship to the University of North Carolina, graduated with a degree in chemical engineering, then came back home to take over the grill when his father died suddenly. Many folks thought he was wasting a great deal of talent and ability, but Mark had to be the happiest man I'd ever known, and that had to count for something. Mark was a great guy who had a thirst for knowledge that was strong and constantly being fed by his love of books.

The owner himself greeted me near the door. "Come to scout out the competition?" he asked me with a grin.

I looked around and smiled. "There's no competition here."

"You got that right."

I tapped the book in his hand and saw that one finger was marking his place. "What are you reading these days?"

He held it up for me to see: *The Impact of Social and Economic Derivatives of Postmodern Imperialism.*

"Well, it looked interesting when I checked it out," he said with a smile.

"I can't imagine how," I laughed.

"You know me—I like a little of this, a little of that." He marked his place with a sheet from an order pad, and then put the book aside. "What brings you to the grill?" Then he must have realized the only reason Maddy and I wouldn't be at the pizzeria. "That's a pretty stupid question, isn't it? Sorry about what happened last night."

"Thanks." What more could I say to that? "It's tough, for a lot of reasons."

"Any idea when the police will release your place?"

I shrugged. "I'm hoping I'll be able to open back up tomorrow."

Mark nodded. "So, in the meantime, you decided to grace my place with your presence. I'm honored, ladies."

"You should be," Maddy said.

Mark took Maddy's hand in his, and, I swear, he kissed it.

She reddened with a slight blush that I hadn't seen in many years, though my sister didn't protest his attention.

"Maddy, you get lovelier every time I see you."

"It defies nature, doesn't it?" she replied.

"If you two don't mind, I'm going to find us a table," I said as I shook my head.

They both laughed at me. They were clearly sharing an inside joke that I wasn't privy to, but I hadn't come to Brian's to have my ego stroked. It was a good thing, too, since there was none of that coming in my direction.

Mark said, "Take any booth that's free. I'll send somebody over in a second to take your order."

As Maddy and I moved toward an empty table beside Sandi and her lunch companion—a young man I recognized as Jamie Lowder—I asked Maddy, "What was that all about?"

"Mark and I like to joke around," she said. "It's nothing more than that."

"Come on, I saw the way you blushed. It's something."

She waved a hand in the air, dismissing my comment.

"Let's forget about the past and focus on the task at hand, shall we?"

I nodded, vowing to bring it up again later. I wasn't about to let my sister get away with anything, especially given the way she liked to tease me mercilessly with much less ammunition.

I pretended to spot Sandi Meadows as we walked by her table. Putting on an air of sympathy, I said, "Sandi, you're so brave being seen out in public like this so soon after what happened."

We were closer to her now, and I could see that she'd been crying recently. At least she was showing some emotion, for whatever it was worth. I added a little softer, "I'm so sorry for your loss."

"Thank you," she said as she dabbed at her cheeks.

"Don't worry about Sandi. She's a champ. She's going to be fine," Jamie said.

"I don't doubt it," I answered. "Still, it has to be difficult losing your boyfriend in such dire circumstances."

"They weren't dating anymore," Jamie said, with an edge to his voice that I hadn't expected. "The two of them broke up weeks ago."

Maddy said, "Gosh, Jamie. I didn't realize you were her spokesperson. Does the job pay anything, or do you do it for free?"

Leave it to Maddy to poke a stick into the hornet's nest.

Jamie snapped, "She's my friend. It's my right to protect her."

"And a fine job you're doing," Maddy said. "Since you're so gallant, we have a few heavy cases in the back of our car. Would you mind bringing them into the diner for us? It would mean a free pizza for you later."

Jamie was notoriously cheap, and at the offer of free food, he quickly abandoned his post. "Sure, I can do that."

Before he got up, he looked at Sandi and asked, "Are you going to be all right?"

"Don't worry about me. I can manage," she said.

Maddy winked at me, grabbed my car keys, and then Jamie followed her out of the grill. I had three minutes to ask questions without Jamie interfering, and I planned to take full advantage of it. Sometimes my sister was absolutely brilliant. There were no cases in the back of my car to be unloaded, and I was sure that Maddy would express her surprise and disappointment when she discovered she'd "forgotten" them back at the pizzeria.

I slid onto the seat Jamie had just vacated. I had to work fast if I was going to get my questions in before he returned. "It must be terrible losing Wade that way."

"Murder's a horrible thing," she said softly.

"Especially after the fight you two had last night," I replied. "You must have been the last person to see him alive."

Her head snapped up as she stared at me. "What are you talking about? Wade and I never fought."

I shook my head. "That's not what I heard. A friend of mine was driving by Wade's place last night and he saw you slap him, and then he heard you screaming at Wade on the front lawn. From what I heard, you were using some pretty stiff language, and you threatened him, too."

"He was kissing that skank Katy Johnson," Sandi said, the grieving ex-girlfriend gone for a second to be replaced by a woman fully scorned. "He deserved it."

"To be murdered?"

"Of course not, but I had every right to yell at him. He shouldn't have messed around with her, and I made sure he knew it." She paused, took a deep breath, and then she added, "I didn't want him to die, though. I had nothing to do with it."

I nodded. Glancing out the window, I could see Maddy pretend to search for the proper key, but I wasn't sure how long she could keep that up before Jamie got suspicious.

"You're a real saint," I said. "Are you trying to tell me that it was an act of compassion, smacking him like that where everyone could see it?"

"Sure, I slapped his face, but I wouldn't hit him with a rolling pin. I wouldn't have been able to, even if I'd wanted. I'm not that strong."

"You know, it's amazing what you can do if you're running on emotion."

"Are you accusing me of killing him, Eleanor?" Her voice had gotten louder, and I noticed that most of the folks in the diner were listening in on us.

There was a deadly look in Sandi's eyes, and though we were in a fairly crowded place in broad daylight—not to mention the fact that I outweighed her by at least forty pounds—I felt a little nervous.

"I'm not accusing you of anything at the moment, but people will talk, and right now, you're the subject of conversation. It's easy to stop it, though. Just tell me where you were last night, and I'll make sure everyone knows you couldn't have done it."

"She was with me," Jamie said, surprising me by his sudden proximity. I'd been so focused on watching Sandi's reactions to my line of questioning that I'd forgotten all about him.

"Is that true?" I asked her.

Sandi never got the chance to respond.

Jamie snapped, "I just told you, didn't I? Now get up, you're in my seat."

All pretense of politeness was gone.

I did as he asked, and then turned to Sandi. "If that's a lie, trust me, we're going to find out."

Sandi stood abruptly and left the grill without looking back, though Jamie gave us enough glares to more than make up for the deficit.

"Should we follow them?" Maddy asked.

"No, I think it's time to give them some space. I'm not sure how much further I should push Sandi until I have more evidence. I saw something in her eyes that scared me a little, and I'm not afraid to admit it."

Maddy nodded. "I don't have any trouble believing that. I hope that was the right thing, getting Jamie away so you could question Sandi alone. I didn't have a chance to check with you first."

"Actually, it was brilliant," I said.

Maddy looked to see if I was being serious or sarcastic, and when she saw that the praise was genuine, she smiled at me. "I have my moments."

Outside, we watched as Sandi and Jamie raced out of the parking lot. A second later, Mark approached us.

"Are you two going to order, or are you still busy running my customers off?"

"Sorry about that," I said. "She didn't like talking to me."

"I can't imagine why not," he said as he removed the plates of half-eaten food and wiped the table down. "What can I get you two?"

I looked at Maddy, and then I said, "Well, we do have to eat somewhere. It might as well be here."

"Be still, my heart. I can't take that much open praise," Mark said.

"Quit fishing for compliments," Maddy said. "You know we like your food."

He just smiled as he slid two menus in front of us.

After Mark was gone, I asked Maddy, "Are you seriously not going to tell me what that's all about?"

"I keep telling you, it's nothing. You've got an overactive imagination, Eleanor."

"And you don't?"

She laughed. "You've got me there. I guess it's just the family curse." After we ordered, Maddy asked, "Do you believe Sandi was really with Jamie last night?"

"Not a chance," I said. "He was clearly covering for her."

"But is it something we can prove?"

I bit my lower lip, then I said, "I don't see how we can yet, but that doesn't mean we should be willing to just let it go. That girl has a mean streak a mile long, and if she thought she was being replaced by someone else, I could easily see her killing Wade."

"So we've got at least one viable suspect. Who do we go after next?"

"I'd like to talk to Art Young, but I'm afraid he's going to make Sandi look like a cooperative witness."

"I've been thinking. You're right. We could ask Bob to do it for us," Maddy said.

"Maybe we shouldn't dump this on him."

"I'm sure he wouldn't mind."

I grinned at my sister. "Especially if you asked him."

Maddy clearly didn't like the tone of my teasing. "He's a friend, nothing more. I keep telling you that, and yet you refuse to believe it."

"That's because I see the look in your eyes whenever he's around. Why do you keep turning him down? He's not going to keep asking you out forever."

"Do you really want to go there? Because I've got questions about your love life, too. What are you going to do about David Quinton? Don't you think it's time you called him back and made things right? It might take a little groveling, but you can do it. So what if he never re-turned your last call?"

That was hitting a little too close to home for my taste. Despite my earlier protests, I'd kept hoping David would call me back and set up another dinner, though it was clear I hadn't welcomed it before. We weren't dating—at least not what I'd call dating—but over the past few months, we'd gotten closer, and I missed him, whether I was willing to admit that to my sister or not.

"Okay, let's make a new rule. From now on, we don't talk about the men in our lives," I said.

"Or even the men *not* in our lives," Maddy said as she extended a hand across the table. I shook it solemnly, and after a few moments, she asked, "So, what does that leave us to talk about?"

"Wade Hatcher is a subject that comes to mind," I said. I was about to expound on the thought when our food came. Burgers thick with toppings of lettuce, onions, tomatoes, and pickles were placed in front of us, and plates of French fries and onion rings soon followed. Maddy and I rarely got a chance to eat out, and we were taking full advantage of it.

As we ate, our conversation seemed to deteriorate into monosyllables.

Mark approached a handful of minutes after he'd served us. "How is it, ladies?"

"Excellent," I said after swallowing another bite of burger.

Maddy just nodded as she devoured another onion ring.

He laughed. "That's what I like, happy customers."

After we finished stuffing ourselves, Maddy asked, "Where do we go now?"

"I don't know about you, but I need a nap." I wasn't used to eating anything like the feast we'd just enjoyed.

"Come on, woman, shake it off. We've got work to do. How often do we get a free day to investigate a crime without worrying about the Slice?"

I got out enough money to cover both bills, along with a healthy tip. "It would be nice to have a day off without thinking about anything, but there's not much chance of that, is there?" I said.

"Dream on," Maddy replied. When she saw how much money I'd laid out, she said, "Hey, you don't have to buy my lunch, too."

"I think your smooth move getting Jamie out of the way deserves some kind of special recognition for a job well done."

She smiled. "If that's the case, then it was at least worth a steak, don't you think?" Maddy bit her lip, and then added, "Speaking of steak, that's precisely the way that Jamie was looking at Sandi, like a hungry bear eyeing prime rib. You noticed it, didn't you?"

"I thought I saw something there too, but he said they were just friends."

"He lied," Maddy replied.

"Probably," I answered. "But how do we prove it?"

"I'm just saying, maybe we should keep an eye on both of them. Jamie should be on our suspect list, too."

"Honestly?"

She nodded, obviously getting enthusiastic about the idea. "What better way to make room for his own play than to get rid of his competition? Whether Sandi and Wade had broken up or not, it's pretty clear Jamie knew he'd never get anywhere with Sandi as long as Wade was around."

"That sounds kind of drastic, killing a rival for a woman's affection."

"I'm just saying."

"You're absolutely right," I said. "We need to put him on our list. We should talk to Roger Henderson, too."

"Wade's boss?"

"Sure. He might know something we don't, and even if he doesn't, we need to meet him and see what he has to say about Wade."

"By all means, then, let's add him to the roster," my sister said.

After saying good-bye to Mark, Maddy asked me in the parking lot, "Do we go after Jamie now?"

"No, he's still with Sandi, and it's no good tackling them together. We need to get him alone when he's not so worried about protecting her. Maybe he'll let his guard down then."

"How about Roger Henderson, then?"

"Why not? He's as good a place as any to start." Art Young, the loan shark, was really the number one name on my list, but I wasn't in any hurry to brace him without reinforcements.

We drove to the accountant's office, an unpretentious place in what passed for a strip mall outside town. Henderson Accounting wasn't much more than a glorified storefront, with barely enough room for two desks, two computers, and a potted plant that hadn't been dusted in years.

A thin, nervous-looking man in his forties stood as we came in. "The pizza business must be good if you need an accountant," he said as he tried to offer us a smile.

"We're doing okay," I said. I'd seen Roger in the Slice on occasion, and he'd even asked for my business a few times in the past.

"You must be if you're ready to let me take over your bookkeeping."

I was about to tell him no, when Maddy said, "We're considering it, but given your current status, we're not sure you can handle the work all by yourself. It was tragic about Wade, wasn't it?"

I saw where Maddy was going, and decided it couldn't hurt anything to play along. "How are you ever going to replace him?"

"It will be tough, but I'll manage. Wade will be missed around here."

"Were you two close?" Maddy asked as she walked up to the desk.

Roger shrugged. "You work in an office this size, you get to be friends, or it drives you crazy." He paused, then Roger added, "I've got a new employee starting next week, so it won't take long to bring her up to speed."

"That was quick," I said.

"What can I say? The business is bigger than either one of us. I'll miss him, but it's my company, and Wade was just an employee." He hesitated before adding, "I know that must sound callous, but I have to move on."

"Where were you when it happened?" Maddy asked. "I can't imagine how you must have felt when you found out."

"I was home watching a movie," he said.

"Alone?" I asked.

He nodded. "I don't date much these days." Roger practically rubbed his hands together when he added, "If you'll start bringing me your bills and deposits, I'll handle everything. If I may, I'll take your corporate checkbook now so I can familiarize myself with your assets."

This was going too fast for my taste. "Thanks for the offer, but I need a little time to decide," I said.

"The sooner we get started, the quicker I can relieve

you of the burden of watching your money." The man sounded sincere, and I found myself nearly taken in by his presentation of concern.

"Thank you," Maddy said. "We'll be in touch."

He forced business cards on us before we could manage to escape.

Once we were outside, Maddy said, "He's good at what he does, isn't he?"

"I don't know what kind of accountant he is, but he's a pretty pushy salesman."

My sister nodded. "At least we've had a chance to talk to him. Could you see him killing Wade?"

"Anything's possible, but unless I hear something else about him, there's no reason not to believe him, but something's bothering me."

"What?"

"I can't help thinking that he was trying to sell us something more than his accounting services in there. He pressed me awfully hard for my company checkbook a few minutes ago, don't you think?"

"He must be delusional if he thinks you're making enough money to have a company checkbook."

"That's beside the point. I had a feeling he was kind of desperate for our business."

Maddy shrugged. "You might be right, but I don't know what it means just yet. What do we do in the meantime?"

I thought about it for a second, and then I took a deep breath and said, "I think we ought to pay Bob Lemon a call, if you really don't mind asking for his help dealing with Art Young."

"I wouldn't have offered if I did," she said.

As we drove to the attorney's office, I wondered how

far he'd go to impress Maddy. This was above and beyond the call of love, and he had every right to refuse us.

But I hoped he didn't. I wasn't all that anxious to tackle the closest thing we had to a gangster in Timber Ridge without at least some kind of backup.

Chapter 6

"Sorry, ladies, but I won't do it," Bob said as soon as he heard our request. In his early fifties, Bob had a fair amount of gray hair, and a huge crush on my little sister. He kept fit by walking around town whenever he could, and I often saw him pass by the pizzeria on his lunch hour, logging in a great many more miles than slices of pizza.

"Why not?" Maddy asked. "I've never known you to say no to me before, and I have to say, I'm not all that fond of hearing it."

He shook his head, whether because of her request, or her reaction to his refusal. "It's too dangerous. I don't approve of the way you two butt into police business, and as an officer of the court, I'm certainly not going to help you."

"Then we'll go see him ourselves," Maddy said. "Don't think you can keep us from doing it, either."

I wasn't all that fond of the new plan, but my sister was right. We needed to talk to Art Young, and though it would have been easier with Bob's help, we couldn't let his refusal stop us. Greg was in trouble that seemed to grow deeper with each passing hour, and neither one of us was about to abandon him in his time of need.

"I'm serious. You can't go," Bob said, the frown across his brow growing deeper. "I won't let you."

Maddy laughed. "How on earth do you think you can stop us?"

Bob reached for the telephone. "I can call the police chief."

Maddy arched one eyebrow. "Go ahead. But I'm warning you, if you make that call, don't bother coming around me anymore. What little chance you have with me right now will be gone forever, and I mean it. Look at my face, Bob. I'm not bluffing."

It was clear to me that she meant every word of it, and I hoped Bob realized it, too.

"I guess I don't have much choice, then, do I?" He dialed the telephone, and Maddy started for the door. Bob held up one finger, commanding her to wait. I was actually shocked when she did just that.

"This is Lemon. Is he in?"

After a long pause, Bob said, "Art, I need a favor, but you're under no obligation to give it. I have two women in my office who want to talk to you. No, it's nothing official. They're friends of Wade Hatcher's, and they're digging into his murder."

I shook my head and mouthed to Bob, "The truth," and he added, "Strike that. They are more like friends with his brother. The police aren't looking at any other suspects, and these women believe he's innocent." Bob frowned as he listened a few moments, then he answered, "Okay, I suppose I have to. If you want to put it like that, I'm calling in the favor you owe me." After another pause, he said, "My office is as good a place as any. That's fine. We'll see you in ten minutes."

Bob hung up the telephone, and then he stared hard at Maddy. "You should know that this goes against every principle I have, and just cost me the only leverage I have on this man. You'd better make good use of the opportunity."

Maddy shocked all three of us by going around his desk and kissing him full on the lips. "Does that convince you that I appreciate it?" she asked.

Bob looked a little off-balance as he replied, "Maybe I should go against my principles more often."

Maddy grinned at him. "Maybe you should."

"I hate to break this up," I said, "but I have a question. Just how dangerous is this man?" I knew we had to talk to him to find out his exact arrangements with Wade, but it wasn't going to be easy without accusing him of some pretty bad things.

"Don't kid yourself," Bob said, suddenly going sober. "He's trouble. But you should be fine here in the office. Just don't push him. If he doesn't want to answer your questions, he won't. He's doing this as a favor to me— don't forget that."

"What exactly did you do for him in return?" I asked.

"That's privileged information," Bob said. "Just know that it cost me something to get him over here, so don't let me down. I like Greg too, you know."

"You're nothing but a big sweetie deep down inside, aren't you?" Maddy asked.

"I'll never admit to that, not even under oath."

Ten minutes later, Art Young walked in. I wasn't sure what I'd been expecting, but it was nothing like the impression the man gave when he came into Bob's office. He wore a nice Italian-cut suit, and his shoes were at least ten times more expensive than my best pair. His light blond hair was carefully styled, and there was a subtle waft of cologne in the air whenever he moved.

Art shook both our hands in turn, then turned to Bob. "This is truly that important to you?"

"It is," Bob said.

He nodded, and then turned back to us. "Ladies, what can I do for you?"

"We want to know what your relationship with Wade Hatcher was," I blurted out, my carefully crafted question poised on my lips flittering away in the wind.

I'd half-expected him to storm out of the office, but instead, he smiled at me. "Direct and straight to the point. I like that. You run A Slice of Delight, don't you?"

"I do," I admitted.

"You make very good pizza," he said.

"Thanks."

"Your sauce could use a little more oregano, though."

I raised an eyebrow. "Then again, it could be perfect the way it is."

He openly laughed at my rebuke. "Maybe you're right." Then he turned to Bob. "Don't you have something to do outside? Surely there's a brief that needs to be filed. If nothing else, you can chase an ambulance or two for a few minutes while we chat."

"I'd be more comfortable staying," Bob said. Though his inflection hadn't changed, there was an edge of steel in his voice that I hardly recognized.

Art's eyebrows shot up. "I'm sure you would," he said in a measured cadence after a moment's pause, "but if they want to discuss such delicate matters, I'd rather you weren't present for my remarks, if it's all the same to you."

"It's okay," I told Bob. "We're just going to talk."

"That's right," Art said, laughing a little. "It's just going to be a friendly little conversation. In fact, why don't we use first names? It's much nicer that way."

Bob looked at me, then at Maddy. When we both nodded our approval, he stood and said, "I'll be in the next room if you need me."

After he was gone, Art said, "I trust you ladies aren't wearing any police wires."

Maddy said, "You can search us if you'd like."

"That won't be necessary," he said. "Your word will suffice."

"Do you honestly mean that?" I asked, intrigued by his faith in us. "We could be lying to you."

He nodded; then he said gently, "But if you were, I'm sure you are both aware of the torrents of destruction that would come down on your friend's head."

"Do you mean Greg Hatcher?" Maddy asked.

Art shook his head. "No, I'm talking about our mutual acquaintance waiting patiently in the other room, Bob Lemon."

I started to call him Mr. Young, but then decided to keep it as friendly as he'd suggested. "Art, I know you don't typically divulge your business dealings with strangers, but we're trying to help a friend, and you could give us some information that will make that easier."

"I thought he was your employee."

"Can't he be both?" I asked.

"Not in my line of work."

"Well, he can in ours," I said. "I understand his brother owed you some money."

"He might have," Art said, being careful with his words.

"Was he late paying you back?" Maddy asked. "Did you have a problem with him? Is that what happened to Wade Hatcher?"

Art shook his head. "That's the problem with folks these days. They watch two or three *Sopranos* reruns and think anybody who chooses to operate on the edges of the law is a thug by definition. I help people sometimes who can't generate cash flow in more conventional ways. I like to think of it as a service I provide to the community."

My sister asked, "Are you saying you don't kill people?"

Art looked at Maddy, who'd reddened slightly after blurting out that last bit. "Please. I'm not a barbarian."

"So, if someone owes you money and they don't pay you, you just write it off as a bad debt," Maddy said. "Is that what you're saying?" What had gotten into my sister?

I was about to comment when Art replied, "No, I don't have the backing of the FDIC, so I can't afford to take a loss that a bank might. But I certainly give someone every opportunity to pay me back before any drastic measures are taken. How else could I guarantee repayment? Your friend's brother made his first payment a day early. He was shaping up to be a good investment, and someone canceled the loan without my consent or approval. Trust me, I'm as upset that Wade Hatcher was murdered as you are, maybe even a little more. I'm the last person here who wanted to see him harmed, whether you're inclined to believe that or not."

Art's cell phone rang as he finished speaking, and after a brief whispered conversation, he said, "Ladies, it's been a pleasure, but duty calls."

He smiled at me, then lowered it a notch as he nodded toward Maddy. Bob was back two seconds after Art left, and he looked honestly relieved to see that we were all right. "How did it go?"

"He told us he didn't do it," I said, "and oddly enough, he made a pretty compelling case. I believe him."

"Don't be fooled by the fancy clothes and the stylish haircut," Maddy said. "No matter what he says, he's still a thug, and I trust him about as far as I can throw either one of you."

"I'm not necessarily a big fan of the man, either," I said, "but he treated us with nothing but respect."

"I don't care," Maddy said. "Somehow that made it even worse."

I asked Bob, "What do you think? Should we believe him?"

"Within reason," the attorney said after giving it some thought. "He wouldn't hesitate to lie to save himself from arrest, or maybe even a little embarrassment, but I didn't hear him, so I don't know if he was telling the truth or not."

"Have you become some kind of human lie detector?" Maddy asked, still rubbed raw by our conversation with Art Young.

"In a way. Over the years, I've become pretty adept at studying people's body language. It's amazing what folks give away without even realizing they're doing it. I've caught my clients lying to me before, and when I call them on it, they admit that I'm right most of the time, so I must be pretty good at it."

"I don't know how you do it," Maddy said to Bob.

"It's easy, if you know what clues to look for."

"I don't mean that," she protested. "I mean dealing with criminals all day long, day in and day out."

"Everyone's entitled to the best defense they can afford, and believe it or not, I represent innocent people as well. It's not a pretty sight to see someone chewed up by the legal system when he doesn't deserve it, and I do all I can to make sure that doesn't happen. I'm sorry you don't approve of my chosen profession." The last sentence was said clearly enough to prove that he wasn't sorry at all.

"Bob, I didn't mean anything by it," Maddy said, softening her words. "I'm sorry."

"It's fine. I've got a tough skin. As a lawyer, I have to have one, don't I? Now, if you'll excuse me, I've got work to do."

Maddy looked flustered, but it was clear that she was—for once in her life—at a complete loss for words.

Fortunately, I wasn't. "Bob, I don't know what this has cost you, but I greatly appreciate you doing it."

"I just hope it helped," he said.

Once Maddy and I were out on the sidewalk in front of my car, I asked, "What was that all about?"

"I don't know," Maddy said. "I'm just having a bad day, I guess. That man in there made my skin crawl. I can't believe you were able to stay so calm when we were talking to him."

"Everybody's the hero of his own life story," I said. "I read that somewhere and it stuck with me. I don't think he realizes he's a bad man, and reacting the way you did to him wasn't getting us anywhere. I'm kind of surprised you went after Bob that way, especially after he did us such a huge favor."

"I know I owe him a better apology than the one I just gave him," Maddy said. "I just don't know what to say. I had no right to treat him that way, but how do I make it better?"

"You could always take him out to dinner," I said, half-joking.

"You're right," Maddy said. "Hang on, I'll be right back."

She headed back into Bob's law office, and I found

myself standing alone on the sidewalk. I felt kind of like an idiot doing that, so I walked over to my car and got in. Without starting the engine, I turned on the radio and searched for a station that actually played music instead of the bombardment of talk radio we seemed to be getting lately.

Three minutes later, Maddy walked out and looked around for me. I tapped my horn, and she came over to the car.

As she got in, I asked, "How'd it go?"

"He had plans tonight, but I convinced him to change them. We're going out at seven. Can you believe that?"

"As far as I'm concerned, it's about time," I said.

Maddy started laughing, so I asked her, "What's so funny?"

"That's exactly what Bob said when I asked him out."

As I started the engine, I asked, "Where should we go now? Or do you need time to go home and get ready for your date?"

"That's hours away yet. I don't need that much time."

"I don't know. It's been a while. You might be out of practice."

She shook her head. "It's like riding a bicycle, Eleanor."

"And goodness knows you've rode your share of those," I said.

"Okay, that's about enough of that," she said. "We're getting close to breaking our rules of conversation. What should we do with the time we have left?"

"I'd like to talk to Sandi Meadows again, but I think she needs a little time to cool off. It might be worth our time to speak with Jamie Lowder, too. But do you know who I'd really like to talk to? Katy Johnson."

"Do you honestly think she could have killed Wade?"

"I do," I said. "She was in our restaurant last night, so she could have grabbed the key while she was there, and she had reason enough to be angry with Wade."

"If you locked the door in the first place, which neither of us is sure about, and if she was mad enough to kill him, then I suppose it's possible. That must have been a pretty heavy blow, and frankly, I'm not sure Katy's strong enough."

"She thinks Greg's her soul mate, he told me that once. If Katy believed that Wade ruined it forever, she could do it. It's amazing what people will do when they don't think they have any other choice."

My cell phone rang, and when I looked at the number in my display, I was surprised to see that the chief of police was calling me. Had he already found out that I'd talked to Art Young? I was sure he wouldn't approve, not that I cared what he thought one way or the other.

The phone rang again, and Maddy asked impatiently, "Aren't you going to answer that?"

"I'm not sure," I said as it rang once more. "It's Kevin Hurley, and I doubt I want to hear what he's got to say."

"Give it to me, then," she said as she snatched it out of my hand. "Eleanor Swift's phone," she said.

After a slight pause, she said, "Yes. Okay. Fine. I understand. Thanks. Good-bye."

She handed the phone back to me without a word.

After thirty seconds, I finally broke down and asked, "Aren't you going to tell me what he had to say?"

Maddy smiled at me. "The Slice is now officially ours again. We can reopen any time we'd like."

"But you've got a date tonight," I protested.

"Bob will understand," she said.

"No," I said suddenly.

"Of course he will," Maddy replied.

"I mean, no, you're not going to tell him. We don't

have any dough made, and I used the last bit in the freezer I'd been saving. Besides, we both deserve a night off. For tonight, we're going to keep the place dark and see how the other half lives."

"I'm going out on a date, but what are you going to do?" she asked.

"Don't worry about me. I'll find something," I said. "I can't remember the last time I rented a movie, made some popcorn, and lost myself. I'm looking forward to having a night by myself. No offense," I added hastily.

"And none taken. If you're serious, that's fine, but if not, I'm sure Bob wouldn't mind if you joined us."

I laughed at the suggestion. "I doubt you could be more mistaken. Don't worry about me, Maddy. I'm a big girl. I can make it one night by myself."

"I know that," she said. "But we still have some time to kill before my dinner date. What should we do?"

"Let's track Katy Johnson down," I said. "I want to talk to her."

I was about to pull away from the curb when a ham-fisted woman I'd never cared for slapped my windshield. I briefly considered driving away, but I knew Greg wouldn't like it if I ran over his mother's foot.

I turned the engine off, and then got out to ask Clara Hatcher what her problem with me was this time.

"What can I do for you, Clara?" I asked as I faced her. She was a dour woman who either didn't realize or couldn't care less that the clothes she wore would be better off in a Goodwill bin than in her closet. It wasn't just that the styles were outdated. She carried thirty pounds more than the outfits could contain, displaying an odd set of bulges and rolls whenever she moved.

"Where's Greg? I know you're hiding him from me, but I have a right to see him."

"I don't have the slightest idea where your son is," I said. "I'm sorry about Wade." Greg had told me many times how his mother had thought that Wade was the perfect son, despite his troubled youth, while Greg was the outcast, even though he'd never done anything to give her a moment's unease.

"Don't talk about my son. You aren't allowed to. You're not doing Greg any favors, you know that, don't you? He killed my boy, and he needs to face his punishment for what he's done."

"Greg's your son, too," I snapped. I could see Maddy getting out of the car, but I wasn't about to stop. "He deserves love just as much as Wade did."

Clara lashed out with a speed that stunned me and smacked me hard across the cheek. In a voice filled with more rage than grief, she snarled, "I hope he gets the death penalty."

She turned away before I could say anything in response. I stood there rubbing my cheek, feeling the burn on my face where her hand had slapped me.

"We can't let her get away with that," Maddy said as she started after her.

I put a hand on her shoulder. "I don't like Clara, either, but we've got to take it easy on her. She just lost her first-born son."

"And she wants to see her only other child put to death. I'm not willing to cut her any slack at all." Maddy stared at my cheek. "That's going to leave a mark."

We got back into the car, and I checked my face in the visor mirror. There was an angry handprint still there, a glowing afterimage of the impact. "I always thought Greg was exaggerating about his mom, but if anything, he was holding back," I said. "She lived and died by Wade, no matter what he did. Greg told me that when his brother was fourteen, Wade used to steal the family car and joyride. When he was fifteen, Wade started drinking, and by sixteen, he was doing drugs. All the while, Greg was getting straight A's and going to Sunday school. He told me once that he had to hide his money in his Bible to keep Wade from stealing it, since he was sure it was the only place he knew his brother wouldn't look."

Maddy nodded. "Did you know that Wade stole Greg's varsity-letter jacket and traded it to another kid for drugs, and Greg never got it back?" She paused, then said, "He never forgave him for that, either."

"I can't say I blame him. What a loser."

"The mother or the firstborn son?" Maddy asked.

The cheek was starting to ache. "Right now, I'm not sure which one I was talking about."

"Then let's say a little bit of both."

I rubbed my cheek, and then I asked, "Did you see her eyes? I honestly think that she's a little insane."

"It's tough to be a little crazy. That's like saying you're kind of pregnant." She sat there a moment, and then added, "I wonder if she could have done it."

"Kill her own son?"

Maddy nodded. "It's happened before."

"I honestly think Wade could have burned down her house and she would have found a way to punish Greg for it."

"Maybe she did," Maddy said.

"I don't follow."

"Wade was in the pizzeria, and we don't know why he was there yet. Who knows who else was there? It was dark, and the two brothers had the same build. What if whoever killed Wade thought they were getting rid of Greg? He was hit once from behind, remember?"

I couldn't believe what I was hearing, but then again, I couldn't deny that it was possible Maddy was right, though not necessarily about the killer's identity. "No matter how unenthusiastic she is toward Greg, I still can't see her killing him."

"What if she did it to protect Wade? I'm pretty sure that in Clara's twisted mind, Greg was expendable."

"I'm not willing to concede that, but it does shed a whole new theory on what might have happened."

"What's that?" Maddy asked.

"If it was a case of mistaken identity, Greg's in more trouble than we realized. No matter who killed Wade, they could have been intent on killing Greg, instead."

"We've been looking at this all wrong, haven't we?"

I shook my head. "No, we just haven't seen the entire picture. Maybe whoever killed Wade knew who they were hitting, but maybe they didn't. Just because we've added Greg to the list of targets doesn't mean we can ignore Wade as the intended victim."

"So now we have to track down motives for murdering two people instead of one," Maddy said.

"One murder, two possible victims," I clarified.

"This whole thing just got a lot more confusing, didn't it?" She looked at her watch, and then said, "I know we said we were going to go looking for Katy Johnson, but could it wait until tomorrow? We can track her down before we open the pizzeria tomorrow."

"What else did you have in mind?" I asked.

She frowned for a second, and then Maddy said, "Would you drive me back to my apartment? Honestly, I want to take a long, hot soak in the tub and forget about this, at least for one night."

"That sounds like a good plan. Are you looking forward to your date with Bob?"

As I started driving back to her place, Maddy paused, then said, "You know what? I am. It might be nice getting out again."

"Even after Bob back-talked you?"

Maddy laughed. "Especially since then. I've been waiting for him to show some spine, and I'd just about given up all hope. I don't like being ordered around, but I don't like being around a sycophant, either."

I smiled. "Men have to walk a fine line when they deal with you, don't they?"

"I'm not denying it, but I'm worth it."

We got to her place, and I didn't even shut off the engine. "Have a good time. I'd say call me when you get home, but I'll probably be asleep already."

As she opened her car door, she said, "How are you going to be able to get to sleep wondering about what happened on my evening out?"

"Believe it or not, somehow I'll manage."

After she was out of the car, I called out, "Be good, Maddy."

"Now what fun would that be?" she asked with a laugh.

I drove away, ready to spend a night at home alone. It was a rare treat for me, and I planned to take full advantage of it, regardless of the pall in the air from Wade's murder. I couldn't let a homicide investigation interfere with my temporary moment of solitude. For one night, I was going to emulate my little sister and think about me, instead of the rest of the world.

*   *   *

I got home and was unlocking my front door when I heard someone call out to me. I turned around and found Patty Louise walking down the sidewalk toward me, carrying a basket in one arm and a newborn strapped onto her chest.

"Hey, stranger," I said as she approached. "I haven't seen you in a while. How's life been treating you?"

"I'm just about finished with my maternity leave," she said, "and I wanted to come by before I went back to work part-time."

I could smell the heavenly aroma coming from her basket, and it was all I could do not to openly salivate. I managed to restrain myself though, and asked her, "How's Madison doing?"

She pivoted around so I could see that her baby was sound asleep. "She loves to sleep when I walk, which is wonderful during the daytime, but it drives me crazy at night. I must walk twenty miles a day." Patty smiled at that. "It has helped with the baby weight, though."

Patty was a runner, and I doubt she'd weighed more at nine months than I did all of the time.

Finally I couldn't ignore the basket anymore. "I can't believe you don't weigh more, being around your wonderful bread all the time." I normally bought all my bakery goods from the grocery store or from Paul's Pastries, but my bread for home consumption was the single exception, when I could get it. Patty was a neighbor of mine who had two very special talents in life. She could work with numbers like nobody I'd ever seen, and she could make sourdough bread that would melt in your mouth.

"Oops, I almost forgot. This is for you," she said as she extended the basket to me.

It took every ounce of resolve I had, but I didn't lift the

dishcloth to stare at my bounty. "I wish you'd let me pay for this."

"I'd rather barter," she said. "As long as you trade pizzas with me, we're in good shape."

"Consider this an open store credit, then," I said as I hefted the basket.

"Well, I'd better be going," she said as Madison started to wake up. "If I don't keep moving, she lets me know her disapproval with a wail that makes dogs run and cats hide."

"Bye, and thanks again," I said as she quickly retreated.

I went inside, peeled away the cloth covering my gift, looked at the two lovely brown, crusty loaves of sourdough bread, and then I covered them back up. It wouldn't do to start eating it the second I got it. A long bath didn't sound all that appealing to me at the moment, so I took a quick shower, instead. After that, I was hungry, but going out somewhere was the last thing I wanted to do, and I'd promised myself that I wasn't going to sit down with my fresh bread and a stick of real butter, one of my favorite indulgences in life. My jeans were getting a little too snug for that, and I didn't like where that was going. Since I couldn't order pizza, and nothing else I could have delivered appealed to me, I decided to get into my sweatpants and one of Joe's old shirts and make myself an omelet. Honestly, the meal wasn't nearly as classy as that. Instead of prepping a lot of ingredients—something Maddy and I did every day at work—I scrambled a couple of eggs, threw a bit of grated cheese into the mix, then searched until I found a couple of mushrooms in my fridge. There was a bit of ham there, too, so I diced that and added it to the mix.

It was wonderful, especially coupled with Patty Louise's

homemade sourdough bread. After all, I had to have some kind of bread with my meal, and I made a little butter last me the entire meal.

Even after I did the dishes, it was just past six, and I was beginning to feel like I had a long night ahead of me. It surprised me to discover that I was bored, something I rarely had the luxury of experiencing in the course of a normal day.

Maybe that was the reason I liked running the pizzeria. It kept me busy during the loneliest time of the day, and by the time I got home at night, I was so worn-out that I didn't have time to dwell on the fact that I was alone. I missed Joe at night more than any other time of day. It had taken three weeks after he'd died for the scent of him on his robe to wear off, but I still found myself putting it on whenever I was especially sad.

Tonight was going to be a robe night for sure.

As I got it out of the upstairs closet, I wrapped myself up in it, able to put the sash around me twice. It was an old black fleece robe with images of cabins, moose, snowflakes, and snow-covered trees, and I'd begged him to let me replace it a dozen times. He'd refused, and now I was glad that he had. A new flannel robe would lack all of the character of this old thing, and if I closed my eyes, I could still see my husband walking through the snow in it toward our Charlotte newspaper in the mornings, the steam coming from his breath and his hair disheveled, though he never seemed to care.

That brought a few tears, but just a few. I missed my husband, but at least I was confident that we had enjoyed a good life together, a nearly perfect fit, though our time was cut a great deal shorter than it should have been. My sister had told me in confidence one night soon after the funeral that she'd been searching her whole life for what

Joe and I had found, but she doubted she would ever manage it.

I hoped she did, and there was even a possibility that maybe she was on her way tonight.

There was one thing I knew for sure. I couldn't spend my life looking back. Joe wouldn't have wanted me to live that way, and I knew in my heart that it wasn't fair to me, or my memories of him. I would have to move on.

Just not today.

My science teacher was asking me why I couldn't understand my test, and I had trouble explaining to him that I didn't read German. He told me his exams were always in German, news to me, because I'd taken French. Everyone in class was laughing at me, and I kept wondering why no one was answering the phone when I woke up.

That's when I realized that I had dreamed all of it, except the ringing of the telephone.

"Hello," I said, barely awake. I'd fallen asleep on the couch watching a movie, which I could see was over when I glanced at the screen.

"Stop digging around, or you're next," a voice whispered on the other end before the phone hung up.

I hit *69, wondering who had called, but it was blocked, and I didn't have the resources to trace it, anyway. Kevin Hurley might be able to track it down, but I wasn't exactly in a position to ask him for any favors at the moment.

Someone Maddy and I had spoken with over the past few days was clearly upset by our meddling, but I didn't have the slightest idea who it might have been. The quality of the call had been so poor that I couldn't even tell if it had been a man or a woman on the other end.

But their intent was clear. We'd gotten close to someone who was clearly upset by our investigation. But just as obvious, the caller didn't know me very well, or my sister. A warning wasn't a red flag to us; it was a green light. If pushing a little got this kind of response, I was all for shoving harder still.

I thought about calling Maddy and telling her about it, but then I remembered that she was probably still out on her date, and knowing my sister, I doubted she'd welcome the interruption.

I got up, turned off the television, and double-checked all of the doors and windows to make sure that they were locked. I felt safe after I did, but just in case, I wedged a chair under my bedroom door and somehow managed to fall asleep.

Chapter 7

"**I** can't believe you didn't call me the second it happened," Maddy said the next morning as we sat in my kitchen, eating the donuts she'd bought and brought over to the house. "This is really serious."

"Come on, there's a good chance that it was just a prank," I said. Given the light of day, I had begun to doubt whether the threat had even been real.

"You and I both know better than that." She grabbed the phone and pushed it at me. "Call him."

"Bob? Why? Did something happen on your date last night? I'm still waiting for a report from you, and I'm not sure it's all that appropriate to call him for an update, if you're not willing to tell me about it yourself."

"You can keep on waiting," she said, "because I'm not giving you one. You need to get the police chief to track that call."

"I don't want to any more than you want to tell me what happened on your date last night."

Maddy frowned, and then she finally nodded. "I'll make you a deal. You call Kevin Hurley, and I'll tell you all about my date."

"Do you mean that?"

Maddy said, "Every last detail. Go on."

I dialed Kevin's number at the office—doubting he'd be in yet—but to my surprise, he answered almost immediately.

"You're working some long hours these days," I said.

"Better here than at home," he said.

"Is there trouble in paradise?" I knew that Kevin and his wife had more than their share of problems, but it was odd that he'd tell me about them.

"It's never been paradise, and we both know it," Kevin said with an inordinate amount of frankness. "What can I do for you today, Eleanor?"

"I don't think it's anything, but someone called my house last night and threatened me. Maddy thought I should give you a call."

"For once, I agree with your sister," he said. "About what time was it?"

"It was a little after eleven," I admitted. "Listen, I don't want to keep you from your work."

"I'll call you right back," he said, and then the police chief hung up before I could say anything else.

"What did he say?" Maddy asked.

"Believe it or not, he agreed with you."

She looked genuinely shocked by the declaration. "Well, I suppose it was bound to happen sooner or later. Is he looking into it?"

"If I had to guess, I'd say he was checking telephone records. That's probably going to take some time, so tell me about your date."

Maddy shrugged. "You're right—a deal's a deal. Bob picked me up, we ate, and I was back home snug in my living room in time for the eleven o'clock news."

"The question is, were you alone when you watched?"

"Of course I was," Maddy said. Her nose crinkled for a second, and then she added, "I invited him in, but he had an early day today."

She might have been satisfied with that weak rendition of her evening, but I wasn't about to let her get away with that.

"I want details," I said. It wasn't like Maddy to be reticent about anything, and I was guessing that she either had a wonderful time, or it was too dreadful for her to talk about.

Just as she started to speak, the telephone rang.

Maddy grinned. "Saved by the bell."

"Not saved, delayed," I explained as I picked up the phone.

It was Kevin Hurley.

"That was fast," I said.

"It's not as complicated as the movies would make you think," he said. "We might not have state-of-the-art everything, but we've got a crackerjack phone company that does. The call to your house came from a pay phone."

"So we'll never have any idea who made that call."

"Eleanor, don't you want to know where the telephone is located?" he asked.

"Does it really matter?"

"I think so," he said. "Whoever called you used the one on the promenade near your pizzeria. I'm guessing they came by to catch you alone at night so they could give you that warning in person, but when you weren't working, they decided to call you at home."

"You're giving me the creeps," I said.

"Good. If it makes you more cautious, then I'm all for it."

I was about to thank him for his quick work, when he added, "Enough of this foolishness. You've got to tell me where Greg is hiding."

"I told you before, and it's still true. I don't know where he is."

"Eleanor, I could arrest you for obstruction—you know that, don't you?"

"Hey, you know where to find me. I'm not exactly ducking you. I seem to be getting a lot of threats over the telephone lately."

He clearly didn't like that at all. In a cold voice, he said, "That wasn't a threat, it was a promise."

"I'll see you when I see you," I said, then hung up.

Maddy was studying me as I turned to her. "What was that all about?"

"He thinks I know where Greg's hiding. It wouldn't surprise me if he has the house staked out watching for him."

Maddy peeked out the window. "I don't see anybody, but maybe his deputies are just that good."

"I don't know how I keep getting myself into these jams," I said.

"You're just talented that way, I guess. Did he tell you to back off?"

"Of course he did."

"And are we?"

I looked at her. "What do you think?"

Maddy smiled. "I think it's time we hit the streets again. I've been thinking about what you said, and you're right. We need to talk to Katy Johnson."

"I'm ready if you are."

"I'll drive," Maddy said as we walked out front. "I know where she lives."

"Then maybe you should be the navigator," I said. "You usually seem to be the one who drives us places."

Maddy shrugged. "Fine, I don't care. You drive."

"That's better," I said.

We got into my car, and then I asked, "Where exactly am I going?"

"The apartment complex in back of Bleeker Street," she said. "I just found out that Katy's in 14A."

As I drove to the other side of town, I said, "You know, I'd hate to live in an apartment again."

"Some of them are really nice," Maddy said. "I always stay in one after I get divorced. It makes the transition a lot easier."

"I didn't mean anything by it," I said. "Joe and I lived in an apartment until the house was in good enough shape for us to move in. I just never felt like I was putting down any real roots until we got the house."

Maddy looked out the window instead of at me. "Some of us don't like roots. They keep us too tethered to a particular place for too long."

"But you always come back to Timber Ridge, don't you?" I asked. I'd never really thought about it before, but it was true. While Maddy's marriages had taken her all over the United States, whenever she divorced, she always came home to our little part of North Carolina.

"It's just a coincidence," she said.

I didn't believe it for a second, and I was pretty sure she didn't, either. But if my sister didn't want to talk about it, I'd respect that, at least for the moment.

We drove in silence until the brick apartment complex came into view. It was named Oakcrest, though I couldn't see an oak tree anywhere, and the place had been built on the flattest part of Timber Ridge, so that took care of the crest.

"This isn't so bad," Maddy said as we got out. "It's not as nice as my place, but for the money, it's a decent deal."

"Did you think about living here when you came back home the last time?" I asked as we walked in. When she'd first come back to town—soon after her latest divorce, and Joe's untimely death—I'd offered her a room in my house, as much for her benefit as mine, but she'd turned me down. It was a wise decision. As much as I loved my sister, we couldn't live together and work side by side at the Slice, certainly not as adults. Whenever one of us was lonely, or just felt like getting away, we'd have a sleepover at one place or the other, but the uniqueness of it was what made it fun.

"No, but I looked at it. It's a different kind of place than where I am now."

"Less upscale, maybe?" I asked as we walked toward the front open-air stairway.

"No, more transient," she said. "These places are rented month to month. Mine is a yearly lease."

We walked up to 14A, and as I knocked on the door, it swung open.

The place was empty, cleaned out of all personal possessions.

"She's not here," I said.

"That's pretty obvious," Maddy answered.

"So you got some bad information."

She raised an eyebrow at that. "It was good as of last night."

"Are you trying to tell me that she moved out this morning?"

"How should I know?" Maddy asked.

As we were talking, a thin, sallow man in his forties walked into the apartment.

He smiled at us, and then said, "Ladies, we're not

ready to show this unit yet, but we've got a lovely two bedroom on the other end of the building that just opened up. Why don't you let me take care of a few things here, and I'll meet you there. I'm the building manager."

"Isn't this where Katy Johnson lives?"

"Lived," he said. "She moved out this morning, after being here eight months. Funny thing, though, she still had fourteen days of rent she's already paid. I've had plenty of folks sneak out a few days past their lease, but not many who go with money still on the books."

"Did you happen to see her?"

He nodded. "I was taking out some trash and found her by the Dumpster. She was in a hurry to get out of here, let me tell you. I started to tell her that she could have her security deposit back after I checked her place over, but she told me to keep it. That girl was in some kind of hurry to get away." He looked around the place, and then said, "It needs a coat of paint, but that's not her fault. I've been meaning to get around to it, but I never seem to have the time. Now, this unit on the end I was telling you about would be perfect for you two."

"We're not looking for a place to rent," I said.

"Then why am I standing here talking to you when there's work to be done?" he asked with a smile. "If you'll excuse me," he said, "I've got to get this place ready to rent."

"Do you mind if we look around anyway?"

"Suit yourself," he said. "I've got to go get my painting supplies."

When he was gone, I looked at Maddy, then studied the abandoned apartment and said, "This doesn't look good for Katy."

"Maybe she just needed a change of scenery."

"And maybe she's on the run."

Maddy frowned as she looked around. "Come on, Eleanor, would you live here if you had any other options in the world? This place is more than a little depressing."

"Apparently, it didn't bother her that much for the past eight months. There had to be another, more compelling reason for her to leave so abruptly."

"The timing is a little off, I've got to give you that." Maddy started digging through a box of Katy's discards.

"What are you doing?"

"Looking for a clue about where she might have gone," Maddy said. "Don't be afraid to get your hands dirty, princess. Dig in."

I chose another box near the front door. "While we're at it, let's keep our eyes open for a motive to murder."

"We don't have all day," Maddy said. "The manager will be back any second, and I'm not sure he'd appreciate us pawing through this."

She was right. There were too many discarded papers in the boxes. I took everything but paperwork out of mine, then dumped Maddy's box inside, too. It was so full I could barely close the cardboard flaps, and on an impulse, I threw the old telephone book on top of all of it.

"And how are we going to get that past the building super? I don't think this guy misses much."

I shoved her toward the door. "That's where you come in. Go charm him while I smuggle this to the car."

She started to protest when the manager came back into view.

I shoved the box behind the door as my sister told the manager, "I never got your name."

"It's William Stratford," he said. "And you are?"

"Single, William," my sister replied. "How about you?"

The poor man actually blushed. "I never had time for a wife, what with my career and all."

It was all I could do not to laugh out loud at that, but Maddy never even skipped a beat. "Business is important, but you must be awfully lonely."

He couldn't even look her in the eye. "I get that way from time to time."

Maddy threaded her arm into his. "Why don't you tell me about it while you show me this apartment vacancy you've got? I can suddenly see some real advantages to living here."

If she batted her eyes any harder, I was afraid she was going to take off like a helicopter.

He bought every bit of it, though, and when they left, I doubted that he even remembered I'd come with her.

Once they were gone, I did one last check of the place, but if there were any clues to Katy's sudden disappearance that weren't in the box, I'd have been surprised. I carried the whole thing outside, nearly tripping over the paint cans in the outdoor hallway where the super had abandoned them.

I put the box in my car, and then waited impatiently for my sister to come back so we could leave. It was almost time for us to get to the Slice, and I didn't want to be late. There wasn't going to be any rushed dough today. We'd been closed—through no fault of our own—and I wanted everyone who came in to remember why they bought their pizzas and subs at our place, and not somewhere else.

I was about to give up on her when Maddy came tearing down the sidewalk. She got into the car, and then said in a panting voice, "Let's go."

"What happened? Did the shy Mr. Stratford get a little fresh with you?"

"It turns out that he isn't all that shy when no one else is around."

I laughed loudly. "You can't be serious."

"Trust me, I wouldn't lie about that. I wonder if that's why Katy left. With that masher for an apartment manager, I doubt she felt very safe."

"I still can't believe it," I said.

At that moment, I saw William Stratford come around the corner, so before he could get any closer to the car, I put it in gear and drove off.

I looked back in my rearview mirror, and then told Maddy, "Turn around."

"Why?" She did as I asked, and no doubt saw Mr. Stratford standing in the middle of the parking lot, waving frantically at us, or, more likely, at my sister.

"The things I do for you," Maddy said.

"It's for the team, and I take my own share of hits," I said.

Maddy nodded. "I know, I know." She shivered once, and then asked, "Is there any time to go back to my apartment before we open?"

"Why?"

"I need a shower after that encounter," she said.

"Sorry, but a good washing up in the sink is going to have to be good enough. We've got work to do."

"More crime solving?" Maddy asked.

"No, pizza making," I said. When I saw my sister's frown, I added, "Don't worry, as soon as we get the dough started and you've got the toppings prepped, we'll dig into that box and see what we can find."

"It's a deal," she said. "But here's another thought. Why don't you prep the kitchen, and I'll start searching for clues?"

"Maddy, I need you to stay focused. The sooner we get our work done, the sooner we can start looking."

"Spoilsport," she said.

"You know it."

When we got to the pizzeria, I parked in back, as was my custom, and Maddy went around to collect our box of what, hopefully, were clues about Katy's vanishing act.

We were both in back of the car when I heard a voice I'd been hoping I wouldn't hear for a while.

There was no dodging it now, though.

I had no place to run.

"Where have you been?" the police chief asked me as I turned around.

"I'm sorry, I didn't realize I had to check in with you wherever I went, Chief," I said. I tried to shield the box from him, but it was clear he was curious about what was in it. I decided to tell him before he asked. Not the truth, but something that might ease his suspicious nature, not that he wouldn't be right on the money this time. "It's just some old stuff for recycling," I added.

He nodded, then reached out and took the telephone book on top. Was Katy's name anywhere on it? I hoped not, because I was going to have a hard time explaining why I had it, and worse yet, the contents of the rest of the box I was holding.

He leafed through it, and then flipped it back on top. "I'll take it for you. I'm going to the recycling center this afternoon."

He made a move for the box, and then Maddy quickly appeared and said, "Thanks anyway, but we've got some trash to sort out first. Was there a reason you were looking for my sister, or are you just serving and protecting everyone in Timber Ridge?"

"I just want to make sure you're all right being here alone after the murder and the robbery."

"I've nearly forgotten about it," I lied. I doubted I'd ever be able to get rid of that image of the gun shoved in my face, or the body on the floor of my kitchen, but he didn't have to know that.

Kevin looked long and hard at me. "Eleanor, why don't I believe you?"

I shrugged. "It's just your nature, I guess."

Maddy laughed. "If I'd have said that, you would have thrown me in jail."

Obviously not the least bit amused, Kevin answered, "I'd have to have more cause than that." He paused for a few seconds, and then asked, "How was your big date last night, Maddy?"

She reddened slightly. "How on earth did you hear about that?"

"Don't kid yourself," he said sternly. "There's not a whole lot that goes on around here that I don't know about."

That stung Maddy a little, I could tell by the way her breath sharpened. I needed to stop this little trade-off of jabs before she said something I'd later regret. "Thanks for checking on me, but if I'm going to have dough ready by noon, I'd better get started on it right now."

He tipped his cap to me. "I understand."

We started to walk away when he called out, "By the way, has either one of you seen any sign of Greg Hatcher this morning?"

"No," I said simply, and Maddy shook her head as well.

"How about last night?"

"I haven't spoken to him since you and I talked last," which was the plain and unvarnished truth. Whether the chief of police believed me or not wasn't my problem. It felt good to be able to tell him the truth, even if it was a change of pace for me recently.

"If you hear from him, call me," Kevin said.

"So, the real reason for your concern becomes apparent," Maddy said.

"Why can't it be about both things?" he asked.

"I'll let you know, Chief," I said.

He seemed content with that, and after we turned the corner, I said to Maddy, "Do you always have to go out of your way to antagonize him?"

"No, but usually it's worth the trip. I'm not about to let him bully you while I'm standing right beside you."

I looked at her a second. "Are you sure it's not because he brought up your date with Bob Lemon?"

"That's irrelevant," she said.

I shoved the box into her arms as we neared the door. As I did, a piece of paper fluttered out of the telephone book. Maddy took the box, and I retrieved the paper.

As I looked at it, Maddy asked, "What does it say?"

"Give me a second." I opened the paper and found a telephone number written on it. "It's just a number," I said as I showed my sister.

She put the box down on the ground in front of the pizzeria's door and pulled out her cell phone.

"What are you doing?" I asked her, though I was pretty sure about the answer.

"I'm calling it, what do you think?"

I reached for her phone, but she must have anticipated the move, because she pulled it out of my reach at the last second.

"Hang on," she said as she moved it to her ear. "It's ringing."

I pulled her phone away enough so we could at least both hear. After four rings, a voice came on. "Hello, this is Wade Hatcher. I'm not here, but if you'd like to leave a message, you know the drill."

There was something about that voice that tweaked my memory. I was still pondering it when Maddy said, "It's no surprise that Katy had Wade's number."

"Hang on a second," I said as I waved a hand in the air in front of her. To my continued shock and amazement, my sister actually did as I'd requested, but whatever tenuous connection I'd made was gone.

"Never mind. I thought I heard something in his voice that I recognized, but I was wrong."

Maddy wasn't about to accept that, though. "Let's listen to it again."

"It's no use," I said.

"Come on, you have to at least try."

She punched redial, and a few seconds later, it was back.

It took me a full ten seconds, and I had to focus sharply on the inflection of his voice, but then it hit me.

"He's the one who robbed me," I said.

Maddy looked at me as if I'd just announced I was going to sell the business and move to Alaska. "How can you be sure? I thought you said he whispered when he held you up."

"He did, but there's something in the quality of his voice that makes me believe that he's the robber."

Maddy was quiet for a few seconds, and then she said, "My first reaction to hearing that recording was that he sounded an awful lot like Greg."

I'd realized that myself, but I didn't say it aloud. "Greg didn't rob me."

"Are you sure? I'm nearly as big a fan of his as you are, but how can you be sure it was Wade and not Greg?"

"Because I know Greg Hatcher, and he's not going to rob me. He knows if he needs money, he can have whatever I've got, no questions asked."

"The voices are similar," Maddy repeated. "I'm just saying."

"No, I don't believe it. He could no sooner rob me than . . ."

I left the sentence hanging in the air, but Maddy finished it for me, anyway. "No sooner than kill someone?" she asked. "Is that what you were about to say?"

I nodded, too appalled to speak it.

"Maybe we don't know Greg as well as we thought we did."

"He didn't kill anybody," I said, but it was pretty clear my voice was losing conviction as shades of doubt began to creep into my mind.

"Still, I think we both need to be careful when Greg comes back."

"Don't you mean 'if'?" I asked as I unlocked the door.

"No, he'll be back. There's not much doubt about that. I'm just wondering when it's going to happen."

Maddy retrieved the box, and after she was inside, I relocked the door so we could work in peace. She carried it back into the kitchen, and then deposited it on a stool by the counter.

We both kept ignoring it as I measured the warm water and yeast out for the first batch of dough. As I added other ingredients to the mix, my gaze kept going back to the floor where I'd seen Wade's body. I couldn't get the image out of my mind, and I was beginning to wonder if I'd ever be able to wipe it clean. The sight of his body lying there, the bloodied rolling pin, and the thin-crust pizza were burned into my retinas.

And then I asked a question I should have been wondering about from the moment I saw the crime scene: "Where did the pizza come from, Maddy?"

She looked confused by the question. "You make them every day."

"I'm talking about the one I saw beside the body."

"I just assumed it was one of ours," she said, a frown creasing her lips.

"The kitchen was clean, though. Nobody made it after I left, or there would have been dirty dishes."

"He could have cleaned up after himself," Maddy said uncertainly.

"If Wade even knew how to make a pizza, he wouldn't be able to clean up so we wouldn't realize someone had been in our kitchen. Look around. Is there a single thing out of place back here, except for the fact that the rolling pin is missing?"

I looked again as Maddy scanned the room. Finally she said, "No, it's how we leave it at night."

"And not even Greg knows our routine back here," I said, with more than a little relief in my voice.

"That means someone brought a pizza with them after we closed. Who would do that?"

"And, more important, why?"

I wiped off my hands and grabbed the telephone.

Maddy asked, "Who are you calling?"

"I need to know if Kevin held on to that pizza."

I dialed his number, and he nearly growled at me when he answered.

I didn't let his tone bother me, though. "Do you still have that pizza you found beside Wade's body?"

"Of course I do, it's evidence. Don't tell me you want it back."

"I've got a hunch I never made it in the first place," I said. After I explained my theory to Kevin, he said, "Don't go anywhere. I'm going to get a big cooler, and then I'll bring it by."

"I'll be right here."

After I hung up, Maddy asked, "Why would someone bring a pizza from some other place to a pizzeria?"

"I'm not sure, but I'm going to give it some thought until I can figure it out."

I went back to my dough, and my thoughts kept returning to the box of Katy's discards as I worked. I was hoping that if I distracted myself enough, my subconscious might give me an idea of how the errant pizza had ended up in my business. The box was intriguing as well. Could there be a clue to what had happened to Wade Hatcher buried among Katy's papers? And would Maddy and I be clever enough to find it, if there was? I had my doubts about both counts, but we had nowhere else to be at the moment. As soon as we got a little downtime, we'd have to start digging into the pile and see if we could make any sense of it.

There was a pounding on the back door two minutes after the first batch of dough was rising.

I looked at Maddy as I wiped my hands on a dish towel. "That was fast."

"Don't forget, he's got flashing lights and a siren. It's probably great for getting through traffic."

I opened the back door and saw that Kevin had a cooler in his arms. "It's the only one I could find on short notice."

The cooler had the Carolina Panthers football team logo on it. "That's fine with me. I'm a huge Panthers fan."

"I didn't know you liked football."

"It's fun, but what I really like are football fans. You wouldn't believe how much pizza we sell whenever there's a game." I held out my hands. "Let's see it."

"You have to put these on first," Kevin said as he handed me a pair of latex gloves.

"Are you serious?"

"It's evidence, and while I doubt a piece of pepperoni could hold a fingerprint, in this day and age, you can't be so sure."

I donned the gloves, and then opened the cooler. The pizza was wrapped in lots of plastic, so it was difficult to tell much about it. "I need to see it without the wrapping."

Kevin nodded, and then took the pizza back from me. He was wearing gloves himself, so I couldn't fault him for his caution with me. Maddy was watching everything with an air of wonder and amusement on her face, but fortunately, she was keeping her comments to herself, at least for now.

After the wrapping was off, Kevin handed it back to me, but I refused it.

"What's wrong?" he asked. "The wrapping's off, just like you asked."

"That's not one of mine," I said emphatically.

"How can you be so sure? You haven't even really looked at it."

"Maddy, do you want to tell him?"

She nodded, then glanced at the pizza. "Look at the crust. That one was baked in a gas oven. We use electric."

"And you can tell that from one glance?"

Maddy frowned at him. "Can you tell a revolver from a shotgun?"

"Of course, I can."

"That's your business, and this is ours. We didn't make it. I'd say Drakes in Goshen's Landing, if I had to guess. Eleanor, what do you think?"

"It looks like one of theirs to me. The question is, who would bring a pizza from somewhere else here?"

Kevin studied the pizza for a second; then he said, "Maybe it was a killer who wanted to lure someone else here for a pizza, but didn't have one on hand." He wrapped the pizza back up, then said, "Thanks for your help, ladies."

"You're welcome," we said, though he probably didn't hear us. No doubt he was about to pay a call on one of our competitors, which was fine with me. Let them explain a patrol car in front of their pizza place, for a change.

We went back to work, but ten minutes later our day was interrupted again. Someone was rapping steadily on the front door of the pizzeria.

"Are you expecting anybody this morning?"

"Not me. Do you think Kevin thought of something else?"

Since all of our deliveries came through the back door, it was odd to have someone trying to get in before we opened, especially without calling ahead first.

I looked around for my favorite rolling pin, and then I remembered that it was now evidence in a murder investigation. Second best was a large cleaver we sometimes used for chopping, and as I peeked around the kitchen door to the dining area, I saw Slick standing outside with a big box on a handcart.

He waved, and I put the cleaver back on the counter.

"The safe's here," I told my sister.

Maddy kept working. "Nothing like locking the barn door, and all that," she said.

I shrugged. There was nothing I could do about the last robbery, but I could make it harder for someone the next time they tried, though I hoped that never happened again. Being robbed at gunpoint was something I didn't need to experience again. When I'd heard Wade's voice on his answering machine, it had sent chills through me. I didn't care that his voice was close to Greg's. I knew he was the one who'd held me up, and though I understood that he could never rob me again, the peace of mind he'd stolen, along with my cash, was irreplaceable.

I unlocked the door and held it open for Slick. As he pushed the handcart in and I relocked the dead bolt behind him, he said, "Surprise, surprise. It came earlier than I expected. Where do you want it?"

It was bigger than I'd remembered. Seeing it in his shop out of context, I thought I'd be able to tuck it under my desk. That was clearly not going to happen. Where on earth was I going to put it? "I don't have a clue where it should go."

"Most people put them in their offices," he said helpfully.

"If I do that, there won't be any room left for me," I admitted.

"Why don't we leave it here for now and see what we can come up with?"

I agreed, and we walked back through the kitchen, where Maddy was still working at prepping our toppings for the day.

Maddy smiled at him. "Hey, Slick. I see you running every day. You think you're ever going to catch what you're chasing?"

"You never know until you try, now do you?" He looked at the green pepper she was slicing. "That looks good."

"Want a nibble?" she said, offering a green ring to him.

"No, I'd better not," he said with some reluctance.

"Go on, we've got plenty," I said. "Besides, you can think of it as your delivery fee."

"Does that mean I can't charge you for bringing it over?" Slick asked.

"No, of course not. I didn't mean anything by it."

Slick laughed. "Eleanor, I'm not going to bill you for wheeling this thing a hundred paces down the promenade."

"Then take two pepper rings," I said.

He laughed, and did just that. "Man, that's good."

"You really know how to live it up, don't you?" Maddy said.

"I try." He looked around the space, then stepped into my office.

Maddy asked me, "What's he doing?"

"Slick's trying to figure out where to put our new safe." I then admitted, "It's a little larger than I thought it would be when I saw it at his place. I don't want to hear a word from you, do you understand?"

Maddy didn't laugh, which was to her credit. "Why not put it in the storage room? We can keep stuff on top of it, and nobody would look for it there."

I shrugged, not sure if I wanted to stumble on the big iron box every time I needed flour.

Slick rejoined us. "That place is no good."

"I told you so."

He kept looking around, and then pointed to our storage room. "What's in there?"

"It's for storage. Maddy just said that's where we should put it."

Slick nodded, then ducked in for a few seconds before reappearing. "It's going to be a tight fit."

"Maybe this is a bad idea," I said. "I don't really have that much to put into it, you know? Buying the safe's going to cut into that, too."

Slick waved a hand in the air. "I'm giving you my best discount, so don't worry about that. I can make it work, but I won't be able to drill until the weekend. Let's put it in place and see how it fits for now. Any chance you two could move some of those boxes out so I can get it in?"

I nodded, so Maddy and I started working at disassembling our carefully arranged storage. By the time we had everything out—and a path for Slick to bring the safe through—there wasn't a free square inch of space on the floor around me.

Slick managed to maneuver the cumbersome unit close to the storage room door, and after removing the cardboard around its exterior, he said, "As soon as I get this in place, we can restock everything."

I frowned at all of the boxes and containers on the floor and all of the free counter space. "If it will fit back in now."

"Don't worry. Leave that to me. We'll make it work," he said.

"Not before we mop the floor in there first," I said. "I hate to make you wait around while I do it, but I'm not going to pass up the chance to clean that floor while I have the chance."

Slick nodded. "Tell you what. Call me when you're finished, and then I'll come back and put everything in place."

"We won't be that long," I said. I was torn between getting my pizzeria back in working order and taking advantage of a cleaning opportunity when I had the chance.

He appeared to think about it a moment, then asked, "Do you have a newspaper? I can go out and grab a booth while I'm waiting."

"I've got the Charlotte paper," I said. "Will that do?"

"I'll read the list of ingredients on the side of a box if I have to," he said with a smile. "I'm kind of addicted to reading."

"There are worse things you could be addicted to," I said.

"You've got that right. Running and reading are about my two favorite things to do in the world."

I mopped the floor in record time, and Maddy followed along behind me with a few old towels we kept on hand for the spills that seemed to happen with somewhat irritating frequency around the pizzeria.

Slick was studying the menu when I walked back out into the dining area. "Did you read the paper that quickly?"

"What can I say, I'm a speed reader. When's the last time you made up a new menu?" he asked as he tapped the old one on the table in front of him.

"It's been about a year," I said.

"How have you managed to keep your prices so low all of that time?"

"I hate the hassle of having new ones printed up," I admitted.

"You should use my guy."

"You have a guy for menus?" I asked, just a little bit incredulous.

"No need for menus in a sporting-goods store," he said, "but I've got a great graphic artist that could make your life easier. As a matter of fact, I've got a guy for just about everything."

"Thanks, but I'd rather design it myself."

Slick shrugged. "Okay, but if you change your mind, I'll give you Sylvia's number."

"Who's Sylvia?" I asked, wondering how our conversation had sidetracked to someone else.

"She's my guy," he said, deadly serious.

"How is she your *guy*?"

Slick laughed. "Anybody I've got who does something

better than anyone else is *my guy*. I don't care if it's a man or a woman or a blue-tailed butterfly." He grinned at me as he added, "You're *my guy* for pizza."

I smiled. "I'm not sure if that's a compliment or not. Honestly, it sounds kind of sexist to me."

He didn't seem put off by my remark. "I guess it all depends on how you look at it."

"Then you're *my gal* when it comes to safes. Everybody's going to be *my gal* from now on."

"Call me whatever you'd like," he said, "just don't call me late to supper. Now let's get that baby installed."

I followed him back into the kitchen, and he was as good as his word. In five minutes, all of the shelving units were back in place, though they were still bare.

"Let me help you restock this," he said as he moved the cardboard and the hand truck out into the dining room.

"Thanks, but we've got it," I said.

"Eleanor, I don't mind helping a bit."

"I know, but Maddy and I are pretty particular on how our storage room is set up, and in all honesty, it would take us longer to give you instructions than it would just to do it ourselves."

"I can respect that," he said.

He lingered a little longer, so I asked, "Do you need me to pay you now?" I'd been hoping he'd bill me so I'd have a chance to work up my savings a little, but I'd manage somehow if he needed his money up front.

"No, that's fine. I'm happy to send you a bill," he said.

"Then what is it?"

"Listen, Eleanor, I'm feeling a little bad about our earlier conversation. I didn't mean any disrespect before."

I honestly wasn't sure what he was talking about. "What do you mean?"

"About the guy thing and all," he reluctantly admitted.

"Sometimes I shoot my mouth off without thinking, but in general I'm pretty harmless."

"Slick, it would take a lot more than that to offend me, but you are sweet to apologize." I bussed his cheek, which elicited a quick grin.

"If I'd known I'd get a kiss, I'd have offended you a lot sooner than that. Now, will somebody let me out of here? I've got a sports shop to run."

I walked him to the door, and as I was propping it open so Slick could get his handcart out, someone was coming down the promenade toward my pizzeria, with a look I wasn't about to mistake for anything but anger.

Chapter 8

"We need to talk," Jamie Lowder said as he approached me. The anger was clear in his face, and I suddenly wished that Slick had stuck around just a little bit longer. It wasn't that Slick was all that physically imposing, but I didn't think Jamie would do anything if there was a witness standing right beside me.

"Sorry, we're not open for business yet," I said, watching Slick retreat.

"This isn't business. It's personal." There was a bristling edge to his words that made me fight the urge to run inside and lock the door. I was more than a little scared, but I wasn't going to let myself be bullied in front of my own place.

"What is it, Jamie? I don't have time for this. If you want a fight, you've picked on the wrong person today." I snapped out my words with force, and that somehow got his attention.

"Hey, take it easy. I'm not trying to upset you. I just want you to back off Sandi. She feels bad enough about what happened to Wade. You don't need to make things any worse for her right now."

"I can't be responsible for how she feels," I said, easing my tone a little. Jamie was pretty imposing, and as he spoke, I kept imagining him in my kitchen with a rolling pin in his hand, standing over Wade Hatcher's lifeless form. "You were pretty eager to give her an alibi yesterday," I added.

"It was the truth," he said, his temper rising again. This guy had a short fuse, and I needed to be a little more cautious than I had been so far. But being timid wasn't going to get me any information I didn't already have.

"All I'm saying is that you both had reasons to want him dead." I said it flatly, not an accusation at all, but a simple statement of fact.

"Why would I hurt him?" Jamie asked. "I didn't even know him all that well." He looked truly puzzled by the accusation.

"Come on, be honest with me. With Wade out of the way, Sandi's free."

"She was already free," he said. "They broke up, remember?"

"For how long, though? The only way there was room for you in her life was to get rid of Wade, once and for all."

He started toward me, and I flinched, though I hadn't wanted to.

"That's crazy," he said. "You need to shut up about things that don't concern you, do you hear me?"

"I'm not saying you did it, but it's something the police have to be wondering about as well, don't you think? Are you sure your alibi with Sandi is good enough to hold up under their heavy questioning?"

I saw his gaze shoot downward, and while it wasn't tangible proof, I had a pretty good feeling that he'd been lying about being with Sandi the night of the murder.

After a moment's pause, he said, "You're not the police though, are you? If they need to talk to us, they know where to find us. Stop messing with this, Eleanor. You're in over your head. It could be dangerous."

Had it been Jamie on the phone the night before threatening me? "What's wrong? Did you get tired of calling me, so you decided to come down here in person to threaten me this time?"

"What are you talking about? I never called you."

"How can you prove that?" I asked.

"How can you prove that I did?" he asked in response. "This is insane. I didn't kill Wade Hatcher, and neither did Sandi."

"Then you don't have anything to worry about, do you?"

Maddy came out, and it felt good to have her presence beside me, though I doubted the two of us combined were any physical match for him. "What's going on?"

"I just told your sister to stay out of my business," Jamie snarled at her. "And I'm telling you, too."

"Okay then, your work is done here. Now shoo."

She pulled me back inside and locked the door of the pizzeria. Jamie stood there another two seconds, and then he stormed off down the promenade.

"My, my, my. He's got a temper, doesn't he?" Maddy said.

"More than I realized. To be honest with you, I was a little scared standing out there all alone with him, even if it was in broad daylight."

Maddy nodded. "He's a bit of a bear, isn't he? We can't keep him out forever, though. If he wants to come after us, we're opening up in an hour and a half."

"We'll deal with that when it happens, but I don't think he'll be back."

"Why not?" Maddy asked, clearly perplexed.

"He said what he wanted to say, and I gave him something to think about. He's hiding something—that much is clear."

"But what?" Maddy asked.

"That's the question, isn't it?" I brushed my hands on the sides of my jeans, and then I said, "It's got to be time to get back to my dough."

"That's why I came up front. Your timer just went off."

"Then let's get to it," I said. "Standing here talking about this isn't going to do us any good."

"Not only that, but we've still got a box of papers to sort through before we open."

"Don't worry," I said. "I haven't forgotten about that. Give me ten minutes, and then we can get started."

"I'm ready now," Maddy said with a grin. "But you're welcome to join me as soon as you're finished with your work. I've waited as long as I'm going to wait."

I laughed, to ease the tension in my heart more than at my sister's feeble humor. "You win. Start digging and I'll be right with you."

Maddy didn't join in my laughter. "Wow, he really must have shaken you up."

"I just told you that he did," I said.

"Yeah, but I didn't realize how much. I've never won an argument that fast in my life, at least not with you."

"Mark it on your calendar—it's not going to happen again soon."

"Then I'll relish the victory while I can. Come on, Eleanor. Everything is going to be all right."

She put her arm around me, and we walked back into the kitchen together. I was glad to have Maddy with me, and not just for the help she gave me in running the pizzeria. She was a part of me; sometimes I thought the better part. Together, we could handle just about anything that came our way.

Including tracking down a killer and making him pay for what he'd done.

Maddy was just getting started on the box when we heard pounding on the front door.

"He just doesn't get the hint, does he?" Maddy asked.

"No, but I'm going to make sure he gets it this time."

My sister put a hand on my arm. "You're not seriously thinking about going out there again, are you?"

"I won't let someone bully me in front of my own pizzeria," I said.

"At least call someone for backup."

"Who do you suggest? Do you honestly think the police chief is going to trot right down here to look out for me? Besides, I don't need a man to protect me. I've got this," I added as I reached out and grabbed the cleaver again.

"And I've got my stun gun," she said as she dove into her purse.

"I don't want you coming with me," I said as the pounding repeated itself.

"Well, I don't want donuts to go to my hips, but I've got a feeling they're going to, anyway."

I raised an eyebrow. "There's barely an ounce of fat on you, and you know it."

Maddy said, "It was an expression, okay?"

I looked at my own hips. "Not with me it's not."

Instead of answering, she started for the kitchen door. "If we're going to do this, let's go right now."

I caught up with her as she walked out into the dining room, ready for trouble. Instead of finding Jamie outside, though, Jenny Wilkes stood by the door, armed with nothing more dangerous than a bouquet of pink roses from her shop, Forever in Bloom.

Maddy lowered her stun gun, and I put the knife down on the counter, where the drink machine was. As we approached the door, I wondered what had possessed David Quinton to send me flowers. I'd been pretty clear that he needed to back off, but apparently he wasn't listening. What did I have to do, send them back to him shredded?

As I unlocked the door, I said, "I don't want those."

"Hi, Eleanor. I'm fine, how are you?"

Jenny was a petite blonde barely into her thirties, and she was a die-hard romantic. She had the perfect personality for running a floral shop, where love was always in the air.

"Sorry," I said as I stepped aside and let her in. "It's just been one of those days, and those flowers aren't making it any better."

She looked startled by my declaration. "Is that any way to talk? Flowers always make everything better."

"Not today they don't," I said. "I was serious before. I don't want them."

Jenny smiled at me. "Then isn't it a good thing that they aren't for you? Maddy, it appears that you have a not-so-secret admirer."

As she handed the flowers to my sister, I felt like a complete fool. "I'm sorry. I'm just not myself today."

Jenny patted my shoulder. "That's okay. But it's good to know how you feel if anyone ever does try to send you flowers." She paused a second, then said, "Eleanor, I didn't mean that how it sounded—honest, I didn't."

Maddy laughed. "Come on, when you get in a zinger like that, it's important to take full credit for it." My sister breathed in the scents of the flowers, then smiled. "I don't even have to see who sent them."

"It was Bob Lemon, wasn't it?" I asked.

When Maddy didn't answer, Jenny shook her head. "Don't look at me, because I'm not telling."

"What is it, some kind of privileged florist-client thing?" I asked.

"You're joking, but believe me, you wouldn't imagine the men who send flowers to women around here who aren't their wives."

I'd never thought of it that way. "Have you ever had to testify in court?"

"Once," she admitted. "The husband was buying flowers from me and having them sent to Hickory. His wife found out, though. I hated seeing my flowers used as a weapon like that. It made my heart sick."

Maddy pulled out the card, read it quickly, and then chuckled. "I'll spare you the suspense, Eleanor. They're from Bob."

"What did he have to say on the card?" It had been so long since I'd gotten flowers from anyone, I suddenly realized that I missed the gesture. My late husband, Joe, was many things, but a romantic was not high on the list of his attributes. He'd rather tell me that he loved me by giving me a new hammer, or maybe a heavy-duty spatula, but the only time he'd given me flowers had been the year before he died. After some prompting, he'd finally admitted that they'd been marked down 75 percent two days after Valentine's Day.

Maddy said, "I'd show you what it says, but you wouldn't understand."

"Contrary to what you might think, I'm not all that dense, Maddy," I said.

"Fine, have it your way." She handed me the card, and I read, *Umbrellas are better than butterscotch only when it's raining. Bob.*

"What is that supposed to mean?"

Maddy smiled. "I told you that you wouldn't get it."

I handed the card back to her. "No sane person would. Aren't you going to give Jenny a tip?"

Maddy looked flustered. "Of course I am," she said. "Just let me get my purse."

"It's not necessary," Jenny said. "Most people don't tip the store owner."

"I'd like to think I'm a little better than most people," she said as she ducked in the kitchen to grab her purse.

While she was gone, Jenny said, "Eleanor, I was sorry to hear about you and David Quinton."

"Why? What did you hear?" I asked as a knee-jerk response. "Cancel that, I don't want to know."

I couldn't believe it when she actually respected my wishes. A part of me had been hoping she'd tell me, anyway. It mattered what folks in Timber Ridge thought of me, and I hoped it was all good, though I knew for a fact that wasn't entirely the case. Some people thought that living in a small town meant being friends with a lot of people, which was true. However, it also meant that enemies made in the course of a lifetime were there forever, a thought that was more than a little oppressive at times.

Maddy came back out with a five-dollar bill clutched in her hand.

Before she could even give it to Jenny, the florist said, "That's too much."

"Nonsense. I think it's perfect."

Jenny shrugged and accepted the offering, giving up the fight pretty quickly, in my opinion.

I let her out, and then locked the door behind her.

Maddy took in a deep breath of the pink roses and baby's breath florets, and said, "I just love these, don't you?"

"They're nice," I admitted. "How did he know pink roses were your favorite?"

Maddy looked surprised. "I suppose I assumed that you told him."

"He didn't ask me," I admitted.

Maddy smiled gently. "The man is managing to surprise me more than I ever could have imagined. I like that in a suitor, don't you?"

"To be honest with you, it's been so long since I've had one, I've forgotten what it's like."

"Nonsense," Maddy said as she put them on a counter in the kitchen. "David Quinton would send you flowers every day if you gave him the slightest amount of encouragement."

"That's not something I'm prepared to do," I said.

"Then in the meantime, you can enjoy mine with me," she said as she spun the vase around until she had the perfect view of them. Clapping her hands together, she said, "Now, why don't you get busy with your work while I dig into Katy Johnson's box of discards, and we'll see if I can figure out what happened to her."

I finished my prep work and joined Maddy as she dug into the box of papers. We worked quickly together, discarding old dry-cleaning receipts, auction notices, and even a few parking tickets, which still hadn't been paid. I doubted if Kevin Hurley would reach out the long arm of the law toward her to collect thirty or forty bucks, but with our chief of police, it was hard to know for sure.

I'd just about given up when I saw a yellow piece of paper that had slipped down between one of the folds in the bottom of the box. Retrieving it, I saw that it was from Jenny Wilkes at Forever in Bloom.

"What's that?" Maddy asked.

"It's a receipt for flowers," I said. The date was less than two weeks ago.

"So what? I bet even Katy got flowers every now and then."

"No, that's not it," I said. "This is a bill."

"So Katy sent flowers to someone else. It's a little odd, but I don't really think it's all that significant, do you?"

I tapped the paper. "That's the thing, though. This isn't Greg's address."

"Who lives there?" At least I had finally gotten my sister's attention.

"I'm not sure," I admitted, "but it may give us an idea about where she could have gone."

Maddy nodded. "You're right. That might be important. But this could be, too."

"What is it?" I asked as I laid my receipt down on the counter by the telephone.

Maddy waved a piece of notebook paper in the air. "This must have been on top originally. Give me the phone."

"You're not just going to call without coming up with an excuse, are you?"

"Planning is for sissies," Maddy said.

"Hey, just because I like to prepare for different contingencies doesn't mean that I'm a sissy."

She patted my arm. "I didn't mean you." Maddy dialed the number, and then she held the telephone so both of us could hear.

"Calvin's," a gruff voice said.

I didn't recognize the voice, or the name.

Maddy asked, "Is Calvin there?"

When I looked at her, she just shrugged. It was pretty clear she didn't know what to do next, either.

"Lady, Calvin's been dead three years come August, so I might have a little trouble calling him to the phone."

"What exactly is it that you do?"

I didn't blame her for asking the question, but I wasn't sure what kind of response she was going to get. To my surprise, the man said, "You need it, we rent it. We've got everything from backhoes to pickup trucks. You can rent by the hour, by the day, or by the month."

"I've got a question for you. Did you rent something to Katy Johnson late last night or early this morning?"

The man's voice hesitated, and then he asked, "Who wants to know? That stuff is confidential, you know."

Maddy didn't know what to say, so I grabbed the telephone from her and said, "This is her mother, young man, and if you've helped an underage girl run away from home, the police will want to speak with you."

Maddy started to laugh, and I held up a finger for her to be quiet. After a moment, the man's tone shifted. "Ma'am, she had proper ID when I carded her."

"It was fake," I said. "My baby's just seventeen years old."

He stammered, and then finally admitted, "She brought the truck back an hour ago, so she couldn't have gone that far." He hesitated, and then added, "There was an older woman with her when she brought it back. I thought it was you. Her mom, that is."

"Clearly you were mistaken," I said.

Maddy asked me something, but I couldn't understand her. She tried to get my attention again, so I said, "One moment, young man."

I covered the telephone with my hand, then looked at my sister and asked, "What's so important?"

"Find out how many miles she put on the truck."

That was actually pretty brilliant. I nodded, then pulled my hand away from the mouthpiece. "Young man, how many miles were on the rental agreement?"

"Hang on," he said. I heard him tearing through some papers, and he came back on the line and said, "She went twelve miles from the time she got it to the second she brought it back. That's not much, is it?"

"Don't you worry, I'll find her," I said as I hung up on him.

"That was brilliant," I said to Maddy. "What made you think of that?"

"I don't know. I was just playing a hunch. How far did she go?"

"Twelve miles total," I said.

"So she's still in Timber Ridge."

"It looks like it. Should we go check on this address?" I held up the florist's receipt as I glanced at the clock and saw that we had twenty-seven minutes before we opened.

Maddy grabbed her purse. "I'm game if you are. Let's go."

We locked the place up, and then took Maddy's car to track down who Katy had sent flowers to.

On a hunch, when we got into the car, I told Maddy, "Reset the trip meter."

She asked, "Why?"

"I'm curious to see if we come up with a twelve-mile round-trip."

"Do you think she's at the same address she had the flowers delivered to?"

I shrugged. "It's a thought."

"And a good one at that," Maddy said. "I'm surprised I didn't think of it myself."

"Wait until you tell someone else this story," I said with a smile. "In that version, I don't doubt that you will."

She laughed as she drove off. "You know what? You're probably right."

We got to the address on the outskirts of Timber Ridge, closest to the mountains. The houses were farther apart, and a bit run-down. If there was a part of our area that classified as the other side of the tracks, this would be it.

We pulled up to a row house that hadn't been painted in thirty years. There were garish lawn ornaments scattered among the weeds, and I wouldn't have been surprised to find a garden gnome crinkling his porcelain nose in disgust.

"Should I go by myself, or do you want to go with me?" I asked.

Maddy shook her head. "Kiddo, I'm not about to let you have all of the fun. What should our lie be this time?"

"I hadn't even thought about not telling the truth," I admitted.

Maddy said, "Eleanor, if Katy's hiding here, what makes you think whoever owns this place is going to give her up just because we asked nicely?"

"You're right," I said.

I could have used more time in the car to come up with something, but a middle-aged woman in a flowery housecoat came out onto the front stoop and stared at us. "It looks like we're on."

"We still haven't come up with a story yet," Maddy hissed.

"I'll improvise," I said as I got out of the car. My sister didn't have any choice but to follow me.

We were three steps onto the woman's property when she said, "Whatever it is you're selling, I'm not interested. I've got nothing to say to either one of you."

"That's too bad," I said. "We have something for Katy Johnson, but if you don't want to talk to us, that's fine."

Maddy was looking oddly at me, but the woman on the porch couldn't see it.

I said to my sister loudly, "You were right all along. We'll keep it and split it. It's not our fault that we couldn't find her."

I barely turned around when the woman asked, "You can't do that. Whatever you've got belongs to my niece."

"You don't even know what I'm talking about," I said as I kept walking away from her.

"I don't need to. I've heard enough already."

I turned, and then looked at her a few seconds before I spoke. "I'm not about to hand it over to you. I don't even know who you are."

"I know you," she said. "You run that pizza joint downtown, the Spike."

"It's called A Slice of Delight," I said, correcting her.

"I guess that does make more sense," the woman said. "I'm Katy's aunt. Whatever it is of hers that you have, hand it over and I'll see that she gets it."

"Sorry, but I wouldn't feel right about doing that. We went by her place this morning, but she moved out in the middle of the night."

The woman shook her head in obvious disgust. "There was too much going on there. She needed to be somewhere she felt safe."

"Like here, with her aunt?" Maddy asked.

"I never claimed she was here," she said.

"But you know where to find her."

"I might," the woman answered cagily.

"Then find her and tell her I've got something that belongs to her, something she's going to want back."

Katy's aunt seemed to think about that, and then finally said, "If I don't know what it is, I'm not going to tell her."

"It's money," Maddy said. Why on earth had she chosen to say that?

It certainly got her aunt's attention. "How much are we talking about here?"

"More than I'm comfortable telling you about," I said. "The next time you see her, you need to tell her to come by the pizza place." I took Maddy's arm, and as we started to walk away, I turned and added, "If we don't see her by this time tomorrow, tell her not to bother at all."

We left as the woman continued to protest. Maddy was around the block before she turned to me and laughed. "You certainly knew how to get her attention, didn't you?"

"You're the one who brought up money. Now we're going to have to pay her when she shows up."

Maddy said, "If she shows up, I'll give her a ten out of my purse."

"Do you honestly think that would warrant us tracking her down?"

"Then you pitch in ten yourself and we'll make it a twenty," Maddy said.

"No, ten sounds good to me," I said.

Maddy frowned at me, so I added, "But twenty's better. I can live with that."

"So can I," she answered.

I looked at my watch. "We've got thirteen minutes to get back to the restaurant. Think we can make it?"

"With time to spare," Maddy said as she proceeded to exceed the speed limit.

"I don't want you to get a ticket," I said. "If we're a few minutes late, who's going to know?"

"You will, for one," she said.

"True. Okay, go ahead and push it a little."

"If I get arrested for speeding, will you split that with me, too?"

I laughed. "No, you're on your own there."

"Then maybe I should slow down," she said as she did just that.

Despite her decreased speed, we got back to the pizzeria with three minutes to spare, which would have been in plenty of time, if someone we both knew hadn't chosen that moment to step out of the shadows in the alley behind the pizzeria and move quickly toward us before we could make our way inside.

"Greg, what are you doing here?" I asked our deliveryman as he hurried to us.

"I had to talk to you," Greg said. "Katy's gone."

"We know," Maddy answered. "We went by her place first thing this morning, and she's moved out."

"Do you have any idea where she went?" Greg asked. "I'm going crazy with worry."

"Why are you so concerned about Katy?" I asked him.

"She could be the key to everything. I need to talk to her before the police do, but I can't find her. Do you have any idea how frustrating that is?"

Maddy said, "I'd think you had enough trouble yourself without borrowing any from your ex-girlfriend."

"You might think that, but you'd be wrong. I'm not about to let Chief Hurley hang this on me. I need to talk to Katy. If she didn't kill Wade, she might know who did. She loved me once—at least she said she did—so maybe she'll talk to me now. What else have you two been up to?"

"We talked to Art Young," I said.

Greg's face went pale. "Tell me you're joking. Have you two lost your minds?"

"Actually, Eleanor thought he was kind of charming," Maddy said.

"Yeah, and a black widow spider has a pretty little hourglass on its belly. That doesn't mean it's still not deadly."

"We were careful," I said. After I explained how we'd gotten Bob Lemon to intercede for us, Greg was a little mollified.

"I don't like you taking chances on my account," he said.

"We've been talking to Sandi Meadows and Jamie Lowder, too," I said. "They're quite a pair, aren't they?"

"You'd better believe it."

I took a breath, then said, "We talked to your mother, too. She sounds like she wants you to get the electric chair."

Greg laughed without an ounce of humor in it. "Good old Mom. She's never been my biggest fan, but you'd think with just one son left, she might try a little harder with me."

"I think she honestly believes you could have killed your brother," I said.

Greg shook his head. "I don't doubt that's what she thinks for a second. If I ever get put on trial, I surely won't use her for a character witness."

"You're taking that particular bit of news rather calmly," Maddy said.

"Do you honestly think it's news to me? My mother gave me a tenth of everything she lavished on my brother. They both thought he was entitled to it, even if it meant hurting me. Now that he's gone, I don't have any doubt that she'll come after me herself if she gets the chance.

Listen, there's something I need to talk to you about, and I didn't feel right leaving you a message on your machine. There's one more suspect that we haven't considered yet, somebody had their own reason to want to see Wade dead."

Before he could tell us, there was a quick burst from a police siren, and we looked up to see Kevin Hurley barreling down the alley toward us.

Greg sprinted away before we could stop him, not that either Maddy or I wanted to. The chief blasted past us, then came back in three minutes with an angry scowl.

"You let him go," he snarled at us as he got out of the car.

"We nearly had him talked into giving himself up when you came bombing up the road," Maddy snapped. "It's your own fault you didn't catch him."

"Do you expect me to believe that?" Kevin asked.

"We don't care what you believe," I said. "Come on, Maddy, we're late opening our restaurant."

As we ducked through the passage to the front of the shops, I turned to look at Kevin Hurley.

He was still standing there beside his patrol car, watching our every step with an unhappy look on his face.

Which was probably a pretty good description of how he'd be behaving from here on out.

Chapter 9

When I walked back into the Slice, I leaned down and smelled Maddy's roses without realizing what I was doing.

"You really should call David," my sister said behind me.

"What makes you say that?"

"Eleanor, if you're ever going to get roses of your own, you're going to have to do something to make it happen. David's a good guy. You should at least give him a chance."

It wasn't like I hadn't been thinking the exact same thing myself. "Okay, I give up. I'll call him again."

"What? You're actually listening to me?"

I started dialing as I said, "I listen to you all of the time."

Maddy didn't respond, but she lowered her chin and stared at me.

I added, "Just because I listen doesn't mean I have to do what you say."

"That, I believe."

I felt a little nervous as I phoned David. What was I going to say to him? I had to apologize for the way I'd been acting lately, but I wasn't sure I could bring myself to do that. Still, if I wanted there to be any hope of something developing between us, I had to take this step, no matter how uncomfortable it made me feel.

His secretary, Joanna Hearst, picked up on the fourth ring. "Hi, Jo, it's Eleanor Swift. Is David in?"

"Hey, Eleanor. You honestly didn't know? He's gone."

I felt my heart seize up a little. "What do you mean? Has something happened to him?"

"Not as far as I know," she said a little curtly. "I spoke with him three days ago, and he seemed fine then."

"Where did he go?" I wanted to add *and why didn't he tell me* but somehow I managed to restrain myself.

"He's in Raleigh. The company is asking him to transfer, and they've given him two weeks there to see how he likes it. I thought you knew about it."

"He must have been too busy to tell me," I said, trying to keep the hurt feelings out of my voice.

"Listen," Jo said, "nobody was rooting for you two more than I was, but sometimes these things just don't work out."

"Is it a done deal? Is he taking the job?"

Jo hesitated, and then said, "I'd probably get in trouble if anyone knew I was telling you this, but you have a right to know. The last time we spoke, he told me that maybe a fresh start was what he needed. I don't know a hundred percent that he's made up his mind to move, but if I were a betting woman, that's where my money would go. I'm really sorry to have to be the one to tell you."

"That's fine," I said. Almost as an afterthought, I added, "If you talk to him again, tell him I called."

"I will. Is there anything else you'd like me to tell him?"

A thousand different things went through my mind. I

wanted him to come back to Timber Ridge and forget about moving, but I couldn't tell him that, not unless I was willing to give him more of a chance than I had so far. I thought about saying that it wasn't fair that he would leave, even though I had no right to say anything of the sort. In the end, there was only one thing I could tell him, and I wasn't ready to say good-bye, not yet, anyway. "No, just tell him that I called."

Jo sounded disappointed in my response, but I wasn't about to say something else just to make her happy. She was a born romantic, and after fifteen years with her husband and four children, it was clear to everyone that she loved him more than the day they were married—something she used to tell me every time the subject came up.

Good for her. I had a feeling I'd had the love of my life, and he was gone. No one in the world knew how hard Joe would be to replace than I did, not that my husband had been perfect—far from it. But he'd been mine, and I'd been his, and it seemed as if that would be enough, just like the vows said, "As long as we both shall live." The only thing was, neither of us knew how short that time would be.

"What happened?" Maddy asked as I hung up the phone.

"David's moving to Raleigh," I said.

"When did all this happen?"

"Evidently, right after I told him off."

Maddy frowned. "Gee, Eleanor, do you think there might be some kind of connection there?"

I tried my best to ignore her, something that was hard to do on my best day, but she obviously wasn't about to let up. "I can't control what that man does or does not do. If he wants to go, I can't make him stay."

"We both know that's a big fat lie, don't we?"

I whirled around to face her. "Maddy, it's true that I

could probably get him to stay, but what I'm not willing to do is to dangle false hopes in front of him. I'm not ready to let go of Joe, and to be honest with you, I'm not sure I ever will be. David understands that. If he wants to move to Raleigh, I won't stand in his way."

"Is that the truth, or are you just too proud to ask him?"

"I'm done talking about this," I said forcefully.

Maddy nodded, and it appeared that she was actually going to respect my wishes. It wouldn't be the first time, but I probably could count the others on one hand.

It was time to finish up the last-minute preparations for the day, and if an errant tear fell along the way, that was all right, too. Just because I wasn't ready to commit to David didn't mean that I wouldn't miss him when he left, especially knowing that I might be letting a chance at happiness slip away forever.

Josh Hurley came bustling in two minutes after we opened and grabbed an apron from the rack. "Sorry I'm late," he said.

"Why aren't you in school?"

Josh's parents had been pretty clear that they didn't want him ducking out early to work at the Slice, and I agreed completely.

"It's a half-day today. I told you a couple of days ago, remember?"

"That felt like a year ago," I said.

"I know a lot's been happening. I can still work, can't I?"

"It's fine with me," I said. "I'm sure Maddy could use the help."

Josh smiled, and I could see echoes of his father in his

grin. "You've got that right. She was a lot happier to see me than you seem to be."

"That's not true," I said. "Now, are you going to stand back here chatting with me, or are you going to work?"

"You know me, I'm all about the work." He glanced over at the empty oven and said, "If you want to make me a cheeseburger pizza sub, I wouldn't say no."

"I bet you wouldn't." I gave my employees a free meal every shift they worked, and Josh always took full advantage of it. I didn't pay them much, and it was a way I could supplement their incomes without costing me a lot myself. "Go help Maddy. I'll let you know when it's ready."

"That's why I love coming here," he said.

"For my smile?"

Josh grinned. "That, and the food."

After he disappeared through the kitchen door, I grilled a hamburger patty on the stovetop, then quickly assembled a sub by spreading pizza sauce on a hoagie roll, adding the hamburger patty—now topped with a thick slab of provolone cheese—then slid it onto a wire rack and onto the conveyor. While that was making its way through the oven, I decided to make something for myself. I split another hoagie in half, swiped sauce on both sides, and then added some sausage and pepperoni. It joined Josh's sandwich on the conveyor, and I decided to peek out front to see what was going on. I'd make something for Maddy, too, so we could eat before the lunch crowd hit.

The place was as quiet as it had been before we opened, and I began to wonder if we'd make enough to pay Maddy and Josh, when the front door opened and a group of senior citizens came pouring in. They were as happy and rowdy as a gaggle of teenagers, and I realized that the sandwiches I'd made for Josh and me were going to have to wait. At least I hadn't made anything for my sister yet.

Maddy came hurrying into the kitchen a few minutes later. "I need six extra-large specials," she said. "Nobody's having subs or sandwiches today."

She looked at the two subs I'd made for Josh and me now sitting to one side. "Which one is yours?"

I pointed to the sausage sub, and she picked it up and took a large bite of it.

"Hey, I just said that was mine."

"You have time to eat back here," Maddy said after she swallowed. "I have to grab it when I can. Why didn't you put peppers on it?"

"I didn't feel like peppers," I said. "Sorry, I'll try to do better next time."

"No worries, this is fine." She took another big bite as I started working on pizza crusts.

Josh came in as Maddy walked out, and he wolfed down half his cheeseburger sub so fast, I couldn't swear that he actually ate it.

"Gotta get back to them," he said with a grin.

Soon I had the pizzas lined up on the conveyor, so I had a little time to clean up my prep station. Almost as an afterthought, I made myself another sub and put it at the back of the line. I wouldn't get to eat as soon as my employees, but at least mine would still be hot when I ate it.

Two hours later, the crowds had all subsided, and we were finishing our preliminary cleaning before we took our afternoon break.

Josh carried a tray of dirty dishes and glasses back into the kitchen, and then said, "I'll see you in an hour."

"Don't you want to earn a little extra this afternoon?" I asked as I looked at the growing pile of dishes in the sink.

"Sorry, but I've got to scoot. I'm meeting somebody."

"Anyone we know?" Maddy asked as she joined us.

"No, it's just somebody from school."

"A girl, I take it," I said.

Josh grinned at me. "Trust me, I wouldn't be rushing out of here to meet a guy. See you."

I started to walk him out when Maddy said, "You get going on the dishes and I'll lock up after him."

"I'm not sure that's a very good deal."

She smiled at me. "I don't know what you're talking about. It sounds great to me. Back in a few seconds."

"I'm counting on it," I said as I started running water in the sink. It was going to cut into our break, but I couldn't come back and face all of those dirty dishes, and it wouldn't wait until this evening. We would need some of our plates and glasses if we had any kind of crowd at all, something that I needed to stay out of the red.

Maddy was as good as her word, and she took up her position drying as I washed and rinsed the dirty plates and glasses. I'd saved the flatware for last, and I had a draining basket for that, so I didn't need my sister's help.

As she started drying the plates I handed her, she said, "What are we going to do with our break today?"

I glanced at the clock. "We won't have a lot of time left after these are finished. Besides, I'm not sure who else to talk to about the case. Greg is going to try to find Katy, and I don't doubt he'll do a better job of it than we did. We've talked to Art Young, Sandi Meadows, and Jamie Lowder, and unless we're serious about adding Greg's mother, Clara, to our list, I'm fresh out of ideas."

"There's something else we haven't talked about lately," Maddy said. "I still think it could have been a case of mistaken identity when somebody killed Wade."

Both our gazes went to the floor where Wade had been found, and pulled away just as quickly. I doubted I'd ever be able to see the kitchen the way I had *before* someone had been murdered there.

"I keep wondering about this inheritance the brothers were fighting over." I said. "I can't help but think it might have had something to do with the murder."

"Eleanor, just because Wade is dead doesn't mean that Greg inherits his brother's share."

"It doesn't mean he won't, either," I said. "Maybe somebody thought they were doing Greg a favor by getting rid of Wade."

"That leads up back to our core group of suspects, then, doesn't it?"

I shrugged. "I guess so, but if that's what happened, then the motive for the crime has changed. We're really right back to where we started from, aren't we?"

Maddy nodded. "I see your point. This is a real mess, isn't it?"

I held a plate out to her. "I just wish we could clean it up as easily as we're washing these dishes."

"If only life were that simple."

Ten minutes later, we had the kitchen respectable again, with clean dishes, plates, and flatware back where they belonged.

"Do we have time to do anything?" Maddy asked.

"Maybe take a quick nap," I said.

She looked around the kitchen. "Unless we're willing to stretch out on the counter, I don't think there's room for us."

"It's a health code violation, anyway," I said.

"So, what's the next best thing to sleeping?" Maddy asked.

"Pastries," I said, and she laughed.

"I was going for something less specific, but I like the way you're thinking. Do you think Paul is still open?"

"There's only one way to find out. Let's go see."

As Maddy and I locked up, I saw Paul standing at his own door.

We rushed over to him, and I asked, "Are you closing?"

He nodded. "I've got a few things left, but I'm ready to go home and grab a shower." He grinned at me as he added, "I've got another date."

"What's her schedule like?" I asked him.

"She works third shift, so we've got a window of opportunity to go out before she heads out to work and I go home and sleep. Who knows?"

"It's worth a try, isn't it?"

"That's why I'm going." He looked down at the box in his hands and asked, "You ladies wouldn't care for a treat, on the house, would you? I'm getting tired of my own pastries, if you can believe it."

Before I could answer, Maddy wrestled it out of his hands. "Absolutely. We'd be delighted."

"Yes, we would," I added, and grinned at Paul. "Thank you, kind sir."

"You two are always good for me. Now, if you'll excuse me, I don't want to be late."

"Thanks for the goodies," I said as Paul left.

"You're welcome."

Maddy started to open the box, and I put a hand on hers. "What are you doing?"

She shrugged. "I just want to take a peek."

"Let's at least wait until we're back inside the Slice."

Maddy reluctantly agreed, and I let us back into the restaurant. "I'll grab a table, and you get two mini-cartons of milk."

"That sounds like a plan. One thing, though. No looking until I get back."

"Spoilsport," she said.

I raced back to the kitchen cooler, pulled out two small cartons of milk, and then rejoined her.

I studied the box for a second, and then asked, "Did you peek?"

"Not yet, but I am now," she said as she threw the box lid backward.

Inside were nine stunning chocolate éclairs.

I looked down at the treats, glorious in their golden tones, glazed with shimmering chocolate, and said, "You know, I suddenly feel like having an éclair."

"What a coincidence. I do, too," Maddy said as she grabbed two and put them on napkins. "If it's all the same to you, I'd rather not dirty another dish if I don't have to."

"You're a woman after my own heart," I said as I bit into one. The rich vanilla custard oozed out, and it was a treat for the nose, as well as the eyes and the palate.

We each had one, and then Maddy said, "My sweet tooth is satisfied. What do we do with the rest?"

"We could save them for Josh," I suggested.

"Or take them home with us tonight."

I looked at the treats, and then said, "You know what? They're a little too rich for me as a steady diet. One was great, but two would be overkill."

Maddy nodded. "I know exactly what you mean. It's no wonder Paul gets tired of them now and then."

"But we never get burned-out on pizza, do we?"

"At least we haven't so far," Maddy said.

Josh knocked on the door a good twenty minutes before he was due back at work. When I let him in, I asked, "What happened?"

"She stood me up. Can you believe it?"

"I'm really sorry," I said, remembering that just because he was a teenager, it didn't mean that he didn't hurt as much as the rest of us did. "Did you try calling her?"

"Forget that. I'm not going to beg," he said.

"Pride's a dangerous thing," I said, and I saw Maddy's eyebrows shoot up. Before she managed to shift the conversation back to my life, I told Josh, "There are fresh éclairs from Paul, and we saved you some."

"How many are there?" Josh asked as he looked longingly at the box.

"There's only seven left," Maddy said facetiously.

Josh shrugged. "I guess that will do, but don't you two want a couple before I start in on them?"

"We've already had ours," I said. "Help yourself."

Josh dove into the box, and I started back toward the kitchen.

"Where are you going?" Maddy asked. Then she looked over at Josh, who was already on his second éclair, with no signs of slowing down. "It's a little like a shark feeding on chum, isn't it?"

"That doesn't bother me," I said, "I've been around teenage boys since we opened the pizzeria." I lowered my voice as I added, "Thanks for not saying anything in front of Josh just now."

"What, about how it's easier to give advice than to take it? I'd never say anything like that, Eleanor."

"You know what? I think you just did," I said as I grabbed a couple of the small milk cartons for Josh.

Maddy smiled. "I guess you're right. Here, I'll take those out to him. You've got to get ready to open."

"I do need to restock some of the toppings," I said.

After Maddy was gone, I thought about what I'd told Josh. The advice applied to me as much as it did to him, but there was nothing I could do about David now. It was too late for my pride to matter one way or the other at this point.

But if I was being honest with myself, I had to admit that I hoped David decided to stay in Timber Ridge.

I just wasn't ready to ask him to do it.

We were well into our dinner crowd, and the kitchen was hopping, when Maddy came back. "Eleanor, you need to take a break," she said.

I looked at the orders piling up. "Yeah, and a long soak in a hot tub would be nice, too, but I'm not getting either one of them anytime soon."

"Art Young is here, and he wants to talk to you. He says he may know something about what happened to Wade."

"Send him back," I said. "I'll talk to him while I work." I had three or four minutes I could squeeze out of my time, if I absolutely had to, and from the sound of it, that was exactly what I needed to do. I was a little nervous about being alone in my kitchen with a known hoodlum, but at least it was on my home turf. Before he came back, I hid knives and any heavy objects, which I could find, in places where I could get my hands on them in case I needed to defend myself.

Art was wearing another nice new suit when he came back into my kitchen.

"Sorry to interrupt you like this, Eleanor. I know you're busy."

"That's fine. I've got a few minutes to talk, if you don't mind me working. Maddy said you might know something that could help us."

He nodded. "I've been asking around, and it turns out that Wade was dipping into the till at work."

"How much could he have taken?" From what we'd

seen of Roger Henderson's office, I doubted it could be that much.

"It was nothing noticeable at first, just a little here and a little there, from what I understand. He was pretty careful not to take too much from any one client, but over time, it added up."

"Could he have stolen enough for someone to kill him for?" I asked as I prepared another pan with pizza dough.

"From what my sources are saying, his murder has gotten people curious, and none of them like what they've found. I doubt it would reach twenty grand all together, but it could be a great deal more. In some circles, that's enough to kill for."

"Are the police looking into it?" I asked.

Art Young shrugged. "While I'm not privy to what the police are doing, I understand that they've focused mostly on your deliveryman, so there are angles that aren't being followed up on. I thought you should know."

"Why are you helping us?" I asked, and then I realized that it was a pretty impertinent question.

"Honestly, I like your spunk," he said, "and I enjoy your pizza, too. Isn't that enough?"

"Excuse me if I'm being rude, but it hardly seems like it is, don't you think?"

I was pushing it, and I knew it, but I had to know if he had an ulterior motive to helping Maddy and me in our unofficial investigation.

He paused longer than I was comfortable with, and then said, "Let's just say someone deprived me of income, and I'd enjoy knowing who it is I should blame."

"We're not going to find out who killed Wade just so you can exact your revenge," I said. I was nervous, but I hoped he couldn't tell.

Art Young shook his head. "You underestimate me,

Mrs. Swift. My motives might not be completely altruis-
tic, but I'm not opposed to seeing someone punished by
the courts instead of by more primitive methods." He
looked at me a second, then said, "I just thought you'd like
to know."

"You were right." He was almost to the door when I
called out abruptly, "Can I make you a pizza while you're
here? It's on the house, as a sign of my appreciation."

The thought amused him, for whatever reason, and a
slight smile touched briefly on his lips. "Why don't I take
a rain check? Not that I don't appreciate the offer."

"Call it in any time," I said. "Thank you for coming."

He saluted me with two fingers, then left. I had a buzz
of new thoughts circling around in my head, not the least
of which was the fact that a known bad guy had decided
to make our investigation a pet project of his. He'd given
me food for thought, regardless of his true motive, and I
knew Maddy and I needed to talk to Roger Henderson
again, and sooner would be better than later.

Josh came bursting back into the kitchen half an hour
before we were set to close. "Eleanor, is there any way
that I can take off now?" he asked, nearly out of breath.

"Where's the fire? Have all of the customers left?" I'd
been filling orders steadily most of the night. It was good
to see that most of my customers weren't holding the
homicide that had occurred in my kitchen against me.

"No, there are a few people still wandering in, but I
talked to Maddy, and she said she could cover everything
up front."

"You still haven't told me what the emergency is," I
said.

"Melissa came in." He looked absolutely glowing as he said it.

"I'm sure that's great news, but I don't have a clue who Melissa is, and why we should all be so grateful for her arrival."

Josh grinned. "You're so funny—you know that, don't you? Melissa is the girl I told you about earlier. She's the one who stood me up."

"And yet you seem to be remarkably happy to have her here now."

"You don't understand. She didn't really stand me up today. She thought we were meeting tomorrow. Everything's great. It was just a little misunderstanding. Please, Eleanor?"

How could I say no to him? "Go on, get out of here before I change my mind."

He shocked me by kissing me on the cheek, and then he threw his apron at the hooks on the wall and jetted out of the kitchen. I could remember how it felt to be young, to be surging with emotions, and I wondered how any of us ever survived it.

After he was gone, Maddy came into the kitchen to place a late order. As I worked it up, I said, "Josh was practically floating when he left here, wasn't he? That was awfully sweet of you to cover the rest of the night shift for him."

Maddy smiled. "Admit it. You're just as much a romantic as I am."

"Why do you say that?" I asked as I layered sauce on the dough.

"He's not here, is he?"

"That's a point," I replied. "This has been the longest day, hasn't it?"

Maddy nodded in agreement. "I'm going home and soak in a hot tub. Then I'm going to crash on my bed until my alarm jars me out of it tomorrow."

"That sounds like a good plan," I said.

She left to cover the front again, and I started cleaning up early. I did that sometimes, working on the dishes and the prep area, doing all that I could ahead of time during slow periods at the restaurant. We weren't a place that was constantly packed, which was something I was grateful for. I couldn't stand being busy all of the time. For one thing, I'd have to hire help in the kitchen, something I was reluctant to do, and for another, it would mean losing the personal touches I liked to add to my creations. I was fully aware of the fact that my food was quickly consumed, and almost as quickly forgotten, but that didn't mean I couldn't add my own artistry to it.

When Maddy came into the kitchen to retrieve the last pizza order, I was elbow deep in hot, sudsy water.

She smiled as she said, "I see you're getting your hot soak in early."

"What can I say? I couldn't wait." As I finished washing another plate, I asked, "How's it going out there?"

"This one changed his mind, so it's a takeout now. That will clear us out."

I glanced at the clock and saw we had less than fifteen minutes to stay open. "Let him have it, then let's close up early tonight. We're both tired, and I don't see much more business coming our way tonight."

Maddy frowned at me. "Are you all right?"

"I'm fine," I said. "Why do you ask?"

She shook her head as she said, "I don't know. You're usually pretty set about staying open as long as the sign says."

"If you're that dead set against it, we can keep the place open."

Maddy boxed the pizza quickly as she said, "Don't get me wrong. I'm not complaining."

"Good, then it's settled."

She came back in two minutes later after delivering the pizza. "That's it. We're locked up for the night."

I kept working on the dishes. "Would you mind taking care of the dining room?"

"I'm on it," she said. Before she went out front, Maddy propped open the door with a wedge so we could talk while we worked. I finished the dishes, then joined her out front so I could get started on the deposit. It felt good not having to go by the bank in the dark, and I was happy again that I'd taken the plunge and bought a safe, even if it did have an after-the-fact kind of feel to it. The drawer cash balanced out with the report, and I slid the money and receipts into the safe. I'd chosen Joe's birthday for the combination, something that would remind me of him every night, and let me feel that, though he was gone, my late husband was still very much a part of this place.

"We're finished," I said. "Can you believe it?"

"I'm pinching myself right now," Maddy said. "Why don't we get out of here?"

"I'm right behind you," I said.

We made it to our cars without event—something I was always thankful for, lately—and as I drove home, I wondered what tomorrow would bring. There seemed to be a lot of things swirling around in my life lately. Running the pizzeria was enough for anyone to deal with, but with a murder investigation added to the mix, I couldn't believe how many directions I was being pulled in. I could shut the restaurant down for a week and track down clues, but if I did that, Kevin Hurley would be certain to notice. I doubted our chief of police would be all that thrilled about what Maddy and I were up to. Besides, I couldn't afford to go without the income that long.

But even if I could, I wouldn't do it. I loved making pizzas too much, which probably helped explain why I hadn't had a vacation since my husband had passed away.

I pulled into the driveway and parked. As I got out of the car and walked up to the front door, I saw a movement in the bushes that wasn't from a gusty wind or a nosy cat.

Someone was hiding outside my house, and as I turned to run back to my car in the dark, a hand grabbed me from behind.

Chapter 10

"Greg Hatcher, you nearly gave me a heart attack."

"I'm sorry," he said. "I didn't want you to run off on me."

"What are you doing here? I thought we decided it wasn't safe for you to just show up on my doorstep."

"I'm not alone," he said.

I peered into the darkness, but I couldn't make out who was there. He looked back into the shadows, and said, "Come on. It's all right."

A figure hesitantly walked out of the bushes, and I could see that Greg had not only found Katy Johnson, he'd brought her with him to my house.

We couldn't just stand out there all night; someone was bound to notice. "Come on in, and hurry."

"Are you sure?" Greg asked.

"You're already here, so I don't have much choice, do I?" I hurriedly unlocked the front door, hoping that Kevin Hurley hadn't staked out my house. If he had, I knew we could expect a visit from the police any minute.

Once they were both inside, I bolted the door and asked, "Did anyone see you come here?"

Greg shook his head. "Don't worry. We were careful. I've been watching the cars on your street for the last hour, and not one of them has shown any signs of life. We're safe."

"If my neighbors haven't been spying on you, then we should be okay." I took a second to look at Katy, who had clearly had better days. "Where have you been?"

"Hiding in my aunt's basement," she said. "I almost came out when you were there, but I was afraid."

"Of what, exactly?" I asked. "Maddy and I weren't there to hurt you. We're just trying to find out the truth."

"So are we," Greg said, speaking for her. "Katy didn't kill my brother any more than I did."

I was surprised that he believed her, but I wasn't so sure myself. I was going to make it a point not to turn my back on her, though at the moment she looked nothing like a killer to me.

Greg said, "Eleanor, I hate to ask, but could we possibly get something to eat? The money you loaned me is just about gone."

I looked hard at Greg as I said, "I don't know what you're talking about. I never loaned you any money."

He nodded. "That's right. I meant to tell you. I took some money from your cookie jar without you knowing it." Greg grabbed a pad I kept by the phone and scrawled something on it. When he handed it to me, I read it. *I owe you $200. Greg Hatcher.*

"Thanks for that," I said. I dove into my refrigerator after making sure Katy was at least ten steps away, and then I started pulling out ingredients. "Sorry, the best I can do are sandwiches and cold drinks. I haven't been shopping in a week, what with everything going on around here lately. Oh, wait. I could make eggs, if you don't mind a skinny omelet to share."

"Sandwiches would be great," Greg said. He looked at his former gir!friend and said, "Come on, Katy, you can trust her. She won't bite."

Katy didn't look like she believed that, but it was clear she was hungry, and not above accepting handouts.

As I slapped a couple of sandwiches together for them, I asked, "Doesn't your aunt feed you?"

Greg shook his head in obvious disgust as Katy said, "After you left her house, she threw me out. All my stuff's still in her basement, but she said if I was going to cause her trouble, she didn't want any part of me anymore."

I felt bad for her, even though I still realized that she could be a murderer. "Where are you two going to stay tonight?" With the words barely out of my mouth, I quickly added, "Not that the question is an invitation. I'm sorry, but you can't stay with me." Kevin Hurley would have a field day with that arrangement if he ever found out. As a matter of fact, he wouldn't be too pleased knowing that I was feeding them both in my kitchen, though as far as I knew, neither one was actually being sought for arrest.

Greg smiled. "Don't sweat it, I've made other arrangements. I just needed to talk to you before we took off."

"Why? What's going on?" I asked.

"I've been thinking about what you said, and something occurred to me—"

He never got to finish the thought. There was a loud knock at the front door, and someone yelled, "Open up. It's the police."

Without a word, Greg dropped his sandwich, grabbed Katy's hand, and headed for the back window he'd come in through the last time he'd visited me.

A powerful beam of light snapped on outside, and I could hear Kevin Hurley's voice shout, "Not this time.

Stay right there, and don't move a muscle until I get inside."

After I let Kevin in, he scowled at me. "You were supposed to call me."

"They just showed up two seconds ago," I said.

"You were going to turn me in?" Greg asked me, the disbelief thick in his voice.

I wasn't about to answer that question. "Kevin, how did you know they were here?"

"We got a tip," he said.

I glanced over at Mr. Harpold's house, and could see that he was watching my place through his window. I waved at him, though what I wanted to do was shake my fist in his direction. He didn't wave back, but at least he had the decency to duck away from my gaze.

"Great, our one-man Neighborhood Watch is in action," I said dryly.

"He was just doing his civic duty," Kevin said, "which is more than I can say for you at the moment."

"We haven't done anything," Greg said. "You can't arrest us."

"Don't try to tell me that you don't know I've been looking all over town for you," Kevin said. "You haven't made it easy on me." He nodded toward one of his officers. "Cuff him, then put him in the back of my squad car."

"I didn't kill my brother," Greg shouted as he was being handcuffed.

"I don't have an opinion on that yet, one way or the other," Kevin said as Katy started to cry. Everyone ignored her, though.

"Then why are you arresting him?" I asked.

"It's true that he's a person of interest in a murder case,

but that's not why he's under arrest." The police chief frowned as he added, "You know, you should be thanking me instead of yelling at me, Eleanor."

"I can't imagine how that's possible, even in your mind."

Kevin shook his head. "I don't understand you. I thought you'd be thrilled that we caught the guy who robbed you at gunpoint the other night."

"That's a lie," Greg shouted. "Eleanor, I'd never steal anything from you. You've got to believe me!"

"I believe you, Greg. Wade did it," I said loudly. "I heard his voice on his answering machine, and the second I heard him, I knew he was the one who robbed me."

"They sounded an awful lot alike to me," Kevin said.

"It wasn't Greg." I knew in my heart that was true.

Kevin was untouched by the display. "Then why did we find your deposit bag and some of the credit card receipts in his apartment?"

Greg looked shocked by the allegation. "Someone planted them there."

"Gee, I've never heard that before." He looked at Katy Johnson, and then said, "We've been looking for you, too, young lady."

"I didn't rob anyone," Katy said.

Kevin said, "I'm not arresting you for that, so that works out great. But I need you to come down to the station with us so I can interview you about your relationship with Wade Hatcher."

"She didn't have one," Greg shouted.

"Get him out of here, would you?" Kevin said to one of his officers.

"Don't say anything else, Greg," I ordered him. "I'll call Bob Lemon."

After Greg was gone, and another policeman was escorting Katy Johnson out of my house, Kevin lingered.

"You can't be serious about getting a lawyer for the guy who stuck a gun in your face."

"He didn't do it," I said.

"How do you know that? You said you didn't get a good look at the perp, and his voice was disguised."

"Wade had to have done it. I know Greg," I said.

"You just think you do. I have half a mind to drag you down to my office with the other two."

I offered him my wrists. "That would make my night. I've been thinking about adding onto the house, and with the money I'd get from the settlement for false arrest, I might be able to afford a swimming pool, too."

Kevin let that slide. "Were you ever going to call me, Ellie?"

I hated it when he used that nickname. It was an unfair advantage most days, and he knew it. Today wasn't one of those, though. I wasn't thrilled about having the police storm into my house and forcibly remove two people from there.

"I guess we'll never know, will we? Now, if you'll excuse me, I have a telephone call to make."

Kevin shook his head sadly, and then he walked out alone.

Bob Lemon answered on the fourth ring, and when I glanced at the clock, I saw that it was nearing eleven.

"I woke you, didn't I?" I asked.

"No, not at all," he said, the sleepiness thick in his voice.

"Liar," I said. "I'm sorry, but I need help."

"Then I'm your man. What can I do for you?"

"Kevin Hurley just arrested Greg Hatcher for robbing me the other night, and I want you to defend him."

He paused, and then said, "I've got to say, that's really turning the other cheek, Eleanor."

"He didn't do it," I said. "I'm pretty sure his brother did, and then he tried to frame Greg."

"Did Kevin give you any reason he jumped to that particular conclusion?"

I admitted, "He found my deposit bag and some receipts in Greg's apartment."

Bob paused, and then said, "I suppose we could say Wade planted them there."

"Because it's the truth," I said, snapping a little more than I'd meant to. Just because it was late and I was tired and upset, there was no reason to take it out on Bob, especially when I was asking him for a favor.

"Hey, take it easy. I'm on your side, remember? Let me get dressed, and I'll head down to the police station."

"I'll meet you there," I said.

"I'd really rather you didn't," Bob said. "Sometimes you seem to bring out the worst in our chief of police."

"It's mutual, trust me," I said.

"Be that as it may, we don't need to complicate matters any further than we already have."

I could see the sense in that, even if it didn't make me all that happy. "You'll call me as soon as anything happens, promise?"

"It could be several hours before I can get him released," Bob said.

"If you're not going to call me, then I'm going to have to meet you there."

Bob sighed. "I could just lie to you—you know that, don't you?"

"You know better than that," I said.

"You're right, I do. I'll be in touch."

After he hung up, I dialed Maddy's number to bring her up to speed.

She answered brightly, her capacity for late nights continually surprising me. I heard some odd form of music in the background.

"What is that playing?" I asked.

"What did you say?" Maddy replied.

"Turn your stereo down!" I shouted.

There was a pause, and the music suddenly died.

When Maddy came back on the line, I said, "What was that you were listening to?"

"Tomorrow's Sorrow," she said. "They're great, aren't they?"

"I'm just glad I'm not one of your neighbors."

Maddy laughed. "That's why I have a unit on the top floor and on the end. There's no one above me, and the apartment beside me is empty."

"How about the unit below you?"

"Mr. Jenkins is as deaf as a post," she said. "Surely you're not calling to check up on me, are you?"

"The police just left my house, so I wanted to let you know what was happening."

"They aren't arresting you, are they?"

"Of course not," I said. "They handcuffed Greg Hatcher, though."

"Greg's been staying with you all along, and you never told me?" Maddy's voice was nearly shrieking as she spoke.

"He came by tonight with Katy Johnson to tell me something. Come to think of it, he never had a chance. Kevin Hurley arrested him before he could say anything."

"Does he honestly think Greg killed his own brother?"

"I don't know what he thinks about that. He arrested him for robbing me the other night at gunpoint."

"That's ridiculous," Maddy said. "We both know that Wade did it."

"That's what I told him."

"Then we have to call Bob."

"I already did," I said. "He's on his way now to get Greg out of there."

Maddy paused, then asked, "What happened to Katy? She's not still there with you, is she?"

"No, the police took her in for questioning about the murder. Trust me, it was quite a scene."

"I can't believe I missed it," Maddy said, pouting as if I'd arranged to have her excluded from the action.

"Honestly, it wasn't all that great. Anyway, I'll let you get back to your jam session. I need some sleep if I'm going to be able to face tomorrow."

"Is Bob calling you later?" Maddy asked.

"I told him to, but who knows?"

"He'll call. Trust me. When he does, call me as soon as you hang up. I don't care what time it is, do you hear me?"

"Loud and clear. I'll talk to you later."

After we finished our conversation, I went around the house and made sure that all the doors and windows were locked up tight, and then I cleaned up the remnants of the impromptu meal. Katy had devoured half her sandwich, but Greg had only had time for a few bites before Kevin burst in. I hoped they gave him something to eat at the station.

The thought that he had robbed me was a ridiculous one. I knew Greg would never do that. If he needed money, he'd come to me, and if I had any to give him, I would. It was just that simple.

Sure, Wade and Greg had similar voices, and it would be even harder to tell them apart if they were both whispering, but I knew Greg was innocent, no matter what the evidence might look like. But how in the world could I convince anyone else of it?

There was nothing more to do than go to sleep and hope that Bob Lemon called me soon with some good news.

After the time I'd been having lately, I could use some.

In what felt like a lifetime later, I was jarred awake from a sound sleep by my telephone.

It was my turn to be groggy when I answered, though Bob Lemon sounded almost chipper. "I didn't wake you, did I?"

"Of course you did," I said.

"I warned you it might be late."

I stared at the clock until I could get the numbers in focus. It was five-fifteen, and the sky outside was still cloaked in darkness. "That's fine, I asked you to call me. Is he out yet?"

"No, that's going to take a little time. He should be out in time for lunch, though."

"Is that the best you can do?"

Bob said curtly, "It's the best anyone can do, and I'd appreciate it if you'd give me a little credit here."

"You're right. I'm sorry. Did you get to see him?"

"For about two minutes, long enough for him to hire me officially. You owe me a dollar, by the way. I had to loan him one."

"Gladly," I said. "How was he? Was he scared?"

"I think he was angry, more than anything else," Bob said. "He's ready to take on the world. Now, if you'll excuse me, I need to get home and take a shower and change. I've suddenly got a busy morning ahead of me."

"Thanks for doing this, Bob."

"For you and Maddy? I'd do anything for the two of you, and you know it." He chuckled softly as he added,

"Not that I'm not going to bill you for my time. I'll give you my best rate, though."

"Any break you can give me will be greatly appreciated," I said. "I'd better call Maddy and tell her what you've told me."

There was a silence, and then he said, "Actually, I just spoke with her. She called me earlier and made me promise I'd call her first."

"Hey, as long as I'm somewhere there in the loop, I'm a happy gal."

After we hung up, I debated getting up and starting my day, but I had nearly two hours left before my alarm clock went off, so I decided to take full advantage of it and go back to sleep if I could manage it.

To my surprise, it turned out that I could.

Maddy was at my front door before the coffee was even ready. As I let her inside, I asked, "Did we plan to get together first thing this morning?"

"I haven't been able to sleep since Bob called me." She looked at me carefully. "You did, though, didn't you?"

"Guilty as charged," I said as I yawned loudly.

"How could you, with Greg sitting in jail?"

I poured myself a cup of coffee and took the first sip. It was the one I cherished every morning, and sometimes the only thing that could blast me out of my bed. "I couldn't help him then, any more than I can now."

"You haven't changed your mind about him, have you?"

I shook my head. "Of course not. I know Greg would never steal from me. It had to be Wade." Maddy yawned. "Do you want some coffee?"

She nodded, so I poured her a cup as well. Maybe it would settle her nerves, though I doubted anything short of a tranquilizer could do that this morning. After taking a healthy sip, she said, "I can't believe how calm you're being about this."

"Bob is taking care of it, so there's really nothing we can do for Greg at the moment. The only way we can help him is find out who really murdered his brother."

"And how do you propose we do that?"

"We go talk to Roger Henderson," I said. "Art said he'd be a good place to start digging."

Maddy shook her head. "You're taking tips from criminals now?"

"If it will help Greg, I'd use information from anyone, Art Young included. The accountant wasn't very honest with us the last time we spoke to him, was he?"

"No," Maddy said as she finished the coffee. "But I don't feel right just ignoring Greg like this."

"Then go have yourself a vigil at the jail if it will make you feel any better," I said. "I'm going to talk to Roger."

"Of course, you're right. I'll come with you," Maddy said.

We drove to the strip mall where Roger Henderson's office was located, and I was surprised to see a pair of black sedans parked out front.

"That doesn't look good," I said as I got out of my sister's car.

"What do you mean?"

"Check the plates."

She did as I instructed, then whistled softly under her breath. "Government tags. How'd you pick up on that?"

"I don't miss much," I said.

"I'll keep that in mind."

We approached the front door and walked into the office. Roger Henderson was at his desk, but he wasn't alone. A large man in a navy blue suit sat on one side of him, and a prim-looking woman in equally drab attire sat at Roger's station. They all looked up at us when we walked in.

"Sorry, we're closed for business," Roger said.

"What's going on?" I asked.

"Who are these women?" the man asked Roger.

"We're friends of his former employee, Wade Hatcher," Maddy said, which was at least as big a lie as I'd ever told myself.

"Then I'm afraid you'll have to leave immediately," the woman said. "This isn't any concern of yours."

There wasn't really much we could do after that. Maddy and I left, but as we approached our car, Roger called out to us.

We came back to him, where he stood just outside his door. "I told them I needed a cigarette break. They don't have to know I quit smoking three years ago, even though this mess makes me want to light up again every time I think about it."

"What happened?"

"One of my clients called the feds, and they decided to do a surprise audit first thing this morning. I can't believe what they've found already. Wade was stealing from my customers, and I didn't even catch it. I'm looking like a real idiot in there."

"What's going to happen to you?"

He looked startled by my question. "You know what? I never even thought about it. I'll lose the business—that much is pretty certain. But I didn't do anything wrong other than trust the wrong man. They'll have to see that." He looked back at his office, and then he said, "I had to get out of there, but I'd better get back. I can't believe this is happening to me."

"Good luck," Maddy said.

"Thanks, I'm going to need it," Roger said.

After he went inside, we got back into Maddy's car. As she started to drive, I said softly, "It's awfully convenient that Wade is dead, isn't it?"

Maddy nearly drove off the road before she corrected her course. "Convenient for who, exactly?"

"Roger Henderson," I replied.

"It didn't look all that convenient to me back there."

"Think about it, Maddy. With Wade gone, Roger can blame every single embezzlement on him, and who's to say Roger wasn't the one stealing all of that money in the first place?"

"Eleanor, you have an active imagination this morning," Maddy said.

"You have to admit that it's a possibility," I said. "He could have stolen the money from his customers, made it look like Wade did it, and after that, he killed his scapegoat. In a twisted kind of way, it makes perfect sense."

Maddy must have been thinking about it as she drove toward downtown. As we neared our usual parking spot behind the Slice, she finally said, "I hate to admit it, but I can see it. Sis, you've got a skewed way of looking at the world."

"I just know people's actions don't always mirror our impressions of them."

"Then we need to dig into Roger Henderson's life a little."

"I agree," I said. "But since we're here, why don't we get an early start on the day?" It was a full twenty minutes before we had to be at the Slice, and I had to admit, it would be nice to get a jump on things.

"Why not? I can't think of anything better to do."

As I unlocked the front door of the pizzeria, I heard the telephone ringing. Maddy walked in behind me and said, "I'd ignore it, if I were you."

"I can't do that, and you know it." I had a tough time letting any phone ring unanswered, though it wasn't the most convenient obsession I could have had.

"A Slice of Delight," I said as I grabbed the phone.

"I didn't think you were ever going to answer your phone," a familiar voice said, though I couldn't place the woman calling me.

"We're not even due to start for another twenty minutes," I said.

"You don't know who this is, do you?"

"Not a clue," I said. I hated playing guessing games, maybe because I was usually so bad at it.

There was a chuckle on the other end of the line, and I suddenly knew who it was. "I take that back. How are you doing, Emma?"

Emma Corbin worked at the courthouse in the small clerk of courts office that housed every department that covered the legal paperwork in Timber Ridge. She also happened to be a pizza lover, and had been lobbying me for months to have a karaoke night at the Slice, something I'd steadfastly refused even to consider. I liked atmosphere, but that was a little too much for my taste.

"I'm doing fine," she said, "at least better than you are. Listen, you'd better get over to the courthouse right away."

"Why? What's going on?"

She lowered her voice, "I can't say over the phone—someone just walked in—but it relates to Wade Hatcher's murder, and I know you're looking into it."

"How could you possibly know that?" I asked.

"I shouldn't have to tell you that Timber Ridge is a

small town. Not much goes on around here that I don't know." She hesitated, then added, "Trust me, Eleanor. It would be worth your time to come."

"I'll be there in five minutes," I said.

After I hung up, Maddy asked, "What was that all about?"

"Don't start prepping anything yet. We're going out again," I said.

"Good, I was getting tired of being here so long," she said as she winked at me.

Once we were outside, Maddy started toward her car, when I put a hand on her shoulder. "There's no need to drive. We're walking."

"For exercise?" she asked incredulously. My sister's idea of working out was opening the top of a half-gallon of ice cream.

"No, don't worry, you won't have to break a sweat. We're going to the town hall to talk to Emma Corbin. She's got some information about Wade Hatcher."

"It doesn't surprise me," Maddy said as we started off. "Emma knows a little something about just about everything. Did she give you any idea what it might be?"

"I think she was going to, but someone walked in. I can't help wondering what it could be."

"We'll find out soon enough."

Maddy and I walked across the brick-lined promenade, through the parking lot, and across the street to city hall. There were plantings out front, and the ancient brick building's trim sported a fresh coat of paint. We didn't go in through the beautiful oak doors in front, though, bypassing them for a dingy little entrance into the basement in front where the city and county records were kept.

There was a huge counter near the entrance, and most of it was covered with rolled maps, books of different registries, and just about any other kind of document you could ever want. It was tough spotting Emma behind the desk, but not just because of the piles of material. She was barely five feet tall, and if she weighed a hundred pounds, I'd give up donuts and pizza for a year, neither of which was about to happen.

"Good, you're here," Emma said as she moved down the counter toward us.

"What's so urgent?" I asked. There wasn't much time for pleasantries. Not only did we need to get back to the Slice soon, but I doubted we'd have the place to ourselves for very long.

"Clara Hatcher was just here. She filed this with our probate department."

I glanced at the document. "Should you be showing me this?"

Emma smiled. "Once it's registered, it becomes public information."

I nodded. "I'll look at it as long as I'm not getting you in trouble."

"Trust me, I'd never do anything to jeopardize my job," she said. "I love it here too much."

I looked around the basement with its massive disorder, lack of any windows, and harsh fluorescent lights, and then said, "Who wouldn't?"

That got a laugh. "I know it doesn't look like much, but it's my domain, and believe it or not, I know where everything is."

Maddy smiled. "I don't see how."

"Try me. Go ahead, I'm game."

"We don't have time for that," I said as I picked up a copy of the document she was so eager for us to see. It was a simple will for Wade Livingston Hatcher, and it left everything to his mother, Clara.

"I'm not surprised he left everything to his mother," I said.

Emma tapped the document. "Now look at the date."

I did as she asked, and saw that the will had just been written ten days earlier. "That's quite a coincidence, wouldn't you say?"

Emma shook her head. "No, what's odd is that ten minutes after Clara left, someone else walked in with a will that was written two months ago. Want to guess who the beneficiary was on that one?"

"I don't have a clue," I admitted.

As she slid another document in front of me, she said, "Sandi Meadows, Wade's old girlfriend, is the sole beneficiary on this one. She got it all, and from the way she walked in here, she thought she had it made. You should have seen the look on her face when I told her about Clara's version of the will."

"What did she say?"

"She said it was a fake," Emma said. "I don't think so myself—the signatures both match—but when there's a dispute, we kick it upstairs. If I were betting on it, I'd say Clara's version of the will is going to hold up."

I thought about it for a second. "If Sandi didn't know about the new will, she might have gotten rid of Wade to get to his money."

"More important, she'd get her hands on the money left to Greg and Wade by their grandparents."

Maddy said, "That hasn't been cleared up yet."

Emma frowned. "I don't know where you're getting your information, but the rumor is that Wade signed the agreement the afternoon he died. The estate was as good as settled, and he was going to get half of everything as soon as the probate was finished."

"Did Greg know his brother signed off on it?"

Emma looked puzzled. "I would assume so, wouldn't you? Maybe he didn't know yet, if his attorney hasn't told him. That would explain why no one's filed it with me yet, wouldn't it?"

"Hang on a second," I said. "What would have happened if Wade had died before he'd settled the estate with Greg?"

Emma grinned. "That's the question I've been wondering about myself. It depends on the original wording of the document, but most likely, if Wade had died without signing the settlement, Greg would have gotten everything. As it stands now, I'm guessing that if Wade really did sign the settlement agreement, it's part of his estate."

"That's terrible news," I said.

"What's wrong with that?" Maddy asked.

"If Greg didn't know Wade signed, then he had a pretty big motive for murder."

Emma shrugged. "I suppose you're right. Sorry if I got you over here for nothing. I just wanted to help."

"You did," I said. "Thanks, Emma."

"I'll keep you informed," she said, "if anything else comes up, or if any more wills for Wade Hatcher come across my desk."

As Maddy and I walked back to the Slice, I said, "We've got new motives for old suspects. I'm not sure if we're any better off now than we were before."

"I don't believe that for a second. The more information we have, the clearer things will get. I'm sure of it."

"I hope you're right," I said. "What do you think our next step is?"

"We need to talk to Clara again."

I shivered a little at the thought. "She's not exactly our biggest fan, is she?"

"If you think she disliked us before, just wait."

"Wonderful," I said.

We were back at the Slice, but before I had a chance to unlock the door, Clara Hatcher herself stormed toward us, with a fierce look of anger burning on her face.

It appeared that our conversation with her about Wade's last will and testament was going to happen sooner rather than later, and in a pretty public arena.

Chapter 11

"You two busybodies had better butt out of my business, or you're going to regret it, I promise you that."

"Hi, Clara. How are you?" I asked, mimicking my best level of sincerity. "You're looking nice this morning."

"Cut the small talk," she said. "I heard you were just at the courthouse sniffing around a few minutes ago."

"Wow, that's fast, even for Timber Ridge," Maddy said.

"You stay out of this," Clara said to my sister. "I'm talking to her."

"Well, this is your lucky day. You get two sisters for the price of one."

Clara snapped, "You both think you're so clever, but everyone in town is laughing at you. You know that, don't you?"

"I doubt that," I said. "Why are you so angry? All we're doing is looking into your son's death. You should be cheering us on, not trying to get us to stop."

"It's a police matter," Clara said. "As long as you keep interfering, they can't do their job properly. My son deserves the best he can get, and you're not going to be able to provide it."

"We're looking out for the son you have who's alive. He's in jail right now, did you know that?"

A look of triumph crossed her face for just a split second, and then vanished so quickly that I began to doubt I'd seen it. "They got him?"

"Not for murder," I said.

"Why was he arrested, then?"

I wasn't about to answer that, but Maddy said something before I could stop her. "The chief arrested him for armed robbery."

Clara frowned. "I never did think that boy would turn out to be any good, always acting like he was better than the rest of us. Who did he rob?" She paused for a beat, and then actually laughed. "It was you, wasn't it? He held a gun on his own boss. I guess this changes your tune about him."

"He didn't do it," I said, angry that Greg's mother could turn against him so deeply, especially when he was such a fine young man. "Wade did."

The words were like scalding water thrown in her face. Clara reached out and grabbed my jacket in her hand and pulled me toward her. It was as if I had no strength of my own to resist her.

"Take it back," she said, the words hissing out of her like escaping steam.

I pulled myself away from her, but I couldn't keep my voice from shaking as I said, "I won't, because it's the truth. They arrested Greg, but Wade is the one who robbed me. How does that fit into your attitude about your sons?"

Maddy put a hand on my shoulder, but it was too late to stop me.

Clara looked as though she wanted to kill me just then, and there was no mistaking it on my part.

She stared at me, then said hotly, "Mark my words, you'll pay for trying to sully my son's good name."

I couldn't believe this woman, and I wasn't about to stand there and take any more grief from her. "Clara, do you honestly think I'd say it if it weren't true? Wade was no good. I'm not saying he deserved what he got, but I don't think it should be all that much of a surprise to you that something bad happened to him."

Her face had gone pallid as I spoke, and I instantly regretted losing my temper with her, but it was too late to make amends.

"Why don't you do the world a favor and crawl into a hole and die," Clara said before she stormed off down the street.

It took me a second to catch my breath after she was gone. Confrontations always left me like that, a little weak from the strain, but to my credit, I'd stood my ground with the woman and hadn't backed down.

Maddy started after her as she said, "She's not getting away with that."

I reached out and grabbed my sister's arm before she could get to Clara. "It's not worth the bother."

"Maybe not to you, but I'm not about to let her talk to you that way."

"Maddy, I don't like her any more than you do, but she just lost a son, and as sad as it is to say, Wade was clearly her favorite."

My sister shook her head in disgust. "If I live to be a thousand, I'll never understand how a woman can turn her back on her good son and idolize her bad one."

"It's a mystery to me, too."

I looked around the plaza and saw that there were a

few people standing around, watching us. I wondered how much of the earlier confrontation they'd seen. "Let's go inside, okay?"

"That's fine with me," Maddy said.

We walked into the Slice, but things I normally took great pride and satisfaction in doing were merely performed, not savored. The confrontation with Clara had left me queasy and unsettled, and I hated her just a little for taking one of my life's joys from me, no matter how temporary it was.

Maddy came back into the kitchen two minutes after we were supposed to open for the day.

"What's wrong?" I asked.

"You're not going to believe who our first customer is."

"I'm really not in the mood to guess," I said as I brushed an errant strand of hair back behind my ear. ·

"Clara Hatcher is sitting at a table by the front window."

That I had to see for myself. If she wanted to continue our fight, I was going to do it before we had a restaurant full of customers. The last thing I wanted to do was air any more dirty laundry in front of the residents of Timber Ridge.

"Where's my soft drink?" Clara said when I walked up to her.

"What are you doing here, Clara?"

She raised an eyebrow as she looked at me. "Is that how you treat all of your customers?"

I nodded. "It is for the ones who come in looking for trouble."

"I don't know what you're talking about," she said. "We've said all we need to say, and as far as I'm concerned, the subject is closed. Now, are you going to serve me my Diet Coke, or do I have to go have my lunch somewhere else?"

"We'll serve you," I said.

I nearly bumped into my sister as I came back into the kitchen.

Maddy asked, "What did she want?"

"A Diet Coke," I replied.

"I heard that much myself. What did she say to you?"

"She said that our argument was over, and she came here to eat."

Maddy looked skeptically at me. "Do you believe that?"

"Not on your life, but I can't throw her out without a good reason."

Maddy said, "I keep telling you, we need to post a sign that says we refuse to serve anyone we choose without a reason."

"I'm not doing it," I said. "Now, are you going to get her drink, or do I have to?"

"Don't worry, I'll take care of her."

I touched her shoulder lightly before she could leave the kitchen. "No extras in it, Maddy, and make sure it's in a clean glass."

"Spoilsport," Maddy said. "I was going to fill it with lemon seeds just to see if she could tell. The woman's got such a natural sour disposition, I doubt she'd be able to tell the difference."

"Come on, I'm counting on you to take the high ground."

"Fine, be that way."

Two minutes later, Maddy had delivered the drink and came back with an order. Clara was having a personal-sized pizza, along with one of our house salads with honey mustard dressing. As I prepped the salad and handed it to Maddy, I peeked out the door. The place was starting to fill up, and we'd have our hands full soon enough. It appeared that Clara wasn't going to cause a scene. If that was her intent, she would have done it now that she had acquired an audience. Thank heaven for small favors, anyway.

As I worked steadily to fill the orders, I mostly forgot about Clara Hatcher. It got that way when things were busy, and we were having a record lunch crowd. That always made me feel good, and all was well until I heard the first scream coming from the dining room.

When I raced out the kitchen door, the first thing I saw was Clara Hatcher standing over her plate, screaming her head off. "There's a roach in my salad."

Her tone was hysterical, and it was clearly upsetting our other diners.

People were getting up to leave in droves when I said, "Let's all stay calm. I'm sure it was an isolated incident."

"Thanks, but I don't feel like taking any chances," Yancey Grober said as he threw his napkin down on the table. "I've kind of lost my appetite."

"I'm not all that hungry anymore, either," Bill Hayes said.

His wife, Enid, chimed in. "We're so sorry, Eleanor."

This was getting bad. "Folks, I'm sorry about what happened. You're all free to go, and nobody owes me a cent, but I'd appreciate it if you'd stay."

Of course, no one did, and I honestly couldn't blame them.

As Clara left the Slice, I could swear she shot a smile at me that no one else could see.

* * *

"This is a disaster," I said as we cleared away the plates and glasses from the tables where our former customers had been sitting. "She planted that bug on purpose."

"Well, I didn't do it," Maddy said. "Even though I have to admit that I'd been thinking about doing something to her myself."

"She beat you to it," I said. "How can we possibly get anyone to believe that we didn't serve her a disgusting bug?"

"I doubt they'll just take our word for it," she said.

"I've got an idea," I said. I looked in my address book and found a number. After dialing it, I prayed the person I needed to speak with was in his office, and not out somewhere having lunch.

He answered on the second ring. "This is Jason Pine, county health inspection department."

"Mr. Pine, this is Eleanor Swift at the Slice of Delight in Timber Ridge."

"Ms. Swift, we're not due to inspect your restaurant for another month."

"I know, but I need you to come today. Right now, if you can manage it."

"Is there a problem? The reason I ask is that most people don't actively seek our inspections of their establishments."

I said, "I just had a customer who claimed she found a roach in her salad."

He paused, and then said, "I can't imagine your restaurant having a roach problem."

"It doesn't," I said, nearly shouting into the phone. "She planted it, and I need you to prove it."

"I'm not sure what I can do," he said. "I have no way of knowing whether it was on your premises or not."

"Would you come right now? Please? This could cost me my restaurant, and you know I don't deserve it."

I didn't think my plea was going to work, but finally he said, "I'll be right there. Take my advice and lock your doors immediately."

"Consider it done, not that there's much chance anyone's going to come in now, anyway."

"I'm on my way."

Maddy looked crossly at me. "You called Pine? Have you lost your mind?"

"Who else can prove that we didn't serve someone a roach?" I asked. "Whether you like him or not, we need him."

"I guess so," she said. "What do we do in the meantime? Should we start cleaning up?"

"Ordinarily I'd say yes, but we need to show him our kitchen, warts and all. If he gives us a bad rating, we'll just have to live with it."

I started for the kitchen when Maddy asked, "Where are you going? You just said you're not going to clean."

"I'm not, but on the off chance there really was a roach in her salad, I want to find it before Jason Pine does."

He arrived at the pizzeria in thirty minutes, really just a little under that. I thought whimsically that the inspection would be free, based on a pizza chain's old advertising campaign. I thought about sharing that thought with him, but from the stern look on his face, I could tell he wasn't in the mood for my offbeat kind of humor. Jason Pine was a balding, thin, and sallow man, who displayed his short height like a challenge, daring anyone to say something to him about his lack of stature. He carried a black clipboard that had been known to make grown men faint in the past, and I felt queasy looking at it even now.

"Have you touched anything?" he asked.

I shook my head. "No, sir. As promised, this is exactly as we left it." It was true, too. Maddy and I had searched the kitchen more thoroughly than we ever had in our lives, and there was no sign of any infestation at all.

He nodded, then asked, "Where was the customer sitting?"

I pointed to Clara's table, and he examined the roach before picking it up with a pair of tweezers. When he flipped it over, he said, "I've seen enough."

"Come on, aren't you even going to look in my kitchen?" I could see my reputation as a restaurateur going in the drink with a surprisingly small amount of effort on Clara Hatcher's part.

"There's no need."

He got out his clipboard and started jotting notes down. Maddy started to say something, but I knew whatever she came up with would just make it worse. I put a hand on her shoulder, then shook my head in warning. She didn't like it, but my sister abided by my request to leave it alone.

"That should do it," he said, then tore the top copy of his sheet and handed it to me.

I looked at it dumbly, and then saw that it absolved me of all guilt in the matter.

Maddy was about to explode, so I knew I had to say something quickly. "How do you know she was lying about finding the roach in her salad?"

He picked the offending bug up with his tweezers and turned it over so I could see. I just wasn't sure what I was supposed to be looking at.

"It's clear enough, wouldn't you say?"

"I'm sorry, I don't follow you," I said.

Impatiently he took a pen from his pocket and pointed toward the roach's sternum. "Someone swatted this roach and killed it, then carefully cleaned up the evidence. See how the carapace is slightly crushed here, and then again here? Whoever did this was clever and cleaned it well, but a trained eye can always tell." He sniffed the roach, then said, "This insect has been dead less than an hour, so that eliminates it coming in with your food supplies."

"How do you know it didn't come from our kitchen?" Maddy asked.

"I've seen your sister's work space. For this to have been your fault, you would have had to step on the insect in back, rinse it yourself, and then carefully place it in among the salad greens. If that weren't unbelievable enough, you would then have to call me to find it, something no restaurateur would ever do. I'll take a look around if you'd like, but I stand by my report."

He went into the kitchen, and as I started to follow, he said, "I'll do it alone, if you please."

Once he was gone, I hissed at Maddy, "Why did you ask him that?"

"I honestly wanted to know how he knew," she said.

"Well, next time look it up online."

Two minutes later, Mr. Pine came back out. "That countertop could use a good scouring, but I'm satisfied in my original assessment."

"Thanks for coming on such short notice," I said.

"It's my job," he said.

After he was gone, Maddy asked, "What good is that going to do us? Clara's already done her damage."

I handed her Pine's report. "I've got a plan. Run over to

Harlow Printers and have one of these blown up to about three by five feet tall. Then have him run off five hundred copies regular-sized."

"What are you going to be doing while I'm doing that?" Maddy asked.

"I'm going to start making everything in sight," I said.

"Do you honestly think that's the answer? I know making pizzas soothes your nerves, but you can't afford to start giving your stuff away."

"You know what, Maddy? That's exactly what we're going to do. Now get busy, we need to nip this before it's all over town."

"Don't kid yourself—all of Timber Ridge knows what happened today."

"Then we'll fix it before people actually believe it. Now go!"

She did as she was told, and I got busy making pizzas, sandwiches, and salads, then putting them in take-out boxes. I'd be lying if I said I didn't keep my eye out for any more unwelcome visitors, but as the health inspector had proclaimed, we were clean.

Thirty minutes later, I had an extremely large supply of prepared food when Maddy came back from the printer. I looked at the full-sized copy and smiled. "This goes in the front window," I said.

"I'm surprised you didn't have the printer make up sandwich board signs for us to wear while you were at it."

"If I'd thought of it, I would have."

Jason Hurley came in as were planning our strategy, and as soon as he heard what we were doing, he volunteered his services pro bono.

"I can't let you work for free," I told him.

"You don't have a problem with me doing it," Maddy said.

"That's different. You're family."

Jason said, "That's how I think of you, too. I'm sure if Greg were free, he'd be doing this, too. Let's get this food delivered before it starts getting cold."

He took bags and boxes, then put a stack of flyers on top of the pile. As he headed for the door, I said, "Remember, explain to them that we got a clean bill of health, and the food is in appreciation of our customers who are willing to give us another chance."

"What happens if nobody takes it?" he asked.

Maddy said, "Trust me, I doubt you'll find many people around here who are willing to turn down free food."

We each grabbed food and flyers, and started out on foot to distribute both. We'd fan out later and use our cars to deliver more food after we ran out this time, but for now, I wanted everyone around us to know that we'd been set up, and we weren't about to stand still for it.

Three hours later, the supplies in my pizzeria were nearly exhausted, and so were the flyers I'd had Maddy make up. Josh, my sister, and I sat at a table in front—though not the one where Clara had been—and shared drinks and stories about our afternoons.

"I can't believe it actually worked," Josh said.

"I told you, didn't I? Never underestimate the willingness of our neighbors to take free food."

"We're not out of the woods yet," I said, cautioning them. "We'll have to see how many show up for our dinner schedule."

"They'll come," Maddy said confidently, "though they might be expecting more handouts from us."

"They'll be disappointed, then. I'll have to tap into my emergency funds to cover what we gave away today."

"Clara Hatcher should have to pay," Josh said, his temper coming to the forefront.

"We'll deal with her, trust me," Maddy said.

I didn't like the way that sounded. "What did you have in mind, Maddy?"

"We're not going to just roll over and take this little stunt, are we?"

I shook my head. "Hardly. I just don't want to do something that will get us into this any deeper than we already are."

"She started it. We're going to finish it," Maddy said.

"Fine. While you're planning and plotting, I'm running to the grocery store to get fresh supplies for tonight. It's too bad Paul is already gone."

"I saw him there when I went by the bakery the last time," Josh said.

"Then let's go ask him if he has any old bread," Maddy said. "We're going to toast it, anyway."

"Okay, I'll go ask him."

"You shop. Josh and I will handle Paul," Maddy said.

I was too tired to argue with her, so I grabbed my purse, made a quick list of the supplies I needed, and headed out to the grocery store. We might not have many customers tonight, and I certainly wasn't going to turn any of them away who were brave enough to come, just because I hadn't had the foresight to stock up on my supplies.

When I got back, Josh was waiting for me by the door, our cordless telephone clutched tightly in one hand.

I pretended to ignore it as I handed him a bag of groceries after I unlocked the door. He took them from me, then immediately put them down on a nearby table.

"Josh, if I'd wanted them there, I could have done that much myself."

"My dad just called," he said as he thrust the telephone out toward me. "He needs to talk to you."

I couldn't say I was all that surprised. "Well, he knows where to find me. If we're going to have anything to feed our customers tonight, I have to get started on fresh dough right away. I'm pushing it as it is." I'd run out of the dough I'd made that morning giving away our products, and I was going to have to make my quick-dough recipe if there was any hope at all of providing pizza to customers—something kind of essential in a pizza parlor.

"It sounded important," he said, the stubborn determination strong in his voice.

"Josh, I'll let him know you delivered the message, but I can't drop everything and call your father whenever he demands it. If I did, I'd never get anything else done."

"It's about Greg," Josh said. "Maddy's in the back getting as much ready as she can for this evening, so you've got a little time. Call him," he said as he pressed the house telephone into my hands.

I nodded as I realized that it was the only way I was going to get him off my back. "Take these into the kitchen," I ordered him, probably being a little testier than I should have been, but I was in no mood to talk to Kevin Hurley.

Unfortunately, I knew his number by heart.

"It's Eleanor Swift," I said the second he answered. "I just got your message."

"Where have you been?"

"Wow, I didn't realize I had to check in with you every time I left the restaurant. Is that a new policy for everyone in Timber Ridge, or are you just trying to make me feel extra special?"

"You need to come to my office." There was no tone of request in his voice at all, strictly a superior giving orders to a subordinate who couldn't say no. If he thought that was true, it was time to dissuade him of that opinion immediately.

"Last time I checked, I didn't work for you. That tone of voice might work for members of your police force, but it's not going to work on me."

"You need to fill out some paperwork, Eleanor. Let's not make a big deal out of this, okay? But I need you to do it as soon as possible."

"What's it about? Josh told me it had something to do with Greg Hatcher."

"Josh talks too much," he said.

"Well, was he right? Does it?"

"Yes," Kevin admitted reluctantly, from the catch in his voice.

"Is it his release papers?"

"You know better than that," Kevin said. "I need you to swear out a complaint against him."

I couldn't help myself—I laughed heartily. "You're kidding, right?" There was a long pause, and I added, "You're not, though, are you? Have you completely lost your mind, Kevin?"

"I'd prefer it if you'd call me Chief Hurley while I'm conducting official police business," he snapped at me.

"Well, I'd prefer winning the lottery over paying taxes, but I don't think that's going to happen, either."

"Does that mean you won't do it?"

"Most emphatically," I said. "I refuse to put my friend and employee in jail, especially since I don't believe he committed the crime."

"You're too easily duped by the people around you— you know that, don't you?"

"I'd rather be too trusting than skeptical of everyone close to me," I replied, adding a little too much zing to the accusation than I should have. I had a hard time keeping my temper in check around Kevin, probably because of the history between us. That same shared past most likely made him a little cockier with me than he was with other business owners and residents of Timber Ridge, so we were even.

"You're making a big mistake," he said.

"Good. That's the way I like it. I'd rather fail spectacularly if I'm going to lose, anyway. That way, at least it's memorable. Does this mean you're going to let Greg go?"

"I don't have much choice," he said.

"Thanks for that, anyway."

Kevin paused, and then said, "Don't thank me. I'm not doing you any favors. He robbed you once, and I don't doubt he'll do it again."

"You're wrong," I said flatly, tired of the way he assumed the worst in my employee and friend.

"Only time will tell," he said, then hung up before I could get in a reply.

I walked into the kitchen and hung the telephone back up in its cradle.

"What did he want?" Josh asked.

"He asked me to come to his office and sign a complaint against Greg. When I refused to press charges, he read me the riot act about how foolish I've been acting."

"Did you tell him it wasn't an act?" Maddy said, smiling to take the bite out of her words.

"No, but I've got a hunch he already knows."

Josh looked at me oddly. "Are you telling me you said no to him?"

"Pretty much, but I did it a lot more colorfully than that," I said as I started a fresh batch of yeast rising in warm water. I was going to have to push the dough a little harder than I liked, but it would be acceptable, and I knew to most palates it would be fine.

"He hates when you do that," Josh said.

"I don't doubt it for an instant. Now, are you ready to get busy setting tables up for our customers, or am I going to have to send you home?"

He grabbed an apron, and after he tied it in place, Josh saluted me. "I'm getting right on it, ma'am. Anybody who can stand up to my dad and live to tell about it deserves at least that much respect from me."

"I'd say I deserve a lot more," I said with a smile. "How about you, Maddy?"

"I always merit respect," she said as she sliced mushrooms.

"I was talking about me," I said as I started measuring out the flour I'd need.

"Aren't you always? Don't you ever get tired of the same subject all of the time?"

"You'd think so, but no, not so far."

Josh shook his head as he alternated looking at us. "I don't understand you two one bit."

"You weren't meant to," I said.

"We women are mysterious creatures," Maddy added.

Josh decided to cut his losses and do as I'd asked. I didn't blame him. Sometimes I had trouble following the conversations Maddy and I had, and I was often the instigator.

"So we get our happy family back," Maddy said. "I'm

willing to bet Greg comes here before he even goes home."

"I'm not a sucker; I won't take that bet."

"Where does that leave us?" she said as she finished the mushrooms and started working on the green pepper slices.

"We still need to find out who killed Wade Hatcher," I said, "but there's a new item on the list as well."

"If you don't say we need to get back at Clara Hatcher, I'm going to be very disappointed in you. I think forgiveness is nice and all, but retribution's kind of cool, too."

"Don't worry, I couldn't agree with you more. One way or another, she's going to pay for that little stunt she pulled today."

"That's the spirit. What should we do to her?"

"I'm not sure, but there's no rush. I'm willing to wait until we have the perfect act of retaliation."

"You know what they say about revenge," Maddy said.

"What's that?"

"It's a dish best served cold."

"Then we're going to freeze her out."

"Thatta girl," my sister said.

I wasn't sure how we were going to get Clara back for her little stunt, but we'd find a way.

In the meantime, it was time to concentrate on getting ready for our dinner crowd, if anyone bothered to show up.

We were busy enough, something I was eternally grateful for as the evening progressed. Clara might have done some damage to our reputation, but I honestly believed that our quick response had saved the pizzeria.

I was preparing a meat lover's delight pizza by spreading a thick layer of sausage, meatballs, salami, prosciutto, bacon, and pepperoni on top of sauce-coated dough when the kitchen door opened.

Bob Lemon walked in, followed closely by Greg Hatcher. Greg hugged me, and then practically twirled me in the air when he came in.

"Put me down, you big goof," I said, laughing.

He did as I instructed, and then said, "I can't believe I'm free." He slapped Bob Lemon on the back as he added, "This man is a genius."

"I didn't do all that much," Bob said. "Eleanor's the one you should thank."

"Tonight there's enough praise for everyone," he said. "I've been slinking around town like an abandoned ferret, and now I'm back out into the light. I hated being on the run like that."

"You didn't make things any easier on yourself," Bob said, the scolding tone clear in his voice.

"I know, I know. What can I say? I panicked. But everything's good now."

Bob frowned slightly. "Slow down, Greg. Just because the police chief released you on the robbery charge doesn't mean that he still doesn't like you for your brother's murder."

"You can't upset me tonight if you try," he said. "I'm free right now, and that's all that counts."

"Just don't do anything stupid," Bob said. "If I know Kevin Hurley, he's going to be watching you day and night."

"I'll behave myself. I promise."

Greg grabbed his apron, and I asked, "You're honestly not thinking about working tonight, are you?"

"Why not? Josh has been covering for me long enough. I thought I'd send him home, if you don't mind."

How could I say I didn't want my customers to see Greg at the pizzeria, when I'd gone to such great lengths to tell Kevin that I knew he was innocent? In the end, I just couldn't do it. I either had to support him all of the way, or take back everything I'd said before.

"I don't mind a bit. I'm sure he'll be thrilled."

"I know that for a fact. He's got a new lady in his life. Boy, a guy lays low for a few days and the whole world goes crazy."

After Greg disappeared, Bob said, "You're doing a brave thing here."

"I know Greg didn't rob me any more than he killed his brother," I said.

"I'm not talking about that. Aren't you concerned what people will say when they see him working here?"

"Bob, if Clara can't scare them off with her phony roach story, I doubt seeing Greg waiting tables is going to affect them."

He shrugged. "It's your business, and I mean that literally. I just wanted to stop by and see how you were holding up."

"I'm doing great," I said. "Thanks for all you've done for Greg. I can't tell you how much I appreciate it."

"It's been my pleasure. Now, if you'll excuse me, I've got to be going."

"Don't tell me you've got a date. I thought you were seeing my sister, and I know she's not free tonight."

He laughed. "Do you honestly think I'd do anything to jeopardize that? No, I'm afraid I'll be wading through paperwork most of the night to make up for being out of my office all day."

I grabbed a hamburger pizza sub off the assembly line and cut it in half, then slid it into a to-go box. "Take this for the road."

"What about the person who ordered it?"

"I can make another one in a heartbeat," I said. "You deserve at least that."

"I wish I had the willpower to say no, but I can't."

"I expect you to bill me promptly for the full amount, so we'll call this a bonus for not being mad at me for waking you in the middle of the night."

"We can talk about that later," he said as he took the sandwich and left the kitchen.

As I prepared a replacement sandwich, Maddy came back.

"What's going on with my hamburger pizza sub?"

"I gave it to Bob," I said. I'd expected Maddy to scold me for doing it, but she just smiled.

"That's a wonderful idea. He did a lot of good for us today, didn't he?"

"It's nice having Greg back. Did he really tell Josh he could leave for the night?"

Maddy laughed. "Are you kidding me? Josh was so happy he tore out of here without even taking off his apron."

I smiled, and then it faded just as quickly. "Maddy, Bob asked me if we were doing the right thing having Greg work out front after what's been happening lately."

"Bob tends to err on the conservative side," Maddy said. "Don't hold that against him."

"Don't tell me you agree with him," I said.

"Did I say that? Eleanor, I understand where he's coming from, but I think you're doing the right thing. Timber Ridge needs to see that we stand behind Greg, and the sooner they do, the better off we'll all be."

"That's the spirit," I said. "Your sub will be out in a couple of minutes."

"No rush. It's for Stephen Haley. He's on a date with

some woman from Westchester County, and I doubt he even realizes I haven't served him yet. Love is in the air out there, Eleanor."

"Just make sure none of it gets back here," I said as I took a pizza off the conveyor and cut it into eight slices. I handed it to Maddy and added, "By the time you get back, Stephen's sub will be ready."

"I'm on it," she said.

Greg came back and placed an order, and I couldn't help but respond to the silly grin on his face. "You're happier than I've seen you in a long time," I said.

"I have good reason to be, don't you think?"

I remembered what Bob had just told me. "Greg, you know you're not out of the woods yet, don't you?"

"I know," he said. "But I also fully understand that you and Maddy believe in me, and that's really all that counts."

"We've got your back." I took a deep breath, then said, "Greg, there is one thing we need to talk about."

"Then let's talk."

"It's about Wade. Do you know if he actually signed the settlement papers for your grandparents' estate?"

"What? What are you talking about?"

"There's a rumor going around town that Wade signed the papers the afternoon he was murdered."

Greg stared at me, his mouth dropped wide open. "Where did you hear that?"

"I can't really tell you that," I told him, not wanting to reveal that Emma was my source.

"All I can say is that if he did, he never told me, and Bob didn't, either. Why don't you ask him?"

"I can't," I admitted. "He's got attorney-client privilege with you, so you're the only one who can ask him if it's true."

"Then what are we waiting for?"

"You can probably catch him at his office," I said.

Greg took out a card, dialed the number, and then waited. I didn't even pretend to ignore what he was doing.

"Bob, it's me. Yeah, I'm fine. It's about Wade. Did he sign the agreement? Okay. No, that's all right. Thanks."

"So, did he?"

"If he did, Bob isn't aware of it. But he told me that didn't necessarily mean that Wade didn't."

"I don't understand."

Greg shrugged. "Bob said Wade asked for a copy of the agreement so he could study it. If he decided to sign it, and he had it witnessed, it could be enforced once it's filed at the courthouse, and Bob wouldn't know anything about it."

"Would your brother do something like that?" I asked.

"Who knows? Wade never was easy to predict. If I had to guess, though, I'd say no. He was pretty adamant about getting more than his fair share. He would have had to be pretty desperate to sign it."

"Wouldn't you say that's what he was?"

Greg shook his head. "I have no idea what drove the guy to do the things he did, and I'm not going to waste any time worrying about it."

I wanted to tell him about the legal ramifications of a signed document, but I didn't have the heart to ruin his good mood.

"Why do you bring it up, Eleanor? Is it important?"

"Who knows?" I admitted. "I wonder if your mother would know."

A look of disgust crossed his face. "Well, I'm not about to ask her. I can't believe what that woman did to you. I'm so sorry."

"It's not your fault," I said.

"No, but I still feel responsible." His frown faded for a

moment. "If you want to get her back, I've got some great ideas."

"You know what? I might just take you up on that."

"I'm hoping you do. We'll have a great time, that's for sure."

He vanished again, and I found myself smiling as I worked to fill the new orders. Our pizzeria had been missing something when Greg had been gone, and it suddenly felt whole and complete again.

I just hoped things stayed that way, but with the ongoing murder investigation, none of us could be sure of tonight, let alone tomorrow.

But for once, I planned to enjoy it while it lasted, without another thought about any troubles that the next day might bring.

That turned out to be a wish that wasn't going to be fulfilled anytime soon, but I didn't realize it at the time, and in a way, I was just as happy that I hadn't known what was about to happen next.

I would be engulfed in it soon enough.

Chapter 12

"Greg just took off," Maddy said as she came back into the kitchen later that night. It was three minutes past closing, but usually our wait staff helped us clean up at the end of the night. "I hope you don't mind. I told him it would be all right if he slipped out a little early."

"Of course it is," I said. "We were lucky to have him come in at all. For a while there, I thought it was just going to be the three of us, but things really perked up at the end, didn't they?"

Maddy nodded. "I don't often say this, but you were right."

I cocked one ear toward her. "I'm sorry, I missed that last part. What did you just say?"

Maddy smiled at me. "You were right. I thought it was a waste of time giving away all that free food this afternoon, but it appeared to do the trick."

"I didn't know what else we could do," I said. "A rumor can break a restaurant, and it doesn't have to be true to do it."

"We win and Clara loses. That's a combination I can live with."

"Don't kid yourself," I said as I dug my hands back into the soapy water. I'd been doing the dishes when she'd come into the kitchen. "We lost customers today that we'll probably never get back. I'm not about to let Clara get away with it."

"Wow, and usually I'm the mean one," Maddy said.

"I'm not being mean—I'm protecting this business."

She said, "Don't get me wrong. I wasn't criticizing. I approve."

"This is the last thing my husband loved, and I'm not about to sit back and see it destroyed."

Maddy's voice softened. "You're wrong about that."

"What do you mean?"

"Eleanor, he loved you the most."

"I know that," I said, "but this place was a part of him, too."

"And it will live on," Maddy said. "I'll work on the front while you're doing dishes, and we'll have this knocked out in no time."

"That sounds like a plan," I said. As she wiped tables down and swept the front, I finished my kitchen cleanup. I'd started it early, so for once, I finished before Maddy did. I was about to go out front to help her wrap things up when I spotted our specials board. It was a whiteboard with dry-erase ink, and in the summer months, we used it out front to announce our specials for the day, which were usually what we had too much of from the day before. It was another way of attracting summertime customers, and I enjoyed embellishing the board with some artwork, too.

But for some reason, the clean board seemed to be calling out to me. I grabbed a black marker and drew a line down the center, from top to bottom. On the left side, I wrote, *What We Know,* and on the right, I put, *What We Don't.*

I'd barely started my list when Maddy came back. "That wasn't as bad as I thought it would be," she said as she put her apron away without even glancing in my direction. "Are you ready?"

"You go on without me," I said. "There's something else I want to do tonight."

That got her attention. Maddy pulled up a bar stool as she looked at what I was doing and said, "I've got nothing to do at home, but even if I did, I'm not about to let you have all of the fun without me." She studied the board's headings, and then she said, "I hope this is about Wade Hatcher's murder."

"What else could it be?"

"Are you kidding me? It could be anything from what really happened to Elvis to who shot J.R."

"I didn't realize there was any doubt about Elvis, and I thought *Dallas* cleared all of that up before they went off the air."

"Wade it is, then," Maddy said. "Why are both sides under your headings blank?"

"Give me a second. I'm just getting started."

Maddy nodded. "The first thing we know is that someone killed him right over there."

"This isn't the Obvious Board," I said. "I was thinking more along the lines of suspects and motives."

"Okay, that makes more sense," Maddy said. "So, what exactly do we know so far?"

I uncapped the marker again and spoke as I wrote under the KNOW side. "Wade could have been murdered because of jealousy, revenge, retribution, or by accident."

"I doubt whoever took a rolling pin to his head was

trying to accomplish anything short of killing him," Maddy said.

"I meant 'mistaken identity,' and you know it."

"Go on, then, let's match some names with the motives."

Under JEALOUSY, I wrote down *Sandi Meadows* and *Jamie Lowder.* For REVENGE, I added *Katy Johnson.* RETRIBUTION got *Art Young* and *Roger Henderson,* and finally, coupled with ACCIDENT, I put *Clara Hatcher.*

I studied the list, and then asked, "Is there anyone I'm leaving out?"

"I can't imagine, unless you want to put Greg's name down, too."

"No, I'm not even willing to think that. Besides, what would he think if he saw this and his name was on it?"

"You're right there. I doubt it would make him happy," Maddy said. "Okay, now that we have a list, what do we do next?"

"Maybe it's time to stir the pot," I said.

Maddy looked around the kitchen. "I thought we were done cooking for the night."

"I'm not in the mood for your bizarre sense of humor. You know what I'm talking about. We need to figure out a way to get the killer to reveal himself to us without endangering our own lives."

"That's going to be a neat trick," Maddy said. "How do you propose we do that?"

"I'm not sure yet, but I'm going to figure something out."

"I believe that. There's only one person I know in Timber Ridge who's more stubborn than I am, and I'm looking at her."

"I'm going to take that as a compliment."

"That's how I meant it. So, are we going to stir the pot tonight, or will it wait until morning?"

I frowned at what I'd written, and then I turned the board around so no one would see it. "I don't know about you, but I need some time to come up with something good."

"Then let's get out of here," Maddy said. "It's been a long day."

"And tomorrow's not going to be any better. Why don't you come by my house around seven tomorrow morning so we can get an early start?"

Maddy wasn't exactly a morning person, but she agreed quickly to my suggestion. "I'll see you then."

As we walked out of the pizzeria, I said, "I thought I'd have a little more trouble convincing you."

"We don't have a lot of time, and we can't just sit around waiting for Kevin Hurley to make an arrest. If we do that, Greg's going back to jail, and it's going to take a lot more than Bob Lemon's blustering to get him out the next time."

As we approached our cars, it started to rain. Maddy waved at me as she raced to her car, and I got into the Subaru just before the deluge hit. We sat there, side by side in the dark waiting for it to ease up, but evidently my sister got tired of waiting. As she drove off, I decided to head home as well. Otherwise, I would be sitting out there alone in the dark with the rain pounding down around me, and that wasn't anything I wanted to do. It never eased up, and as I pulled into my driveway, a flash of lightning lit up the sky. Was there someone on my porch, or had I just imagined it? I sat there trying to think of what I should do when there was another flash, and I saw that the porch was empty. Pulling my jacket off and throwing it over my head, I made a mad dash to the front of my house, and though no one was there, I didn't dawdle getting inside. It wasn't until I had the heavy oak door dead bolted behind me that I think I actually started breathing again.

I'd been thinking about homicide too much lately, and it was starting to affect my imagination. The sooner we cleared up Wade Hatcher's murder, the happier I'd be. I liked my simple life of running the Slice with my sister. I knew in my heart that investigating murders should be left to the professionals, even though I felt I had to step in from time to time. I just wished Kevin Hurley would focus on someone besides my best employee.

But if he wasn't, I was going to have to do it myself, along with some help from my sister.

I was ready the next morning at six forty-five and began to regret not offering to pick Maddy up at her apartment. My sister wasn't the most punctual woman who'd ever lived, and early mornings were not her best time.

I was just about to call her at seven to tell her I was on my way when she pulled up and parked behind my car. Before she could get out, I left the house, being careful to lock the dead bolt behind me as I went.

"No coffee?" Maddy asked, clearly disappointed by our sudden departure.

"We'll get some at Brian's. My treat."

"How about some eggs and a biscuit to go along with it?"

I nodded. "Okay, but I never knew you could drive such a hard bargain."

"Just be glad I didn't hold out for the Hungry Cousin's Sampler."

We'd shared one of Mark Deacon's specials once and still had food left on our plates. The portions of bacon, sausage, ham, and eggs were enough to feed a lumberjack, but Maddy had been certain we could polish one off by ourselves.

She'd been wrong.

As she drove to the diner, my sister said, "I didn't realize there were this many people out running around this time of day."

"Just think; Paul's been at his pastry shop for three or four hours by now."

"That's why he's still single," Maddy said. "I don't know a woman alive willing to put up with that schedule."

"I'm sure there's someone out there for him, even with his crazy work hours. He's not ready to give up on romance, and I don't blame him."

"How can you sound so positive?"

I shrugged. "I'm a firm believer that there's someone for everyone out there."

"Sometimes even more than one," Maddy said.

"Hey, I wasn't taking a shot at you. I promise."

"Sis, it's not like I haven't thought the same thing myself. I've had some near misses, but I'm still looking for my Joe."

"He's out there," I said as I patted her shoulder.

"Well, I wish he'd quit dillydallying around and make himself known to me, because, honestly, I'm getting tired of looking for him."

I laughed, glad that my sister was so easy to talk to. Sometimes that personality trait was a real thorn in my side, but on other occasions, it was exactly what I needed.

We got to the diner, and the parking lot was nearly full.

"You've got to be kidding me," Maddy said as she found a place to park. "This just isn't right."

"Mark told me once that he did a better breakfast trade than lunch and dinner put together, though he didn't make nearly as much money doing it. Evidently, folks around here aren't as willing to pay top dollar for their breakfasts."

"So, why does he stay open in the mornings?" Maddy asked as we got out of her car and started toward the door.

"It keeps his customers happy, and he admitted to me that he liked getting up early every day."

"If I had my way, I wouldn't get up until the crack of noon," Maddy said.

"Not me. The older I get, the more I like getting up early every morning."

We walked into the diner, and I thought we were going to have to take a seat at the bar when Hank Parkinson waved us over to him. Somewhere in his early seventies, Hank was dressed in worn but clean blue jeans, a flannel shirt, and a burgundy baseball cap that had ALASKA blazed across the front of it in bold white letters.

"Take my booth, ladies," he said as he shoved his dishes to one side. "I was just leaving." He took a last sip of coffee, then stood.

"We don't want to rush you," I said.

"Nonsense. Chivalry's not dead, at least not as long as I'm still living in Timber Ridge."

Maddy leaned toward him and kissed his cheek. "If you were thirty years younger, you'd have to watch out for me."

He smiled at her. "Darlin, if I were thirty years younger, you wouldn't be able to keep me away. I guess it's just a matter of bad timing, isn't it?"

"It's the story of my life," Maddy said as Mark came over with a large gray plastic tub.

"Let me clear that for you," he said as he quickly dispatched the dirty dishes and wiped down the table.

"I didn't even have a chance to leave you a tip yet," Hank said.

"You can catch me next time," Mark said.

"You're putting an awful lot of faith in me. How do you know I'll be back?"

Mark grinned at me. "Where else would you go? I heard you've already been thrown out of all of the nice places in town."

"You've got a point there." Hank tipped his hat toward us, and then walked over to the cash register.

"He's something, isn't he?" Mark asked.

"I think so," Maddy said. "I wonder if he was serious about chasing me."

"I don't know what he said," Mark said, "but I wouldn't assume he was kidding. The man has more energy now than I ever had in my life. I don't know how he does it."

"Flirting with women like us probably helps," I said.

"It couldn't hurt, could it? Do you two know what you want?"

"We'll split a Hungry Cousin's Sampler," Maddy said.

"Cancel that," I said quickly. "I'll have two eggs over easy, a biscuit with sausage gravy, and coffee."

"Party pooper," Maddy said.

Mark smiled. "Not everyone's as brave as you are."

She nodded. "You'd think at least some of it would rub off on her, though." She glanced at the menu, and then said, "You might as well bring me what she's having."

"Got it," he said as he jotted our orders down and left. While we were waiting for our food, I said, "I've been thinking about the list we made last night."

"Me too," Maddy admitted. "That's about all I seem to be able to think about lately."

"Come on, that's not true. What about your new boyfriend?"

I'd said it offhand, but she got serious as she looked at me. "One date does not make him my boyfriend."

"Sorry, I didn't mean to offend you."

"It's not that," she said. "I just hate that term. I'm a grown woman. I don't have boyfriends."

"What would you like me to call him, then?"

"Bob has a nice ring to it," she said.

"Then Bob it is."

Mark brought us our breakfasts, and we enjoyed our meal together, discussing the weather, the price of gasoline, and whether winters were milder than they were when we were kids, but we didn't touch on boyfriends or murder until we were out in the parking lot again.

"Where to now?" Maddy asked.

"I'd like to talk to Katy Johnson again. I'm not sure I'm willing to accept her spin on things, no matter what Greg thinks."

"How about Sandi and Jamie?" she asked as we approached her car.

"Why should we start with them?"

She pointed to the other end of the parking lot. "Because they just drove up."

"Okay," I said, taking a deep breath. "Let's go poke a stick into a hornet's nest and see if we can get something going."

"You first," she said.

I walked over to their parking spot and saw that they were clearly in no hurry to leave their car. They were in a deep discussion about something that was bordering on a fight. I held back, hoping to hear something before they noticed I was standing there.

It was a lovely morning, and I was glad that one of the windows was partially cracked. If they'd both been rolled up, I wouldn't have been able to hear anything but a muffled exchange, but as it was, their argument was easy to pick up.

"You have to tell the police chief," Jamie said. "The cops need to hear what you've got to say."

"You know as well as I do that I can't do that. What are they going to think?"

Jamie asked, "Who cares? It's going to be a lot better if they find out from you. If someone else tells them, it's going to make you look bad."

"I can't do it," Sandi snapped.

She happened to glance out her window and spotted Maddy and me. With a quick shake of her head toward Jamie, she got out of the car.

"What do you two want?"

"Don't mind us," I said. "Go ahead and finish your conversation. We can wait."

Jamie glared at me. "How much of that did you hear?"

"Enough to be interested in hearing the rest of it," Maddy said.

"Come on," Jamie said as he grabbed Sandi's arm. "We're going in."

"That sounds great," I said. "I'm kind of peckish myself." If I had to choke down another breakfast, even though I was full, I'd have to find a way to do it for the cause.

"You're not invited," Sandi said.

"The funny thing about a public restaurant is that we don't have to be invited in."

They glanced at each other, then pivoted and got back into their car.

"Don't leave on our account," I said.

Neither one of them commented, and as they drove away, I noticed Mark standing nearby looking at us. "Are you two still driving away my customers?"

"I'm sorry," I said. "We were just talking."

He shrugged. "You know what? I don't mind. There's something about that girl I never have warmed up to."

"It's Jamie I don't care for," Maddy said. "I hate the way he treats her."

"Neither one's a prize," Mark said. "Just do me a favor. Don't run anybody else off, okay? I've got bills to pay."

"We won't let it happen again," I said.

"Come on, Eleanor, you know we can't promise him that."

Mark laughed. "I guess it's crazy to even ask, isn't it?"

We got in Maddy's car after Mark was gone.

"What do you make of that?" I asked.

"I understand him not wanting to lose customers," Maddy said. "You really can't blame him."

"I'm talking about Jamie and Sandi, you nit," I said.

"They're hiding something, aren't they?"

I nodded. "But what could it be? From the sound of it, Sandi knows something that might be relevant, but she's not telling. Can you believe Jamie's trying to get her to tell someone about it?"

"You heard him, he wants her to spin it in their favor," Maddy said. She started the car, and then said, "Where are we going? That might be nice to know, if I'm supposed to drive us there."

"Why don't we go to Roger Henderson's office? I want to talk to him, but I need to make a telephone call first."

"Who are you going to call?"

"I'd tell you," I said, "but you wouldn't like it. Why don't we just let it be a surprise for now?"

He picked up on the first ring, and I was surprised to catch him at his desk this early. "Hey, Kevin, it's Eleanor Swift."

"Eleanor, trust me, you don't have to identify yourself. I know your voice. What's going on?"

"I've got a tip you might want to look into," I said as Maddy shook her head in my direction. I knew full well she didn't approve of me sharing anything we learned with the police, but there were questions they could ask that we couldn't—if I could just convince him that it might be important.

"Go on, I'm listening."

"I just heard that Sandi Meadows has some information that might be relevant to your investigation, so I thought you might want to drop in on her at work today and ask her."

"Where'd you hear this?"

"Jamie Lowder was talking to her outside Brian's urging her to tell you something, but it was pretty clear she didn't want to."

He paused, and then asked, "How did you happen to hear that? I doubt Jamie would say anything to her in front of you. The whole town knows he's had a crush on her since the third grade."

So our chief of police wasn't as clueless as I thought. "He didn't exactly know we were listening," I admitted.

"Don't tell me you've stooped to eavesdropping," Kevin said.

"Maddy and I were in the parking lot, and we happened to overhear them arguing. Talk to her, don't talk to her. I don't care."

"Take it easy," he said. "I shouldn't have said that last bit."

"No, you shouldn't have," I said, and then I hung up on him.

When I looked over at Maddy, she was smiling at me. "Wow, you really spanked him that time, didn't you?"

"He called us a couple of snoops," I said.

"Well, he was right, wasn't he?"

I studied my sister for a few seconds. "Whose side are you on?"

"If you have to ask that, I think I'll take you back home and go see Roger by myself."

She started to turn in toward my place. "I'm sorry. Kevin just pushed me a little too hard. I know I shouldn't take it out on you."

"No, you shouldn't," Maddy said without any trace of rancor in her voice. She was like that, able to detach herself from situations that made my blood boil. And yet sometimes my sister took offense at the mildest slight. There were times I could understand men's frustrations with women. If they only knew that sometimes we didn't know the reasons we acted the way we did any better than they did. I wasn't sure if the knowledge would make things better, or infinitely worse.

When we got to Roger's business, there was only one car parked out in front, and it wasn't one of the black sedans we'd seen the day before.

I said, "I wonder if the feds know he's here all by himself?"

"Maybe we can use that," Maddy said. "Do you feel like taking another swing at the hornet's nest?"

"I've got my stick all ready," I said.

"Hang on a second. I'm going to park out of sight so he doesn't know we're coming." She pulled up beside the building out of anyone's clear line of vision, and we got out and headed for the bookkeeper's office.

When we walked in, Roger had a cash box out on his desk and was obviously counting money. The second he saw us, he jammed the money back into the box and slammed the lid shut. "What are you two doing here?"

I decided to ignore his direct question, a skill I'd learned from my local congressman. "Wow, for somebody who's supposed to be broke, that looked like a lot of money."

"This is all I've got in the world," he said. "I know the embezzlement wasn't my fault, but I still feel responsible. After all, Wade was my employee. I'm going to pay back what I can, even if I'm not obligated to."

"That's big of you," I said.

"It's not much, but it's what I can do. Is there something I can help you with? The auditor's due in any minute."

I suddenly didn't feel like poking him anymore. "No, we just wanted to stop in and see how you were doing."

"Just peachy," he said, the sarcasm dripping from his voice.

Once we were outside, Maddy said, "You gave up too easily in there. What about poking the nest?"

"It felt like kicking him when he was down," I admitted. "Can you believe he's trying to make some kind of restitution?"

"Frankly, no," Maddy said. "Who's to say that was his money he was really counting? Or how he managed to get it?"

I shook my head. "You don't trust anybody, do you?"

"Me, a hundred percent. You, about eighty-five. Everybody else in the world is on probation."

"Wow, I know I should feel honored, but somehow I don't."

We were still sitting in Maddy's car when a long black limousine pulled up in front of Roger's business. I kept waiting for the passenger to get out, but instead, Roger came out and handed a thick envelope through an open window in back of the car.

As soon as he made the handoff, the car sped off, and Roger hurried back inside.

"What was that all about?" I asked.

Maddy put her car in drive, and then said, "I don't know, but I'm going to find out."

She started heading in the direction that the limousine had just taken, but we were three blocks away before we both realized that we'd somehow lost them.

"How did that happen?" Maddy asked. "He was right there."

"I don't know. Did you realize that someone in town had his own limo?"

"I didn't have a clue," she admitted. "That's really odd, isn't it?"

"It's just one more thing to add to the list."

As she wheeled the car around, I asked, "Where are we going?"

"I don't think we're finished with Roger Henderson, do you?"

"Not on your life."

We got back to Roger's office, but to my surprise, his car was gone. "Where did he go?" I asked. "He was just here."

"Cars keep disappearing on us, don't they?" Maddy frowned. "Is there anyone else we can run off before we start work at the Slice this morning?"

"I'd like to talk to Katy," I said. "Clara's the only other

name on our list, but I'm not really in the mood to go up against her first thing in the morning, are you?"

"We don't seem to be faring too well in the exchanges, do we?" She paused a moment, then asked, "Then what should we do?"

"Greg's coming in at noon, so we can ask him about Katy then. As for Clara, I'm still trying to figure out how to get her back for what she did to us."

"I've got an idea," Maddy said.

"Do you care to share it with me?"

She shook her head, but I didn't like the grin she had. "Trust me, the less you know about this, the better. There's something to be said for plausible deniability."

"Normally I'd say don't do anything we might regret, but right now, I honestly don't care."

"That's the spirit," Maddy said.

As my sister started driving, I realized we were going in the opposite direction of the Slice. "Where are we headed?"

"Just have a little patience."

It took me a minute to realize that we were heading for Clara's house, and I wondered what my sister had in mind, but I wasn't going to find out just yet.

She wasn't home, and from the look of the newspapers piled up on her front porch, she hadn't been there for at least three days.

But where could she have gone? We'd seen her around town, so she hadn't gone far.

Then it hit me. If she wasn't staying at her own place, there was only one other place she might be.

"Come on," I told Maddy. "I think I know where she is."

We got back in the car, and I said, "Head over to Wade's house."

"Do you honestly think she'd stay there, instead of here?"

"Where else could she be?"

Maddy nodded. "It's as good a place as any to start looking for her."

When we got to Wade's, I was surprised to see a line of trash in front of the place. It appeared that Clara had decided to clean house in the most basic sense of the term.

"Wow, that's kind of harsh, isn't it?" Maddy said as she surveyed the discards of Wade Hatcher's life.

"You'd think she'd make the place a shrine to him," I said.

We walked up onto the porch as Clara was heading out with another box. When she saw us standing there, she dropped the box onto the porch floor, clearly spooked by our sudden arrival.

"What do you two want?" she asked as she edged back toward the front door. "I've got to warn you, I'm armed."

"Do the police know that?" I asked.

Maddy said to me, "Relax, Eleanor, we're fine as long as she doesn't have a rolling pin in her hand."

That was pretty mean, even for my sister. I wasn't any happier with Clara than she was, but it was a quick, painful cut, nonetheless.

"I'm ordering you to leave my porch," Clara said.

"This isn't your property," I said. "You can't order us to do anything. I'm not even sure you should be here doing this yourself."

"He was my son. It's my right to put things in order again."

Maddy reached for her cell phone. "Let's see what the chief of police has to say about it."

"Call him. I don't care." Clara slammed the door in our faces, and Maddy put her telephone away.

"Aren't you going to call Kevin?"

She shook her head. "It was a bluff that didn't work."

"Should we call Sandi Meadows? From what Emma told us at the courthouse, there's a legal dispute about which will is the valid one."

Maddy nodded. "That's even better than what I had in mind for payback." She took out her phone, called information, and phoned Sandi at work.

After a few seconds, Maddy said loudly, "Your inheritance is walking out the door over here at Wade's. His mother's decided to do some spring cleaning."

She held the phone away from her ear, and I could hear Sandi yelling.

When there was a break, Maddy said, "I just thought you should know"; then she hung up.

"What should we do next?" I asked.

"Now you can call the police. Things might get ugly, so it could be a good thing having Kevin here."

After I told the police chief what we'd seen as we just happened to be driving by Wade's place, I turned to Maddy. "Is there anything else we should do, or is it time to make pizza dough?"

"Are you kidding me? I'm not about to miss this. Let's go sit in the car and wait for Sandi to show up."

We did as Maddy suggested, and four minutes later, Sandi Meadows drove up, with Kevin close behind in his squad car.

She didn't even look at us as she raced up the stairs to the house.

But Kevin did.

It might have been my imagination, but as he turned away, I could swear I saw him smiling.

Chapter 13

"The show's about to get started," Maddy said four minutes later. I looked over at the front porch and saw Sandi coming out of the house, with Clara right behind her. Kevin Hurley stood there stoically, and we watched as Clara appeared to confront him.

They were too far away for us to hear what they were saying, but Kevin evidently began scolding her pretty hard, because Clara's face turned three shades of red, the last one with a touch of purple in it. She finally reached into her purse and handed him something.

"What did she just give him?" Maddy asked.

"I'm willing to bet that those were the keys to the house," I said, and, sure enough, Kevin turned and locked the door behind all of them.

Clara was fuming as she stormed toward her car, and I wondered what kind of retribution she'd have for us next. As hard as it was to believe, though, she was so mad that I don't think she even saw us there.

"Duck," I said as she started to pull out.

"I don't care if she sees me," Maddy protested, but I pulled her down with me, anyway.

"I know you don't, but the last time we crossed her, she did her best to have us shut down. There's no need for her to know that it was us stirring the pot."

"Be that way," Maddy said.

As Clara drove away, there was a tap on my window, and I looked up to see Kevin Hurley staring down at us.

As we sat back up, I rolled the window down.

"Good morning, Officer," I said in my politest voice.

He shook his head, and it took me a second to see that he was trying to suppress a laugh. "I'm not sure she could have been any madder without actually exploding," he finally managed to say.

"What did Sandi say?" I looked around for her car, and noticed that while we'd been hiding, she'd left as well.

"She wasn't happy about it, I'll tell you that. I've decided to keep everyone off the property until this gets resolved. They're both threatening lawsuits and legal action until we're all old and gray."

"How can you keep them out?" Maddy asked.

"I'm designating it a potential crime scene," he said.

"But Wade was killed in my pizzeria," I said.

"That's what it looks like, but who's to say he wasn't killed here and then someone moved the body?"

"Do you think that's possible?" I asked, holding out for the slightest glimmer of hope that he hadn't died in my shop.

"There's not a chance of it," he said, "but they don't have to know that, do they? I owe you one for calling this in."

"Enough to let us inside and look around?" I asked.

"No, not that much."

He got into his squad car before I could ask him if Sandi had told him her little secret, but it was just as well.

I knew there was no way he'd tell me, and as things stood now, it looked like I was doing a public service for the good of the community, instead of the self-serving act of retaliation that it was. Not that Kevin had missed my rationale. He knew me better than I liked to admit.

"My, my, my, we've had a busy morning," Maddy said.

"And our real work hasn't even started yet. Is there anyone else we can antagonize before we get started on making pizza today?"

Maddy considered it a few moments, then admitted, "Not that I can think of. If we knew where Katy was, we could make it a clean sweep."

"I've got a feeling we'll know that soon enough. Come on, let's go make some pizza dough."

"We might as well," Maddy said as she started the car. "I think we've done enough damage for one day. I just hope something comes from it."

"Even if it doesn't, it's better than just sitting around waiting for something to happen, wouldn't you agree?"

"Absolutely," she said.

As Maddy and I prepped for the day in the Slice's kitchen, there was a pounding on the back door.

I started to open it, when my sister said, "Should you do that?"

"It could be our vegetable delivery," I said. "He was supposed to come yesterday, but he never showed up."

"We need a peephole so we can see who's out there before we let them in," she said.

"My, aren't you being just a little paranoid?"

Maddy shook her head. "I don't think so. Somebody killed Wade Hatcher not ten feet from us, and we've been doing our best to aggravate everyone we suspect. How hard would it be for someone to come back here and do the same thing to us that they did to Wade?"

The pounding started again, and I began to open the door when Maddy's paranoia struck home. Was she being paranoid, or perceptive?

"Who is it?"

A muffled voice called back, "It's Greg. Open up."

As I moved the wooden beam blocking the door, I said, "See, it's just Greg."

"But that doesn't mean we shouldn't start being a little more careful than we have been," she said.

"Agreed."

As I opened the door, Greg came in. To my surprise, he wasn't alone. Katy Johnson was with him, shadowing his footsteps.

"I'm glad you're here, Katy. We were hoping to see you today," I said when we made eye contact.

"Why? What do you want with me?" Apparently, she had had a rough night, based on the disheveled state of her hair and her faded complexion.

"We just have a few questions about what happened the other night," Maddy said gently.

Greg moved in between us and Katy, clearly blocking us from her. "Listen, she didn't come here so you two could interrogate her. She had enough of that yesterday from the police."

"I understand," I said. "But there are some gaps in the timeline we've been making, and Katy could help us fill them in." I looked past Greg and stared directly at Katy as I added, "You do want to help prove Greg is innocent, don't you?"

Greg shook his head in disgust. "Are you serious? I never would have brought her here if I thought you were going to grill her." He handed Katy his keys and told her, "Go back to my place. I'll be there in a little while."

"You're not working today?" I asked.

"I was planning to, but I just changed my mind."

"So much for your heartfelt gratitude," Maddy snapped.

I thought about saying something to her, but then again, I happened to agree with her at the moment.

Katy tugged at his arm. "Come on, Greg. I appreciate you trying to protect me, but it's okay. I don't mind answering their questions. I don't have anything to hide."

He turned to look at her, and I saw his expression soften. "Are you sure? You don't have to say anything if you don't want to."

Maddy started to say something else, but I touched her arm lightly and she kept her comment to herself. We had to let the two of them work it out, or we were going to drive them both away, and while I could do without Katy's presence in my restaurant, I needed Greg.

She bit her lower lip for a second, then said, "I want to help if it means figuring out who killed your brother."

Greg nodded, then turned back to us. "Okay, ask your questions, but don't bully her. She's had a rough time of it lately."

I couldn't get over how protective he was of her. It appeared that he'd forgiven her for the kisses she'd given his brother, though I never would have believed it. I knew young hearts could be malleable, but I couldn't believe the way Greg was acting right now.

"When was the last time you saw Wade?" I asked.

"It was when Greg came to the house. I took off after him, but he wouldn't stop and give me a chance to explain."

"I was mad," Greg said. "You can't hold that against me."

"I don't," she said. "I just hope you'll be able to forgive me someday."

"I told you, I won't talk about that until whoever killed my brother is caught."

She nodded, and then started to cry. "I still can't believe it happened. Hang on a second. I need to get myself together." She ran out of the kitchen into the dining room, but none of us made any move to stop her.

I saw something in Greg's eyes, just a flash of something gone before I could categorize it. "What's going on? What are you up to?"

"I don't know what you're talking about."

I walked up closer to him and said, "What game are you playing, Greg? You're not about to forgive her, are you?"

Greg shook his head in disgust, but he refused to answer my direct question.

Maddy was about to speak, but I shook my head curtly, and she obeyed my request for silence.

Finally, he said, "Do you want to know the truth? I couldn't turn her away when she came to me for help, no matter how much she hurt me. I loved her at one time, but the second I saw her kissing my brother, she was dead to me."

"Then why protect her?" Maddy asked.

"She's got nowhere else to go," Greg said. "I can't just turn my back on her."

I patted his shoulder. "You're a good man, Greg Hatcher."

"Don't give me too much credit," he said. "There's another reason I'm keeping her close to me."

"Why?"

"If she did it, I don't want her running away. She's got to pay for what she did, if she killed Wade."

I was taken aback by the admission. "Do you think it's possible she did it? If she's a killer, you're not safe being alone with her."

"As long as she thinks there's a chance I'll take her back, I'm as safe as can be. Besides, I'm trying to get her to trust me enough to open up. I'm sorry I've been treating you both so rudely this morning, but it's the only way my plan is ever going to work."

I frowned. "You're taking a real risk, no matter what you think. Greg, forgive me for saying so, but I know how you felt about your brother. *Why* are you doing this?"

"Sure, there wasn't any love lost between us. But until we figure out what happened to him, folks around here are going to think I'm a murderer, and I can't have that. I love Timber Ridge, but if Wade's murder goes unsolved for very much longer, I'm not going to be able to stay."

"You really wouldn't leave, would you?" I asked him. I couldn't imagine not having him around.

"I don't have much choice. The whispering behind my back is already driving me crazy. My Sunday school teacher from grade school crossed the street a few hours ago so she wouldn't have to say hello to me. How much more of that do you think I can take?"

"Believe me, I know what you're going through."

"Then I shouldn't have to tell you what it's like." He gestured to the dining room and added, "I should go out there and check on her."

"I don't like this," I said.

"I agree," Maddy added beside me.

"It's not my first choice, either, but it's all I've got. Maybe she'll loosen up and talk to me now. I need to know if she killed him."

"Be careful," I said.

He grinned at me. "I always am. Well, almost always."

Greg went up front, and I looked at Maddy. "What should we do?"

"Greg's a big boy. He can take care of himself."

I looked hard at her. "Just like Wade did?"

She didn't answer, but the creases around her mouth deepened.

Greg came back in a minute later. "Would one of you let us out? We're going to take off."

"So, you're not working, after all."

"Don't worry. I'll be back before we open," he said. Lowering his voice, he added, "I think she's ready to tell me something, and I don't want to lose this chance."

"Go, then," I said.

I let them out, and then I came back into the kitchen. Maddy moved aside when I came through the door, and it was clear that she'd been watching us.

"I don't like it," she said.

"Neither do I, but there's not much we can do about it."

It seemed to take forever, but true to his word, Greg came back a few minutes before we were set to open.

Before I could even ask, he shook his head. "Sorry, I didn't have any luck with her. She clammed up the second we left, and I couldn't get another word out of her. It's so frustrating, I could scream."

"We'll join you," I said.

"What do we do now?"

"We make pizza," I said, "and try to figure out what our next move is going to be."

Maddy came back with an order, and as I prepared the two panini sandwiches and put them on the press, she said, "I told you they were for takeout, right?"

"No, but that's not a problem."

"They're for Roger Henderson," she said, "and he's acting odd."

"What do you mean?"

She shrugged. "He kept asking me about this morning. He wanted to know if we'd told anyone about the cash we found him counting. I told him we hadn't, but I'm beginning to think I should have said we took an ad out in the paper."

"Why would we do that?"

"If he thinks he can shut us both up, he might just believe that he's going to get away with something. Is that a chance we want to take?"

The kitchen door opened, and I saw Roger himself walk in, with Greg on his heels. Greg explained, "I told him he couldn't come back here, but he wouldn't listen to me."

"That's fine. It's okay."

"Are you sure?" Greg asked as he scowled at Roger.

"I told you, I just want a word with Eleanor," Roger said.

I motioned for Greg to go, and though he didn't look happy about it, he did as I asked. After he was back out front, Roger said, "I didn't realize he was so protective of you."

"Greg's a good man to have around."

"Then he's nothing like his brother, is he?"

I wasn't about to defend Greg's honor any more than I had to, and certainly not to Roger Henderson. "What can I do for you?"

"It's about this morning," he said.

"I told him we didn't discuss it with anyone, but I didn't realize you'd already told the police chief," Maddy said.

"You told Hurley?" he asked me.

"It came up in our conversation," I lied.

Roger seemed to lose some of his urgency. "I just want you to know that I'm doing everything I can to pay back the people who lost money because of what happened."

"You already told us that," I said.

He nodded, and as he started to go, I asked, "Is that what you were doing this morning in the parking lot out in front of your business? Paying back one of your customers? I didn't realize any of your clients could afford their own limousine."

That stopped him in his tracks. "What are you talking about?"

Maddy said, "Come on, Roger. We saw the envelope, and I'm betting it wasn't full of coupons or trading stamps."

"It was part of my restitution," he insisted.

"Then you won't mind telling us who you were repaying, would you?"

"I'm afraid that's confidential." He glanced over at the sandwiches I'd been making. "I've changed my mind. I don't want those anymore."

"That's fine. Just pay me the twenty dollars you owe me and we'll call it even."

He raised an eyebrow, but Roger dug into his wallet and pulled out a twenty. As he laid it on the counter, he said, "If I were you, I'd forget about what you saw this morning outside my office, and I wouldn't share anything else with your police friend."

"Is that a threat, Roger?" Maddy asked.

"No, but not everyone in this world is as nice as I am."

"Yes, my sister and I were just saying what a prince you were."

He looked at us both a second longer, then shrugged. "Fine. Just don't say I didn't warn you."

"We won't," I said as he left.

Greg came back instantly. "Is everything okay?"

"We're fine," I said. "Would you like a couple of sandwiches? They're on the house."

He nodded. "Sure thing."

"Don't you want to know what kind they are?" Maddy asked.

"Not necessary. If Eleanor made them, I'm sure they're great." He added with a grin, "Besides, I skipped breakfast. Anybody mind if I take my break now?"

"Go on," Maddy said. "Find a table and I'll bring them out to you."

"You don't have to do that," he said.

"I don't mind waiting on you after the time you've been having lately."

"Cool," Greg said.

As I plated the sandwiches, Maddy asked, "What do you suppose that was about? I can't believe Roger tried to warn us off digging into the limo's owner."

"To be honest with you, it makes me ten times more curious about who was in that car."

"But how do we find out?" Maddy asked as I handed the sandwiches to her.

"I'll check around," I said. "Hey, I just had a thought. Maybe Bob would know."

"I'll ask him tonight," Maddy said as she started to walk away.

"Hang on a second. Since when did you have a date tonight?"

Maddy smiled. "Since about ten minutes ago. He came by to ask me in person. You don't mind if I cut out a little early, do you? Greg said he'd stay behind and help you clean up after closing time."

"Go. Have fun. You have my blessing."

"Thanks, Eleanor," she said with a smile.

I was happy for my sister, and hoped that maybe she was finally on the right track with her love life. Goodness knows she deserved it. But where did that leave me? The only man I'd had even the slightest interest in since my husband, Joe, had died was probably going to move away, and I had to wonder if at least part of the reason was my fault. If David left Timber Ridge, would he be taking my last chance at love with him?

I honestly didn't know, and with Wade's murder weighing heavy on my mind, I wasn't sure I wanted to. I had enough to think about at the moment without dragging my heart into it.

Our customers were getting used to our closing time between lunch and dinner, and I was starting to enjoy it myself. It was nice to have a break during the middle of the day, and most folks took theirs for granted.

Maddy came into the kitchen as I stored the last of the pizza and sandwich toppings into the refrigerator. "We're all set. Greg just took off."

"He's coming back, though, right?"

"He told me he was," Maddy said. "He wants to go to his place and talk with Katy again on his break."

"Does he really think she's going to admit anything to him?"

Maddy shrugged. "He has hopes, and I wasn't about to say anything to him. I still think he's taking his life in his hands."

"I know, but we can't keep him from doing whatever he wants, can we?"

She grabbed the house phone. "I know one way. We can tell Kevin Hurley what's going on. Maybe then he'll step in."

Maddy handed me the telephone, but I didn't take it. "Do you honestly think he'll listen to me?"

"There's more of a chance of it than him listening to me," she said.

"I guess you're right there. Fine, I'll try."

Kevin wasn't in his office, though. When his voice mail came on, I left a message to call me.

"What do we do now?"

Maddy said, "I think we should find Clara and poke her a little more."

"Do you honestly think there's something she's not telling us?"

"I don't know, but I just feel like giving her a hard time. Who knows? Maybe if we ask her enough times, she'll actually tell us something."

"I guess it's worth trying," I said, "though I'd rather not see her again if I had the choice. There's just something wrong with that woman."

"Wrong enough for her to kill her own child?"

I bit my lip, and then I said, "I have no idea, but I have to admit, she could be capable of it."

"That alone earns her a spot on the list."

As we walked out front, I turned to lock the door when I realized someone was walking toward us.

I could imagine a hundred different people in Timber Ridge who might like to chat with me, but I never would have picked Sandi Meadows out of the hat as one of them.

"Eleanor, can we talk?" she asked softly.

"Sure, what's up?"

She looked at Maddy, and then asked my sister, "I don't mean any offense, but would you mind if I spoke with Eleanor alone?"

Maddy looked at me for a clue as to what to do, but I didn't know what to tell her.

I finally nodded. "Why don't you go over to Paul's? I'll catch up with you there." We hadn't made plans to go to the bakery, but I hoped she'd take the hint and stay where she could see me. Not that I thought Sandi would do anything in broad daylight on the promenade, but I decided I couldn't be too careful.

Maddy caught on immediately. "Sure thing. I'll go ahead and order you an éclair and a coffee."

"I didn't think the pastry shop was still open," Sandi said.

I glanced at my watch, and saw that we still had seven minutes before Paul officially closed. "We've got just enough time, if we make this quick," I said.

Maddy walked toward the pastry shop, and I asked Sandi, "What was it you wanted to talk to me about?"

"It's about Wade," she said. She looked around the promenade. "Can we go somewhere? I feel kind of exposed standing here."

Going somewhere with her alone was the last thing I wanted to do. "Let's sit at this bench. That way, we'll be comfortable."

"Are you sure you don't want to go back into your restaurant?"

"I'm positive," I said. "Now, what is it you want to tell me?"

"Jamie believes that Katy killed Wade," she said, the words tumbling out of her like a floodgate released.

"What? Why?"

"There's something I have to confess right up front," Sandi said. "He wasn't with me the night Wade was killed, at least not all of the time. I was so upset that he offered to go get me some mint chocolate-chip ice cream.

He knows it's my favorite thing in the world, and he told me it would calm my nerves. I've got to tell you, I was a real wreck after I heard about Wade and Katy."

"That still doesn't explain why he thinks Katy did it."

She lowered her voice as she explained, "Jamie was passing by the promenade on his way to the grocery store, and he saw Katy go into the pizzeria after it was closed for the night. She had a Drake's pizza box with her."

"He knows all of this, and he hasn't gone to the police?"

Sandi said, "Don't you see why he doesn't? If he admits that we weren't together every minute that night, the police might think he's lying to protect me. Jamie's afraid to say anything, but I'm getting worried about Katy. I wanted someone to know what really happened, in case something bad happens to us."

"Why tell me?"

Sandi shrugged. "I didn't know who else to go to. I know you're digging into the murder. I'm really frightened, Eleanor."

"You've got to tell Kevin Hurley," I said.

"I can't."

"Then I will," I said. "The police chief needs to know what really happened that night, Sandi."

"Don't tell him. Please," Sandi asked, pleading with me.

"If you won't do it yourself, I have to."

Sandi fought back the tears, then said, "At least give me until tomorrow to convince Jamie that telling the police is the right thing to do. If the chief of police comes to him with this, he'll deny it to protect me. The only way anybody's going to believe it is if he comes forward himself. Will you do that for me, Eleanor? All I'm asking for is twenty-four hours."

She had a point. I knew Kevin Hurley, and if I came to him with this story, he'd tend to think I was lying to protect Greg, or at the very least I was mistaken.

Still, I couldn't let her take the risk. "I don't like it. It's too dangerous."

Sandi touched my hand. "Please, Eleanor, I'm begging you not to say anything. Katy doesn't know that Jamie saw her, and she won't know about it until the police come to talk to her. I just need some time to convince him to come forward."

I really didn't have any choice. "Okay, but first thing tomorrow, I'm calling Kevin Hurley, whether Jamie's ready to admit what he saw or not."

"Thanks so much," she said, the relief flooding her face. "I won't forget this kindness you're doing me."

"I just hope I don't live to regret it," I said.

"You won't. I promise."

She suddenly stiffened, and I saw Jamie Lowder hurrying toward us. Sandi whispered, "Don't say a thing. He doesn't know that I was going to tell you."

I nodded in his direction as Jamie approached, but it was as though I wasn't there. He looked hard at Sandy as he said, "There you are. Don't take off like that, okay?" There was an edge to his voice that gave me a start. It wasn't a request; it was clearly an order he expected to be followed.

"I'm sorry, Jamie," Sandi said. "Eleanor and I were just chatting."

"About what?" he asked, finally looking at me.

"The Strawberry Festival," I said. It was the first thing that came to me after spotting a tattered banner from the event.

"What about it?" Jamie asked.

"I told her she should run for Strawberry Queen next

year," I lied. "She's certainly pretty enough, don't you think?"

"If she wants to enter, she'll win," Jamie said. "But we're running late. Come on, Sandi, let's go."

As she stood, she reached out a hand and gently squeezed my shoulder. Sandi mouthed the words, "Thank you," and then they were gone.

I'd promised not to say anything to Kevin Hurley about what Jamie had seen, but that didn't mean I had to ignore it completely, either. If what Jamie had told Sandi was true, that meant that Greg Hatcher was harboring a murderer, and I wasn't about to let her strike again. At the very least, I had to get him away from Katy. If she snapped again and something happened to him, I'd never be able to live with myself.

Maddy met me halfway between the bakery and the pizzeria, and I saw she was holding a bag from Paul's shop. "I caught him just in time. Éclairs sounded good, so I got us a couple." She took one look at my face and asked, "What's wrong, Eleanor?"

"We have to go to Greg's apartment."

She looked at her watch. "What's the rush? He'll be back at work in thirty minutes, or maybe a little less." Maddy smiled. "That's pretty funny, given our line of work. Greg will be back in thirty minutes or less, or his pizza's free."

"Sorry. I can't appreciate your little joke at the moment. We need to go get him now."

"Why? What's the rush?"

"I think Katy killed Wade, and I don't want her to make it a clean sweep with the Hatcher brothers. We have to warn him before it's too late."

*   *   *

As we drove to Greg's apartment, I brought my sister up to date on what Sandi had told me.

Maddy asked, "I still say we should tell Kevin Hurley about this. We're in a little over our heads, don't you think?"

"Sandi said she'd deny it, and even if she didn't, the police wouldn't believe me. You know what? She's probably right. Kevin thinks I'd say anything to protect Greg. No, this has to come from Jamie, since he's the one who saw Katy going into the Slice around the time that Wade was murdered."

"It's too important to keep to ourselves," Maddy said as she drove way too fast to Greg's place. For once, I was happy that she had a lead foot behind the wheel. I just hoped we weren't too late.

"I gave her until tomorrow morning to convince him to come forward," I said. "It will have a lot more credence if Jamie volunteers the information himself. Trust me, I know Kevin Hurley. It's true."

"We're still taking a chance," Maddy said.

"As long as we get Greg away from Katy, we should be fine. I don't think she suspects anybody saw her going into the pizzeria after hours."

"Then how are we going to get Greg away without alerting her that we know what happened?"

As I thought about that, Maddy said, "If you're going to come up with something, you'd better do it fast. We're almost there."

"We'll tell Greg there's an emergency, and we need him at the Slice."

"What are we going to say? That there's a fire or something?"

I shook my head. "No, nothing as dramatic as that. I'm going to make up a giant pizza order."

"We've never made a giant pizza before," Maddy said as she pulled up in front of Greg's apartment.

"It's not one big pizza—it's a lot of little ones."

"We haven't made tiny ones before, either."

"Maddy, are you seriously jerking me around at a time like this? The pizzas aren't small, they're normal-sized. It's the order that's big."

"Fine, make them whatever size you want. Just make sure it sounds convincing," she said as she pulled up in front of Greg's apartment.

I took a deep breath, and then opened the car door. "Why don't you stay here? If something happens to me, tell Kevin everything I just told you."

"Forget it, Eleanor," she said. "I'm going with you."

"Are you sure? It's not right that I'm putting your life in danger."

"What's not right is trying to leave me behind." She took her cell phone out as we got out of the car and punched two numbers in.

"Who are you calling?" I asked her.

"I dialed nine-one, so now all I have to do is hit one and we're connected."

"That's not a bad idea," I said.

"Don't look so surprised. I get them every now and then myself."

We approached Greg's door, and after nodding to Maddy, I knocked.

It took forever, but Greg finally came to the door. He opened it slightly, and I could see that the chain was securely in place.

"What is it?" he asked. "I've got another half hour on my break."

"Sorry, but we just got a huge pizza order, and I need your help."

Greg looked back inside and called out, "It's okay. It's just Eleanor and Maddy."

There was no response, and Greg said, "Hang on a second."

He shut the door, and I kept waiting to hear the chain slide out of position so he could let us in.

Only he didn't.

After I realized that he wasn't going to open the door for us, I started pounding frantically on the door. "Greg, let us in."

I just hoped he'd do it in time, but I had a bad feeling in the pit of my stomach that I'd lost my last chance to save him.

Chapter 14

It seemed to take him forever to come back, and I was just about ready to have Maddy hit that final one on her telephone when the door finally opened.

"She's gone," he said. "She took off out the back. Sorry, but Katy said she wasn't in the mood to face either one of you right now."

"Good, I didn't particularly want to see her, either," I answered. "Come on. We need to talk."

"Let me get my jacket," he said.

"It's not that cold out," I answered, imagining Katy lurking in the closet with another rolling pin, or maybe a knife. I wouldn't put it past her to slip back inside the second Greg's back was turned. I was willing to admit that my imagination was running on overdrive, but it still didn't ease the growing sense of dread I was feeling.

Greg shrugged, and I was sure he thought I was more than a little crazy, but I didn't care. At least he followed us out of his apartment.

"Why don't you ride with us?" I asked.

"Then how am I going to get home tonight? I said I'd come back to work, you two don't have to escort me."

"That's not it," I said, keeping my voice low in case Katy was lurking somewhere around outside. I had the strangest feeling that we were being watched, though I fully realized I was just being delusional. "Come on, Greg. Don't argue."

"Okay, I'm coming," he said.

We got into Maddy's car, and she started to drive.

I turned around in the front passenger seat and looked at Greg. "There's an explanation for why we just rushed you out of there. We have reason to believe that Katy killed your brother."

"I know, you said that before," Greg said.

"Yeah, but now we have some proof. Jamie Lowder saw Katy going into the pizzeria the night Wade was murdered with a pizza box from Drake's in her hands."

"Do the police know yet?"

I shook my head. "Sandi Meadows told me that she's trying to convince Jamie to come forward on his own so it will have more credibility with Kevin Hurley."

"And you're just going to let her take her time doing it?"

"No," I said. "I gave her until tomorrow morning to make him talk to the police, and if she hasn't had any luck by then, I'm going to tell him myself. You can't go back to your place tonight, Greg. She might decide you're expendable."

"Where am I supposed to go?"

Maddy said, "He's got a point. He probably shouldn't come home with either one of us. After all, this small town has a thousand eyes, and we've got enough trouble as things stand now without adding any grist to the rumor mill."

"I guess I could crash with Josh again," Greg said. "But I don't even have a toothbrush, though."

I fished a twenty out of my wallet. "Here."

"I'm not taking your money," Greg said.

"How about if I put it on your tab?"

Greg nodded reluctantly as he took the offered bill. "Okay, but I'm paying you back every cent that I took."

"Am I arguing with you?" I asked with a smile.

"No, I noticed that, too," Greg replied. "I still think you're overreacting."

"So let me," I said. "I'm asking you for a favor. Do this for me."

"For both of us," Maddy added.

Greg shrugged. "You know I have trouble saying no to you two."

"That's why we don't ask for much," Maddy said.

We got back to the pizzeria, and I realized that I needed to talk to Slick while I had a few minutes. I'd gotten his bill in the mail, and it was for substantially less than the amount we'd agreed on. I wasn't about to let him get away with it, and I needed to settle things immediately.

"Could you drop me off at Slick's on the way?" I asked Maddy.

"That's not a bad idea. Are you going to pick up another baseball bat for protection?"

"No, I think I'm covered. I need to talk to him about the bill for our new safe."

Greg asked, "What happened? Did he charge you too much?"

"Actually, he didn't charge me enough."

He looked at me oddly. "And you're complaining about that why, exactly?"

"You wouldn't understand," I said.

"You're right there. Do you want me to go with you?"

"Thanks, but I'd rather you went with Maddy to the Slice. Don't worry, I'll be along shortly."

Maddy said, "Besides, we've got to start working on that giant pizza."

It was Greg's turn to stare at her. "Do I even want to know?"

"It's an inside joke," I said.

"Most things are with you two," he said.

Maddy let me off at Slick's, and then drove to the parking lot in back of the Slice. I went in and found the store owner counting a massive amount of tennis balls.

"I thought those things came in cans."

"They're supposed to," Slick said. "But somehow I got a shipment already opened. I should have known that deal was too good to be true."

"They usually are, aren't they?" I fought back my smile and added, "I got your bill today."

He knew instantly why I was being stern with him. "Before you get upset, I got a special deal from my guy. He had a surplus of safes, and he passed the savings along to me."

"We agreed on a price," I said, not backing down an inch.

"Come on, Eleanor, if I charge you more, it's going to foul up my whole bookkeeping system, and since Roger Henderson cut me loose, I don't know what I'm going to do."

"Did you lose much money?" I asked.

"I didn't think anybody knew about that," Slick said.

"I happened to stumble onto some information," I admitted.

Slick shrugged. "I lost a little, but Roger paid me back out of his own pocket, so I'm good. I told him he didn't have to make full restitution, but he felt bad about what happened, and I couldn't talk him out of it."

"He actually gave you your money back?"

Slick nodded. "I'm not the only one, either. He paid Paul back, too."

So his story had been true. That still didn't explain the limousine and the thick envelope I'd seen go into it, but at least part of what Roger had told us had been the truth.

"I'm not set up to take any more money from you," Slick said. He added with a grin, "Sorry. I'd really like to help you."

"I bet," I said. I looked around the shop for something to buy, and saw a pistol on the counter.

"I didn't know you sold guns," I said.

He looked puzzled, and then Slick picked up the weapon. "It shoots darts, can you believe it? People will buy the craziest things."

"How much is it?" I thought the threat of it might be enough to dissuade someone from robbing the pizzeria. I didn't want a handgun there, but this certainly looked real enough.

When he told me, I asked, "Is that the full retail price?"

"No," Slick admitted. "I'm giving you the merchant discount."

"I'll pay full retail," I said as I slid the money onto the counter.

"Then I'm not selling it to you," Slick said. It was clear from the set look on his face that he was serious.

"Fine," I said, tired of battling him. "Charge me whatever you want. I'll take it."

As he rang up the sale and put it in a bag, I said, "You're a tough bargainer, you know that, don't you?"

"Especially with you," he said. "Don't try to slip anything over on me, young lady."

"I won't," I said, not even trying to hide my smile.

I was in a better mood than I had any right to be in as I walked out of the sporting-goods store.

But that suddenly changed when I saw the same black limousine I'd spotted outside Roger Henderson's business pull up to the curb in front of Slick's store. When I saw Art Young start to get out, I had a very bad feeling.

"So you're the mysterious limo owner," I said as the driver held the door open for him. "I should have known."

"Good afternoon, Eleanor."

"Have you been extorting money from Roger Henderson?"

He looked at me for a long three seconds, and then he said calmly, "If you're going to use that tone of voice with me, I ask that you at least have the decency to do it in my car."

All the while, the burly driver had been watching us. With a slight motion from Art Young, he sprang to get the door again with a quickness that didn't look possible for a man that size.

As we stood there near the promenade, Art asked me, "Are you going to get in, or is this conversation over?"

I looked around for someone to witness what I was about to do, but no one was watching. Where were Maddy and Greg? How about Slick? I would have to be out of my mind to get inside.

"No thanks," I said. "You might be surprised, but I'm not that stupid."

I'd expected a snappy retort from him, but instead, he looked hurt. "Please, you have nothing to fear from me. You should know that."

"I don't know anything anymore, but I'm not about to put myself at risk if I don't have to. Thanks, but no thanks."

He gestured toward his driver again, who closed the door and got into the car.

Art Young looked at me; then he said, "At least we can talk over there, away from prying eyes."

I didn't know who had the prying eyes he was talking about, but it was a reasonable request. We found a bench nearby and sat down. From anyone watching us, it probably looked like two old friends sharing a bit of afternoon sun, but there was nothing friendly about our conversation.

Once we were settled, he asked, "Now, may I ask what has driven you to treat me with such rudeness? I was under the impression that we left things rather cordial the last time we spoke."

"That was before I knew what you were involved in."

He raised an eyebrow. "And what exactly do you know?"

I thought about it, and then I finally admitted, "Not much. I saw Roger Henderson hand you an envelope full of cash this morning in front of his shop."

"You saw me?" he asked.

"Well, I saw that limousine of yours."

Art pondered that a moment, then said, "I could deny that I was in it, but I won't treat you like a child. All I ask is that you reserve that same attitude toward me."

"Tell me the truth. Did you have anything to do with Wade Hatcher's murder?"

There, it was finally out.

I expected half a dozen possible reactions, but the one I got actually surprised me. Instead of being outraged by the accusation, he started to chuckle.

After a moment, he said, "Excuse me, but you caught me off guard. No, I had nothing to do with the murder, as I've already told you."

"Then why were you taking cash from Roger Henderson?"

"I can think of a dozen lies I could tell you, but I have no reason to hide the truth. He was paying off a wager, one I'd warned him not to make, but took nonetheless. It's usually out of my range of responsibilities, but I made an exception for him."

"You took advantage of him, you mean."

That struck a chord of anger in him, something that he suppressed as quickly as it had appeared. "Just the opposite, as a matter of fact. He begged me to put him in contact with a friend of mine. When I refused, he told me he'd do it himself. Not only would he have lost his money, he probably would have managed to get himself killed, and since he owes me money as well, I didn't see that as a prudent alternative."

I was really confused now. "How can I believe you?"

"You could ask Mr. Henderson himself, but I doubt he'd tell you. I could give you the name of my associate, but that wouldn't end well for either one of us." He spent a few seconds thinking about it, then said, "Let's go over to my driver. I won't say a word, and you can ask him where I was the night of the murder. Since he'll verify that Roger and I were in Charlotte together, it should satisfy you."

"I don't know."

"Come now, Eleanor. I have no reason to have arranged an alibi in advance, since I never dreamed anyone would ask me my whereabouts. What have you got to lose?"

He was right, and he was telling the truth. I knew it in my heart.

"Okay, let's go ask him."

The driver must have been watching us, because as we

approached him, he popped out of the car like he was on springs.

Art looked at him and said, "Tell her whatever she wants to know." He then turned away and walked back to the bench we'd recently vacated.

"Where were you the night Wade Hatcher was murdered?"

He got out his log, looked at it a second, then said, "I was driving Mr. Young and an associate to Charlotte. We left at eight P.M. and returned at two A.M. the next day."

"And who was the associate?"

That got a raised eyebrow, but he was a good employee and did as he'd been told. "Roger Henderson."

"Thanks."

He nodded. "Is that it?"

"Yes, that's everything."

I was about to turn away when he said softly, "Be very careful."

"I am, believe me."

I rejoined Art on the bench and said, "Thank you. I'm sorry if I was rude to you earlier. It's been a pretty difficult past few days for me."

"Do you believe me?" He looked honestly surprised.

"The truth is that I did before I talked to your driver. I don't know how, but I can tell when you're being straightforward with me and when you're not."

"How is that?"

"I'm not exactly sure it's something I could put my finger on, but I knew."

"I'm serious," he said. "Sometimes in my life, I need to be a little disingenuous, so if there's some way I'm giving things away, it would be a very good thing to know."

I thought about it; then after a minute, I said, "You seem a little uncomfortable with the truth. I don't know if you mean to, but when you're hiding something, you look me straight in the eye. The only times you don't are when you're telling the truth."

He looked surprised by what I said.

"I'm sorry," I said quickly. "I didn't mean to offend you." I kept thinking about what I'd heard about Art Young, but I still had a hard time coupling the actions with the man in front of me.

"You didn't," he said with an expansive smile. "In fact, you've done me a rather important favor. Now I'm in your debt, Eleanor."

"You don't owe me anything," I said, startled by his comment.

"That's where you're mistaken. I pay my way as I go, and I expect those around me to do the same. Good afternoon."

He was gone before I knew what had happened.

I found Maddy working in the kitchen when I came back to the Slice. Greg was setting up the tables out front, and I just nodded to him as I blew past him.

"You're not going to believe what just happened to me."

Maddy asked, "Did Slick give you an even bigger discount when you protested?"

"You know him, don't you?"

She looked at the bag I still clutched. I'd forgotten all about it during my conversation with Art Young. "What's that?"

"It's protection," I said.

I pulled out the dart gun, and she pulled back. "You actually bought a pistol after your rant at me? I didn't even know he sold those."

"It shoots tiny little darts," I said.

"What good is that going to do?"

"I don't know," I said, rethinking the purchase. "I just thought it might be a good idea to have something on hand around here besides a baseball bat."

She took it from me, broke the gun free of its packaging, carefully loaded it, and then said, "Who knows? It might come in handy after all, but I still don't think it's something I'd have a hard time believing."

"That wasn't what I was talking about," I said. "I just had a long conversation with Art Young. He gave me alibis for Roger Henderson and himself for the night Wade was murdered."

"And you believed him?" Maddy asked.

"I do," I said. "He had proof to back it up."

After I told her what Art had said—and the driver had verified—Maddy nodded. "Okay, that's good enough for me too, then. Katy looks guilty right now, but I feel better eliminating some of our other suspects. I can't believe you had the nerve to confront him like that."

"He's been very polite with me," I said.

"So far."

"He actually told me that he owed me a favor, if you can believe that."

Maddy frowned. "Why would he owe you anything?"

"I told him how I knew he was telling the truth."

"I don't understand."

"I'm not sure I do, either, and I was right there when it happened."

Maddy knew to accept that for what it was worth. "So, where does that leave us in our investigation?"

"Do you mean in case Katy didn't do it?" I thought about it for a few seconds, then said, "We can take Art Young and Roger Henderson off our list, so if we're still saying Greg is innocent—"

"Which we are," Maddy said as she interrupted me.

"Which we are," I agreed. "That leaves Jamie, Clara, and Sandi."

Maddy said, "Sandi came to you with what Jamie saw. That should clear her."

"And if what Jamie told her was true, it clears him as well," I said.

"I still can't see Clara killing her own son, even if it was a case of mistaken identity."

"Then that points us right back to Katy Johnson," I said.

"Until something more convincing comes along," Maddy agreed. "Should we really wait until morning to bring Kevin Hurley in on this?"

"I don't see what it can hurt," I said. "It looks solid to us, but you know Kevin. He's going to want more to go on than thirdhand information to change his mind that Greg is guilty."

"Then we wait," Maddy said. "In the meantime, I'm canceling my date with Bob tonight."

"Why would you do that?" I asked.

"With Katy on the loose, I don't want her coming after you when you're alone."

"Don't be silly. She doesn't have any reason to want to harm me." I picked up my dart gun and said, "Besides, I have this. Don't look for excuses to break your date. Go, and have a good time."

"That sounds like an order to me," Maddy said.

"Think of it as a strong suggestion."

"You've been spending too much time with hoodlums lately," my sister said.

"Art Young doesn't seem like a hoodlum to me."

"From what I hear, those are the ones you have to watch out for."

I didn't deny it, but for some odd reason, I wasn't afraid of Art Young—though by all accounts, I should be.

Instead, I was afraid of a young woman I never would have imagined had the capacity to murder. It just proved that none of us know what we're capable of doing until we're pushed up against a wall with nowhere to go.

Soon after we opened for dinner, Maddy came back with another order—one of many, so far—and a smile on her face.

"You've got a visitor," she said. "Why don't you go up front, and I'll run the kitchen for a little bit?"

"I don't have time to see anybody right now," I said. I was churning out pizzas as fast I could and still having trouble keeping up. Our conveyor oven was usually just fine for our needs, but when we were busy, I wished I had another one just like it.

"Make the time," Maddy said as she took the pizza dough out of my hand. "Josh and Greg have the front, and I can do this."

"Who is it?" I asked as I wiped my hands on a dish towel.

"It's David Quinton," Maddy said.

I threw the dish towel down on the countertop. "I don't really feel like talking to him right now."

"Get over it then," Maddy said. I'd heard that tone in her voice before, and I knew that she was serious. "This is important."

"Fine," I said in a bit of a snit as I pulled off my apron. "I'm sure he just came by to dump me."

"I didn't think you two were going out," Maddy said. "So how can he dump you?"

"We're not, so he can't. You know what I mean. He's

leaving town. I'm sure he just came by to tell me in per-son. Frankly, I'd just as soon he wrote me a note."

"Well, he didn't, and he's waiting out front for you."

I shot her a dirty look as I walked past her. All she could manage was a grin in return. Maddy was enjoying my discomfort just a little too much for my taste.

I touched my hair lightly as I walked through the door. David was standing there, waiting patiently for me.

"Hi, David. How are you?"

"I've been better," he said a little curtly.

"What happened? Didn't they want you in Raleigh, after all?" Why was my pulse suddenly starting to race? Could it be that I didn't want him to leave?

"They wanted me, all right, but I told them I had to think about it. You know why, don't you?"

I noticed we were gathering a crowd of watchers, in-cluding my two servers. "Come on, let's find an empty table so we can have a little privacy."

I pulled him to a booth, and then shot a warning look at Josh and Greg. I had no interest in having them come over to wait on us—even as a gag—and they both knew it from the way they scurried away.

"Why haven't you said yes?" I asked.

"I don't want to leave you," he said, open and honest, without any guile or guilt. "I can't stand the thought of not being in your life."

I had to admit that, just for a second, I was tempted. And then I remembered Joe, and the way he'd looked the day before he'd died. "I can't give you any more than I al-ready have," I said.

"I'm not asking you to," he said.

David reached out for my hands, but I pulled them away. "That's exactly what you're doing. You think this is going somewhere, and I'm telling you, it's not. If you can find happiness in Raleigh, you owe it to yourself to go there."

The poor man looked as if he was ready to cry. "Don't you want me at all?"

"Not now, maybe not ever." They were the cruelest words I'd ever spoken to someone in my life, and I hated myself a little for saying them. But I owed David my complete honesty, if I couldn't give anything more.

He looked at me intently for a second, and then smiled softly as he said, "You just said 'maybe.'"

"I wouldn't pin my hopes on that, if I were you. It's probably not ever."

"But there's a chance, no matter how slim it may be right now."

I just didn't seem to be able to get through to him. "Listen, I'm not all that special. You can find someone better than me. I've got faith in you."

"What if I don't want anyone better?"

I had no idea what to say to that. I stood and looked down at him, then said, "David, I can't tell you how to run your life, but I hope you'll give what I said some serious thought. You need to make the best decision you can for yourself."

"Even if it's staying here," he said.

"Or leaving," I said.

"Then I guess I don't really have any choice. I'm going to take the job in Raleigh, Eleanor."

"It's probably for the best. I'm sorry, David."

"So am I." For a second, I thought he was going to kiss me, but after hesitating a second, he left the pizzeria for the final time.

I walked back into the kitchen, knowing that I'd ended any chance David Quinton and I had of ever getting together. More than a little part of me was saddened by the prospect, but I'd done the right thing. I knew that in my heart.

So, why did I feel so empty inside all of a sudden?

I was just about to go back into the kitchen to tell Maddy about my conversation with David when I heard the front door of the pizzeria open.

Kevin Hurley walked in and headed straight for me.

Josh tried to cut him off. "Hey, Dad. What's going on?"

"Not now, son. I need to speak with your boss."

"She's kind of busy right now. Is there anything I can help you with? Would you like a pizza, or maybe a sandwich?"

"Joshua, I don't have time for this. Step out of my way."

"Sure thing," he said as he looked at me and shrugged. I had to give him credit for trying. Most of the people I knew would have hesitated facing down our chief of police like that.

"We need to talk," Kevin said.

"Why is that never a good thing when you say that?" I asked.

"Do you want to do this out here in front of all of your customers, or should we go into the kitchen?"

"Do you really want Maddy as a witness?"

"Good point. Let's go outside."

I followed him out of the restaurant, and as I started toward one of the benches on the promenade, he asked me, "Where are you going?"

"Can't we sit? I've been on my feet all day."

"I guess so," he said as he followed me, albeit reluctantly.

Score one for me.

"What's so important that it couldn't wait until later?" I asked. There were a lot of folks out strolling in the early evening, no doubt enjoying the pleasant weather we were having. I saw a couple kissing in the shadows under a tree, and another pair who were chasing their young toddler in and out of some of the lines of shrubbery. One thing led to another, I thought, and couldn't help but smile.

"What's so amusing?" Kevin asked.

"I don't know. Something just struck my whimsy."

"Well, try to rein it in for a few minutes, could you?"

I wiped the smile away. "What's going on?"

"I thought you were going to stop snooping," he said.

"When did I ever promise that?" I asked.

"Sure, you might not have promised anything, but it was implied."

"I'm not even willing to acknowledge that," I said.

"Eleanor, do you really think I don't know what you've been up to lately? It's bad enough talking to all of my suspects, and even a few I'm not even considering, but talking to Art Young is a whole new level of stupid."

"How did you hear about that?" I hadn't seen a soul around when I'd talked to Art, and yet the chief of police knew about it less than four hours later.

"At least you're not denying it," he said.

"Why should I? There's nothing wrong with me talking to him."

"There you're wrong," Kevin said. "He's a very bad man, and people around him have an unfortunate habit of regretting being a part of his world. You're so far out of your league on this one that you can't even see the playing field."

"So far, I've found him to be a reasonable man," I said, aware inside that Kevin was probably right in his assessment.

"I'm sure everyone does, right up to the point where he sticks his knife into them." His face softened, and he added, "Listen, if you're hurting for money, I have some put away. It's not much, but you're welcome to it."

I couldn't believe it. "Is that what you think? Do you honestly believe I'd be stupid enough to ask Art Young for a loan?"

"Why else would you be talking to him, then?" He frowned, and then asked, "This isn't about Wade Hatcher, is it?"

"What if it is? Art's been very helpful to me."

"Art? You two are on a first-name basis?"

"I'm on a first-name basis with most of this town."

He studied me for another second, then said, "There's something else you're not telling me, isn't there?"

How did he do that? "I'm sure I don't know what you're talking about."

"Eleanor, withholding information from a peace officer is a criminal offense, and you know it."

"I don't know anything for sure, and the last time I checked, you weren't interested in my idle speculations."

He clearly wasn't in the mood for my wisecracks. "What is it? I need to know what you found out."

"I can't say anything just yet," I said. "But I have a feeling someone's going to be talking to you tomorrow."

"If the conversation can happen tomorrow, then it can happen right now," he said. "Come on, I don't have all night."

"I'm sorry, but I gave my word. If that means you have to arrest me, then you should go ahead and do what you have to do." I shot my wrists out at him, but I was hoping with all my heart that he didn't cuff me.

After a full ten seconds, he shook his head. "When are you going to learn that this isn't some kind of game?"

"Trust me, I know how dangerous this is."

"I doubt it," he said as he stood up. "And I hope you never do."

"If you don't hear something by nine A.M. tomorrow, come by the pizzeria and I'll tell you everything myself. I promise."

"I just hope it's not too late by then," he said as he walked away.

That made two of us.

Chapter 15

"Are you sure I should go out with Bob tonight?" Maddy asked me an hour before we were supposed to close for the night. "I don't mind canceling."

"It's late as it is," I said. "I've been trying to get you to go for hours. I'm not sure what you can do at this hour of night."

"Don't worry about that," Maddy said, laughing. "We'll find something. I just hate abandoning you like this."

"Greg and Josh are here to cover the front, and we've slowed down to next to nothing. Honestly, if you stay, too, we'll all be tripping over each other."

"If you're sure," she said.

"Don't make me throw my own sister out of my pizza place," I said.

Greg poked his head into the kitchen. "Maddy, your date's here." He looked her over, and then added, "From what I just saw, you're grossly underdressed."

"What is he wearing, a tuxedo?" she asked.

"No, but it's a couple of steps above that outfit."

Maddy threw a wet kitchen towel at him, and Greg ducked back through the door just in time.

"Your aim isn't as good as it used to be," I said.

"That was just a warning shot." Maddy leaned toward me and hugged me. "Don't do anything stupid tonight, Eleanor."

"I was just about to say the same thing to you," I said.

"Dating is something else altogether. See you tomorrow."

"Bye," I said.

After Maddy was gone, I decided to get a jump on the dishes. We were normally slow late at night, and I often contemplated shutting the pizzeria down an hour earlier than we did at the moment, but after instituting the lunch-dinner break we were now taking, I wasn't convinced that it was that good an idea. I wouldn't have to pay salaries to my employees, but they weren't making that much, anyway. The real reason I'd been considering it was because of the wear and tear it was taking on me. Some days it felt like I spent every waking moment either thinking about pizza or homicide, and I wasn't sure either topic was all that healthy for me as a steady diet.

I had the dishes done in half an hour, and the kitchen was spotless. When I walked out front, I found Josh and Greg playing rummy.

They didn't even try to hide it when I walked in.

"This place is really dead tonight," Greg said.

Josh asked, "Do you need any help in the kitchen? I'm so bored I'll even do the dishes."

I knew that was saying something for him. "Why don't you two go on home? I just have to balance the register, and then I'm right behind you."

Greg shook his head. "No way. We promised Maddy we'd walk you to your car, and that's what we're going to do. There's no chance you're walking down that alley by yourself tonight. If something would happen to you, we'd never be able to forgive ourselves."

"I don't need a pair of nursemaids young enough to be my own nephews," I said.

"Think of us as trained bodyguards, then," Josh said.

I thought about it a moment, and then said, "I'm making an executive decision. Greg, you're going to go move my car to the front of the promenade. While you're doing that, Josh and I are going to sweep up and finish cleaning the front. Then you two are leaving, and as soon as I balance the cash register report, I'm going home myself."

Greg started to protest, but I held up my hand to let him know that I wasn't finished. "Anyone who has a problem with that doesn't have to bother coming in tomorrow. Am I making myself clear?"

"I just have one question," Greg said.

I prepared myself for his challenge. "Go ahead and ask it."

"Where are your car keys?" he asked with a grin.

"I'll get them," I said. I went back into the kitchen and grabbed my purse. Coming back into the dining room, I found that Greg and Josh had already started on the cleanup out there. They'd even flipped the OPEN sign to CLOSED.

"We came up with a better plan," Greg said as the vacuum died. "We're going to clean up while you do the register. Then we'll all leave together."

"Greg, I wasn't kidding," I said, keeping my temper in check. I knew he meant well, but the Slice was mine, and when it boiled down to it, Maddy was nothing more than an employee, just like they were.

Greg looked aggravated, but Josh said quickly, "How about this? Run your report, and if it doesn't balance the first time, we'll go and leave you to it. But if it does, you get an escort to your car."

"I'm not in the mood to make a deal with you two," I said.

"Come on, where's your gambling spirit?" Greg asked.

"I run a pizza place with students and my sister as my only employees. You don't think that takes nerves of steel?"

"You've got a point," Greg said. "Just humor us, okay?"

I was tired of fighting about it. I counted out the cash in the drawer and ran the report on the register as they finished cleaning up. It probably wasn't a bad idea having them walk me to my car, but I wasn't sure how I could accept their offer after making all that fuss before.

Unfortunately, it didn't matter.

We were short fifty dollars—a pretty substantial amount in the general scheme of things—and I wasn't about to leave the Slice until I knew exactly what had happened to the missing money. I trusted my three employees implicitly, but money is money, and I knew I wouldn't be able to get to sleep until I figured out what had happened.

They didn't take the news very well.

"Could Maddy have borrowed it without telling you?" Greg asked.

"No, she always asks me first when she does that," I said.

"We didn't take it," Josh said, just a little more defensively than I would have liked.

"I never said you did," I said. "I'm sure there's a perfectly good explanation for it, but I'm not leaving until I know what it is."

"How about if I put fifty bucks in the till myself?" Josh asked.

"That depends on one thing," I said.

"What's that?"

"Did you take fifty out?"

"You know I didn't," Josh said.

"Then it won't work." I chucked my keys to Greg. "Would you mind moving my car for me, after all? I might be here awhile."

He took them, and then hesitated at the door.

Before he could say a word, I said, "Greg, I mean it. Just do as I ask, okay?"

He finally understood that I was in no mood to mess with. "Yes, ma'am," he said, and then turned to Josh. "Are you coming?"

"No, I'm going to wait right here until you get back," he said.

After Greg was gone, Josh said, "Listen, I know you and my dad have had your share of troubles in the past, but if you need him, you should realize that he'll come running and ask questions later."

"Thanks," I said. "I know that."

"Just don't wait too late to call him," Josh said.

I grinned at him. "I appreciate your concern, but how am I going to know when it's too late, until it already is?"

"That's a good point," he said.

Greg pulled into the closest spot to the Slice, but it was still a fair distance away. It didn't seem that far in the daylight, but at night, it could be intimidating. At least the promenade stayed lit for most of the night.

Greg waved to Josh, and he turned to me before he left.

"Be careful, Eleanor," he said.

"Right back at you," I replied.

He waited until I dead bolted the door; then he gave me a "thumbs up" sign, which I returned.

After they were gone, I turned the radio off and started working on the report. I counted the cash three times, but the number stayed off by the same amount. What happened to that fifty dollars? I was about to call Maddy to ask her—date or no date—when a thought occurred to me. I pulled the till all the way out of the register, but I couldn't see anything in the expanse. I was almost ready to shove it back in when I decided to have a closer look. Taking a flashlight from under the counter in back, I turned it on and peered into the opening.

Something was jammed in the back where the drawer slid in, and after some maneuvering that barked up one of my knuckles, I was able to extract a bit of paper from the opening.

Unfolding the money, I saw that it was a fifty-dollar bill, no doubt the missing culprit that had thrown off my balance for the night.

It felt good knowing that there was a simple explanation for the missing money, but even better that I hadn't jumped to the conclusion that someone had been stealing from me. I would rather have lost a hundred times that amount than think bad of one of my employees, and I was glad my faith in them had been justified.

I filled out the next day's deposit, slid the cash and change into the bag, then deposited it all into my new safe. It felt good knowing that I wouldn't be walking around at night all by myself with money in my hands. The robbery was still too fresh in my mind. I saw the dart gun on the counter, and I thought about returning it to Slick in the morning. It had been a silly impulse purchase, and I already regretted making it. I slid the dart gun and its packaging back into the bag it came in, and tucked the whole thing under my arm. As I walked back out front, I turned all of the lights off as I went.

As I walked to the Subaru in the silent night, I was glad that I'd asked Greg to bring my car around front.

There was no way I wanted to walk by myself in the dark tonight. There was something in the air, something unsettling, and I breathed a sigh of relief when I made it to my car and drove back safely to my house.

I'd barely taken my jacket off when there was a pounding at my front door. I put my keys and the bag from Slick's on the table, and then I wondered who was trying to get my attention so urgently.

Peeking out through a side window, I saw Sandi Meadows standing there beating on the door, begging me to let her in.

A stream of blood was trickling down her face.

"Help me!" Sandi screamed. "Katy's after me, and she's got a knife."

My fingers trembled as I unbolted the door and let Sandi in. She stumbled into my house, and I latched the bolt behind her as quickly as I could.

"Go into the living room," I ordered. "We can call the police from there."

I helped her into the other room, and as I reached for the telephone, Sandi said in a hard voice, "Put that down, Eleanor."

And at that second, I knew. There was something in Sandi's voice that made me doubt everything she'd told me before. I suddenly realized that every shred of evidence I thought I had pointing at Katy had come from Sandi. It had all been just a little too convenient, and with the will she thought she had, and the scene Wade had made with Katy, it gave her a double whammy of a motive for murder.

"I have to call Kevin Hurley," I said without looking at her. I wished I'd thought of retrieving Joe's shotgun, but the key to the gun case was in the other room, and I didn't have any time left.

I felt a nudge on the back of my neck, and I wondered if I was about to die, too. When I'd turned my back, Sandi must have picked up the baseball bat I kept by the door for protection. A bat was always my weapon of choice. At least she didn't have a knife or, worse yet, a gun.

I was beaten, and I knew it. I put the receiver back into its cradle and then slowly turned around as the pressure of the bat eased.

"I can't believe the way you played me," I said hoarsely.

"Don't act so surprised," Sandi said. "It's pretty clear you were onto me, so there's no reason to play dumb now."

"Did you actually cut yourself to convince me to let you inside?" I asked, still having a hard time wrapping my mind around what I now knew had to be the truth. I should have seen it sooner, but she'd fooled me for so long with her act of helpless innocence. Once I got past the fact that she'd been playing me from the start, I could see patterns start to emerge. Why hadn't I realized that I had only Sandi's word that Jamie had seen Katy going into the pizzeria after hours? Sandi had been the one to plead with me not to say anything to anyone else right away. She was buying time, and I'd let her. The motive was clear enough, after the fact. She'd been under the impression that she was Wade's lone beneficiary. The murder was a way to exact her revenge for his dalliance with Katy Johnson, and she managed to make herself rich in the process.

Sandi wiped the crimson smudges away from her forehead with her free hand. "It's novelty blood. I got it at a joke shop. It looks pretty real, doesn't it?"

"Why would you want to hurt me?" I asked. "I'm not a threat to you."

"Sadly, you are. You have to understand my confusion. I told you to let me handle things on my own, but after we talked today, you went to Greg's apartment, talked to Art Young, and then had a long conversation with the police. What was I supposed to think? I had a perfect suicide/confession planned for Katy, and then you had to go and ruin it. I had a hunch you wouldn't leave well enough alone. It was a good thing I followed you today."

"You were watching me the entire day?"

"It wasn't all that hard—you're not exactly the most observant person in the world. You looked right past me when you were talking to Chief Hurley on that bench out in front of your shop. Believe me, it wasn't hard to get Jamie to kiss me, and it made for perfect cover."

I suddenly remembered the couple making out on the promenade, and I was surprised to realize that I hadn't identified two of my suspects. The fact that their faces were both obscured still didn't count for much. I should have been watching a little closer, and seeing them kissing would have sent warning bells sounding in my mind, if I'd only noticed.

Sandi waved the bat toward my head, and I felt a shiver run through me. I hated the thought of being bludgeoned to death like Wade had been. I had a hunch Sandi wouldn't take care of me with just one blow. If I let things run their course, I was going to suffer before I died. Panic was starting to sweep through me, but I had to fight it back if I was going to have any chance to survive. But what could I use as a weapon? Since I didn't have the key on me, the shotgun in its sturdy case was as inaccessible as if it had been back at the Slice.

That's when I remembered the dart gun sitting on the table just a few steps away.

It might as well have been on the moon.

There was no way I could get to it without getting past Sandi first.

Unless I could trick her into letting me over there.

"Okay, I give up," I said. It was time for some serious lying. "I've known all along that it was pretty clear that you've been setting Katy up to take the fall."

"Wrong again," Sandi said with a grin. "I originally planned to use Greg, but when he got out of jail so quickly, I decided to make Jamie the killer. Then Katy started acting like an idiot, and I realized that it was time to improvise. I didn't give up on Jamie, though, in case Katy managed to beat the rap, so I've been busy working up solid motives for each of them."

"When did you plan to kill Wade, and why did you do it at my pizzeria?"

Sandi frowned at me. "Why should I tell you anything?"

"Wouldn't it feel good for someone to know how brilliant you've been in manipulating events? It's not like I'm going to be around to tell anyone."

"You've got a point. Dear old Wade decided to cheat on me, and he honestly thought he could get away with it. Come on, with Katy Johnson? Honestly? He had to be kidding. The fool didn't think I'd find out, but when I did, he came crawling back to me on his hands and knees. He begged me to forgive him, but I had that image of him kissing Katy burned into my brain. How could I forgive him—let alone forget what I'd seen? He had to pay for what he did."

Then, much to my surprise, she started laughing.

"What's so funny?" I asked.

"He paid in more ways than one, didn't he? The idiot confessed to me that he loved me so much he'd named me in his will so I'd get everything if anything happened to him. Can you believe that? I didn't even know it until the day before I killed him. He thought it was a grand romantic gesture, but it wasn't going to wipe out that memory. Without realizing it, Wade sealed his own fate by telling me that. He didn't have much money before, but when he finally settled his grandparents' estate with Greg, Wade was suddenly worth a lot more to me dead than he'd ever been alive. He signed the settlement, and I witnessed it. I've been waiting for somebody to get arrested for his murder before I filed the paperwork. What a fool Wade turned out to be."

"Why kill him at the Slice, though?" I asked as I started slowly moving toward that table where the dart gun was resting. Sandi didn't seem to notice it; she was so caught up in bragging to me about how smart she'd been.

"Greg was always my first choice to frame for the murder, so what better place could I have picked? His apartment was too hard—I could have never gotten Wade to meet me there. But your pizza place was perfect. Wade would have done anything to put something over on his brother."

"How'd you even get the key to the place? It was locked when you got there, wasn't it?"

"There are more keys to this place floating around than you know. Wade stole one from your office when he was there fighting with Greg about the will while you were on one of your lunch breaks, and you didn't even know it. He bragged to me that he could come and go as he pleased, and no one would know."

"So you got a pizza from one of my competitors and used it to lure Wade there."

She nodded, clearly pleased with my deduction. "I was wondering if anyone would catch that. I had to get Wade to the pizza place if I was going to implicate Greg, and what better way to do that than to offer him a romantic dinner so we could make up? He thought it was bold and daring, which made me that much more attractive to him. I ordered the pizza, and then I got rid of the box before I went into the Slice. Everything would have been perfect, if you hadn't kept butting in. You were eliminating my frame-ups as fast as I made them."

"You had to know I wouldn't stand by and let Greg go down for it."

"Why not? He's just an employee, Eleanor."

"That's where you're wrong. He's family."

If I survived this, I was going to have to change the lock to the pizzeria's door, but at the moment, that seemed like a very small problem that was very far away.

I was two steps from the table where the dart gun was hidden when Sandi said, "What do you think you're doing?"

"I feel like I'm going to pass out," I said as I pretended to feel dizzy. "I need to lean against the wall."

"Don't worry, Eleanor, you're not going to have that problem for very long," Sandi said with a smile as she lovingly stroked the bat. "I just love a blunt weapon, and the fact that it's yours will prove that the little break-in I'm about to stage wasn't premeditated."

"You don't have to do this—you know that, don't you?"

"If you're waiting for reinforcements, you're just wasting your time. No one knows we're here. By the time anyone finds you, I'll have a new alibi all ready for the police."

She was probably right, but as long as I could keep her

talking, I still had a chance. "Did you put Wade up to the robbery, too?"

Sandi laughed. "Please don't give me that much credit. He must have come up with that one on his own. I wouldn't be surprised if Greg told him about the late-night deposits one time, and Wade realized it would be an easy way to come up with some fast money. He was a fool to borrow from Art Young."

"Why did he? From everything I've heard about Wade, he wasn't stupid."

"Don't count on it," she said. "First he stole from his boss and some of their clients, and when he borrowed money from Art, he had to have a way to pay it back. I still can't believe he had the guts to rob you."

"But why did he need so much money in the first place?"

Sandy looked pleased with herself as she answered, "Can I help it if I have expensive tastes? I warned him when we started dating that it wouldn't be cheap keeping me happy, but he didn't believe me."

"So he'd commit armed robbery just to keep you happy?"

"He would have done anything for me," Sandi said. "He was willing to walk through fire, if I asked him to." She shook her head. "Wade never suspected a thing. The second we walked into the kitchen, he turned his back to me and I hit him with the rolling pin. It was amazing how fast he went down."

Was that a smile on her face as she described the murder? She'd actually enjoyed killing him! I liked my chances of surviving the confrontation less and less.

"I'm getting tired of this, Eleanor. Don't worry, it won't hurt much. At least not for very long."

Sandi started to move toward me with the bat—swinging it back and forth like she was going for the fences—but I wasn't close enough to the dart gun to grab it yet.

"Did you ever love him?" I asked.

She shrugged. "I'm not even sure love's real. When Wade wouldn't settle his grandparents' estate with Greg, I told him he needed to come up with some other way to buy me something nice if he expected me to stick around. I was getting bored with him, and the only reason I stayed was because I kept hoping that he'd settle the estate with Greg, and I'd get that money for myself."

"How many people have you hurt along the way? How many times have you lied?"

"That's not very smart, Eleanor, making the girl with the baseball bat angry."

She started toward me, so I pretended to cower, not that it took that much acting. "I'm just trying to understand," I whimpered, edging closer and closer to the hidden gun.

"Pay attention, then. I planned to get my hands on that money, one way or another." She grinned as she added, "He laughed when he told me about robbing you. Wade said it was amazing how fast you handed over your money when he held that gun on you. You're nothing but a coward, aren't you?"

Sandi looked around the room, and then said, "There's not much of value here, is there? If I'm going to make this look like a robbery, I'll need to grab some goodies along the way."

"I have money in the kitchen," I said. I had, too, at one time before Greg had depleted it. Still, if I could distract her long enough, I might be able to get back to that dart gun.

"It's back here," I said, leading her toward the kitchen.

I thought about lunging for the gun as I walked near it, but Sandi was closer. I was going to have to wait.

I reached for the cookie jar and realized there were just a few singles I'd recently added to it. I had to make sure Sandi didn't know that. Doing my best acting, I glanced furtively over my shoulder as I looked inside it, and I could almost feel her hot breath on my neck.

"What else do you have in there?" she asked with sudden suspicion.

"Just the money," I said, trying to make my voice sound like I was lying.

"There's a gun in there, too, isn't there?"

"No," I said, letting my voice crack.

"Get out of my way," she said as she shoved me aside.

As Sandi reached into the jar, her eyes were off me for just a second. It was all that I needed.

I raced for the dart gun, pulled it out of the bag, and then turned to face her with it. She was faster than I had expected. Sandi was just a few steps behind me when I got to it.

"Drop the baseball bat," I ordered.

Instead of doing what I'd commanded, Sandi slowly stared at me. The frown on her face was quickly replaced with a smile when she looked closer at the gun in my hand.

"Eleanor, that's just a toy," she said. "But that was a nice try."

"It shoots, trust me," I said. Maddy had been playing with it earlier. Was it even loaded? I'd been counting on using it to bluff her, but now it appeared that option wasn't going to work.

"I don't believe you," she said.

As Sandi moved toward me, I pulled the trigger, not sure what would happen. A dart fired from the gun, and struck her arm. I'd been aiming for her heart, but it was close enough.

Or so I'd hoped.

She howled for a second as she reached down and plucked the dart out, threw it on the floor, and then hissed at me, "You'll pay for that."

Sandi suddenly lunged at me with the bat.

As she did, I threw the gun at her head. It didn't hit her straight on, but the force of the strike was enough to stun her.

I should have grabbed the bat, but I turned toward the front door, instead, and started fighting the dead bolt as she screamed in frustration and anger behind me.

It was no use. I wasn't going to be able to open the door. I heard her take a deep breath and felt her presence too close to me. At the last possible moment, I jumped to one side, afraid that my reactions were a little too late.

I made it, though, just barely. The baseball bat crashed against the front door on the exact spot where my head had been a second before.

As I glanced into Sandi's eyes for a split second as I whirled around, I saw madness there.

The time for talking was over.

I raced into the kitchen, tearing open the drawer where I kept my knives. I might go down, but it wasn't going to be without a fight. I was spinning around when I saw her. She swung the bat down toward my arm, and if she'd made contact, I was sure she would have shattered the bones in it.

I pulled out of her way, but I didn't get off completely. The bat struck the knife in my hand, sending it sliding across the kitchen floor.

Before she could react, I took my precious Garfield cookie jar and threw it at her. It shattered as it hit her forehead, and for a second, I thought I'd succeeded in knocking her out.

All it managed to do was make her even angrier than she'd been before. There was real blood dripping down her forehead now, and she swiped it away with the back of her forearm. If I could manage to interfere with her vision, I might just make it out of this alive.

The blood flow seemed to energize her, instead of weakening her. Sandi took a full swing at me, and I tried to get out of its path again, but this time it caught me in the ribs. It was a glancing blow, but it still nearly put me on the floor. I'd deflected most of it, but I still might have broken some ribs from the attack.

She pulled the bat back over her head one more time, and then snarled at me.

"Get ready to die."

I might be murdered in the next five seconds, but I wasn't going to go down without one last fight.

I lunged toward her and somehow managed to get my hands on the bat before she could bring it down on my head for the killing blow. Sandi fought me, but all those hours kneading pizza dough by hand paid off. As we struggled for control, we lost our balance and fell onto the kitchen floor.

I'd like to think that I was winning when we both heard a tapping on the back window of the kitchen, where Greg had come and gone a few days before.

Instead of Greg, though, Kevin Hurley was standing there, his gun leveled straight at Sandi's heart, and she seemed to lose the last bit of fight in her.

After Sandi Meadows was handcuffed and led away by another police officer, Kevin asked me, "Are you okay?"

"I'm still a little shaky," I admitted, "and my ribs are

killing me, but besides that, I'm fine. I've got to admit, though, I'm glad you showed up when you did."

"Josh called me. He started worrying about leaving you alone tonight, so I promised him I'd check in on you. It looked like you had things under control, though." He frowned slightly, and then added, "I had Sandi on my list of suspects, but between the two of us, she wasn't that high up."

"Don't beat yourself up about it," I said. "She had everybody fooled." I'd explained her raving rationales to him, and he shook his head at the grand scale of her delusions.

Josh and Greg came bursting into my house a few seconds later.

"What happened? Did Katy try to hurt you?" Greg asked.

"No, it was Sandi all along," I said. "How did you two hear about it?"

Josh looked sheepish as he admitted to his father, "We were listening to your scanner in the basement, Dad."

Kevin nodded. "I'd say it's too little, too late, wouldn't you? You boys should never have left her alone tonight."

"Don't be too hard on them," I said. "I made them go."

"Dad's right," Josh said. "We shouldn't have listened to you."

Kevin actually smiled at that. "If either one of you could do that, you'd be a better man than I am."

Maddy and Bob Lemon were next as Kevin and I finished our interview. The adrenaline had worn off, leaving behind a throbbing in my ribs and my head that I couldn't stop.

My sister tried to hug me as soon as she walked in, but I pulled away. "Sorry. She whacked me pretty hard in the ribs with my baseball bat."

"Eleanor, I'm so sorry I wasn't here for you when you needed me."

"Hey, Maddy, none of this was your fault. Sandi just snapped. She was pretty smart, though. Somehow she'd managed to give motives to everybody but herself. That girl was playing us all along. When we came to Greg's defense, she started laying the groundwork for accusing everyone else who'd made it to our suspect list."

Bob said, "I should have realized it was about the money. It usually is."

Kevin nodded in assent, but I disagreed, "Don't kid yourself. It wasn't just about the money. Wade put things in motion himself when he set up that kiss with Katy so Greg could see it. He wanted to hurt you after you pushed him into signing off on the agreement. Sandi witnessed it, and she told me that she was just waiting to file the papers until after the murder investigation died down."

"But why bring Katy into it in the first place?"

"I don't know, but if I had to guess, I'd say that it was his way of getting back at you for not giving in to him, and it ended up killing him."

"What a mess," Greg said. "At least Mom will be happy. Her favorite son's killer will be going to jail, and my mother is getting Wade's money, too."

Bob shook his head. "That's not true. She won't see a dime of it."

"Why not?" Greg asked. "He signed the papers, and then he had it witnessed, even if it was Sandi. The money's not rightfully mine."

"That's where you're wrong. I thought you knew. You and your brother had to each live thirty days after the agreement was filed for it to go into effect. It was a clause that might have saved your brother's life, if he'd only told Sandi about it."

I shook my head. "It didn't change anything, not really. She would have waited. I never could have imagined what a cold-blooded killer she'd turn out to be."

Josh asked, "So, who gets the money now?"

"That's not a question you have any right asking," Kevin told his son.

"It's all right," Greg said. "It doesn't really matter, does it?"

Bob put a hand on his shoulder. "Actually, it does. The papers weren't filed yet, so as things stand, you inherit everything."

"That somehow doesn't seem fair, does it?" Greg asked.

"Would you rather that your mother get half of it? If you want her to have your brother's share, you're perfectly within your rights to give it to her."

"I wouldn't make any hasty decisions just yet," Maddy said.

"Don't worry, I'm not going to." To Greg's credit, he seemed more interested in why his brother had died than who had inherited his money, something I wasn't sure I'd be able to say about his mother.

Maddy looked at Kevin and asked, "Chief, is this a crime scene, or can we put on a pot of coffee?"

Kevin frowned. "Sorry. There's evidence of an assault here, so I'm going to need my crew to get photos and video of the scene. You're going to have to stay somewhere else tonight, Eleanor."

"She can stay with me," Maddy said. "Why don't you all come back with us to my place? We can put on some coffee and make a party of it."

"I've got a better idea," I said. "I've got some leftover dough back at the pizzeria. Does anyone want a pizza?"

Kevin said, "Eleanor, have you lost your mind? You almost died tonight, and you're talking about making pizza? You should go to the hospital for X-rays."

"I might a little later, but right now, I feel like having pizza."

He shook his head. "I don't understand you, woman."

"It's a good thing that's not your job, then, isn't it? You're more than welcome to join us."

"Thanks, but I've got to start processing the scene after I lock Sandi up. You all go ahead, though."

After Kevin drove off with his prisoner, the rest of us headed back to the Slice.

As soon as we walked in the door, Josh said, "I'll turn on the music."

"I'll get the tables ready," Greg chimed in.

Bob, Maddy, and I moved into the kitchen. As I got out some chilled dough left over from the day's pizza making, I winced from the pain in my ribs.

Maddy took the dough from me and said, "Sis, your job is to sit on that bar stool and watch me work. If you give me any lip, you're going to the hospital for those X-rays, and you're going to miss your own party."

"Don't worry. I'm not in any position to fight you on it."

As Maddy worked the dough into pans, Bob said, "I'm glad you're okay, Eleanor."

"Me too," I said. "I'm just sorry I ruined your date."

"Don't worry," Bob said. "There will be other opportunities for us."

Maddy looked at him and said, "You sound awfully sure of yourself."

"That's because I am," he said. Before Maddy knew what he was doing, Bob took her into his arms and kissed her soundly.

He was smiling as they broke it up. "Now, if you'll excuse me, I'm afraid I need to head home. I've got a big day in court tomorrow. Good night, ladies."

After he left, Maddy was still smiling.

"What was that all about?" I asked.

"I'm not sure, but I think I like it."

She looked at the dough she'd formed into the pan, then said, "Now, what should we put on these? I think tonight calls for a kitchen-sink pizza, what do you say?"

"Agreed. Everything we can find goes on it," I said as I leaned over and turned on the conveyor oven.

"I can't believe I wasn't there for you," Maddy said softly as we waited for it to warm up.

"You're with me now. That's all that counts."

She was in one of her rare serious moods, something I could understand, given what had happened tonight. "I don't know what I'd do without you, Eleanor."

"Let's just hope and pray you don't have to find out anytime soon," I said.

"I'm being serious," Maddy insisted.

"So am I."

The kitchen door opened, and Greg asked, "When's the pizza going to be ready? We're starving."

"It won't be long," I said.

"Excellent. While we're waiting, Josh and I will be out front playing cards."

"We'll bring it out as soon as it's ready," I promised.

With nothing to do but wait, I had a little time to think. That's when I started to realize just how close I'd come to dying tonight. No doubt, most folks would think I was crazy for coming back to the pizzeria after what had happened.

But for me, I needed this more than anything, good memories to wipe out the bad ones. The people and things I loved in the world were gathered in that kitchen, and a part of me wanted the night to last forever. I knew I'd have to have those X-rays sooner rather than later, but right here and right now, there was nowhere else I'd rather be.

While we waited for the pizza, Maddy asked, "Is there any chance David would come by to join us?"

I suddenly realized that I hadn't told her about my earlier conversation with David. "Trust me, that's not going to happen."

"What did you say to him, Eleanor?"

It was time to come clean with her. "We had a long talk. He's taking the job in Raleigh."

I wasn't sure what I expected from Maddy, but I was still surprised when she just nodded.

"No lectures on my behavior?" I asked.

"Not tonight. I know I was pushing him on you. I just want you to be happy."

I hugged her, despite the pain in my head, my ribs, and my hand. "Having you here is all I need."

After a moment, she pulled away, and a sudden smile sprang to her lips. "I don't know about that. I can think of something else that might bring you a little joy."

"No more fix-ups," I said.

"This is something completely different."

"Then I'm listening."

"We still need to even the score with Clara Hatcher, and I've got a few great ideas. Are you game?"

I loved seeing the laughter in my sister's eyes. "That depends. Are they like some of the childish pranks you come up with now and then?"

"Oh, yes."

I didn't even hesitate as I replied, "Then count me in."

MY THIN-CRUST PIZZA CRUST RECIPE

When my family is in the mood for something different, I like to make mini-pizzas with thin crusts. You can make regular-sized pizzas with this recipe, but sometimes it's fun to shake things up. I've used my pizza stone in the oven to make these at times, but with thin crusts, I believe you can honestly taste a difference between pizzas made in your conventional oven, and ones made in my small portable brick pizza oven. It was an investment buying one—and I made quite a few pizzas before I bought mine—but I figure I've saved its cost many times over making my own pizzas at home. I do feel that a pizza stone is needed at the very least, and these produce very good crusts, both thick and thin.

This pizza has a light and flaky crust, that my family thinks beats all of the chains.

This recipe yields four 4" mini-pizzas, two 7-inch small pizzas, or one 14-inch pizza. Keep toppings to a minimum, or the crust won't get as crispy as you might like it to be.

1 cup warm water
packet active dry yeast (around $\frac{1}{8}$ ounce)
$1\frac{1}{2}$ teaspoons white sugar
$\frac{1}{2}$ teaspoon salt
3 tablespoons extra virgin olive oil
3 cups bread flour (for its high gluten content)

Preparation

In a large mixing bowl, combine the warm water, yeast, sugar, olive oil, and salt all at once, mixing until the yeast dissolves. Start adding the flour to the wet mixture in the bowl, ½ cup at a time, stirring as you go. I personally like to use a wooden spoon for this process. After the dough is thoroughly mixed, knead it on a floured counter for another few minutes, or until the dough is elastic to the touch. If you're making mini-pizzas, divide the dough into four equal parts and roll them into balls. Let everything sit ten minutes, and while you're waiting, turn your oven (brick or conventional) on to preheat, with the stone in place so it will be nice and hot when you bake your pizza.

While you're waiting, it's a good time to make your sauce. For a good and quick recipe, try my basic thin sauce that follows. Since it doesn't have to heat on the stovetop, you have plenty of time.

After the dough has rested for ten minutes, it's ready to use immediately. Shape each ball with a floured rolling pin, until you have a round piece of dough approximately the size you need. I like mine to be thin, around ⅛ inch thick. Add your sauce, any toppings you'd like (though I do it sparingly), and a blend of cheese. My favorite mix is 3 parts mozzarella to one part provolone. I like to cover the dough thoroughly, but it's really just a matter of taste.

Bake the pizzas at 425°F for 11–17 minutes, or until the crust is starting to turn a dark gold on the edges and the cheese is bronzed on the top. It's probably not necessary, but I like to turn the pizza a time or two as it bakes, starting about 8 minutes into the process.

When it's ready to come out, the crust will be darkened somewhat on the bottom, and still be flexible enough to check it by lifting one edge up with a peel or spatula rated for high temperatures. Enjoy!

My Basic Thin Pizza Sauce

This sauce is quick and easy, but it doesn't lose anything in taste. I like to use it with my thin-crust pizza, but you can use it just as easily on a thick crust. A little goes a long way, so you'll probably have some left over. I keep it refrigerated for a few days, but it never has time to go bad, since crusts are so easy to make.

15 ounces tomato sauce (I like Contadina brand with Italian herbs, but any sauce will do)
1½ tablespoons extra virgin olive oil
1 teaspoon Italian seasoning (it needs oregano, basil, and rosemary, but can have marjoram, thyme, and sage as well)

Preparation

In a large mixing bowl, combine the ingredients until they are well mixed, and there you go! Premade pizza sauce works fine, too, but I like to add my own special touch to my sauce, and I like the way this blend tastes.

I don't heat this mix, and use it straight out of the bowl.

With thin crusts, I use the sauce sparingly, since a little seems to go a long way for my family. Like everything else, though, it's all a matter of personal taste.

Though it's an unseasonably chilly October in Timber Ridge, North Carolina, Eleanor Swift is warm and cozy in A Slice of Delight—her scrumptious pizzeria. But when snooty Judson Sizemore breezes into town to open an upper-crust pizza parlor nearby, Eleanor's biggest worry is that her beloved restaurant's days may be numbered . . . until she hears Judson's days have come to a most gruesome end . . .

Since half the town saw Judson causing a ruckus in A Slice of Delight before he expired, Eleanor and her saucy sister, Maddie, are the prime suspects. The only way out is to prove their innocence. Soon, a little surreptitious sleuthing reveals that the dough behind Judson's impending pizzeria came from Timber Ridge's resident recluse: crusty oddball millionaire Nathan Pane. It turns out he's Judson's long-lost uncle . . . and someone is after him, too.

As Eleanor digs deeper, her suspect list grows longer than the local soccer team's pizza order—and life in the once quiet town heats up like Maddie's five-alarm Volcano pie. Could it be Judson's gold-digging sister? Or her secret boyfriend? Between working on the case, keeping her customers happy, and even finding time for an old flame, Eleanor's plate is full. But with an unhinged murderer closing in, she'll have to move very quickly—and very carefully—because the killer is already *much* closer than she thinks . . .

**Please turn the page for an exciting sneak peek of
A PIZZA TO DIE FOR
coming next month!**

Chapter 1

The pizzeria was dark, and nothing moved among the scattered tables and chairs in the dining room or the counters and work areas in the kitchen. There was just a whisper of light filtering in through the windows in front, but back near the oven, most of the light had already dissipated into darkness.

At first, it was hard to make out the identity of the body lying on the floor, but after a closer look, it was clear to see the one thing that would shake the very core of the citizenry of Timber Ridge, North Carolina.

There on the floor was the pizzeria owner, and a status of dead or alive was too difficult to determine at that moment.

I knew it was bad news the second I heard there was going to be another pizzeria opening in direct competition with mine in our sleepy little town of Timber Ridge, North Carolina, but I never thought it would lead to murder. It was alarming enough that someone was going to try to steal my customers, but opening another pizzeria on the promenade a thousand feet from A Slice of Delight was just too much.

There was going to be trouble; I was certain of it.

I just didn't realize how much when I first heard the news.

"It's freezing out there," my sister, Maddy, said as she walked into A Slice of Delight before we opened one morning toward the end of October. "What happened to the concept that we're living in the South where it's supposed to·be warm?" Maddy was tall, thin, and lovely, and whenever we stood side by side, I felt every extra pound I carried on my shorter frame. "I didn't think it was supposed to get this cold until January."

"You know our weather," I said as I continued kneading the dough I'd been working on. "It can change in an instant this time of year. It could just as easily be in the seventies and sunny tomorrow."

"Then again, it could be snowing," she said as she rubbed her hands together.

"Aren't you going to take your coat off and stay awhile? It's going to be tough to prep the veggies if you're bundled up like that."

"You turn up the thermostat and I'll take off my jacket."

I walked over and raised it one degree, but I really couldn't afford to heat the entire place when it was just the two of us, and Maddy knew it. Our operation was marginal, and we both knew it. We could stand one bad month, but two in a row could shut us down for good, and I wasn't about to give up my pizzeria without a fight. My late husband, Joe, and I had worked too hard establishing the place for me to give up on it.

My sister acknowledged my gesture by finally slipping off her coat. As she did, Maddy said, "Eleanor, I still wish that you and Joe had bought one of those wood-fired ovens instead of the conveyor system we've got. It would be nice to be able to warm ourselves up by the fire."

I laughed. "If you're that cold, go ahead and turn on that space heater in the corner. Sorry, but it's just going to have to do. Joe and I looked at wood-fired ovens when we first opened this place, but we couldn't afford the initial investment, let alone the hassle of collecting wood, keeping the fire going, and hauling off the ashes. Besides, you have to admit that it's a lot easier to make a pizza, put it on the conveyor, and then just wait for it to come out the other side. With a wood-fired oven, we'd have to be checking every pizza and sandwich constantly, and I know for a fact that you don't have the attention span that would require."

She smiled. "That may be true, but you've got to admit that I have other attributes."

"Too many to name," I agreed. "I hate to burst your bubble, but I heard on the radio that we might get a hint of snow flurries this weekend."

"Whatever happened to this global warming that everyone was making such a fuss about?" she said as she washed her hands and started prepping the vegetables and meats for our pizzas and subs.

I loved the morning hours before we opened. It was the only time of day that Maddy and I had a chance to work together and chat, and as much as I objected sometimes to her subject matter, it was great having her close. My sister had been a real sport, moving back to town when my husband died to help me out in my darkest hour. It just so happened she'd been between husbands at the time, but I had a feeling that she would have found a way to come back anyway. Having her at the pizzeria made all the difference to me.

"Come on, you remember how much we both loved snow when we were kids," I said, trying to lighten the mood as I formed the dough into balls and stored them in the refrigerator until they were needed later in the day.

"I was quite a bit younger then," she said.

"Hey, so was I," I protested with a grin. "If you get to be younger, Sis, then I do, too."

Maddy studied me for a few moments, and then she said, "What's gotten into you today, Eleanor? You're awfully chipper for it being first thing in the morning."

"Halloween is next week," I said. "How can I not be excited about that? You know it's my favorite time of year."

She laughed. "You used to come up with some unique costumes, I'll give you that. Remember the ghoul-friend outfit you wore in high school?"

At the time, I'd been dating the guy who would become our current sheriff, and I wasn't certain I liked any reminders of the time we'd been a couple. Kevin Hurley had been handsome, a smooth talker, and younger than me. Against my better judgment, I'd gone out with him for quite a while until I'd caught him cheating on me with the girl who was now his wife. The Halloween we'd been together, he'd refused to dress up, so I'd donned zombie makeup and then created a sign with an arrow pointing to the left. Instead of it saying, I'M WITH STUPID, it proudly stated, HIS GHOUL-FRIEND. Kevin hadn't been all that amused, but I'd refused to take the sign off until Halloween was over.

"Those days are long gone," I said.

"Thank goodness for that." Maddy paused, and then asked me, "Did you hear that?"

"Hear what?"

"Someone's pounding on the front door."

"They can just wait until we open," I said. We'd been working hard prepping the place, and we were close to our opening time. I didn't realize how close until I glanced at the clock and added, "They just have to wait ten minutes. It won't kill them to stand out in the cold that long."

"It's your place," Maddy said. "I know how you hate not answering a door or a ringing telephone."

At that moment, my cell phone rang.

"How did you do that?" I asked my sister as I reached for my telephone.

"I'm just that good," she said with a sly smile.

"Hello?" I asked, after I'd quickly washed my hands and then dried them on one of our towels.

"Eleanor, have you both gone deaf? Would one of you mind coming up here and opening the front door and let me inside? It's freezing out here."

"Greg? What are you doing here? You're early." Greg Hatcher was our delivery guy and inside waiter, a student at the nearby college, and one of the best employees I'd ever had. Though he'd recently come into a substantial amount of money, I'd been relieved to learn that he had no intention of quitting his job at the pizzeria. It appeared that he enjoyed being with us as much as we loved having him around.

"Let me in where it's warm, and then I'll explain."

I was about to ask him more when he hung up on me.

"Wow, Greg's less of a fan of the cold weather than you are," I told Maddy.

"At least some of us around here have some common sense," she answered.

I shook my head. "It's October. I'm not sure what you

both expect, but I for one like changing leaves, brisk weather, and snuggling up by a fire."

As I walked out front, Maddy asked, "I thought he wasn't supposed to be due for another half-hour?"

"He's not, but evidently he's got something to tell us."

Greg came in stamping his feet and rubbing a hand through his always-short haircut as though he was trying to warm up his scalp. He was built like a linebacker, solid and strong, but underneath that exterior was a young man who had a good heart, a deep soul, and a real desire to make the world a better place. I would never have admitted it out loud, but of all the high school and college employees I'd had over the years, Greg was my favorite. Josh Hurley, the police chief's son and the remainder of my current staff, was a close second, and I dreaded the thought of my favorite team breaking up someday, as they always did, sooner or later.

"What's so urgent?" I asked him out front as he took off his jacket.

"I found out what's going in The Shady Lady's place," he said as he rubbed his hands together. I didn't like it, but I had to admit that it was a fact of life that businesses on the promenade had a way of coming and going. I loved where A Slice of Delight was located, nestled in a blue building among a series of shops that were lined up in a nearly continuous block of storefronts, with a large brick promenade out front that made it easy to stroll around from place to place. I'd seen pictures of the location from the turn of the century, and it was decidedly strange to see a dirt street out front instead of those weathered bricks.

The Shady Lady's demise didn't surprise me. How on earth Myra Clark had stayed afloat selling just lamps, shades, and accessories had been a constant source of amazement to me. Since she'd closed her doors a month ago, the windows had been soaped over, and despite the buzz of activity around the place and the proclivity of townsfolk to dig out the most carefully guarded secrets, no one had an inkling about what was going in.

Apparently until now, at any rate.

"What's it going to be, another clothing store?" Maddy asked.

He shook his head. "Trust me, you could both take a thousand guesses, and you'd never get it."

"It's not going to be another restaurant, is it?" I asked.

"How could you possibly guess that?" Greg wanted to know. "I thought I was the only one who knew."

"I don't know anything," I said. "I was just guessing. Then it's true?"

"I'm afraid so," he said.

I shrugged. "I've got to admit that I'm not happy about having competition so close to the Slice, but we'll be okay. We've got a loyal fan base who love our pizza. They won't desert us." I wasn't sure I meant it, though. There were months where we barely squeaked by as it was. With another restaurant so close, it would make my life harder than I liked.

"I'm not so sure," Greg said as he handed me a flyer. "That's not the worst part of it."

What I saw printed there was enough to make my stomach drop.

Announcing Our Grand Opening This Saturday at noon! ITALIA'S offers a wood-fired oven and a professional pizza maker who will spin your crust into the air as you watch amazed! Come by for the show, and for a sample of what real pizza should taste like! We'll have free food, drinks, and prizes, so don't miss it!

"We're dead," Maddy said as she read over my shoulder.

"Not yet," I said. "Grab your coat."

My instruction surprised her. "Where are we going? We're supposed to open in ten minutes, Eleanor."

"Sorry to disappoint anyone who's in the mood for a slice, but this can't wait. We need to see just what we're going to be up against."

No one answered the door when I knocked at Italia's, which shouldn't have come as a great surprise to me, since the sign still wasn't up, and the windows were soaped over, not letting even a speck of light through.

As he jammed his hands into his pockets, Greg said, "We're wasting our time, Eleanor. It's pretty clear that no one's here."

"Come on, we can't give up that easily," I said. "They have to be taking deliveries in back if they're going to open so soon. Let's go check it out."

Though her legs were longer than mine, Maddy had trouble keeping up with me as I raced around the promenade. "Sis, I don't think I've ever seen you this fired up," she said.

"No one's threatened my way of life before," I said. "You know what they say. This isn't personal. It's business."

The three of us went around back, passing the pharmacy and the bank along the way, and I was surprised to find the back door of the new pizzeria standing wide open. I knocked on the steel frame, but again, no one answered.

I started to go in when Maddy grabbed my arm. "Hang on a second, Eleanor."

"Why should I? It's not like I'm going to tear the place

up or threaten anyone. I'm just going to offer a friendly welcome to our new neighbors."

"Is that all?"

"Of course not," Greg said as he brushed past us both. "She's going to mop up in there. Let's go. I'll lead the way."

Greg was being entirely too enthusiastic, so I put a hand on his shoulder. "I appreciate the gesture, but this is my battle, remember? I'm going in first, and I'll do the talking."

"Do you honestly see that happening in your wildest dreams, Eleanor?" Maddy asked.

"If you don't, then you both need to stay out here while I deal with it myself," I answered. From the tone of my voice and the expression on my face, they both knew I wasn't kidding.

"Fine," Maddy said, "but don't think for a moment that you're going to keep us standing out here while you go in and have all the fun by yourself."

"Do you agree to those terms, too, Greg?" I asked.

"You bet," he said with a grin. "It's going to be fun sitting back and watching you work. Let's go."

We walked inside the back room, and I had to admit that though I'd meant every word I'd said, I still felt better having Maddy and Greg with me.

At first I thought no one was there, but then a man wearing blue jeans and a flannel shirt came out of the front with a small bucket in one hand.

He looked startled to see us there. "Can I help you?"

"Do you own this place?" I asked, trying to keep my voice calm, though I wasn't nearly so tranquil on the inside.

He grinned at me. "No, ma'am. I'm the mason. I had

to come by and put a few finishing touches on the pizza oven's façade before the grand opening. If you haven't seen it yet, you should sneak a peek. It's a work of art, if I say so myself."

"Is the owner around?" I asked.

"He just stepped out," the mason said. "Excuse me, but I've got a window of opportunity here before the grout hardens, and it's closing fast. If I don't get to it, I'm going to have some nasty chisel work ahead of me."

After he was gone, Maddy asked, "Now what do we do? We're not going to just leave, are we?"

I looked at my watch, and saw that time was running out. I wasn't exactly sure how long the owner of Italia's would be before he showed up, and I couldn't wait around all day. We might just have to come back on our lunch break, but I wasn't all that pleased about doing it that way. I was ready and primed, spoiling for a fight, and I was afraid if I waited, I'd lose some of my fire. On the other hand, I couldn't afford to alienate any of my customers by opening the Slice late, especially with this place opening up so soon.

I was about to tell my sister that we were going to have to go back to the Slice when a tall, elegantly dressed man came in.

He took one look at us and sneered as he asked, "Are you the wait staff? I told the agency that you need to dress up for the interviews." He took in our apparel once more, and before I could say anything, he added, "It doesn't really matter. I'm not sure you're what we're looking for, but thank you for stopping by."

"I'm not here for a job interview," I said, the blood beginning to roar in my ears. "I own A Slice of Delight."

The man frowned as he shook his head. "Then you shouldn't be back here in my kitchen. So sorry, but you'll have to wait for our grand opening celebration before you can come spying on me."

"We weren't spying," Maddy said, despite my warning. Oh, well. It wasn't as though I actually expected her to abide by her agreement to remain silent. I knew in my heart that it was just too much to ask of her.

"Funny, that's what it looked like to me." The pizzeria owner walked us toward the back door, and Greg looked at me questioningly before he allowed himself to be moved. With Greg's size and strength, I would have loved to see the man try to physically remove him, but that wasn't the way I wanted to fight this battle.

I wanted to make one try at being nice, even though I felt little goodwill toward the man. I put out a hand and tried to give my best smile. "It appears that we got off on the wrong foot. I'm Eleanor Swift."

He looked distastefully at my extended hand, then he refused to take it. "I'm Judson Sizemore," he said. "Pleased, I'm sure."

"Not as much as you might think," Greg said, nearly growling out his words.

I had to handle this fast, before things got ugly. "What made you decide to open a restaurant in Timber Ridge?" I asked.

"Do you even have to ask? It was clear that this town was in desperate need of some authentic cuisine," he said.

"What we serve is good enough for the people around here," Maddy said with a frown.

"Perhaps they believe that now, but I daresay their tastes will change when they sample what we offer." He offered me a slight smile with a hint of condescension in it. "Perhaps you'll find another niche in the marketplace."

"Okay, I tried being nice," I said. "Clearly that didn't work. It looks like it's time to go to Plan B."

"And what might that be?"

"Don't worry. You'll find out soon enough," I said, since I had no idea what I'd meant myself. I turned to Maddy and Greg, and then said, "Come on, we're leaving."

"Fine by us," Maddy said.

As we walked out the door, I saw that Judson Sizemore had followed us.

Once we were outside in the alley, a delivery truck was just starting to unload when Judson called out a question to me. "Was that a threat you just made, Ms. Swift?"

"No, I wouldn't look at it that way. Think of it more as a promise," I said.

As we walked back to the Slice, I stared at the blue brick exterior. I'd been saving enough money to get it repainted to a more appetizing color, but that money was spoken for now. It was going to have to go into a war chest in a life and death struggle for my restaurant.

I was about to enter a battlefield, and I couldn't afford to be cash-strapped when I went to war.

"I can't wait to hear what you have in mind. What's Plan B?" Maddy asked me as I unlocked the front door of the Slice and we walked inside.

"I have no idea," I admitted as we moved back into the kitchen. It was officially one minute past opening, but no one had been waiting to get in, and we had things to talk about. Flipping our CLOSED sign to OPEN could wait a few more minutes.

"Not even a clue?" Greg asked. "Come on, I know you better than that. I can think of a thousand things we can do about this, if you need any suggestions."

"It can't be illegal," I said.

Greg nodded. "Got it. Then that narrows it down to a hundred, but that should still be enough to run him out of town."

"I won't stand for anything unethical, either," I added.

Greg frowned at me as he asked, "Then what am I supposed to do if you keep taking away all of my options?"

Maddy looked at me as she said, "Eleanor, this is no time to be squeamish. We can't let Mr. High-and-Mighty back there get away with it."

"I agree," I said. "But if I drag myself down to his level, I don't deserve to have a business. There has to be a way we can beat him fair and square. Don't we have loyal customers?"

"I would certainly like to believe that," Maddy said with a shrug. "But do you really want to bank on that?"

Her answer surprised me. "What do you mean?"

"Come on, Sis, I love the Slice almost as much as you do, but Judson's offering a wood-fired oven and a guy who tosses the crust in the air like it's some kind of show on the Food Network. Our sad little conveyor stashed away in back can't compete with that, and you know it. We need to upgrade to the big guns."

"We can't," I said, some of the fight going out of me. "If we have to do that, we've already lost. I just don't have that kind of money."

She frowned. "Then we're out of luck."

Greg said softly, "I can finance it, and we all know it. If money is all that it's going to take, trust me, it's not a problem."

I'd actually forgotten how much money he had; Greg had been living hand to mouth for so long that it was hard not to still think of him as a struggling college student. "Thanks, but I can't let you do that." It was time to open the restaurant. I couldn't delay it any longer, and besides, I needed to defuse the bomb Greg had just hurled.

He clearly wasn't all that pleased with my reaction to his generous offer. "Why not? I've got more money than I'll ever need, and if you can use some of it, I can't think of a better way to spend it."

I stopped in my tracks, twenty feet from the Slice's front door. "Greg, I cannot express how much I appreciate your generous offer, but I can't accept it, and we both know it."

"If she won't take it, I will," Maddy said.

"What do you need money for?" Greg asked, clearly concerned about my sister's well-being.

"*Need* might be a little strong, but I saw a new sports car on television the other day that I'd look just darling in."

I knew that Maddy was trying to ease the tension in the air, but it wasn't going to work by joking about money.

"I'm sorry, Greg. Win or lose, I have to do this within the limits of my own financial resources. Joe and I never believed in mortgages. That's one of the main reasons we bought a house that was such a wreck and fixed it up ourselves. In a world full of credit, we've always believed in paying as we go, and I can't change the way I do business now just because things are getting scary."

He shrugged. "I'm sorry, Eleanor. I didn't mean to offend you. I just thought it might help."

I gave him a big hug, and was quickly joined by Maddy. I wasn't sure what it would do to his reputation around town to have two women in their thirties embracing him so publicly near the Slice's front window, but if he minded, he didn't show it.

Maddy ruffled his buzz cut with one hand as she said, "You're not half bad; you know that, don't you?"

"Can you get her to accept the offer?"

My sister laughed. "I wouldn't even try. She's absolutely right. It's her place, good or bad, sink or swim."

"Then if we go down, we go down together," Greg said.

"But we still have some fight left in us," I said, suddenly buoyed by the show of support. "Let's figure out a way to beat him fair and square."

"I guess we could always try," Maddy said, and then added with a grin, "even if you are taking all the fun out of it by not letting us fight dirty."

I answered with a grin. "How about if we keep those ideas on the back burner in case things get really desperate."

"Really?" Maddy asked.

"Of course not," I replied. "But that doesn't mean they aren't fun to think about."

GREAT BOOKS, GREAT SAVINGS!

When You Visit Our Website:
www.kensingtonbooks.com

You Can Save Money Off The Retail Price
Of Any Book You Purchase!

- **All Your Favorite Kensington Authors**
- **New Releases & Timeless Classics**
- **Overnight Shipping Available**
- **eBooks Available For Many Titles**
- **All Major Credit Cards Accepted**

Visit Us Today To Start Saving!
www.kensingtonbooks.com

All Orders Are Subject To Availability.
Shipping and Handling Charges Apply.
Offers and Prices Subject To Change Without Notice.